THE
BOND

a novel

D0817307

THE BOND

A Novel

ROBIN KIRK

Goldenjay Books

Publisher's Cataloging-in-Publication Data
Kirk, Robin.
The Bond.
p.____ cm.____
ISBN 978-1-947834-31-6 (Pbk.), ISBN 978-1-947834-32-3 (Ebook)
1. Science Fiction. 2. Young Adult Fiction. 3. Fantasy Fiction. I. Title
813.6 | LOC PCN 2018910335

Goldenjay Books

Published by Goldenjay Books
an imprint of Blue Crow Publishing, LLC
Chapel Hill, NC
www.bluecrowpublishing.com
Cover Design by Lauren Faulkenberry
Cover Photo Credits: Tithi Luadthong/Shutterstock, Sleepwalker/Shutterstock, and Efes Kitap/Pixabay

Praise for THE BOND

Fans of *The Handmaid's Tale* and *Never Let Me Go* will devour *The Bond*.

-Lisa Williams Kline, award-winning author of ONE WEEK OF YOU

An adventure and a masterful exploration of what it means to be a human being.

-Constantine Singer, author of STRANGE DAYS

Kirk brings the reader into an intricate, well-imagined world—a landscape so credible it instantly feels like a classic.

-Beth Kander, author of ORIGINAL SYN

Kirk's dynamic world-building will transport you to a place you've never been before.

-A.M. Rose, author of ROAD TO EUGENICA and BREAKOUT

A rollicking adventure story whose underlying questions make for a read that is as thought-provoking as it is highly entertaining.

-Carolyn O'Doherty, author of REWIND

A riveting, dark, post-apocalyptic romp that hooked me from its very first line. Set in a dark and unsettling world populated by cyborgs, genetically engineered humans, and mutants, at its core *The Bond* is a story of Dinitra, who must make an uneasy choice, her loyalty, bravery, and humanity tested in the process.

-Katya de Becerra, author of WHAT THE WOODS KEEP

Contents

Acknowledgments	xiii
1. Brave	1
2. Perfect	10
3. The Rule	18
4. Chronicler	26
5. Legionship	33
6. Trisk	40
7. Holdfast	46
8. 12	53
9. Tracker Map	63
10. Two Hearts	69
11. Tribute	80
12. Sons	90
13. The Rift	99
14. Petal	108
15. Daughter Feast	116
16. Mother-Bond	128
17. Sil	138
18. Ash	147
19. Death Machines	159
20. Great Quest	169
21. Shape language	181
22. The Fall	189
23. Fir	200
24. Gemstones	212
25. Mother's Kiss	224
26. Susalee	233
27. Renegades	237
28. Cheese-seller	245
29. Labyrinth	256
30. Queen	264
31. Anku	272
About the Author	279

To Frances and Ray
& my own ferocious 12
RoZee

Love often takes the form of menace, and safe havens are reached, if they are reached at all, only after terrifying adventures.

Stephen Greenblatt, MY BROTHER'S BOOK

All that will remain of us is what is written down.

Robert Harris, DICTATOR

Acknowledgments

Authors know their books benefit from the generosity of many people. I am indebted to my parents, Frank and Judith Kirk, who instilled in me a love of story, reading, and wild places. Frances and Randolph Starn introduced me to a version of the Black Stairs in the Trinity Alps, now part of the rock, stream, and wood of the Weave, Bounty, The Deep, and the Eastern Wastes.

In the book's earliest version, Anne Allison and Cathy Davidson urged me to free Kesh from the background. Joe Neff, Alison Jones, and Rick Mashburn read draft after draft with admirable fortitude (and the staff of our haunt, Blue Corn, always welcomed "the writers" with attentive service). For their perceptive reads at all stages: the Bapties, Eden Herzog, Monica Roe, Laura Wagner, Lisa Poteet, Ellen Reagan, Alex and Maggie Perron, and Katie Grimm.

My advisers at the Vermont College of Fine Arts saw what needed praise and rethinking: April Lurie, Alan Cumyn, and Margaret Bechard, who bought me my very own carnivorous potato. I owe a special thanks to the Magic Ifs, who helped me be brave. YAM. A residency with Robert and Maureen Barker at Artcroft in the Kentucky Knobs inspired me to expand my world. Wildacres, along the Blue Ridge, gave me time to refine that world. For final corrections, I benefited from a month's residency at Seoul Arts Center-Yeonhui. My agent, Mickey Choate, believed in me despite all evidence to the contrary. His death robbed the literary world of an author's champion and a book enthusiast. I miss him to this day.

The editing of Blue Crow's Katie Rose Guest Pryal and Lauren Faulkenberry was smart, unsparing, and entirely wonderful, and I am so grateful these talented writers saw something in my story. Adam Versényi put up with far too many writing-related rants with grace, love, and wine. My daughter, Frances, made me want to write books worthy of her love. The bright soul of my son, Ray, animates every page. When he saw the very first draft, he asked: why not write more of this story? So I did.

Brave

My gray is for the fog that oozes over the Black Stairs: ash and egg-white binder. My purple is eggplant skins and vinegar, steeped for a week.

I brewed the paints special to paint Asta's gift. By the Mother's breath, if I don't finish soon, I'll be a hank of hair sticking from a block of ice because of this freeze.

My hair: walnut shell. Ice: mica bound with pounded chalk.

I make fists, wiggling my fingers to warm them. The boulder does double duty as a seat, table, and something to hide behind. Collegium students aren't supposed to be on the green on graduation day, especially so near the Moorings.

No other spot has this view. Plus the boulder has a crack where I wedge my paints. The crack is stained from all the times I've painted here. Most important of all: Asta and I first met here nine years ago. She was the one who told me the mountains are called the Black Stairs.

For the billionth time, I inspect them. The peaks aren't so much pure black as gray-black, when coals burn to ash. I dab in a bit of green for the trees covering the lower slopes. Once the painting's dry, I'll hide it in Asta's trunk, among her shifts and socks. She'll discover my gift when she unpacks in her new home tomorrow. It's my way of telling her how much I love her. How much I already miss her.

I'll never finish if I blubber.

We were six years old on our first day at the Collegium. The professors told us we could wander only as far as the boulder and definitely not beyond, into the pines encircling the green like spiky armor. I wanted a better view of the Collegium's high black walls and turrets. Close up, I'd noticed how each stone precisely fit to the others around it, as if the Mother herself chiseled them. As young as I was, the stones filled me with wonder. I wanted to fit, to belong, just like my Sower intended.

I don't remember the ship that delivered me to the Collegium or the Keeper I'd left that morning. I remember Asta perfectly: perched on the boulder, knees to her chest. Asta examined me— my brown boots, brown face, brown curls. I'd never seen a girl with hair as white or with eyes as piercing: gray rimmed in black.

"They're higher than I expected," she said abruptly.

The curl of hair she'd been sucking glistened against her neck. "That's the end of the Weave," she said. "Beyond those mountains, it's only scrags and beasts to the poles."

I felt happy and fearful and curious at once. Then and there, I vowed to paint the Stairs.

"You could call them the start, too," I told the girl. "If you were on the highest mountain and looked back, you'd see fields and such. Farms. Our Mother. Us standing here at the start of everything."

"I'm sitting, actually," Asta corrected me. "It's more accurate to say there is no single start to anything."

Accurate? This girl must be sowed for counting, I thought. I liked her. She saw things other girls didn't see.

"Are you coming up?" she asked. "The view's better."

Asta told me her name and I told her mine. We've been best friends ever since.

Asta knows me better than anyone. And I know her. I'm the only person Asta allows to touch her, the one person she'll whisper to when she's afraid. Some girls have special friendships and sneak into each other's beds at night, when no one's looking.

That's never been our way. It's more like we hold each other inside, in our minds.

The lump in my throat is sour. There's no escaping today's graduation. There's no escaping my separation from Asta. She'll almost certainly go to a Centrum counting house and leave in the morning on one of the capital's golden ships.

And me? With my Compendium, I'll be lucky if my assignment is within a thousand miles of her.

A human avalanche crashes into me: Professor Flicke. She yanks me away from the boulder, black eyes practically vibrating with rage.

My painting–Asta's gift–tumbles away.

"See you not the Legionship a-mooring, you bletherous girl!" With a vicious twist of my ear, she has me on tiptoes. Over the Moorings, a Legionship hovers: lozenge-shaped, all black. The silver nose whiskers lock to the Collegium signal straight as sticks. My painting careens purple-and-white toward the pines.

A kernel from the deep-fried corn cake Professor Flicke ate splats to my forehead. "Those Legionaries have no patience for underfooting students. Especially you. Of all of the Mother's bounteous days, you choose this one to go a-roaming?"

She shoves me toward the Collegium gate. "Get you gone before she sees you."

I don't dare ask who *she* is. Flicke glares at the Legionship, then hustles off, quick despite her bulk.

My paints are smashed: pink button flower and orange woolly worm guts ground into the dirt by Flicke's boot sole. I wipe away the corn kernel. Why didn't I just snap a photograph with my scroll? I shove the still-wet brushes into my pockets. The other girls tease me about the stains on my study robe, the stink under my bed from peels and mashes. So what? I have to paint just like I have to breathe and eat. I just wish painting didn't hurt so much.

The wind shifts. My painting lifts on a gust, then tumbles directly at the Legionship.

"Bless the Mother and all her fruits," I swear. I race for the ship. I can grab the paper and duck into the pines before anyone sees.

Why is there a Legionship here? The Legion is for Arcadium girls, made by Sowers to join the Legion and catch scrags. In my nine years at the Collegium, I've never seen anyone go to the Legion.

The Legionship settles into the Mooring cradle with a hiss. Just as I'm about to snatch my painting, the hatch opens.

My painting sucks inside.

Before I can duck away, a foot emerges. I freeze. The foot is a black blade connected to the parallel silver rods of a shin. Above, a circular knee joint rotates to absorb the legionary's weight. A second blade joins the first.

The legionary's knees bend backwards like a dog's. On her metal thigh, my painting plasters wet side down. The rest of her body is flesh but for a machine arm, her right.

I know this because her right hand flashes silver as she lifts the paper.

"I didn't order a welcome," she says. "Your name?"

I smell machine oil and rosemary. My eyes crawl up the metal legs to the black tunic covering where those legs connect to her flesh. Her face is pale, narrow, and with one ice-blue eye. Her other eye is an empty socket. A pink scar divides her face diagonally in two, like a poorly mended plate.

Three silvery pergama sheaves are pinned to each shoulder. I feel like some experiment she's reviewing. "Have you no tongue, girl?"

Another legionary emerges. She has flesh legs. A black chain links her left nostril to a hoop in her ear. "A lurker!" she crows. "What hey, the Moorings are off limits. I never believed these Collegium girls were so smart."

With three sheaves, the first legionary has to be a commander. My painting left an eggplant-colored smear on her metal thigh. "If you won't tell me your name, I must find out for myself. Show me your tulip, girl."

I tip my chin down to expose the base of my neck. The commander uses her metal finger to trace the tulip tattoo. Her two black blades are tipped with six yellow claws apiece.

"Dinitra 584-KxA." She holds my painting up like some odd

discovery: a plant with feet or a snake with wings. "Is this what you're after?"

I'm in so much trouble that trouble fills me like rain, drowning every response. If I could, I'd sink into the grass and vanish completely.

But I'm a flesh-and-blood girl.

"Looks like her blasted Sower forgot to give her the power of speech," the other legionary comments. Face-chain, I call her. "By the Mother's breath, why waste our time at the Collegium? There are Arcadium girls aplenty an hour south."

The commander's metal joints whir as she lowers to level her head with mine. "Is that true, Dinitra 584-KxA? Did your Sower forget to give you speech?"

"No one knows her Sower." It's the truth but stupid to say out loud.

Face-chain hoots. "Does the sun shine? Is it filthy cold?"

The commander ignores her. "Tell me, Dinitra 584-KxA. Who taught you to draw?"

How do I explain? I've always felt color, tasted it. When I was a second-year, Professor Wylla found me with a flat stone, mashed raspberries, and a stick with a softened end. I was painting (surprise) raspberries. Later, she gave me old paper and glass vials to make paint.

I take a deep breath. "I taught myself."

"Yourself?"

"Yes." Colors and shapes, the distance between shapes, shapes within shapes. Everything useless and a waste of time if you believe the infractions in my Compendium.

"Why not take a photograph and be done with it? You have a scroll."

"Those colors aren't mine."

She considers this. "No one owns colors."

"I find things and make the colors I need."

"Show me what's in your pockets."

I hand her my brushes: eyelash, thumb-on-a-stick for smudging, and the tuft, which I made from vicuña wool. Vicuña soaks up paint like a sponge.

"You're a little Chronicler, aren't you, with your paper and such," the commander says.

I'd rather drink Professor Flicke's sweat than agree. To compare myself with the Chronicler is Egoism, one of the worst infractions. The Chronicler drew the Weave's founding centuries ago, collected now in the Book of Sowers. Every Founder's Day, we take an original stored at the Collegium and parade it around the green. The drawing is preserved between glass and framed in filigreed pergama, more costly than silver at a fraction of the weight.

Face-chain peers over the commander's shoulder. "Why, this thing's good as a map. See there?" She jabs west of The Watcher. "A scrag could cross the Rift with this. It even stinks of scrag."

I've only seen scrags on the news, dirty huddled things. I have no idea how they smell. But I know my own paints. "That smell is vinegar. A solvent."

Face-chain mocks me. "I'm a Collegium girl and I know about all sorts of useless things." She waggles her head. "I'd put this one to shoveling shit in the kennels. Benit's always complaining about the cleaners."

The thought of working for the Legion squeezes my chest. Then I make a terrible mistake. "It's not a map. It's a gift. A goodbye gift."

Face-chain pounces. "A gift for who? Who gave you paper, anyway? Why, this paper should have been tossed into the Cyclon. Waste of resources. You're sneaking, that's it. Sneaking with another girl. Where's she hiding?"

Face-chain scans the green, as if a girl might be waiting to be caught. "Defying orders, wasting time," Face-chain blares. "Wasting *vinegar*!"

"Enough, Trisk." With her metal finger, the commander lifts my chin. "Answer the question, little Chronicler. Who is the map for?"

I can't get Asta in trouble. Or Professor Wylla, who keeps old paper for me. Not on my last day. Not before I say goodbye to Asta, for who knows how long.

The commander has me pinned with her single eye. But I refuse to say another word.

She tucks my painting under her belt. "Give me your scroll."

I unhook the scroll from the chain around my neck. She gives the slender tube a quick twist, then flattens the screen, flashing blue. My Compendium records everything about me from the moment I was sown to every test I've taken and infraction received. And my few miserable merits.

"Time-waster, dawdler," the commander reads aloud. "Poor in factoring. Messy, disheveled and—ah, a lonely merit. In History." She pauses, her one eye staring. "Professor Wylla gives you scrap paper, doesn't she, Dinitra 584-KxA?"

Trisk shakes her head. "That old pile."

The commander points at the ship. "Make sure the refueling pipe is set."

Trisk glares at me before ducking under the ship's belly.

The commander returns to me. "What's the merit for, Dinitra 584-KxA?"

A tap would bring up my entire Compendium. "A wren."

Her eye narrows. "A what?"

"A wren. I mean a wild bird that nested outside Professor Wylla's classroom. She liked the painting."

For days, I'd pull a chair next to the window, where I could watch the nest. I'd use paper scraps to puzzle out the different browns and whites of the wren's feathers, then how to capture both the stiffness of a feather's central spine and the softness at the edges.

When babies hatched, I drew the featherlets poking through loose skin.

Abruptly, the commander turns the scroll screen toward me: grades, rankings, infractions, my few lonely merits. At the top is my formula: a string of code recorded the day my Sower planted me in a Vessel. At the bottom of the screen, an empty rectangle winks. Waiting for my graduation assignment.

"I have the power to enter any assignment I want, Dinitra 584-KxA. Or any assignment you want. Caracol Bay and sea air?

Would you go as far west as the Shield? The Sowers might find your drawings amusing. Just give me the name. Nothing more."

Her friendly tone makes the threat worse. If I name Asta, I get a top assignment. What would happen to Asta? If I refuse, the commander could send me to some filthy outpost. Since I was old enough to remember, I've been told I'd get the assignment my Sower intended when she devised my formula. The thought of choosing makes me giddy, like I've suddenly escaped gravity. I could be a Gardener and grow any plant I need for paint. A Spinner and brew dyes to color fabric.

If she discovered I revealed her name, Asta would regret the day she invited me to climb up the boulder.

The commander's metal finger hovers over the screen. "If you don't give me a name, I might assign you to a containment. You know what a containment is."

The Weave keeps males in containments for our safety. Someone has to feed them, guard them. Seeing a living male would be like coming face to face with a dinosaur, something out of history. I should have never come to the Green. I should have never painted the Stairs for Asta. I should never have taken paper from Professor Wylla in first place. I should never have been sowed at all. Curse the Sower who made me, wherever she is.

The pilot emerges from the Legionship. "By the Mother's eyes!" She looks from the commander to me. "With respect, commander, we need to get you to a heater before your legs freeze solid." The pilot peers at me. "Girl, is Dren still Master Cook here? One dish, what was it, flakes of green. Lamb, if I'm not mistaken."

"Oregano." Oregano makes a lovely green paint.

The pilot nods. "Maybe Dren will give us a quick bowlful to warm up. Come, commander. If you haven't made this poor sprite piss her robe yet, you won't. She's got a bit of spine. I need some lamb stew. With *oregano*."

The commander taps my Compendium. With her flesh hand, she twists the scroll closed, then hands it to me. Trisk and the pilot follow her to the Collegium, skipping to keep up with the commander's long strides.

My painting is still tucked under her belt.

I wait until I'm standing by the heater in the Biotics lab to see what she wrote. There's a tang of singed rubber and alcohol in the air. The glass vials, titration tubes, and pipettes are neatly shelved. Asta is supposed to meet me to help put the finishing touches on my Biotics final.

My screen flashes *Compendium updated.* I expect to see Disobedience or Failure to Respond to a direct command.

The commander issued me a merit. An Exceptional Merit. Even Asta doesn't have an exceptional merit.

This is it: *Brave.*

Brave? As I swallowed my words? As I talked about wrens and vinegar solvents? As I refused to give her Asta's name?

Brave.

I'm an ice block with a racing heart. The commander wanted me to protect my friend.

The commander wanted me to say no.

2

Perfect

Before Asta can even sit on a stool, my story gushes out: the boulder, Flicke, the black lozenge of the Legionship hissing into its cradle. I can't lift my hand higher than the legionary's imaginary elbow to show how tall she is, so I climb up a lab stool. Still, my head's only level with the commander's imaginary shoulder.

A merit can't be erased any more than an infraction. Still, I'm astonished to see *Brave* winking on my screen.

Asta shakes her head. "You're the least brave person I know."

"Right?" The panic I felt at the Moorings comes out as a gurgle. There's even a little snot I wipe away with my finger. I'm afraid of open closets, heights, dogs, bees, waves, and thunder (not lightning). I can add: *afraid of Legionships*. And commanders who step through hatches with machine legs and a single bright-blue eye.

Asta asks, "Brave for what?"

I can't confess I almost got her in trouble for a painting she didn't ask for. The gift was always more for me than for her, so she'd have something to remember me by.

A lie slips from my mouth. "I don't know."

Asta's eyes narrow. "You were painting, weren't you?" She sighs, exasperated. "Dini, the Moorings are off limits on

Graduation Day. By the Mother, for your own safety if nothing else. You have to put away such foolishness. Mother's breath, why take such a risk?"

Her words sting. I can't let *foolishness* be the last thing she remembers about me.

Asta pushes aside a rack of tubes to flatten her scroll on the lab counter. "Why is the Legion here, anyway?"

Asta searches for *Commander, Legion,* and *machine legs*. She taps the most promising result, circling her finger to turn down the volume before the video plays: a clip from last Founders Day. With her machine legs and black blades, the commander is unmistakable. She wears a dress Legion uniform: gleaming black leather with three sheaves on each shoulder, the bright gleam of pure pergama.

Asta whistles softly. "She's not just any commander, Dini. By the Mother's breath. She's Legion Commander. Kesh 544-DxL."

Asta's gray eyes fix on me. "The Legion Commander called you brave. She gave you an exceptional merit. Listen. This is the best thing that's ever happened to you."

Together, we watch the video again. The commander—Kesh 544-DxL—stands among the Sowers. Sowers pluck out their eyelashes and eyebrows, so their faces are like moons of different colors. Next to them, the commander looks like something wrecked. Asta taps older links. Kesh stands beside a hovuck carrying supplies for legionaries fighting north of the Rift, the Weave's border. Kesh speaks about captured scrags on some dusty plain. Each video has a headline. "Legion Commander reviews forces at Holdfast." "Legion Commander rounds up scrags." "Legion Commander announces new Campaign against the rebel captains."

It's news we hear all the time and usually ignore. This time, I listen carefully. "See if there are pictures of her whole," I tell Asta. "Before the legs."

There are none. "Why would the Legion Commander even be here?" I ask. "I thought only Arcadium girls went to the Legion."

A dark thought occurs to me. There's been a terrible mistake. Maybe I should have been an Arcadium student all this time.

Maybe I was never supposed to be at the Collegium. Maybe my Keeper put me on the wrong ship. Collegium girls are supposed to be smart, brewed to manage laboratories, banks, and communications. They make some of the best pilots and controllers on the Signal Way.

Could my whole time at the Collegium have been some awful mistake?

Asta twirls a wet curl around her finger. "A three-sheaf commander does whatever she wants, Dini. You know they have Sower rank. There have only been two three-sheaf commanders since Constance."

I don't say the name Kesh out loud. The name feels spiky as wire ends. Constance defeated the army of men. On the spot where the Centrum stands, she offered terms: surrender, and receive lands to the east. The general's answer was to spit on her. For this, Constance severed his head. In the Book of Sowers, the Chronicler drew Constance next to the stone they set over the buried head to keep him imprisoned forever.

I've always admired that drawing. With just a few lines, the Chronicler captured Constance's exhaustion. At the top of the page, the Chronicler wrote: *We serve the Mother. No price is too high for peace.*

The first Sowers contained the men for everyone's safety. Constance became a Sower and led the Great Quest, to protect the Mother for all time. One day, she promised, Sowers would discover a way to brew new citizens without men. Their terrible violence would be eliminated forever.

"We're thinking about this all wrong," Asta says. "You got an exceptional merit. From the legion commander, no less. How can we make sure this helps you?"

The "we" makes me want to hug her tight enough to make her squeal. But Asta hates to be touched. I tap my finger next to hers, our compromise to show feelings.

"There's nothing to be done," I say. "It's not like any of us can choose."

"Except." Asta lets the wet curl of her hair drop. "You can invoke the Rule."

"What?"

"You know," Asta says, growing more confident. "Students can volunteer for the Legion before their assignments chime."

"Why would any Collegium girl choose the Legion?" We're supposed to get the best jobs.

Asta taps her scroll again. "There was one. Our second year. She made the news."

"I don't remember her."

Asta pauses. "You were in the infirmary. The winter the dog attacked you."

The memory makes me catch my breath. Before the graduation feast our second year, I was collecting walnut shells in the orchard to make brown paint. A wild dog leapt from the brush and seized me by the arm. The dog threw me back and forth as if it meant to tear my arm from my shoulder.

Professor Flicke was nearby. She beat the dog off with her huge fists. A fysic later told me it was one of the Legion's battle dogs gone feral. My scar throbs when I see a battle dog on the news.

Asta peers at me. "Dini, you'd be the first Collegium girl in history to invoke the Rule to a three-sheaf commander. That's almost better than getting some entry-level job in the Centrum."

Asta is nothing if not determined once she's certain she's right. "Seriously, Dini. Even with this merit, your Compendium's a disaster. You'll probably be sent to some awful job in the colonies. You wouldn't be able to move to the Centrum for years. Maybe forever." Asta sighs. "Or you'll be sent to work a Cyclon. Remember when we visited the Cyclon at Fourth Years? No sun, no fresh air. At least in the Legion, you won't be underground for who knows how long."

Her words bring sudden tears to my eyes. Asta never means to be cruel. But she can't lie or soften her opinion to spare anyone's feelings. Every Weave city and town has a Cyclon, all connected to the central Cyclon at the Centrum. The Cyclons generate fuel for heaters and coolers, lamps, kitchen stoves, computers, the ships traveling the Signal Way, and even the Signal Way itself.

The Collegium Cyclon is as wide as the building itself and

buried deep underground. When Asta and I visited, we saw its enormous bladder sagging green and veined over our heads. Fat bubbles lifted through the murk. Bits floated by: bone shards, hair mats, peels, and even human waste. Everything we discard, down to the last fingernail, goes into the Cyclon.

As we watched, a worker in a greased suit and goggles wriggled up into the bladder, to loosen a clog, we were told.

Asta waits as I wipe away a tear. "I have to be honest about these things," she says.

"I know. It's just…" I don't want to argue with her on our last day. I feel like one more thing to be thrown away. "I was fooling myself about getting a decent assignment."

Asta has her own deficits. Allergic to sunlight and dust. Poor in social encounters. But her list of merits is long: detail-oriented, deliberate, easily grasps complex number sequences, outstanding pattern recognition. She doesn't have to think about invoking any Rule. She'll get a wonderful assignment: Central Bank or a warehouse in the capital.

What would I even do in the Legion? Stab a scrag with a brush handle? Splash it with moldy paint?

"Promise me you'll think about it," Asta insists.

"I promise." Here's one merit I should have: I'm an excellent liar.

"We should look at your final so I can leave before Professor Rusta gets here."

The Biotics assignment was to create a simple plant or creature that's useful and also resistant to a natural predator. I mixed a formula for a mole-repelling potato in one of the consoles, cutting the formula this way and that with the injectors. I show Asta the shelf where the potato plant grows from a box of dirt. The vines spindle up the stone walls, leaves turned to the wintry light filtering through a window.

I try to sound Biotics-y. This also keeps me from blubbering. "The leaves are well-developed. There's scaling on the stem, normal for the base variety. The color is robust."

Asta's trying to calm me. "You should mention the quantity of leaves."

Together, we pull the vines down, each tender suckling exhaling mortar dust as it pops free. I carry the box to a lab table. Asta selects a small scoop from a drawer. "Bring me a dissection tray," she says.

The red wax coating the bottom of the tray reeks of preservative. Asta makes a neat pile of dirt on it, then peers into the box. "I see a lump."

My spirits lift. Still covered in dirt, the lump looks like a potato. A real potato. An edible, storable potato no mole should even sniff.

I managed to create a living thing. Maybe I'm not so bad at Biotics after all.

Asta places three more potatoes onto the tray. Under a light, I see that one potato has a swollen seed eye. I poke it with a glass probe.

I swear the potato shivers. The eye has something inside it: serrated and butter-yellow.

Asta pries out the object with a scalpel. "It's a tooth. Look, there's more than one."

I roll the second potato over. With my probe, I poke at a black patch. Fur. "Now what?"

"Maybe they're not all the same," Asta says.

Every single potato has teeth and fur. The largest one even softly growls.

Asta shakes her head. "We have to shave and de-tooth them all. By the Mother's breath, what did you put in this formula?"

"Skunk. A natural predator of the mole. And a bit of orange."

"Orange?" Asta is incredulous.

"For the smell."

"Snake would have been a better choice," Asta says, exasperated. "You could have made the potato shed its own skin. Cooks wouldn't have to skin them. You could have made a potato that grows in water. There are no potato predators in a tank. At least it wouldn't growl! No one wants an orange-flavored potato, Dini. Look at what Susalee did. That's the kind of final the professor wanted."

Susalee's project is an insect-eating flower combining

gardenia, bee, and *Drosera glanduligera*, a carnivorous sundew. The sundew's creamy petals curl around anthers heavy with nectar that slow-drips into a beaker. Pieces of fly wing, the only part of the insect predator the plant can't digest, lie like crusty snowflakes around the sundew's base.

No de-toothing will make my mole-resistant potato pass. Asta's determined to do what she can, though. Her scalpel flashes over the last potato, lumped like a turd.

I wish there were some place I could officially surrender.

Asta's expression is as serious as I've seen it. "The exceptional merit is lucky for you. Invoke the Rule. Otherwise..." She doesn't have to finish: risk a truly terrible first assignment. She gives my hand a quick tap of affection before she leaves.

I dump the potato fur, teeth, and vines down the Cyclon chute. Once the whole mess hits the first bladder, there's a faint, fruity burp. I can erase charcoal lines with the fat of my hand, but there's no way to erase my Compendium.

I give the potatoes a last scrub, then stack them in a glass beaker. I put the turd at the bottom. Maybe Professor Rusta won't notice.

Of course, the first thing she does is upend my beaker on one of the dissection trays. The turd's at the top. Her lips press together in disgust. With a silver tongs, rolls the turd back and forth. The holes where Asta and I pried out teeth are red-rimmed and look painful to the touch.

Professor Rusta slices the turd open with a scalpel. An oily stench fills the room. The potato's inner flesh quivers for a moment, then slumps in a gelatinous mess.

At this moment, my whole life feels like one lumpy, messy turd.

"I don't know a single creature made by the Mother capable of ingesting this horror." The professor marks the potato inedible and potentially carnivorous. *Fail.*

Mariza gets a high mark for a spider that produces web strong enough for armor. The spider's hard carapace is too bitter to appeal to birds or frogs. High pass. Tem's project is sow bugs that eat garbage, then poop a froth that can be molded into soap. At the lightest touch, the sow bugs roll into hard pellets.

"Inedible." Professor Rusta wrinkles her nose. "With that carapace, the bugs would likely pass through the digestive system unharmed. Good work."

Another high pass.

The professor snatches her hand back when the tiny pink tentacles on the nose of Edba's dilidot grasp her finger. "Cyclon tube cleaner," Edba says. "It can scour the narrowest joints."

Edba's creation is hairless, a plus. Professor Rusta gives her a low pass since there are no natural predators in the Cyclon.

With relief, she turns to Susalee's final. Susalee's always been best among the 584s. The professor dips a glass probe into the beaker, half-filled with golden nectar, then dabs the end on her tongue. She allows each of us a taste: a morning fragrant with just-opened flowers and a tangy edge, like just-baked bread.

"Each harvest more efficient, each crop more nutritious and delightful," Professor Rusta says. The Biotics Guild motto. "Perfect."

Susalee earns a merit. Best in class. Susalee even smells like her final: sweet, like honey.

Susalee is exactly the person her Sower intended.

I am a furry, carnivorous potato.

3

The Rule

A scrub at a stone basin doesn't rid my skin of skunk potato stink. There's a single perfect and a thousand and one ways to be less than perfect. Asta would correct me since the true number is infinite. There's an imperfection between imperfections and another one between that imperfection and the original one, and so on.

First-year math. Easy.

As I enter the Great Hall, nothing feels easy. The encounter with the Legion Commander and Asta urging me to invoke the Rule and the Biotics fail drag behind me like a dirty string.

A fourth-year pinches her nose at my smell.

"Watch out for your ankles," I snap at her. "My Biotics final got loose. It bites."

She scurries away.

My mouth is sour with meanness. In my mind, meanness has a color: old scab. My Sower should have mixed snake into my formula so I could shed my skin. Better yet, lizard. I could snip off mistakes and start fresh.

The voice in my head is Asta's. *The mistakes would regenerate exactly the same.*

I make a point of not glancing at Asta's table. I can't bear one more word about the Rule.

Banners marked with 584, our birth year, sway from the rafters. There's a happy buzz as everyone finds their seats. For graduates, this is the last time they'll sit where they were assigned nine years ago. The tableware is festive: porcelain plates in stone chargers, heavy forks and knives, two sizes of spoons, for soup and for jam, and a delicate mother-of-pearl-handled pick, for the sautéed snails only served at graduation. Brilliant purple and yellow irises cultivated just for tonight flare from tall vases.

With each table setting comes a glass of licor, for the toast. Next to it is folded the purple collar we all wear as a sign we've completed our training.

As a younger student, I practiced how I'd react when my assignment chimed. Sometimes, I'd jump and wave my hands. *What a thrill to be called to the Centrum my first year out of school!* I'd pat the imaginary collar. Other times, I'd stare at my face in the mirror and shrug. *I would have been happy with any assignment, to be honest. Really, the praise goes to my Sower and my Keeper and the teachers who made me into a citizen worthy of the Weave. I'm so humbled by this honor.*

I never imagined how my stomach would twist, bubbles of fear rolling up my throat like my own gassy Cyclon. If everyone's happy, why do they clutch their scrolls? No girl ever admits she's disappointed. Or scared.

For the billionth time, I wonder what procedure my Sower fumbled when she sowed me. Were the mistakes in her egg or the male extract? Maybe as I brewed, the lab temperature dropped or rose, or there was an unexpected jolt. Perhaps my Sower left a soapy impurity on the mixing tube.

Are my flaws due to soapy impurities? I'd laugh except we did a whole unit in Biotics on the disastrous effects of impurities on embryos. Maybe the Vessel who carried me drank the wrong tea or didn't eat enough of whatever a Vessel's supposed to eat.

I refuse to invoke the Rule. I'm not brave, no matter what word Kesh entered into my Compendium. If I ever saw a living scrag, I'd dissolve into a murky little puddle of fear. What would I do north of the Rift, with all of the wild beasts? Legionaries like Trisk would laugh at me. Or worse: abandon me.

The girls from my sleeping hall chatter with excitement. Our table is round and, just for tonight, draped in a thick purple tablecloth to match our collars. Mariza's to my left, talking to Susalee. On my right, Tem has placed her scroll beside her plate, her hand resting on top.

To her right is Edba, her scroll flat on the table and still flashing her low pass in Biotics. She's saying to Tem how unfair it is, but in a casual way since a pass is still a pass.

Becke sits opposite me. She's keen to see what Chef Dren has prepared. Becke can always tell what's in a dish, down to how many cloves of garlic or what specific kind of basil—cinnamon, sweet, or lemon? She wants to be assigned to Cut Hill to be a master chef.

"I've heard the Centrum's boring," Susalee's saying. Not that she'd mind the assignment, she adds. The one thing Susalee isn't good at is modesty. Of course, she expects to be assigned the Centrum. "I want something exciting, where I can make a mark."

Becke rolls her eyes. Susalee's planned out every step to becoming a Sower. And why not? Her Sower gave her everything: intelligence, athletic skill, beauty. Even after a long day of finals, her red-gold curls look arranged to catch the light.

One day, Susalee may be Head Sower. It will be her face I see on Founder's Day, plucked clean of every hair.

She'll be just as beautiful. Beneath my feet, the Cyclon thrums slow, slow, fast, slow. Susalee will wear the blue Sower robe and I'll be in a greased sheath made to slither through the Cyclon's bladders.

A server delivers a platter of snails. The other girls spear them at the shell opening, where the soft brown feet glisten with hot butter.

My appetite went down the Cyclon chute with my toothy potatoes.

Tem slips her hand under the table to hold Edba's. The way they look at each other makes me feel a little mushy and jealous at the same time. Will anyone ever look at me the way they look at each other? Being in love isn't allowed until after graduation. Yet most professors look the other way when it's between older girls.

I feel a quick stab of shame. I've been thinking so much about myself I haven't spared a thought for them. Tem and Edba will have to say goodbye before morning. If they're not assigned to the same place, it will be three years before they'll see each other again.

I'm surprised when Tem turns to me. "I'm sorry about your final, Dini. Professor Rusta shouldn't have failed you."

I look down at my plate. "I just wish this was over."

"The Mother is wise."

A reply sticks in my throat. If she's so wise, then why didn't she make me more like Susalee?

The Collegium Director sweeps in, the professors following behind. For the feast, they dress in ceremonial black robes with turbans on their heads dyed according to their disciplines: green for Biotics, gray for Toximetry, white for Computations. Professor Wylla, my favorite, wears the bright yellow of History.

Behind her lumbers Flicke: my tormentor. Her blue Spectronomy turban is askew over her forehead. She gives the students a baleful glare before taking her seat at the head table.

The Director has Sower rank, so she has plucked her face clean of eyelashes and eyebrows. "Please stand to welcome our guests," she announces.

There's a happy murmur as the ship crews enter. They've come to collect their assigned graduates. Minas is first, in swirling, shiny robes. There, chemists and smiths work the metals the Mother provides from her mines.

Next enter the livestock specialists of Starry Plains. They wear sheepskin vests and high leather boots, faces sun and wind-burnt. Despite my sour mood, I smile at Caracol Bay. Fishers and sea gardeners, they wear fantastical hats shaped like starfish, octopi, and sea urchins. The Centrum crew, representing the Weave's capital, is somber in gray tunics with black piping at the collars and sleeves.

There's a gasp of surprise when the Legion enters: black tunics over black leggings and boots laced to the knee. Everyone knows the Legion only takes Arcadium girls, brewed to be strong, fearless, and obedient.

I can hear the tick of Kesh's blades on the stone floor. Because of her machine legs, no chair fits her. Chef Dren herself carries in a high stool.

Kesh surveys the room. I stare at my plate until I'm sure her gaze has passed.

The Director lifts a glass of cordial. We follow, the licor like liquid rubies. "To the Mother," the Director pronounces.

"To the Mother!" The licor burns a stripe down my throat.

The servers return with trays heavy with soup: carrot topped with saffron cream. Becke grins broadly. She's thin as a stick but eats for three.

She sees I'm not eating and waggles her spoon. "If the soup's going to waste, can I have it?"

I push my bowl across the table to her just as someone's scroll chimes. Then another and another. Assignments.

Not for us. From across the hall, I see Asta twist open her scroll. Her face flashes blue from the screen light. She smiles. Normally reserved, her smile's like a belly laugh. The offer must be Central Bank, what she's always wanted.

I touch my scroll, then pull my hand away. What does it matter that I feel the scroll quiver a second before it chimes? The assignment's final no matter what.

Becke claps as the next course arrives: broiled calabaza and snap beans in garlic. Then comes roast chicken, fried potatoes, and loaves of twisted bread. On each table, a server thumps pots of glistening mora and oolieberry jam.

More scrolls chime. Ignoring the excited chatter in the hall, Kesh leaves her stool to speak to the Director.

Edba notices I'm watching her. "I don't understand why the Legion's even here," she says.

I don't want to have to tell the whole embarrassing story so stay quiet.

Tem asks, "Do you think her organs are metal, too?"

Susalee shakes her head. "The Weave's grown replacement organs for years. Whole limbs are still too complex."

Tem speculates about how Kesh's legs connect to her spine: through wired cables or possibly animal-based cultivated nerve.

There's another round of chimes and a final course: Assignment Day cakes, one to each student, chocolate topped in a purple frosting peak.

Becke gives her cake a thorough lick to prevent anyone else from claiming a taste.

I'm looking past her when a girl with a purple collar stands. The girl next to her tries to yank her down, but she pulls away.

The girl's name comes to me: Helma. We were in Computations together. She has a solemn face and a careful way of moving, as if she's hiding an injury. Helma wanted to be a ship navigator, but struggled with numbers.

The chatter stops, the Hall suddenly quiet. Asta's mouth is a perfect O.

Kesh and the Director are still arguing. "I require it." Kesh says. When her voice rings out in the suddenly silent Hall, she searches out the reason.

Helma's voice wavers. "I invoke the Rule."

The Director's chair scrapes the floor. "Is this your doing?" she accuses Kesh. "I'll speak to the Sowers, I tell you!"

"I will be at the Centrum in the morning and will speak to the Sowers myself." The director is not a small woman, but she shrinks beneath the Legion Commander's stare.

Kesh's apparatus whirs as she steps toward Helma. "Do you invoke the Rule of your own free will?"

Helma nods.

"You must speak," Kesh says. "Swear it so the Director standing there may hear it from your own mouth."

"I volunteer."

"You must be willing to defend the Mother with your life. Are you truly willing? Let me see your tulip."

Helma lowers her chin.

"You must say this a second time, Helma 584-WxL."

"I am willing."

"Hand me your scroll."

My skin prickles. I know Asta is staring at me. Do it now, she is thinking. I wish there was a way for me to scream so only Asta would hear: *I will never be brave no matter what the*

Legion Commander says. All I did was protect you from my stupid mistake.

The legionary Trisk, with her metal face chain, escorts Helma from the hall.

Around us, the other girls look at each other in amazement. Susalee has a strange smile as she surveys us. "I have the most extraordinary idea. We should all invoke the Rule. Now, before it's too late."

"That's not funny," I blurt. None of them know Asta urged me to do that very thing, but I feel exposed.

"I'm perfectly serious." Susalee waves a spoon still glistening with jam. "I know I'll get some good post at the Centrum. That's still years away from what I want, to be a Sower."

Becke shakes her head. "Don't you see what scrags did to that legionary?"

Susalee dismisses her with a wave of her jam spoon. "Maybe she was in some crash. I'm talking about us."

Her voice grows more confident. "Six girls invoking the Rule together. I'm amazed I didn't think of it before. We'd make the news. We'd make *history*. Since the Great Quest is almost complete, it's not even so dangerous. Helma's onto something. We should do it now, before our assignments come."

Susalee stands, as if to approach the head table.

"Wait." I take a deep breath. "I don't think that's why Helma did it."

I haven't spoken to Helma since Computations. But I'm sure she's not on any fast track.

Susalee is impatient. "Out with it."

I could say it's because Helma's like me. She knows her Compendium is bad. At least with the Rule, Helma's making her own choice.

I keep it simple. "She wanted to be a Signal Way navigator, but she couldn't handle math."

"I get what's going on." Becke folds her arms. She and Susalee often fight. "Susalee thinks this is good for her. Not for the rest of us. We'd just be tagging along so she can make Sower faster. This won't help any of us. It will help *Susalee*."

Susalee's cheeks turn bright pink *Precisely*, I think. "I want no part of any Rule," Becke says. "I'm going to Cut Hill to be a Master Chef, not some scrag-catcher on the Rift."

Susalee doesn't give up easily. She turns to Tem. "If we invoke the Rule, you and Edba will be together. Tomorrow, you'd leave on the same ship. Think about it."

Edba looks slapped. "Susi, you're being cruel. This isn't a game to us."

"It's not a game to me, either. It's the smart move."

"Smart?" Becke stands, her napkin slipping to the floor. "Susi, you're not thinking about us or even the Weave. You're thinking about yourself, like always. It would be Susalee and those five other girls who don't even have names. I happen to like my legs and I also like my arms, thank the Mother. I don't want metal ones like that commander. You can't manipulate us like you manipulated your Biotics final. The Rule is for girls who are afraid they won't do any better, like Dini said. Girls who have no choice. Shut up, Susi. Shut. Up."

If there were merits for goading Susalee, Becke would have just earned a double. Susalee's voice is savage. "All you care about is what you're going to eat next. This is for Dinitra as much as anyone. Have you thought about that?"

Her words are like a punch. Susalee's using me to get her way.

"We shouldn't argue," Tem says softly. She's our peace-maker. "It's our last night. We're all a little upset."

A hand rests on my shoulder. It's Professor Wylla, from History. "A word, dear girl," she says.

I can't say I'm sorry to leave the Great Hall for the last time.

4

Chronicler

My first year at the Collegium, Professor Wylla supervised my sleeping hall. I was a notorious sleepwalker. Before tucking me in, she'd bind my ankle to the bed frame with a strip of cloth. Late into the night, she'd sit nearby and read from her scroll. Sometimes, she'd whisper into the open screen. I imagined she spoke to a person far away, maybe someone she loved.

In those years, I'd often dream the same, terrible dream. Someone gripped me close. I heard the thud of boots, felt the snap of winter on my cheeks. I had wings in my dream, black and wider than I am tall. Again and again, I'd leap over the Collegium walls, the wings lifting me. Above, I'd see the constellation called the Eternal Keeper, meant to watch over us. Even as I dreamed these things, I felt Professor Wylla's binding and my ankle pulling against it.

Without warning, my wings would turn to smoke. I'd fall and wake gasping just as I was about to smash to the ground.

With stories, Professor Wylla would soothe me back to sleep. Born in the famous Quintennial year, she seemed impossibly old even then. My favorite stories were about the Chronicler. Like me, the Chronicler drew pictures.

Professor Wylla's stories always started, "A long time ago."

My favorite was about when the Chronicler climbed a tree to escape a beating from her father. Every time Professor Wylla said "father," I'd shiver with excitement and terror. Such a thing hadn't been allowed in the Weave for many generations. The Chronicler lived in terrible times, when people were little more than beasts. Males were violent, uncontained.

"The father beat the tree trunk with a stick," Professor Wylla would say. Repetition made the story sweeter. "He sawed at it and chopped with an axe, then beat his fists bloody trying to knock the tree down and seize her. The tree protected her. It was the Mother all along."

The Chronicler never drew herself. I assumed she was a girl like me, with brown skin, curly black hair, and charcoal-stained fingers.

"The Chronicler heard the Mother's voice speaking through the leaves: *Wait*," Professor Wylla would say in her quavery voice. "That night, the Legion swept through the girl's village. Constance herself noticed the girl clinging to a high branch. The girl was small and weak and knew nothing about fighting. But Constance rescued her." That night, Constance herself fed the girl from her own rations. "She asked the girl what she could do. The girl said this: 'I draw.'"

"I draw!" I'd say happily to Professor Wylla.

"Don't I give you my precious paper, child?" Her eyes were rheumy and with drooping folds. Professor Wylla told me to hide my drawing things since others wouldn't understand. "Let them think this is a passing thing."

The first time she said this, I didn't know what she meant. "Like a game of skips," she told me. "Or weaving bracelets from flowers. Things girls do. Things they forget, after a time."

I understood her to mean I should pretend my drawings were not important, even though they were most important things in the world to me.

In Bioregeneration, we learned that paper was made from ground-up trees, their mightiness and life sap boiled, pressed, and dried into sheets. Paper is wasteful, with by-products that poison the Mother's waterways and fields. Yet there were no scrolls so long ago. No Centrum, no Cyclon, no ships or Signal Way. There was paper and a world of violent men.

Constance gave a blank sheet to the girl and a bit of charcoal from her fire.

"Do you know the first picture the Chronicler drew?" Professor Wylla always asked.

"Constance herself."

"Just so," Professor Wylla said, pleased every time.

I'd always loved stories about Constance. By all accounts, she was brilliant, beautiful, and kind. My favorite thing about her, though, was that Constance was left-handed, like me.

"What about paints?" I asked. By then, I was making my own paints. I desperately wanted the secret to blue, the hardest color to make.

"She always drew with charcoal. You know as well as I do, my dear."

Professor Wylla assured me that one day, I'd be known for my drawings.

How naive I was to believe her.

Professor Wylla collected my sketches and clumsy attempts at painting. She'd praise them to the skies. Yet she'd also shut them in a special drawer in her desk. For a time, I hoped others would love them, too. But most professors went out of their way to give me infractions: for stealing leftovers to make paint, for smudges on my study robe, for stained fingers and cuffs. I hid my paintings from everyone except Professor Wylla and Asta.

The sounds of the feast fade as Professor Wylla leads me to the Collegium's third floor and her History classroom. I'm still angry at Susalee for using me to justify the Rule and angry at the others for not defending me. I never want to see those girls again.

In the History classroom, a single light illuminates Professor Wylla's old desk, pulled close to a window. The clouds I saw gathering over the Black Stairs earlier have become a storm. Sleet scratches against the thick panes, rimmed with ice.

Professor Wylla's back curves like a question mark. She points to the eave where the wren I drew long ago once nested. "Do you remember?" she says.

Professor Wylla has no way of knowing I spoke of this same wren to the Legion Commander that afternoon. My skin prickles with shame. For weeks after I finished the painting, I pestered Professor Wylla with questions. Was that how I was born, in a blue shell speckled with brown? Do Vessels have feathers? How big was the nest my Keeper used to cradle me?

Professor Wylla would answer patiently. No, you were not brewed in a shell. A Sower placed you in a Vessel's belly, as human as the two of us standing here. No, neither Sower or Vessel have feathers. How fanciful! Your Keeper embraced you in the nest of her arms just as the Mother intended.

The morning I found the wren's nest empty, I was inconsolable.

"Will they return?" I asked her.

"It's the Mother's will, my dear."

They never did.

The professor settles in her chair, motioning for me to pull the heater close as she piles on blankets. "I remember you kept that nest for weeks afterwards."

"Yes." Until Professor Rusta made me throw it down the Cyclon because it could harbor fleas.

"You know I have the painting still. Bring it to me, won't you?"

In her drawer, my paintings lie stiff and yellowed at the edges, the paint flaking off. Compared to how I draw now, my lines seem crude. The feathers look like wood splinters. The wren's eye is flat.

On Wylla's chin, white hairs curl. "I have something for you."

The fabric on the chair's arms is frayed through to gray stuffing. As a 500, Professor Wylla was among the first Weavers to see in the dark. Her pupils are rectangular from the *Capra aegagrus* enhancement. By the time I was brewed, Sowers had managed to round the pupils again while retaining night vision.

The Bioregeneration lab below gives off a faint whiff of cheese. "Flicke and I are the same year, you know," she says. "Did I ever tell you about my graduation?"

I remind her she told me all she ever wanted to be was a teacher.

She nods. "Flicke was never small and well! You see me as I am, skin, bone, and a hank of hair. How I wept when I thought we'd be parted. It reminds me of that girl, the one with the odd name…"

"Edba."

She nods. "Reminds me of Flicke and I, so long ago. We feared being parted."

Wylla's yellow turban makes her head look like a mushroom cap. "At our final feast, oh! I couldn't stop crying. Flicke wanted to be a Pilot, so she did. Crisscross the Signal Way. Adventure! To the ocean. To the Eastern Wastes. The Rift. Back then, this was the thing, to be a pilot."

For a long moment, I think she's dozed off. I think I might sneak off to see Asta and say goodbye.

Then Wylla speaks again. "How I long to see the Centrum once more, walk the streets! Professor Falyse says she can hear the grass of their green breathe like some great beast, but she's a known fabulator. All I ever wanted was my students and a place to read my books. When Flicke was assigned to Professor, how happy I was. We would be together."

Professor Wylla babbles about how Flicke was going to pilot training once her three years teaching were up. Wylla begged her to stay. Just another three years. They had all the time in the world.

It's no secret Wylla and Flicke have a particular affection. Teachers spend their lives at these schools and sometimes share rooms.

"She came to us, Oh! Such things cannot be allowed. Such things are wrong. We had to stay, the two of us. Flicke, for love of me, oh!"

I'm lost. "Who came? What was wrong?"

From beneath the blankets, Wylla pulls out what looks like a roll of paper. "Dear Dinitra, what life gives us is not always what we expect."

She's speaking in what sound like Chronicler quotes. "I can't take paper with me," I tell her.

Professor Wylla doesn't seem to hear me over the burbling of the heater. "I watch her when the ships land. So much sacrifice."

If Flicke could have pinched or shoved or shouted Spectronomy into my head, I'd be the Weave's greatest light engineer. Even for Professor Wylla, I can't pretend I like her.

Wylla reads my thoughts. "Flicke's a dreadful Professor, I know it. More's the pity, so does Flicke. Her heart's not in it. That's where teaching comes from: the heart. She stayed out of love of me. My dearest girl, it will all soon be clear."

"What will be clear?" It's like a second conversation just out of earshot. Wylla's never called me her dearest girl before. I'm not anyone's dearest girl.

"We've watched over you. Kept you safe these many years, Flicke and I. I grew to love you, those long nights."

Her smile is sweet. "She's come to collect you now."

"Do you mean Flicke?" That can't be right. I'm dizzy or maybe it's the tapping of sleet against the windows. For nine years, Professor Flicke's given me infraction after infraction. Never once did she say she was going to collect me. "Why?"

The professor's goaty eyes seem to see through me to a future I can't even imagine. Professor Flicke once beat off the wild dog that attacked me. This morning, Flicke appeared suddenly at the Moorings as the Legionship landed. "Where is Professor Flicke taking me?" I ask.

Professor Wylla presses the paper into my hand. "Trust what you see, not what you're told, dearest girl. May the Mother protect you."

I start to unroll the gift, but Wylla stops me with her shrunken hand. "No one must know you have this. Promise me."

I'm about to insist: what did she and Flicke protect me from? If Flicke isn't coming for me, who is? Then my scroll shivers. And chimes.

My assignment.

I understand the flashing word even as I understand nothing.

"There's been a terrible mistake." I stand. Wylla's gift slips to the floor.

"Your Mother knows you better than you know yourself," Professor Wylla says.

What could the Mother possibly know that would lead to this? The decision flashes in black letters. The black of shock, the black of the charcoal I use to sketch.

LEGION

"You will come to understand," Professor Wylla says.

Invoking the Rule would have made no difference. Nothing would. Bile sears the back of my throat. I was going to the Legion no matter what. If I could, I'd shove this whole day down a Cyclon tube, a moldy loaf of hours even a mouse wouldn't touch.

LEGION LEGION LEGION

A shape darkens the doorway: Flicke. "Come, you daft knuckle."

Was this what the Director and Kesh argued about? When Flicke hauled me up by an ear on the green, she said: *Especially you.*

I never want to see Professor Wylla again. All my painting, all the times I showed her something precious I made just for her.

She knew I was going to the Legion. She knew and said nothing.

I leave her gift where it fell, on a fold of Professor Wylla's frayed blanket.

5

Legionship

When I enter the sleeping hall, I hear Becke's voice, sharp as one of her junior chef knives. "You always have to have your way no matter who you hurt."

Becke is furiously shoving clothing into her satchel. "I. Will never. Speak to you. Again."

On the next bed, Edba and Tem are holding each other, surrounded by piles of undershifts and socks.

"Where did you disappear to?" Mariza says accusingly.

"Professor Wylla wanted to say goodbye." I can hear girls laughing in the next sleeping hall. "I got the Legion," I say, tears welling in my eyes.

"We all got the Legion, dummy." Mariza gnaws a fingernail. "You'd know if you'd bothered to be here."

"Because someone asked for it," Becke interrupts her. "Because someone had to have her way. Because someone only thinks about herself."

But Susalee seems as stunned as the others.

"That's impossible," I say. "I got the Legion."

Becke grabs her scroll and shoves it toward me. Her screen is the same as mine: LEGION LEGION LEGION.

Trust what you see, not what you're told, Professor Wylla told me. Weakly, I ask, "We're all assigned the Legion?"

Becke spits. "None of this will be on the news. Susalee got what she wanted, of course. And no one else."

One of the professors claps her hands. "Because of this storm, you need to be aloft within the hour or the crews will be stuck for days. All of you to the Portico, packed and ready to fly."

Becke shoves her scarf into the satchel, then pulls it out again. "The blasted Legion. Do they want me to boil scrags to death? Fry them up in a pan?"

She tries to zip the satchel, but a boot lace catches. "Susalee and her outstanding. Susalee and her best student in the class. Susalee and her... *Susalee-ness.*" Becke hurls the boot against a wall and stomps out, dragging her satchel by the strap.

For nine years, we've been told to do our best, work hard, and follow the rules, and we'd be rewarded. We've been brewed and trained for this. The assignment is supposed to be a reward.

Collegium girls don't go to the Legion. That's for Arcadium girls, sowed to be strong and follow orders. Not to make a completely new flower to drip lovely nectar. Not be a chef, like Becke. Not to heal the sick, like Tem.

"Leave your scrolls on the bed for new girls," the professor shouts. She glances anxiously at the high windows, already skinned in ice. "Off with you before you have to climb through the snow to your new assignments!"

I shove my few pieces of clothing into a satchel. Then I gather up every one of my paint vials and dump them down the Cyclon chute. The sound of smashing fits my mood: everything's ruined. If Professor Wylla is to be believed, she and miserable Flicke crept behind my back all my life.

The only thing I ever needed protection from was the Legion.

I'm the last out of the sleeping hall, and I don't look back.

In the Portico, graduates line up according to the ship they'll board. After the Legionship arrived, eight more cradled at the Moorings. Lit by landing beacons, the large ships shake and jounce in the icy gusts. Caracol Bay, Starry Plains—each glowing ellipse is a different color, with different patterns etched on their translucent skins.

Everyone's drawn their hoods and capes tight against the cold. Even if Asta were standing in front of me, I wouldn't know her.

This can't be the way we part, but there's nothing I can do.

Professor Flicke barrels up and down the rows, her turban askew. She pokes girls hard with her finger to make sure no one strays. "No chattering and nattering! Shoulders square. Blast the blastedness of this night! We don't want Starry Plains to go to Pergama, or the Centrum girls to The Spices. Look alive, shirkers!"

The girls assigned to the Centrum board first. Their ship is golden. *Like their futures,* I think sourly. I have to squint against the ice crystals. I mouth a silent good-bye, wondering if Asta is thinking of me.

Through the ship's translucent skin, I see each girl belt in. At the rear, one girl removes her hood revealing bone-white hair. Asta. She presses her hand to the inside of the ship's skin and peers back at the Collegium, as if through the storm she'll see me.

She's saying farewell. The gesture undoes me—such an awful day.

I have to swallow my sobs.

The Mooring cradle releases the Centrumship. The prow bucks up, the directional whiskers whipping as they search for the Signal Way. The rear propellers whine, lifting the stern. For an instant, the whiskers snap into place, connected to the Signal Way.

But a gust shoves the ship sideways. The whiskers lash, then stiffen, then lash again as they search for the lost signal. The ship is a golden oval over the dark pines. I lean forward, as if by this motion I can somehow push the ship higher, to catch the signal again.

In the prow, the pilot's helmet courses with color. The girls, strapped in their seats, stare out, whether at us or at the whirling snow I can't tell.

Again, the Centrumship slips sideways, this time toward the trees. The rear propellers rise abruptly, forcing the ship's prow down. The side rudders flap like caught fish. The ship skids toward the Collegium's massive stone walls.

Suddenly, the ship's whiskers stiffen with an electric zing.

Locked to the Signal Way, the ship levels and rises, a golden smear that swiftly vanishes in the storm.

One by one, the rest of the girls board, their ships fighting the storm, then locking to the Signal Way and vanishing. Soon, it's just the seven girls bound for the Legion.

"I can't feel my hands!" Becke glares at Susalee, as if this, too, is her fault.

Tem's the only one brave enough to say out loud what we're all thinking. "I'm afraid."

Ice needles my eyes. I hear a low churning. Suddenly, something thumps to the Portico flagstones: a rope ladder. The ladder has metal feet that skitter toward us.

A legionary swings down: Trisk.

"Cheer up!" Her grin is pure malice. "It's not every day a Collegium girl gets to climb a ladder!"

"What lunacy is this?" Flicke is furious. "Confound it, these are children, after all. Land so they may board safely."

"Pilot's orders. You saw those idiots from the Centrum almost lost the ship."

"Tell Del to land the ship," Flicke demands.

Trisk makes a show of shouting. "Hey, Del! Land the ship!" She looks again at Flicke. "I guess she can't hear."

Trisk grabs Susalee. "You first, Red."

As I've learned, Flicke is quick despite her size. She grabs Susalee's other arm. The two of them, legionary and professor, drag at Susalee as if they mean to halve her.

"Land the filthy ship," Flicke bellows over Susalee's head. "What's the good of smashing them?"

"What do you care? They're Legion now, blood, bone, and hair. This one here will climb and show the others how it's done."

From above, an alarm blares.

Trisk shouts, "Del wants them loaded before we lose the cruiser. Do you want to explain how your delay smashed us?"

Abruptly, Flicke releases her. Trisk catches the dancing ladder. In the scuffle, Susalee drops her satchel and reaches for it. Savagely, Trisk kicks the satchel into a snowdrift. Susalee can make a sundew drip with honey, win every foot race, best any one of us on an exam. But I've never seen her grasp a bit of ice-coated ladder and climb. The wind plays her like a kite, the ladder twisting and swinging. Her knuckles go white on the rungs. Several times, she slips.

But Susalee does it, vanishing into the storm.

I love her in that instant.

Trisk seizes Becke next. She's bonier than Susalee and not as strong. But somehow, Susalee's bravado is contagious. Becke struggles, but doesn't look down once before disappearing. I'm convincing myself to follow since I want nothing more to do with the Collegium or with Flicke. Plus, the ladder's only getting more slippery.

Before I step forward, Flicke's fingers clamp to my shoulder. "Go last," she growls.

Trisk's eyes are cruel. "Afraid, little Chronicler?"

Yes, I want to scream. I'm afraid of the storm and Flicke and Trisk and the chance, even remote, that I'll be killed by a scrag on the Rift. The others climb, then Trisk returns to me. "Up with the little Chronicler or I'll snag her flesh with the hook and hoist her in!"

Flicke shoves herself between us. "You first," she tells Trisk.

Little icicles tremble on Trisk's face chain. She tries to grab me.

Flicke's a mountain of no. "Touch her and I'll splat you like a bug."

"Try it."

Flicke raises a meaty first. "With pleasure."

"I'll write you up."

"Write away, Arcadium trash. This one goes last."

The ladder gyrates madly. "Mark me, this won't go unnoticed," Trisk tells her. "I'll make sure the Head Sower herself hears of this."

"Tell her what you will. This one climbs last."

Practically dancing on the storm, Trisk climbs the ladder.

"Mother's breath, you misbegotten sprite," Flicke growls. Her lips are specked with freezing spittle. "You smashed her poor heart to bits. I should break your neck here and now."

My answer surprises me. "Get on with it. So much for protecting me all these years."

The gleam in her eyes is just short of murder. Flicke shoves something at me: Wylla's gift. "After all she did for you."

I refuse to take it. Flicke wrenches my arm. "It's my countenance you'll see last here and it's a beauty," she hisses. "For the Bond, I do this, for the Bond and love of her. Get up that ladder or I'll wring your sorry neck." Then she shoves the gift at me again.

This time, I shove it in my pocket.

I'm practically blown up the ladder by her fury. My feet find a rung one out of ten times, then one out of twenty. If Asta were counting, she'd put it at nineteen times my boot swings free.

I climb blind, clenching my eyes against the cutting ice.

A hand grabs me by the shoulders and hauls me up. When I open my eyes, I see a six sets of eyes—the other girls, terrified.

Trisk wastes no more kindness on me than a flour sack. Before I can belt in, the ship lurches. Trisk rams her shoulder into my gut to keep me from flying down to the Portico.

I hear Becke: "We're going to crash."

In the cockpit, the pilot's helmet flashes purple, green, and yellow. The ship shudders. It's as if we're in some balloon pummeled by giant fists.

Trisk hangs from a bar riveted into the ceiling, her body shifting at the Legionship bucks. "Welcome to the Legion, Collegium dreck! On my honor, you lot will be first to die by a scrag's rusty bolt if I hear a single scream."

The whiskers at the prow lash so fast they're a silver blur. "You're too close to the wall!" Trisk bellows at the pilot.

"Blast this ice!" Del stands, then hangs her entire weight on an angled rod beside her seat. The rod doesn't budge. "We should have left hours ago. By the Mother's eyes, this storm will end us."

"Not if I have a say." Trisk hauls on the lever, which shudders down then freezes again.

The Legionship lists heavily to the right. Susalee claps her hand over Mariza's mouth to stifle a scream. Since the ship's skin is transparent, I see all the way down to the Portico flagstones.

Professor Flicke is still there, black robe billowing around her upturned face.

A shattered face stares up beside her. The Legion Commander.

With a squeal, the pilot's lever moves. There's a new sound: like a knife sharpening. It's the whiskers gone stiff as they lock to the Signal Way.

I praise every Transportonics worker and each one of their Sowers. Locked to the signal, the ship can't crash. We rise with prow and stern level, so fast I think I've left my stomach behind.

Becke vomits her feast and mine, yellow and purple swirling on the floor. I grit my teeth to keep them from clacking. The Legionship thrusts up and up, then bursts into a sea of stars.

6

Trisk

With the storm beneath us and the Legionship's whiskers locked to the Signal Way, we fly level as a plank. Becke passes out against my shoulder. I'm so awake I feel peeled.

I'm flying for real: not a nightmare. My wings are the ship, my muscles the propellers throbbing at the stern. Through a headset, the pilot talks to a controller, maybe the Centrum itself. To make double-sure I'm not in a dream, I scrape the base of my thumb until the skin is raw, then lick the spot: salty and warm.

The stench of Becke's puke is oddly comforting. She leaks a slug trail of drool onto my sleeve. I think: not so bad. I could be splattered on the Portico, Flicke complaining, "Who will scrape up this mess of a girl?"

I practice bracing for whatever's next: brace and relax. It's like the second before I put charcoal to paper, when I wonder what sort of line I'll draw. A good one, a shaky one? This moment, then the next, when the world is changed.

Brace, relax.

Asta's gift blew away. Kesh stared at me with her shattered face. *For the Bond*, Flicke hissed, *for the Bond and love of her.*

I can't call Asta, tell her where I am, what's happened. What would she even say? I can't click the links that might tell me what happened to that other Collegium girl, the one who invoked the Rule years ago and flew away on a shuttle.

The one whose fate might hold a clue to mine.

Did she look down on the Weave for the first time and think, *Wonderful*? Or did dread clutch her chest, like it does mine? In Biotics, the space between one thing and the next is called *interstitial*. A spiky word, a path to a wall with no door. Like the distance between my cheek and the Legionship skin, or how far we've already travelled from the Collegium.

Far below, the storm foams. I want to draw the lines of what's happened, but I don't know how any of this connects. I'd smear the whole page with the blackest paint I could brew, so thick the paper would warp, the paint drying and flaking off in chips.

Anyway, I'm done with drawing. I've discarded every drop of paint. I left behind my brushes, my vials. My night shifts, my underwear, my spare boots, the ones with the hole in the toe.

Gone.

Except for Professor Wylla's gift. The roll of paper lies against my thigh like an extra bone. Something I tried to leave behind. Something I didn't want. Even on this dark ship, heading to a place I never wanted to go, I can't shake off my failures, my mistakes. Why can't we wipe everything clean when we get our assignments, start fresh? I'd even change my name.

Dark ship, I'd call myself. *Ladder climber*.

Lesser girl. Less than her, whoever she is.

Little Chronicler.

Soon, we're past the storm. Below, the Weave unfurls in clusters of light. At intervals, the ship's sensors blink red, invisible intersections where we turn. Becke snores, oblivious. When I realized my mole-resistant potato was a failure, I wished my Sower had given me snake skin I could shed. Now, I'm skinned in Legionship. Maybe I never needed my Sower to fix me. I'll have to fix myself.

Brace, relax. What does fixing myself even mean? I've tried trying harder. I've done the sneaking away to paint. I've watched, trying to learn how to be better. Just at the moment I needed to disappear most, a machine leg emerged from a Legionship hatch.

Trust what you see, not what you're told, Professor Wylla told me. I don't trust anything anymore.

Del, the pilot, smiles at something Trisk says. All of this has to make sense. I'm just not understanding how.

Trisk notices I'm staring. She saunters down the aisle with a mocking smile. I don't know a thing about her other than she works battle dogs and loathes Collegium girls.

There's a long bar down the center of the ceiling. Trisk hangs from it, examining me. "Ever hear of the Rift, little Chronicler?"

"Yes." An easy question. The Rift is a gorge that runs down the length of the Black Stairs, splitting the mountain range in half. To the north is Beyond-the-Weave, a wilderness all the way to the frozen pole. I've never given Beyond-the-Weave a second thought. Why should I? That's not where Collegium girls go.

Trisk pushes her face close to mine. "What I can't figure out is why she wants any of you. What use do we have for Collegium girls?"

I flinch when she prods my chest. "The commander stares at you. Why, little Chronicler?"

Trisk might as well ask what kept the Legionship from smashing into the Portico.

"Speak, Dinitra 584-KxA. I'd hear your answer."

"We go where the Mother needs us."

"Ha!" On Trisk's breath, I smell oregano from Dren's stew. "The Legion's not for girls who paint pictures. The Legion's for girls who can shoot. Girls who can kill. Is this the kind of girl you are?"

The only truthful answer is no.

"I have seventeen battle dogs waiting at the Arcadium. My most promising trainer, too! It will be a month or more before I can collect them. Yet here I am, with raw Collegium girls!"

Trisk shakes her head. "Something stinks. None of you have seen a scrag in your life. How will you do anything but run? And a male, in the wild?"

Trisk slaps her thigh. "By the Mother's breath, I'd pay a thousand coin to see the look on your face when you see a scrag in the wild."

Shame prickles my arms. I've never given a second thought to what's north of the Rift. I've never even wondered what the Legion does to keep us safe. Even thinking about wild males makes me queasy.

Trisk wriggles her fingers as if to frighten a small child. "I'd put twenty coin on you running. You might be the smartest sprite in the Collegium. Compared to an Arcadium girl, you're nothing on the Rift."

I suppress a bitter laugh. Smartest?

Trisk is enjoying herself. "I've led hundreds of Arcadium girls across the Rift. I've seen them scrags from the peak of The Watcher! When they see me, hoo! How they run. Lam, Quor, even Timbe of the Living Wood."

She says these names as if I should know what they are. I know The Watcher, tallest peak in the Black Stairs. But Lam, Quor, Timbe? They might as well be in a chapter I never read in History.

"Them warriors piss themselves when they see my dogs. My dogs won every battle: Split Rock, the Caves. Battle of the Bog."

Trisk knows the other handlers are listening. "Let me tell you how it is across the Rift. There are wild beasts like hybas hanging from their fearsome tails in the trees. Lithers slithering from them holes in the ground. To them, you're a tasty morsel. Oh, you'll get tired from the climbing. Slopes of pure scree. One step up and a long slide back. You'll get used to it and think, 'Why, it's only a day in the woods! We're Collegium girls! They're running from our abundant smarts!'"

Trisk slaps her thigh loudly. Del, the pilot, turns to look. "Trisk, you need to help me lock in the switch."

Trisk grabs my hand and squeezes, just where I made my wound. I bite my lip to keep from crying out.

"That's just when you'd be wrong. Them scrags have been watching you the whole time, so they have. From the moment you crossed the Rift, scrags were watching. Traitors, criminals, thieves every one. Some among them Sowers, yes, Collegium girls who turned traitor. Didn't teach that in your fancy places, did they?"

I can't help my shock. "Sowers?"

"*Traitors*. Tell me, how many of us Arcadium girls have betrayed the Weave?"

I shake my head.

"A single one," she says, triumphant.

The ship shudders. Trisk bumps against my leg, missing Professor Wylla's gift by an inch. "The wonderful Weave and the Mother's bounty and all the slurr they teach you in that fancy, fancy place. Well. On the Rift we give our lives," she hisses. "You with your paints. You with your brave. You wouldn't know brave if it came up and bit you on your ass."

If I were seated at an open window and not against the Legionship's skin, I think Trisk might toss me out. "We fight and die for the Mother every day. But do they send us strong Arcadium girls? They make us take weak girls. Puny girls. Oh, I know," she says viciously. "You'll *draw* away them scrags coming at you, killing bred into their bones."

Abruptly, Trisk thrusts her face down. "Here's what I think. A three-sheaf commander thinks she's better than the rest of us. Better than an Arcadium girl, who only knows how to serve. A three-sheaf commander wants a little Chronicler to draw her for the ages. To make herself another Constance. To declare for all she alone pacified the north. She wiped away them scrags. Why? Can you guess why, little Chronicler?"

Trisk's face chain trembles with fury. "Because she wants to be Head Sower, that's why. She's using us, using the Legion, to have her way with the Weave. To have her way with all of us. Not for a minute do I believe we need Collegium girls to pilot the new fleet."

"Trisk!" Over her shoulder, Del glares. "Stop jawing and get on the navs!"

I don't know anything about a new fleet. I don't know anything about the Legion other than what Trisk told me in a spray of angry spit. Trisk jabs a finger at my face. "I'll be watching, little Chronicler. Wherever you are, whatever you're doing. She'll make a mistake, I know she will. I'll be there to catch you both."

Trisk swaggers back to her seat. If I had to paint her, I'd definitely use pepper red.

"Mother be blessed, what was that all about?" Becke whispers at my shoulder. "What did she say about the Legion Commander? About you? About scrags?"

I bend over and puke on top of Becke's crusty remains.

7

Holdfast

A t dawn, the Legionship cruises parallel to the Black Stairs. The prow points east, into the sun. Close up, the mountains don't look like stairs. They are an immense wall. No scrags live south of the Stairs, I tell myself. Telling myself this doesn't convince me I won't see something in the shadows.

That I won't see *men*.

If what happened yesterday with our assignments is any guide, I can't assume anything I've been taught is true.

Becke's voice is thick with sleep. "Where are we?"

"About to go over the Stairs, I guess. Or into. Right now, I'd lay last night's cake on into."

Becke peers out. "By the Mother's breath, it's beautiful."

Below us, the lower tier of the Signal Way is busy with traffic. Tiny transports skip around long-haul freighters, their containers jointed like metal snakes. Either we've descended or the land has risen close to the mountains. I can make out an open market, a village with streets, some stone houses with solar arrays. From the chimneys, smoke spirals.

This is the first time I've seen a Rift village with my own eyes, at least that I can remember. After what Trisk told me, the sight is a comfort. *The Rift is still the Weave*, I tell myself. The Legion is strong. Maybe sending Collegium girls is a good sign. Maybe they need us to manage the new lands that will open up once, as Trisk said, the Legion defeats the scrags. How is this not a good thing?

The ship's shadow slides across a long building. Dozens of tiny faces turn up: a Keeper House. I could have been raised here, before I was brought to the Collegium. I remember kicking a ball across a dusty field somewhere. There were songs. I ate spicy candies from a paper bag.

How dangerous could it be if there are Keeper houses so close to the Rift?

With a groan, the Legionship slows, then stops, hovering. Del is intent over the controls. Liquid spews yellow from a side hatch.

I remember this from Transportonics. Del is lightening the ship by dumping fuel. The Black Stairs must be too high for a fully-loaded ship. The ship's prow angles up as the engines start to throb. At my cheek, the ship's skin hums. The prow rises until I'm pressed flat to my seat back. The ship angles up, the belly now fully exposed to the ridges and rocky spires of the Black Stairs.

Through the cockpit windshield, I see sky and two birds circling. Del has us nearly vertical and still rising. It feels like we're being blown toward the mountains, and as we approach, I see them in even greater detail: spiky, stunted trees, cracks where rock shattered and split. Hitting any one of them would pop us like a child's balloon.

As I brace for the impact, the crags slip beneath us. The Legionship bellies into a narrow valley. Immediately, there's another pass, higher, and another. Over each one, the Legionship groans and lumbers. Someone behind me sobs. The alarm peals, and Becke shrieks so loudly it's like a pin in my inner ear.

Trisk turns to shout at Del. Over the throbbing of the engines, I can't understand a word. I'm fiercely glad we left all of our trunks and satchels behind. If I could wrench open my window, I'd toss out Wylla's gift, my boots, my wool robe. I'd spit just to lighten this blasted Legionship and get us safely over.

The Legionship waggles, our route over the peaks complicated by gusts of wind. We're closer than ever to a ridge, serrated and scraped bare. My breath stops as I spot something seeming to perch on a rock face: a goat. Then three more. The ship is mere feet above where they perch. Higher, a dirty patch of snow clings to an outcropping. I see a dog, then a girl in a muddy cloak. Her face is upturned. She's swinging a rope.

As our shadow swallows her, a stone cracks the Legionship directly under my feet.

Then we're over. A bowl of air cushions us. For a moment we hang, the engines suddenly silent. There's a swoosh of wind over the still-turning propellers. Then Del noses the Legionship down and we plunge.

I wish I'd paid more attention in Physics. Gravity, mass, speed, acceleration. Air is thicker at lower altitudes. Does thick air slow us? Acceleration: the rate of change of velocity with respect to time. Or velocity multiplied by time? Knowing the answer wouldn't loosen the clutch of dread at my heart. Del's helmet goes black as she grins madly at Trisk.

The ship jounces. Del yanks a lever and the Legionship levels and steadies with a shuddering groan.

Del pulls off her helmet and turns to Trisk. "I thought Arcadium girls don't scare."

"By rights, you should be caged!" Trisk's hands harden into fists. "To put such a thing as a Legionship at risk to mock me. Blast you and your Sower and your Sower's Sower until the beginning of time. I live for the day you're downed north of the Stairs and you beg me and my dogs to rescue you."

Del stretches her arms above her head. "Battle dogs are old technology. When we deploy the new fleet, there'll be no use for them. Except in a pot. I ate dog once."

"Shut your trap."

"It's true. They make dog stew at The Spices. With a bit of that green stuff." Del looks back for me. "What was that called again, girl? The green leaf?"

Just the thing to make Trisk hate me even more. "Oregano."

"What was that?"

"Oregano!"

"Your dogs are history, Trisk, that's all I'm saying. I could do this crossing in my sleep. I just wanted a bit of fun. You girls liked it, didn't you?"

None of us dare say no.

Below, a lone Mooring comes into view. Del cradles the Legionship. When the hatch opens, I suck in fresh, cold air.

"Welcome to Holdfast, recruits." Del says. "The fleet is looking for pilots. You could be at the controls of a helio in a month. Trials are tomorrow. Don't miss out!"

From the Moorings, we walk a paved road between two crags. The road enters a tunnel through an elaborately carved arch. At the top, a name is carved into the dark gray stone: HOLDFAST. Beneath the name are three interlocking crescents, the Legion emblem. Below, the Legion's motto is chiseled in the Chronicler's distinctive hand: *We serve the Mother. No price is too high for peace.*

For security, the Weave doesn't allow images of military bastions to circulate. I know that Holdfast is the largest of the bastions and the Legion's command center. The tunnel is wide and angles downhill, with a floor of smooth stone. A few legionaries glance at us, then go about their business. At intervals, smaller tunnels open off the sides.

There are cameras everywhere. Del disappears down a side tunnel, her helmet under her arm as she waves good-bye.

Abruptly, the tunnel widens into an enormous open space. Above curves a broad glass ceiling sectioned into hexagonal panes. As I stare up, it's like looking through the eye of an enormous bee. Far above is a strip of blue sky.

Trisk motions us onto a broad balcony. "We call this the Gallery." She points straight ahead, over the railing and toward a glass wall swirling with mist. Like the ceiling, the wall is sectioned into hexagonal glass panes. "The Rift itself."

The wall is easily the height of three Collegium walls stacked one on top of the other. Beyond-the-Weave is hidden by swirling mist.

A plaza lies a dozen or more levels down. In the middle, the Legion emblem, three interlocking crescents, gleams silver with pergama, the most precious of the metals. Legionaries cross it, busy with their tasks.

In Geology, we learned the Rift was created when two tectonic plates collided centuries ago. There are eleven bastions along it, from SeaWall on the western shore to the Eastern Shield. "Some nights, there are gatherings in the Gallery," Trisk tells us. When she's not angry or mocking, she doesn't look that much older than us. "Troupes with spectacles. Speeches. Whatnot. Eventually, you'll cross a Rail."

The mist slowly boils upwards, fed by the Rift River below. Susalee's eyes are wide with wonder. "A Rail?"

Trisk points toward the glass wall and up. Long shadows reveal themselves then vanish again in the mist: bridges over the Rift, set at different heights and angles. Susalee can't help herself. "How soon will we see scrags? When do we cross a Rail? What weapons will we have?"

Heedless, she answers her own questions. "They bring males across the Rails, don't they? Are there males at Holdfast now? Can we see them?"

My heart skips. It's one thing for Trisk to frighten us with tales. But with Beyond-the-Weave close, males could be nearby.

Trisk's black eyes glitter. "What's your name?"

Susalee is used to being the smartest girl, the professors' favorite. She hasn't seen Trisk the way I have.

"Susalee 584-TxS. Top in my class," Susalee says eagerly.

"Best at everything, you say?"

Susalee picks up the threat in her tone, but Mariza doesn't, even when Susalee squeezes her hand. "Susalee runs fastest. The professors love her. What, it's true, Susi!"

"In Holdfast, recruits speak when they're spoken to. Six infractions for Susalee 584-TxS. Three for your friend, for being irritating. I'm guessing by hair color: Mariza 584-BxB? One more question, Susalee 584-TxS, and you'll be on Cyclon duty for the next six months."

Susalee looks slapped.

I can't help my smile. Maybe the Legion will teach her a little of what it's like to be me. My smile vanishes when I realize: if the Legion is this hard on Susalee, how will the rest of us survive?

Trisk separates us into two groups. "East Quadrant there," she says, pointing to Tem and Helma. A young legionary appears to

guide them. The rest of us—me, Susalee, Mariza, Becke, and Edba
—are to follow Trisk to West.

There's no time for Edba and Tem to say goodbye. Since
arriving at the Collegium as first forms, they've never been apart.
Tem looks over her shoulder once. She sees Trisk watching, so
turns back quickly before disappearing.

I don't think Edba feels me take her hand as we enter West
Quadrant.

Trisk points out baths, a training arena, leather and metal
workshops, and a bakery. Our sleeping hall is on Corridor F,
which tunnels deep into the rock. The room is round with
windowless rock walls. The beds are placed at intervals like on a
dial and separated by heavy red curtains. Especially after a
sleepless night on the Legionship, my bed looks delicious, wide
and piled with pillows. A little heater burbles. The room is
pleasantly warm.

I can hear the Cyclon hum beneath our feet.

"You'll find uniforms and other necessaries in the trunks,"
Trisk tells us. There's one at the foot of each bed. "Change now.
Breakfast is laid in the next room. Lind will be here shortly for
orientation."

Edba raises her hand to ask a question.

Trisk moves as if to open her scroll. "Do you want an
infraction?"

Edba lets her arm fall.

Once Trisk is gone, Edba babbles. "Why separate us now?
What's different about East? When will I see her again?"

"You might as well ask why we're here at all." Becke examines
her bed, then pulls open her trunk. "Let's eat."

As the others put on their uniforms, I slip Wylla's gift into my
trunk. As soon as I can, I'll dump it down the Cyclon. I pull on a
black tunic, thick black leggings, and used boots: leather, thick-
soled, laced to the knee. Each of us has a new scroll. My scroll
rolls like my old one, but also shapes into ball that bounces.

All of our information is there, transmitted from the life fibers
on our necks.

By the time I'm dressed, the others are eating: cold baked fish in lemon sauce, fresh rolls, and one red plum each. To drink, there's sweet coffee in an urn.

Was it only yesterday we were students in the Collegium? Yesterday, I was so worried about my assignment I couldn't eat. Now, I sop up fish sauce with the roll and gnaw every morsel of sweet fruit from the stone at the plum's center. We're drinking coffee when a legionary arrives, bouncing her scroll. She introduces herself as Lind. She's short and pink-cheeked, with bright yellow hair. "Which one of you is Dinitra 584-KxA?"

I raise my hand, feeling optimistic for the first time in weeks.

"You stay behind." Lind points at the other girls. "The rest of you, follow me."

I head back into the sleeping quarters to wait.

8

12

L ater, a different legionary shakes me awake. There are no windows so I can't tell if I've been asleep a minute or hours. I'm crossways on the bed, my mouth thick with the sweetness of the coffee.

"Follow me," she chirps.

I have to skip-step to keep up. The legionary lopes down F corridor, then crosses the balcony and descends zig-zag stairs to the Gallery floor. The great wall is still shrouded in mist. East's corridors look the same as West's: halls, workshops, legionaries doing whatever legionaries do when they're not piloting ships or hunting scrags. I search for Tem or Helma. Once, I think I see Helma hunched in a doorway, but I can't be sure.

The legionary turns up a dark hallway. The floor is slippery with mud. The hallway angles up, climbing away from the Rift. At the end are barred metal doors. I'm grateful for a moment to catch my breath, but the legionary doesn't pause. Beside the doors is a round metal hatch. The legionary needs both hands to spin the hatch open. Using both hands, she grabs the bar above the hatch and swings through.

I have to jump up to reach the bar. On the other side, I land with a splash in a mud puddle.

The winter cold slaps me so hard I cough. It's still daytime:

noon or early afternoon. I look behind me, to sheer gray cliffs. We must be in the same narrow valley where the Legionship landed. Since we went through East Quadrant, the Moorings must be to my right: west. I can't tell if the ship is still there, since the Moorings are blocked by a black cinder cone.

The legionary waits for me. Ahead is a paved path that leads down a steep hill to a stone building. A glass tower stands to one side, built around what looks like a large tree. I can see over the building's roof to a series of pens built end-to-end along the valley's narrow floor.

In the largest pen, legionaries work battle dogs over an obstacle course.

"No," I say. "The last time I was close to a dog, it tried to kill me."

The legionary shakes her head. "Poor you."

Pointing, she names the pens: Northpen, Centerpen, Auxpen, Mainpen. Northpen, she says, is big enough to land the transports that deliver fresh pups and ship out guard dogs destined for the containments. Centerpen has the obstacle course: barrels, fences, and a wide trench.

The kennel keeper is called Benit, she tells me.

"Do you work there?" I desperately want her to say no, since that could mean I'm not assigned there. I have no wish to be anywhere near Trisk.

My fragile hope dies with a shake of her head. "They call me Birdie because I flits here and there, odd jobber. Deliver messages, guests, needful things. Today, I am delivering you, on special orders of Herself."

"Herself?"

"Only one of them with legs like a battle dog!" she grins.

The consequences for being brave feel more painful by the second.

Birdie gnaws a finger. "Listen careful. Them creatures bite through the bars. If they snag you with even a claw, they'll drag you close. Their nature. So you run like this."

Birdie flattens her arms to her sides and wobbles. She looks ridiculous. "If you value your skin, don't dally."

At the kennel door, the stink is so thick I taste it: dog spittle, shit, the bite of cleaning fluid. Inside are dozens of cages that form narrow aisles. Birdie says something, but I can't hear over the howling.

She flattens her arms to her side, waggling at me, then takes off.

Ridiculous.

I do the same.

The dogs push as close to the aisle as possible. I see in blinks: a slab of tongue stabbing at a latch, claws scraping, fangs scraping metal. If my heart could leap from my chest, it would, and wobble leaky behind me.

At least my heart would be a smaller target than my suddenly too-wide body, too-long arms, and too-slow legs.

I waggle to a stop at a small shed. Birdie hoots, "She lives!"

Then I bend over and retch up every morsel of breakfast, including the coffee, gone sour. I've lost a meal twice in twenty-four hours: a new record.

The kennel's far doors are chained open, onto Centerpen. There, legionaries are working battle dogs. Gradually, the caged dogs stop howling. The nearest dog—mud-colored or caked in mud, I can't tell—places its paws in the corner nearest me, lies down, and stares. If I had to pick the worst thing that could happen to me, it would be exactly this.

There's a bang from inside the shed. A woman appears in a dirty wool smock, her bare arms sheathed in sweat. Her expression is neither harsh nor kind. Curious, I guess.

"Turn around and let me look at you," the woman says.

If she's disappointed, I can't tell. "I'm Benit."

Birdie gives me an awkward wave, then waggles back the way we came, dogs howling their farewells.

Benit motions for me to take a seat on an upturned bucket. "She sent word about you just yesterday. I don't mind saying it was a surprise."

For both of us. I don't bother to ask who *she* is: Kesh.

"I'd say you don't know a thing about battle dogs."

Will telling the truth make things better or worse? I'm about to confess my fears when I hear someone entering from Centerpen. I see the dog first: broad head, yellow teeth, ears chewed to nubs. The dog's shoulders reach the handler's hip. The dog is limping.

"By the Mother's blessed breath." The handler is Trisk. "What is this Collegium slurr doing here?"

Benit kneels beside the dog and gently lifts its injured leg. A deep red gash opens the flesh above the knee. "What happened?"

"124 broke the line."

The number 132 is branded on the dog's left haunch. If I had to describe the color of its eyes, I'd say pus.

"Blast you, Trisk." Benit sounds exasperated. "132 is due at the containment by week's end. I can't send her injured."

Trisk is more concerned with me. "Don't tell me we went all the way to the Collegium just to bring back a new kennel cleaner."

Benit moves her hands over the dog's chest, checking for other wounds. "When I need your help, I'll ask for it."

Between the cold and my terror at being so close to 132, I'm practically vibrating. The wild dog that attacked me was smaller than 132 and starving. With one jerk of her jaws, 132 could rip my head off.

Trisk face lights up. "Let's see how brave she is."

She steps back abruptly.

"Don't you do it, Trisk," Benit warns.

Too late. Trisk points at me: "Go!"

132 seems to shrink as she gathers on her haunches. I stand, the bucket falling backwards. 132 leaps, and I see the metal prongs on the inside of her collar pierce her flesh with little blood florets.

Piss wets my leggings. But 132 doesn't reach me. Her shoulders lift almost as if she's levitating, a dog ship borne upwards by an invisible propeller. The reason is clear when I see Trisk hauling back on the leash, her arms bulging. 132 shrieks, then crashes on her back.

Trisk pumps her fist in the air. "The new cleaner pissed herself!"

132 wobbles up. She shakes, a bit of her blood spattering on my Legion tunic.

Benit snatches 132's leash. "I'd piss myself if you sent 132 at me in close quarters. Why don't you do your jig again for the camera so that everyone in Holdfast sees how you hurt this beast?

"You're too soft, Benit." Trisk folds her arms. "You're not hurt, are you, little Chronicler? Better a dog than a scrag, right? You'll have to get used to them dogs if you're going to clean the cages."

Benit scoffs. "The girl's no cleaner."

"What then, mash-pounder? I know: shit collector." Trisk grins.

Benit examines the new wounds at 132's neck. "She'll train the hyba cross."

Trisk turns on her. "The cross is mine. You've said as much."

"Never did and never would have. Herself sent the order yesterday, with this girl's name on it. Which is Dinitra, by the way. Best learn to say it."

Trisk's face chain vibrates with rage. "I earned her, Benit. You can't give her to this, this... *Collegium girl.*"

Even in my wet leggings, with 132 still watching balefully, I feel a jolt of pleasure. Whatever the cross is, Trisk wants it. She can't have it. I'll pay for this, likely more than once. But at this second, I'm fiercely glad I got whatever Trisk wanted.

"You're training dogs today and so you will be tomorrow, unless new orders come," Benit tells her. "When they need you on the Legionship, there you'll go. We do what we're told. Off with you before I tell Kesh you've injured another dog. You'll be the one called shit carrier."

"You wouldn't dare."

"I don't do dares."

Trisk doesn't back down. "Something stinks here. When I find out what it is, don't think I won't remember, Kennel Keeper." Trisk stamps away.

"A pity," Benit says, as if to herself. "She wasn't always so cruel."

Then and there, I confess: the dog attack when I was little, my nightmares. I show the kennel keeper my forearm, rippled pink where the wild dog tore flesh from bone. "I can't work with dogs. Meaning I can't be near them. Meaning this is all impossible." I look down as my leggings, the piss patches cold against my inner thighs. "Please don't make me."

Benit listens while tending 132. From a box, she removes a vial of clear liquid, a needle, black thread, and gauze. Expertly, she forces 132's massive head up, then dribbles several drops of liquid down her throat.

The dog sits heavily, then flops to her side, snoring. As Benit plucks grit from the dog's shoulder with the curved needle, I tell her I'd rather clean, I'd rather make mash, I'd rather carry shit.

Benit strings a curved needle with black thread. "You'll do what the commander says, Dinitra 584-KxA." After flushing the wounds with alcohol, Benit presses the needle through the edge of the gash. "Blast that Trisk. This leg will swell like a peach."

The needle eye, a little thicker than the tip, needs an extra tug to pull through. Benit makes six stitches, tying each one off separately. "You're in luck, though. You're not getting a dog. The hyba cross is entirely new." She gestures at the tall glass tower.

I look over my shoulder at the tower I passed on my way in, wondering why Trisk wants this cross so badly. Everything I'd heard in Biotics about hybas was terrifying. A mix of hyena, baboon, and bearcat, some cubs killed and ate their Sowers. The experiment was discontinued. In class, Professor Rusta told us those Sowers are honored for their sacrifice for the Weave.

Benit finishes by coating the battle dog's wound with orange salve. The salve smells of rosemary. "Rosemary kills infection and keeps a wound from swelling. The orange is arnica for pain. Remember that."

Benit finishes by draping the battle dog in burlap sacking. "She needs to sleep off the forgetting I gave her. Come. I'll introduce you to the cross."

There's no escape.

I follow Benit to the glass tower beside the kennel. Through a connecting door, there's a small enclosure encased in metal mesh beside what I thought was a tree. The tree is actually an elaborate structure made of logs and wooden platforms. At the base is a thick carpet of straw.

Like the other cages, this one has a number by the door: 12.

In the Tower, there's a new scent. Benit grins. "Burnt butter. That's the bit of bearcat in the original hyba."

If you smell burnt butter north of the Rift, Benit tells me, "best to run to water. That's the only way you'll survive. Wild hybas hunt in packs from the trees. Once you actually see a pack, it's too late. But they're terrified of water, that's a certainty."

As Benit talks, a shape separates from the highest platform. I see its body in flashes: a dog-like face with jowls. A black nose. Golden eyes. The hyba cross has a long, furred, muscular tail. She descends by curling the tail around the logs to hang her body, seeming to move in slow-motion.

My heart hammers. I'm terrified of dogs. But this creature is a dog times a million, a billion. I barely hear Benit, chattering on about how decades ago some juvenile hybas escaped a Sower lab near the Rift and made it to Beyond-the-Weave. I can't take my eyes off 12. She's twice the size of 132, with jaws that could easily crush my head.

Benit tells me Kesh captured a wounded hyba on patrol, then brought it to Holdfast. "The thing howled the entire time. Awful racket. Before it died, she extracted enough tissue to make her drafts."

"Drafts." I'm confused. Drafts are first attempts at a writing assignment or a drawing.

"She wanted to make something new for the Legion. Something that would protect us from scrags. And more."

By now, the hyba cross has reached to the straw covering the floor. Her fur is copper-colored. Black stripes cut across her shoulders and flanks. Her ears and tail tip end in white tufts.

"Kesh added dog, to make her trainable. Tiger, for the stripes. Some lynx. You see that in the ear tufts," Benit says proudly.

My carnivorous potato is a child's mess next to 12.

"Or maybe for the quiet? I'm no Sower." Benit murmurs at the beast, and its golden eyes lock to her. "How is my sweet girl? Come here, lovely."

As 12 pads toward Benit, the kennel keeper taps her ear. 12 might as well be hovering over the straw. The straw doesn't even rustle under her pan-sized paws. "When she hunts, even if it's for a ball, once she starts, she never gives up."

The hyba cross sniffs Benit's hand through the mesh, then gently chuffs.

"An adult hyba in the wild is blacker than the blackest pitch. No stripes. We call her color brindle."

I hadn't noticed the door in the enclosure until Benit reaches for the latch. "Ready to go in?"

I feel like officially surrendering. "Does it matter what I feel?"

"Now you're getting the hang of things," Benit says.

12 greets us with a stretch, the black claws digging into the straw as her tail lashes. From her paws to her tail tip, she's almost the width of the enclosure. Benit murmurs endearments as she collects a collar and leash from a hook. "Don't let her size fool you. 12 is still a puppy."

12 shakes herself, then licks her lips, as blue-black as her tongue.

Benit slips the collar over her neck, then then latches it. Without warning, Benit presses the leash into my hand.

I drop the leash like it's made of fire.

12 growls. Swiftly, Benit picks up the leash. She presses it into my hand again. Using the same low tone she did with 12, she says to me, "Calm yourself. Watch me."

Benit raises her forearm to command 12 to lie down. Then Benit pulls her arm back and turns her palm up, bringing the hand to her shoulder. 12 sits. "You have to master her. Show her you are in charge. So far, those are the only commands she knows. Use them."

Benit slips out of the enclosure and beckons me to follow. "Come, let's take her for a turn around the kennel."

I try not to look at the creature pacing at my side. Her brindled shoulder brushes high as my elbow. As we pass the cages, the battle dogs are completely silent, crouching as far from her as they can.

I don't think 12 even notices them. At the same time, she seems to notice everything. Her huge head tracks back and forth, her blue-black tongue dangling as she takes everything in.

At the shed, 132 is still asleep. Benit grabs a pouch of meat nuggets and slips the strap around my shoulder. I'm to give 12 a nugget every time she successfully completes a command.

The thought of putting my hand near 12's jaws makes my knees go soft.

Benit sees me sway and so does 12, who again softly growls.

"Settle yourself, Dinitra 584-KxA," Benit murmurs.

"I need to sit."

"You cannot. If you turn your back on her, you'll become prey. Remember what I said. She never relents."

Benit shows me how to position a meat nugget on my palm, then press my fingers together and back. "From now on, she'll only eat from your hand. She'll walk only with you. You'll be the one who cleans the cage, brings fresh straw."

Benit gently squeezes my shoulder. "She's a little nervous, too. She wants to love you. Let her."

I do as I'm told: palm flat, fingers bent back. 12 sniffs, her golden eyes going from mine to the meat nugget. Her whiskers brush my palm: some long and springy and others bristly and stiff. She uses only the nubby teeth between her front fangs to lift the meat.

"Trisk is probably more dangerous to you than any beast," Benit tells me. "A beast is loyal. But a human? Especially one like Trisk? She's a tricky creature."

"Trisk thinks I shouldn't be here. She thinks I took something from her."

"Did you?"

"I took 12."

"Nothing you can do about that."

"You mean don't turn my back on Trisk?" I'm surprised I can make a joke.

"You are a fast learner." Benit grins.

I'm starting to like the kennel keeper.

Benit says I will be 12's source of everything. "Food. Water. Trips outside. You tell her when to wake up and when to sleep. You and no other. We're hoping 12 obeys like a battle dog. They'd give their lives for their handlers."

Hope? "What about the baboon part? The tiger?"

Benit shrugs. "We'll see."

Benit loads a hovuck with a bale of straw and a bucket of mash, marked with the number 12. The hovuck is old and rattles, barely lifting off the ground as Benit locks in the coordinates for 12's tower.

132 stirs, drawing 12's gaze. A little ridge of copper hair lifts between the hyba cross's shoulders.

"Head back to the Tower." Benit's voice is firm. "12 shouldn't be here when 132's awake."

"What will 132 do?"

"Die when 12 rips out her throat."

In 12's enclosure, my hands are slick with sweat as I unbuckle 12's collar. I feel like I'm outside my body as I hook the mash bucket near the water trough. 12 gives herself one terrific shake, then pads to her meal. She has it down in three gulps.

As Benit instructed, I spread fresh straw. 12 defecates like a rabbit, in little balls. As quietly as she descended, she climbs up the structure. At the highest platform, she turns and lies down. Her tail drips over the side, the white tuft twitching.

Her golden eyes never leave me.

9

Tracker Map

I n Holdfast, no one gives a second glance to a fresh recruit in muddy boots trailing a burnt butter smell. In the Rift, the mist has parted. For the first time, I see the Rails clearly. A gentle snow has made its way down the gorge, coating them in a lacy veil.

For the first time, I see Beyond-the-Weave: a rock face patched in furry green moss. Ferns and other plants root where the rock splits and hang like hair. I glimpse legionaries leaving Holdfast through the glass of the lowest Rail, the thump of their boots like distant thunder.

In our quarters, the rock walls are warm with light. Towels and blankets heap on the floor. I can hear the clinks of forks against plates in the next room.

Before joining them, I change my leggings. I hide the still-damp pair under my bed.

When I slip into a chair, Becke slides me a plate she's saved. "They told us it's hyba meat. They like to scare us into believing there are hybas south of the Rift."

I don't correct her: there are hybas here, at least a kind of hyba.

"The meat tastes like lamb, to be honest." Becke pushes a small dish toward me. "Rose water pudding. The chef here has skill," she admits. "Tasty."

Susalee leans toward me sniffing. "What's that smell?"

My day comes out in a gulp. "They sent me to the kennels. To the battle dogs."

Susalee looks shocked. "Everyone knows you're terrified of dogs. It's all over your Compendium."

"Technically, not a dog. Or not all dog," I say.

"What do you mean?"

"She's more hyba than dog, or so the kennel keeper says. With a bit of extra tiger for the stripes. Hyena, howler monkey, too. Lynx. I lost track of everything that's in her."

Becke grips my shoulder. "How could you bear it?"

Her touch opens the space inside me where the confusion, surprise, and fear of the past two days are packed. "That's not even all of it," I groan. "That awful Trisk was there, the legionary on the ship. She tried to scare me with one of her battle dogs. And she succeeded."

"Didn't you tell them you were afraid?" Susalee insists.

"Do I have a choice? Do any of us?" Only yesterday, we were bickering over the Rule. Only yesterday, Asta urged me to volunteer for the Legion. Only yesterday, I met the three-sheaf commander, saw her metal leg smeared with the paint I'd brewed, from a gift I ruined. Everything's changed except me: same old Dinitra. On the Legionship, I vowed to fix myself, start fresh.

How can you fix something like fear? Fear is so deep inside you can't pull it out.

I try to smile when Tem uses a napkin to wipe away my tears. "It has been a very long day," she says kindly.

"Tell me what you did," I say. "Especially if it has nothing to do with dogs or hybas or nasty legionaries like Trisk."

Susalee tells the story. Lind led them around West and through the Gallery. Like me, they saw the Rails. Most of Holdfast—workrooms, training gyms, the kitchens, and common areas—is tunneled deep into the rock. They saw storage areas for food, cloth, weapons, and machine parts. Pumps bring fresh water to every room. In the baths, the water pools fill with water from sulphurous hot springs.

"Are there other new girls?" I ask.

"We saw some at lunch," Becke says. "We didn't really talk. Lind made us sit at our own table."

Mariza shakes her head. "I couldn't believe the way they looked at us. Like we had horns or tails. You know the type."

On rare visits to Shell Bay from the Collegium, we'd see Arcadium girls buying sweets in the shops. They were tall and broad, built for rough work.

Edba lowers her voice. "If you ask me, they haven't had Collegium girls here for a long time. Why would they? I still don't understand why we're here."

After lunch, they practiced shooting crossbows. "Real ones," Susalee adds, "not the ones we had in Physical Appreciation." Susalee was top sharp-shooter every year at the Collegium. For the first time, they had live strela bolts, fully charged. Since the crossbow fittings are all pergama, the crossbows weigh no more than a paring knife. "Very light on the trigger, too," Susalee says.

"You should have seen it, Dini." Edba nods at Susalee. "With real bolts, the target doesn't collapse like it does at the Collegium. It evaporates in a poof of dust. Like it was never even there."

"Then we got these." On the table, Mariza set a white roll of paper. "It's called a tracker map."

I hide my surprise. The roll looks like what Professor Wylla gave me, what Flicke shoved into my pocket before I climbed the icy ladder into the Legionship. For a moment, I think Mariza must have taken this from my trunk.

They all flatten their tracker maps. On hers, Susalee presses a thumb to the corner. The map's surface glows. Lines, triangles, and colors swim up from under the paper's surface.

"Here's the Rift, here's Holdfast." Susalee's finger taps the map. The shapes are like photographs: Holdfast with the Gallery like a bee's eye, the long, black gorge of the Rift. "It works by combining our formulas and embedding them in the paper. Except it's more than paper because of the light inside. They put energy cells in the paper, kind of like strela bolts. Except the maps don't explode."

"Like your drawings and the strela combined. Sort of," says Becke.

Susalee points to black dots. "We can see each other. Look. Susalee, Mariza, Edba, Becke. Then Lind way over here, in the Gallery. We're all in the same squadron."

I fight the urge to run to my trunk, snatch Wylla's gift from its hiding place. But the professor could not have been clearer. Keep this hidden. No one must know you have it.

Susalee points to a cluster of spots in Holdfast's West Quadrant. "Those are the other legionaries in our squadron. Arcadium, all of them," she adds. "Here's the coolest part. The map knows where you've been. It transmits to and from our life fibers. Our history, I mean. See? Here's the Centrum, where Lind says I was kept before the Collegium."

The Centrum is marked by a black rhombus with a sharp point. Susalee slides her finger to the Collegium, the map's glow following. Silver threads tremble on the map's surface.

"The Signal Way," Susalee says. "Look, ships in real time." Black ovals slowly move along the threads. "This is how we got to Holdfast. This one here?"

Another silver thread connects the Centrum to the Collegium. "That's how I was transported when I was six."

"This is the coolest part." Becke touches her map to the edge of Susalee's map. The seam seems to smudge, then the maps knit together, the seam invisible.

Becke points to a square to the south of the Centrum. "That's where I was kept before being brought to the Collegium. "Cut Hill. You know what that means."

I repeat what she's always said: "Some of the Weave's best chefs come from Cut Hill."

Becke grins. "See, I always knew I was meant to be a chef!"

When Mariza and Edba join their maps, we can see that Edba was kept not far from Holdfast, in a village called Pergama, just like the precious metal. Mariza was kept in the south, at The Spices. "The more you travel, the more places appear," Susalee says. "Lind explained it. The substrate absorbs each new transmission from our life fibers."

"Blah-de-blah, who cares?" Becke squeezes my shoulder. "Once you get your map, Dini, you'll know where your Keeper raised you, too. We'll be able to join them all together, won't we?"

I know what Asta would say: you have to be logical about these things. Not emotional. You have to look at the facts. *Think, Dini.* Why would you not be on the tracker map?

Maybe Kesh took me because she had to. She wanted the others. But the Collegium Director forced her to take me, too. That's why they fought at the feast. They put me in the kennel because I'm expendable. I'm extra: not important.

Right now, the logic seems as relentless as the hyba cross.

"I'm going to bed," I say abruptly.

I take a shower, the burnt butter smell sluicing off me and down a metal drain. When I climb into the bed in a fresh shift— my bed, a Legion bed—the others are still softly talking around the table.

When I wake, the room is dark. A single light glows near the door. It takes me a moment to remember where I am: West, Corridor F. Holdfast, the Rift. I recognize Becke's snores. Something rustles: my feet beneath the sheets.

Bless the Mother for *Capra aegagrus* and my night vision. The stone floors are cold. Professor Wylla's gift is exactly where I left it in the trunk, tucked under a night shift.

The gift doesn't look like paper to me. It looks like a tracker map.

I slip back into bed, pull the blanket over my head, and unroll the paper. Holding my breath, I press my thumb to the corner.

The map gently glows. I take my thumb off and the map goes dark. Why did Wylla have my tracker map? If the other girls were given maps, why am I supposed to hide mine?

Shapes swim into view: the Rift, Holdfast and its glass Gallery, the trembling silver threads of the Signal Way. I see the Collegium, the Centrum. I must have been kept there, too. A little spot marks where I'm bent over in my bed, a single girl in Holdfast.

Then I notice a second spot north of the Rift. In Beyond-the-Weave.

Not possible. Even Asta's logic would fail her. I brush at the map, thinking it's some piece of fluff. No: it's a spot. There's no on/off switch, no reset for a tracker map. I place my fingertips on the spot and spread them.

The spot splits: two spots.

Two people who share this map.

I open my mouth, shut it, open again. Two people on the far side of the Rift. Somehow connected to my formula. How could that be? Are there Collegium girls north of the Rift? Battle dog handlers? Recruits like me?

Why not? Asta's voice, patient and logical. If a tracker map can be infused with different formulas, the spot could be any stranger. Their formula would just be included with mine, as Susalee's was with the others.

Asta's voice again. *You have to admit the possibility this is a scrag.*

"Shut up, Asta," I whisper.

Even thinking the word *scrag* makes me dizzy. I press my thumb to the map again and there it is: two shapes. In those few seconds, they've edged a little closer to the Rift.

I pull my hand away. Whoever has this tracker map might have one, too. One where I appear as a little black spot. Here, hidden under my blankets, in the darkened room.

"Dinitra?"

My heart practically leaps to the floor. I pull the blanket back.

Edba stands by my bed, her face wet with tears. "I had a dream Tem was lost somewhere. I miss her so much, Dini."

I shove the tracker map to the foot of my bed. "Can I get in with you?" Edba asks.

"Of course." I scoot over.

She's shivering, so I wrap her in my arms. "How long were you standing there?" I ask. Could she have seen my tracker map?

Edba is already asleep.

10

Two Hearts

The next morning, I cross the Gallery alone. I'm not even through the hatch and my insides are squeezed tight, my breath coming in little bursts. Flicke's final words before I boarded the Legionship are my only real clue about why I'm here. *For the Bond, I do this, the Bond and nothing more.*

By the Mother's bones, what *Bond*? What does a bond have to do with 12?

The kennel's stink hits me fresh. The dogs howl just as they did yesterday. I wobble to the shed where Benit's pounding fresh mash. She points to the hovuck, already loaded with a bale of fresh straw and 12's portion of mash. "Let's roust her from her beauty sleep."

At the Tower, 12's eyes lock to us. She's stretched along the same high platform. From beneath, she looks more hyba than battle dog. The jaws are heavy like a hyena's and there's something relentless about her eyes, like a tiger. Her tail, hanging like a thick vine, ticks at the white-tufted tip.

I set the mash bucket down outside the gate. Then I throw up breakfast, a lemon-colored smear on the stone floor. Everything smells like burnt butter. Crouching, I see the edge of the tracker map I've stuck in my boot.

My boot was the only safe place I could think of.

"Pretend you've fed her a hundred times," Benit tells me. "A thousand. The only way."

From the wall, Benit takes a long prod from a rack. The tip is head high and glows yellow. "If it makes you feel better."

The prod was a gift from a friend who ran the guard dogs at a containment, she explains. "The closer we get to the Great Quest, the less we need containments or things like these," she says, meaning the prod. "Mind you, the prod is a last resort. 12 would take off your arm quicker than I could flatten her. I couldn't use the prod twice."

12 moves down from her perch. It's like an avalanche in slow motion, the massive head and shoulders leading, the structure creaking from her weight. Last of all comes the white tip of tail, still ticking.

Benit's gaze is admiring. I take a chance.

"May I ask you a question?"

"One."

I choose my words carefully. If I ask about the Bond directly, she'll want to know who told me about it. "These containments," I say. "Where you send dogs. This is where the Legion takes the scrags the legionaries catch in Beyond-the-Weave."

"That's not a question." Benit folds her arms. "Get to it, Dinitra 584-KxA. 12 wants her feed."

The hyba cross reaches the structure's base. Benit has taught her to sit until the gate opens. 12's tail wraps around her paws and ends at her right haunch, the tip raised like a little plant. "It must be hard to work in such a place. A place with men."

I'm testing her patience. "Do Collegium girls know what a question is?" Benit says.

I clear my throat. "Your friend, the guards. They must feel a special, I don't know, a *bond* with the dogs? The dogs protect them, right?" *Idiot*, I think. "A bond against the men. That bond?"

Benit shakes her head. "You're asking if we have a bond with these beasts? Look at her."

12 is working her blue-black slab of tongue around her snout in anticipation of breakfast. "That's the whole point, Dinitra. We build

a bond with the creatures so they'll follow orders. Imagine having to guard men without them. It's bad enough we have to deal with the scrags the legionaries catch. Spitting and snatching! We have to wrap the cages in burlap or else the crew won't load them."

In Replicative Sciences, we learned that Sowers insert a virus into the men they brew for reproduction. They feed the men a supplement to keep the virus dormant until the men are no longer needed. "Is the virus contagious?" I ask Benit.

"That's two questions," she answers roughly. I feel a buttery burst of air at my shoulder. Impatient for breakfast, 12 has broken from her sit and moved to the fence.

"Remember, scrags are sneaky. They run in packs, too, like any wild beast. They try to wheedle their way into the guards' trust. Then they attack." Benit looks from me to the prod. "This ain't made for dogs, girl. That would be cruel. This is for men."

"How did your friend stop being afraid?" Technically, my third question.

Benit takes pity on me. "I see now. You're asking how not to be afraid. One, you don't have to be afraid of men. The Great Quest is almost complete. By the time you're my age, well, men will be a thing of the past. Like..." She shakes her head. "Like war itself. They'll be no more need. The Sowers will win and Beyond-the-Weave will be ours for the taking."

This doesn't help me with my fear of 12.

"You must master your fear," Benit says abruptly. "Once you do, nothing can truly hurt you." Benit looks at 12 lovingly. "There's someone who's been waiting for her mash like a good, good girl."

I do as I'm told: unlatch the gate, step in, latch it behind me, go to the corner, lift the empty bucket from the hook, hang fresh mash. 12 gulps it down.

"You'll take her outside to Auxpen now," Benit says. "Put the collar on her. Slowly."

As I approach with the collar, 12 closes her eyes. The collar is thick leather, of some scaly skin I don't recognize. For an instant I touch 12's ears: softer than goose down.

Her golden eyes stay on me. My hands shake so hard I can't work the latch.

A low growl rumbles in 12's chest

"Easy," Benit murmurs. "One thing fits the other. It always does."

The collar latches.

Benit opens the cage door and I walk through it, 12 padding gracefully at my side.

At the shed, Benit helps me pull on a sheepskin jacket. Hers, she says, for luck.

The morning is blustery. Low dark clouds scud overhead. "I'll watch over you this first week," Benit says. "Then you're on your own."

Auxpen is small, a mesh fence surrounding hardpan dirt. Over the top, Benit has draped netting she vows 12 can't rip through.

12's ears swivel at every sound: handlers working battle dogs in Northpen, birds, the whirring of propellers from the Moorings beyond the cinder cone. Sometimes, I think the thud of my heart must echo in 12's ears.

"Walk the perimeter," Benit orders. "She's full of beans this morning."

For days, walking is all we do. Around the perimeter, on the diagonal. Clockwise and counterclockwise. Once 12's used to Auxpen, she starts to chase after every bird that perches on the netting, every leaf that somehow tumbles into the pen. Each time, the leash rips through my hands, taking a bit of flesh with it. Once, 12 pulls so fast and hard I'm jerked entirely off my feet. She drags me like a loose thread, oblivious.

When I look up, Trisk is standing next to Benit, grinning with satisfaction.

12 sheds several teeth a day, a common hyba trait. Benit told me she has two hearts, giving her tremendous endurance. Each evening, I drag back to my quarters while 12 remains as playful as ever.

The second week, Benit climbs onto an empty licor barrel to demonstrate commands I'm to teach 12. For each correct response,

I give the hyba cross a meat nugget from a pouch belted at my waist.

I might as well eat the nuggets myself. 12 gulps down what I give her, then does as she pleases.

Over dinner one night, Becke pumps me for details. I have the same story: I walk. I get dragged. The hyba cross treats me like a dust speck. All the while my stomach is in knots.

Meanwhile, the others have gone from strela practice to exploring the valley with their tracker maps. In the afternoons, they rotate through piloting, advanced meteorology, and population management.

I shake my head. Population management?

For when the Weave expands beyond the Rift and has to deal with the scrags, Becke tells me. "Sort of like a preserve. Proper food and shelter, at least until the Weave can build cities and such. One day, it will be Weave all the way to the Pole."

One night, they don't come back until the next evening. Becke is breathless with news. They crossed the lowest Rail to bivouac with a patrol. She defines "bivouac": a temporary camp. The legionaries have been tracking scrags for weeks.

That night, the cook made them a special dessert with iron presses buried under the coals from a fire: oolieberry pie. The berry juices bubbled out the sides: delicious.

"I didn't sleep a wink," Becke confesses. "You know, the sky looks just the same from over there. Stupid, I know, to think something as big as a sky would look different. But there she was, the Eternal Keeper: exactly the same."

I listen with as much energy as I can muster. Every hour with 12 sucks me dry. I collapse into bed after dinner, while the other girls visit the Gallery or play Snaps around the table. Once, when Benit goes to meet the transport delivering new battle dog pups, Trisk perches on the barrel and watches me work 12. I see her lean over the lunch Benit's left for me, lift the lid on the soup, work her jaws, and drop a thick wad of spit.

When I tell Benit, she says she'll keep my lunch locked in the shed.

After weeks of 12 dragging me around Auxpen, my palms are

callused. Winter deepens and then starts to fade, leaving a muddy, wet trail. After I feed 12 one afternoon, Benit has me sit by the shed as she coats my palms with the same orange salve she used on 132. I can't help the tears sliding down my cheeks. I'm not as afraid of 12 anymore. I even enjoy her puppy ways, when she wants to play tag or leaps at a bit of dandelion fluff.

But I can't control her. "I have no talent for this," I confess.

"Remember, 12's a child," Benit says. "Repetition, Dinitra. Patience. You're learning her. Believe me, she is learning you."

"Trisk is right. I'm no dog handler."

"12's no dog," Benit answers curtly.

Just then, an alarm blares. The monthly transport is landing at Northpen to collect fresh dogs for the containments. Several handlers pass us. As a rule, containment dogs are low to the ground and thickly muscled, with broad, shovel-shaped jaws.

Benit looks at me closely. "You may be surprised to hear it. Trisk's too rough for 12. She'd get angry. She'd force her. There'd be a massacre of her or the hyba cross. If there's one thing I know about 12, it's this. She works out of love, not fear." Benit wipes her hands on her leggings. "But there's one thing you're right about. Something has to change. In the morning, let's have you make her mash. She needs the smell of you in it, I'm thinking, to know you provide for her."

Benit shows me the ingredients. Meat and meal, of course. For 12, she also adds whole bird eggs, onion grass, ground bone, oolieberries, and dried ants. Hybas are partly nocturnal and sleep through the mornings high in the pines. So Benit adds a dropperful of pine sap, to keep her fur sleek.

Last in is a handful of pebbles. Benit tells me to rub them on my forearm before dropping them into the mash bucket. "Hybas carry pebbles in their stomachs to help grind up bone. In the wild, a hyba leaves nothing behind. She'll scent you on them. Let's see if that helps."

I arrive a little earlier the next morning. By now, a muddy spring has turned to summer. The mornings are bearable, but every afternoon's a furnace. Benit watches closely as I mix ingredients. When I hang the bucket on the hook, 12 sniffs suspiciously, then eats as she normally does, licking up every speck.

When I go to get her collar and leash, there's nothing there. I'm sure I hung them properly the night before.

In the kennel, the other handlers are leashing their dogs for the morning's work when I tell Benit. A little too loudly, she tells me to work 12 without a collar or leash. "You're well quit of them. 12 will work better on voice command alone. You have a natural talent, Dinitra. I've never seen the like."

The prospect of not having anything to control 12 with makes me woozy.

Benit leans close. "Don't worry. I'll be watching. So will someone else."

She means Trisk, and I understand: Trisk stole them. I can't stop Benit from taunting her by praising me so loudly. But Benit herself told me she can't do a thing to help me when I'm alone with Trisk.

12 searches for the collar and leash, then glares at me, as if I'm to blame for losing them. I make a show of picking up an invisible collar, using my hands to stroke along her jaws and neck. I make a fist, as if clutching an invisible leash. I step to the gate.

12 follows in perfect position. Her shoulder is so close she brushes my elbow. As we enter Auxpen, Trisk stares balefully, 132 at her side.

Trisk doesn't give up so easily. The next morning, my pouch for meat nuggets is gone. Again, Benit speaks loud enough for Trisk to hear across the kennel. "She doesn't relish the nuggets, does she? What she does, she does for pure love of you. I've never seen the like. All you need to do is praise her."

She's right, at least for the first hour. Then a grasshopper bounds across Auxpen. 12 tears after it, easily climbing the walls to the netting at the top. As the grasshopper desperately leaps from strand to strand, 12 shreds the netting, strands falling like snow around me. With a leap, she catches in midair the strand where the poor grasshopper clings.

She devours strand and insect alike. Then she refuses to obey any command I give her, leaping around Auxpen in a frenzy of joy.

I'm out of ideas. I stand with my eyes closed. Beneath the burnt butter smell, I catch a scent of summer: green grass, last night's rain, a bit of the pink button flower I used to harvest for paint. *Used to.* I am so tired I could fall asleep on my feet. I sort of do, my thoughts light as a strand of netting. For the first time since arriving, I think I might try painting something. Perhaps the cinder cone east of the kennel. Or The Watcher, this time from the north.

Or 12. I'd have to find charcoal for her tiger stripes. What paint could capture her golden eyes? Ground feldspar and a bit of egg white. For the ear and tail tufts, I'm thinking bleached corn silk I could press into powder.

A cold nose nudges my hand. I ignore her. Should I draw her sleeping or as she leapt for that grasshopper?

Again, a nudge. Then 12 licks my bare finger: her tongue rubbery, a little painful from the lynx spikes on the surface. I let her lick my wrist. On my forearm scar, she's surprisingly gentle. I feel her tail wrap around us both, the end sliding up my chest, the tuft ticking against my chin.

When I finally look at her, her golden eyes are eager. She works her massive brow under my hand, as if I've decided on my own to stroke her.

12 doesn't run away from me again.

After the incident with the grasshopper, weeks fly by. Benit installs larger barrels in Mainpen, to fit 12's massive shoulders and allow her to crawl through end to end. To the obstacle course, Benit adds a tall climbing net. After only a few days' work, the barrels are splintered from 12 charging through. Benit calls in the armorer, to fit them with thick iron bands.

"The only obstacle course she won't destroy are the Black Stairs themselves," I tell Benit proudly.

One evening, Benit hands me a clean rag. I'm to tuck it into someone's pillow, then bring it back in the morning. Susalee agrees to be my test case. When I bring the rag back in the morning, one of Susalee's long, red hairs clings to it.

Benit tells me to rip the rag in two. I tuck one half in my belt, then drape the other high on the climbing net.

"Let her sniff your half." Benit shows me a new hand sign: a fist exploding at the hip. *Find the smell.* "She'll smell that other girl."

I let 12 sniff the rag, then walk her to the climbing net several times to find the half with Susalee's smell.

"Now make it interesting," Benit says. I distract 12 with some simple sits and stays while Benit tucks the half into a link of chain between two barrels. When I explode my fist, 12 bounds to the climbing net, but the rag is gone.

12's tail lashes. If I had to describe her expression, I'd call it disappointed in me.

"Patience," Benit shouts from her seat on the licor barrel.

I try several more times, with no success. I add a gesture: fist explode, arm sweep. I want the sweep to mean "search."

12 cocks her head, tail tip ticking. She might as well be saying, "By the Mother's breath, what are you trying to say, human?"

I repeat: *fist explode, arm sweep.*

12 shakes her head, then does a swift circuit of the pen. Her run is graceful and terrifying, like a boulder able to stop in mid-leap and tear off in the opposite direction. 12 returns to my side. *Fist explode, arm sweep.* She circles Mainpen again, this time with her snout thrust into the air. She freezes, her tail lashing. Her golden eyes go to me.

Fist explode, arm sweep.

She bounds toward the barrels and the hidden rag with Susalee's scent. She tears it away, then chuckles in delight. The chuckle raises the hairs on my arms. But I praise her. As a reward, I throw her a ball, which she tosses into the air, catches, then rips in two. 12 gives herself a terrific shake, then eyes me: *again?*

It's as if I can hear her thoughts and she can hear mine. I hide the rag fifty more times and every time she grabs it and chuckles. Soon, 12 can find a rag blindfolded. Over the next days, I use rags from all of the girls and even mix the rags up, giving her Becke's rag to sniff and hiding Mariza's.

When I do, 12 looks offended at how I've tried to trick her.

I start to look forward to my work with 12. She and I develop a routine—the morning mash, a swift brush, some easy sits and stays in the Tower. We choose the pen to work in depending on the weather and where the other handlers are. She responds to voice commands, clicks, and hand gestures. Sometimes, I know she's read my eyes, springing to action with only a glance.

One afternoon, Benit has me put 12 back in the Tower early so I can watch Trisk and the other handlers run a final training before sending their dogs to a containment. "To show you how advanced 12 is in so little time," Benit adds.

Several legionaries sit on weathered benches outside Centerpen to watch Trisk and the other handlers put their dogs through their exercises. Trisk wears a padded tunic, padded pants, and heavy-soled boots. She positions herself on a little mound at the pen's center, then straps a leather gauntlet over her right arm. Lastly, she pulls on a helmet the size of a mash bucket with a grill to cover her face.

On the opposite side, four handlers line up. Trisk raises her left hand. The first handler in line releases her battle dog. Just before reaching Trisk, the dog launches into the air.

The dog's jaws close on the gauntlet. The dog hangs there, a monstrous extra limb. With her fist, Trisk punches the dog's snout.

The handler shouts "Off!" The dog releases, then trots to her side, shaking its head.

I have no reason to pity Trisk. She spares not a crumb of kindness for me. But I can't help wincing when dog after dog slams into her.

The last one, branded 73, is largest. The dog seems to have learned from watching the others. Just as she's about to reach Trisk, she dodges under the gauntlet and latches to Trisk's hip. Trisk slams to the ground. The dog's pan-sized paws pin her by the shoulders. Trapped by so much padding, Trisk can't move away. The dog settles its jaws around the helmet and wrenches back and forth, metal rivets shrieking.

Benit runs for the prod. She stabs 73, and the dog howls in pain. The dog stumbles off, then sits to lick a blackened circle of fur.

"73's no containment dog," Benit declares. "We'll hold her back for the Legion."

I can't help asking, "Will I have to do this with 12? Fight her?"

"No padding could protect you. Besides, 12 would never attack you." Benit's thoughtful. "Trisk doesn't have to suit up, you know. She could order any trainer to put on the padding. I'll say this for her. She insists on doing this herself. Last summer, she lost three legionaries and their dogs to the scrags. She may not like you, but she's loyal to her squadron."

I watch with Benit as the other handlers pull Trisk to her feet.

"Trisk's got her mean streak," Benit is saying, "but I was shocked when 12 went to some Collegium girl and not to her. I'm not criticizing, mind you. I see the wisdom now. You've bonded like no other pair I've seen. For better or worse."

Bonded. It feels good to know what Flicke meant by the word. "What do you mean by worse?"

"Well, what if you're killed?" Benit is watching Trisk brace for another charge. She parries it easily. "12 won't bond with another human, I'm guessing. A battle dog, that's different. If we lose a handler, the dog passes to a new one."

I'm surprised to feel dismay. I don't think I could bear to see 12 with someone else. In our quarters, I sometimes reach out to touch 12 between the ears, where the fur is especially soft. When I remember she's back in her Tower, I'm disappointed. I miss her.

I think I may even love the hyba cross.

11

Tribute

The next morning, Lind appears as we're finishing breakfast. Since the day will be warm, I'm planning to try a water crossing with 12. Benit told me hybas are famously afraid of water and will die rather than swim or even get their paws wet. I want to see if dog, tiger, monkey, or hyba prevails.

"You've drawn a tribute run today," Lind announces. "Congratulations."

Susalee and the others have been training all week on the small cruisers the Legion uses for short trips from Holdfast. A tribute run is a final test before they're cleared to operate without supervision. It's part of their training to be pilots in the new fleet.

Lind assigns them to the village of Pergama an hour west of Holdfast. Pergama is named for a mine of the precious metal the Weave uses in ships, scrolls, and crossbows: feather-light, pliable, and an excellent receptacle for energy.

Edba brightens. Keepers in Pergama raised her.

Lind says. "It's market day. You'll collect the month's tribute. Just be back before nightfall. With the cruiser," she adds playfully.

She hands Mariza a circle of cord with strands tied to it, like a necklace. Communications can be spotty on the Stairs, so the knots stand for what Pergama must send as tribute. Lind counts them off: the gold strand for jugs of oil, the brown for sacks of grain, the white for bales of cloth.

Mariza has always been good at codes. She runs her fingers over the knots eagerly. "A dozen hinds?"

Lind nods, pleased.

I slip on my boots, careful to keep the tracker map hidden in the shaft of the right boot. Honestly, I'd rather be with 12 than go with them.

Lind turns to me. "You're Dinitra 584-KxA, correct?" She checks her scroll. "Benit's got the hyba cross on a screw worm treatment. You'll go to Pergama with the others."

12 will wonder where I am. "I'd really rather stay," I tell her.

Lind shakes her head. "Orders."

She distributes fifty coin to each of us, to spend as we will. On one side is the face of a Sower, her eyebrows plucked clean. On her chest is a medallion shaped like an upside-down cup: Ω. On the coin's other side is the prow of the Centrum, an enormous rhombus of stone. Fifty coin is enough to buy some vials and perhaps paper, if anyone even makes those things in Pergama.

I decide. The first thing I'll draw is 12.

Lind saves the best news for last. Tem is waiting for us in the Gallery. This will be the first time Edba's seen her in months. We're all embracing Tem and laughing when I realize: I never asked Lind about Helma. Tem herself says she hasn't seen her.

The change in Tem is striking. In six months, she's grown taller, more slender. Tem and Edba are shy together, as if neither one is sure they're still in love. Soon, though, their hands are entwined.

It's a lovely high summer morning, a sweetness in the air. Some shadows still cling to the folds of the Black Stairs as we walk to the Moorings. Susalee nods in my direction as she tells Tem I'm training a battle dog. "What is it again, Dini? A dog-hyba or some such? The only one of its kind."

Tem shakes her head in amazement.

"She's afraid of dogs, right?" Susalee laughs. "Dini's practically got the creature doing flips."

I describe how terrified I was to even enter the Tower. Now,

I'm planning new commands not even experienced dog handlers use.

"You sound proud of her," Tem says.

I haven't thought about it that way. "I've never taken care of anything. I mean I feed her, watch her. It's..." I feel strange telling her that I might love 12. Can a human love a draft? Other than love, the only word I come up with is nice. It feels nice to be with 12.

Nice sounds ridiculous for a 600-pound killer hyba cross. But that's what I say. "It's nice," I tell Tem.

"You haven't told us anything about you," Mariza says to her. "What's the patch?"

Tem wears a red patch on her tunic. "Apprentice fysic." Since we separated, Tem says she's crossed the Emergency Rail five times to evacuate wounded legionaries. It's the lowest Rail, kept open at all times.

"Have you bivouacked?" Becke asks eagerly.

"Biv what?"

Before Becke can explain what bivouacking is, Susalee interrupts. "What wounded?"

There's a new gravity to Tem's gaze. "One legionary broke her leg in a fall. The bone came all the way through the skin. I've treated head trauma. Spear punctures. And hyba attacks." She looks at me gravely. "By the time those legionaries get to us, they're too far gone."

Mariza's always been squeamish. She waves her hands in front of her face. "No details."

Edba looks proud. "It's what you always wanted."

"I would never have thought I'd be happy in the Legion." Tem's gentle smile lights up her face. She leans into Edba. "You're right. This is what I wanted."

Before the Legion, I never would have thought I could work with animals let alone a creature like 12. Since 12 and I have been working so well together, I can't imagine life without her. It's strange to be happy in a place you never expected.

There it is again: *nice*. When we return tonight, I'll rub extra salve into 12's paw pads to make up for being gone.

At the Moorings, Susalee climbs confidently into a cruiser. Hooked to the back is a separate compartment to load the tribute. Mariza takes the nav screen. Edba, Tem, Becke, and I settle in the passenger area. It feels like were a puzzle that's been put back together again.

There's an easy chatter between us. We've known each other most of our lives, but it took the calamity of being assigned to the Legion make us friends. "Do you know how to drive this thing?" I tease Susalee.

"Just you wait."

She dials in the coordinates for Pergama. The cruiser's directional whiskers stiffen as we rise. A clear hood extends and locks over our heads.

"Clear," Susalee says confidently. The cruiser smoothly turns west. Holdfast quickly disappears behind us.

I can't help seeing myself through Asta's eyes. What would she think if she saw me speeding so close to the Rift? Or with 12 in Centerpen as her tail pulls her up and over the climbing net? Asta is probably in a counting house doing exactly what she thought she would do, exactly what she was made to do.

And me? There's a Chronicler saying, *To every foot there is a path, to every eye something to see.* She wrote the words in her distinctive script over a drawing of a button flower seen on Constance's march to the sea. I used to wonder why she'd chosen a common button flower. Perhaps she wanted us to see the flower in a different way, as something worthy of admiring even though it spreads in a great carpet every spring. We walk the path we're given, not the one we think we should have.

I wish I could tell Asta that everything's fine. Somehow, my path led me to Holdfast. And 12. I've found something new to love, yet I still think of Asta and wish her well.

Becke weighs a coin in her palm as she describes what she'll look for: a jam-filled bun or candies like the ones she used to buy in Shell Bay. When she's excited, her leg jiggles.

"Is everything food to you?" Tem teases. She's been told to return with various syrups and essences to treat wounds.

"What will you buy, Dini?" Becke asks. "You were always mixing paints at school."

"Maybe some vials," I admit. "But a jam-filled bun sounds perfect."

An hour west of Holdfast, Susalee coasts the cruiser over Pergama. The village is smaller than I expected, about forty low buildings protected by a high wall. Mariza climbs out first to set the anchor. Once we're locked in, Becke tries to connect the fueling tube. But the spout is bent so badly it won't clamp to the tank. A bit of fuel leaks out and puddles on the ground. The fuel smells of sour milk.

"So much for my appetite." Becke frowns. "Maybe I'll buy socks."

The cruiser has enough fuel for our return. But the bent spout is unsettling. Why wouldn't the Pergamans repair something so simple?

The market is in the village center. I see tired-looking vegetables, battered pots, old gears and levers. Even the bread looks used. A few Vessels, their bellies round, peer at us suspiciously.

"I don't remember a thing about Pergama," Edba confesses. Then quieter: "Maybe that's a good thing."

Under her breath, Susalee says, "This isn't what I expected."

"So much for a jam-filled bun," Becke murmurs.

Tem takes a list from her pocket. "We should get what we've come for and be on our way. I'll find the fysic and meet you at the cruiser."

While Tem looks for fysic's supplies, Susalee and Mariza search for the prefect and the tribute we're supposed to collect. I follow Becke down a row of tables. Becke pauses to peer inside some baskets that look promising for bread. I look over some hinds hanging on a stand. I'm hoping to at least buy a bone for 12.

There's nothing so fine as a glass vial. Or paper.

One butcher is selling scrawny chickens hooked by the necks to a pole. I'm peering around her table for bones when she spies me.

She wears a bloody apron. "You from Holdfast?"

"Yes. I want to buy a bone."

"Soup bone? Bone for carving? Slender bone, marrow bone?"

I don't want to admit it's for a hyba cross. "Any bone will do."

"Trade only," the butcher grumbles. "What do you have?"

My hand goes to the fifty coin in my pocket. "Just coin."

The woman slides a cleaver along a whet stone. "For your boots, I'll give you that bucket of juicy bones." On the ground is a bucket filled with bones still covered in gristle.

"I need my boots."

With a terrific chop, she splits a goat shin. "Then move along. Holdfast should know better than to send girls with nothing to trade."

I've lost any desire to have something from this awful place.

"I'll take your coin." A vendor at the edge of the market is motioning to me. On her table are what look like child's slingshots. The grips are carved from stout branches, y-shaped, and painted bright blue.

She has mottled cheeks and wispy white hair. "Good slingshots for bringing down them dilidots nesting in the trees," she says eagerly.

"Dilidots," I repeat. Edba used the little rodents for her Biotics projects. "Aren't they confined to the Cyclon?"

She waggles her head. "Natural burrowers, those. Juicy, too. Haven't had a Cyclon for years."

She presses a slingshot into my hand. "Cradle's extra springy. Rocks fly far, far."

I'm more interested in how she brewed the blue paint. Blue is hard. I've made a lighter shade with mashed button flower.

The woman strokes my hand as I describe the flower. "Could be!" she says with a wink. "I'll sell you my own dear recipe for twenty coin."

The slingshot handles are pleasingly smooth. The band is old tire cut into strips. The cradle is woven from wool or cotton, a glossy black. Other slingshots have brown or even white cradles of the same sleek material.

"Try it," the vendor urges. She shows me how to pull the cradle back. The weave is a little sticky, perfect for a small rock. I remember the girl that shot a rock at the Legionship. The cradle was set in the center of a thick rope with no wooden handle.

I describe the rope to the vendor. "Huaraca," she nods, eyes narrowing. "That'll take a derak down at fifty paces, so it will. More expensive."

She repeats the word. Wah *RA* Ka. "Only fifty coin," the vendor winks.

"Are you the only one who takes coin?"

The vendor motions me closer. "The metal fixes the dye. Twenty coin and I'll whisper the recipe to you."

I never considered using metal to make paint. "What about this fabric?" I ask, still stroking the slingshot cradle.

"They use a special oil on their hair, so they do," she says. "Extra springy. Twenty coin, my lovely, and the recipe is yours. Got a grip to it, so male hair does."

I think she means a plant: wolfsbane, shepherd's purse. Malehair. "Does this malehair grow near here?"

She cackles. "North of the Rift, ha! Strong and stinky. What sells it to us in exchange for…"

The butcher pulls me away from the table, bloody cleaver in hand. "Stop your jawing!" she says to the slingshot vendor.

The butcher turns on me. "This is our hair, all of it. We cut it and trade it to her, see? You could chop your ringlets and get a fine price. Take this bone for your trouble and get you gone."

The slingshot seller protests, but the butcher shoves a bone under my arm and shoves me away. "Move along, knobbie."

The butcher's hair is fine and blonde. The slingshot seller has wispy white hair. By the Mother's breath, what is a knobbie?

Male hair. She said *male hair*.

In a crude fountain, I put down the bone to scrub my hands. The water is so cold my teeth ache. I don't need Asta's logic to understand. Scrags cross the Rift. Not just scrags: *men*. Men who sell their hair.

They could be in Pergama even now.

I don't have to convince Becke to return to the cruiser. She rattles a tin box she traded for her boot laces. As she walks, the boots flop around her shins. "You won't believe what's inside," she says under her breath.

"You won't believe who comes here," I tell her.

Several children follow us, bare-footed and wild-looking. They carry the wooden slingshots.

I think they might be planning to crack us in the head with the stones lumped in their pockets.

Are they female? My stomach lurches. Could I even tell the difference between male and female? I grab Becke's hand. "Hurry up, before they take aim."

Susalee, Mariza, and Tem are speaking with a tall woman near our cruiser. She wears the tricornered hat of a town prefect. Beside her rumbles a battered hovuck loaded with tribute. Mariza has her knotted strings out and is arguing.

There are four hinds, not fifteen. Three thin bolts of cloth, not an even dozen. There's no grain, no leather. There's not a single bar of pergama. Mariza runs her fingers over the knots marking the tribute Pergama owes.

"I am telling you. I can't send what we don't have." The prefect is painfully thin, with skin gone patchy. Her frizz of hair looks like the color's been drained out. She looks frequently over our shoulders as the townspeople gather. The children pull and snap their slingshots. "The harvest last year was poor as was the one before it. The spring was wet. We lost a crop of early grain just last week. And the goats, well. A whole herd's gone to the hybas."

Benit swore there were no hybas south of the Rift.

Susalee is impatient. "We must call Holdfast. I need to explain why you're unwilling to fulfill your tribute."

The prefect shakes her head. "We haven't had a com link for months. What does it matter, anyway? They took our scrolls."

The crowd is growing larger. The butcher is there, still in her bloody apron. I whisper in Susalee's ear. "We should go."

Susalee snaps at me, "That will be marked against us. You of all people should understand. Let me handle this."

Her words are a slap. She's the same Susalee as before: better than anyone else.

But the prefect doesn't budge. "I have nothing more to give you."

"Let's go, Susi." Tem gently presses her arm. "We'll sort this out later."

The prefect gives us a message for Holdfast. "Don't send anyone else." Then another to us: "If you value your lives, don't stop on your way back. For anything."

Once we've taken off, Susalee puts the controls on auto. She and Mariza climb back to the passenger area. Below us, the valley is drenched in light. The cruiser's shadow flies like its own creature over the fields and farms.

My hands are still cold from the fountain. No matter what happens, Susalee will always think I'm less than her. I was a fool to think that being at the Legion together would bring us closer.

"By the Mother's breath, what does knobbie mean?" Edba asks. "The word followed me everywhere. Knobbie, knobbie."

None of us know what knobbie means. I consider not telling them about the slingshots and the male hair. But it's not Becke or Edba's fault that Susalee is who she is. I tell them: scrags cross the Rift and sell their hair. Males. I confess: I touched male hair.

I spread my fingers and lift my hands palm up, to show how red they are from the cold water. "I scrubbed them. The virus isn't contagious, right?"

Tem's always been best at medical subjects. "It's kept dormant by supplement. Good you washed your hands, though. Who knows what other diseases they carry."

"Not just scrags," Becke interrupts. "Look."

Becke opens the tin she bought with her boot laces. Inside are three long, yellow teeth. The broad ends are drilled with holes, to string a necklace. The points are quite sharp.

I've seen teeth like this before. "Those look like 12's teeth. Hyba teeth. When they shed them, there's always a new tooth behind it. 12 loses a couple every week."

Susalee shakes her head. "Hybas haven't crossed the Rift for years. And males?" She looks at me angrily. "That's absurd."

"This doesn't feel absurd, Susi," Becke says. The tooth has

serrated edges and is as sharp as cut glass. "The vendor told me they collect them in the woods."

For a long moment, we stare at the teeth. I feel lighter, like I could lift out of this cruiser and float back to Holdfast. We were lied to about our assignments. We were lied to about Pergama.

"Edba and I walked by the houses," Tem is saying. "The people looked at us like thieves. No one had fysic supplies to sell. One woman even slammed her door."

"There was no bread, no eggs, no cheese." Edba lowers her voice. "I don't think anyone there's had a proper meal in weeks."

"Scrags don't cross the Rift," Mariza repeats. "No way. Not for a hundred years or more."

"Neither do hybas," Becke says, shaking the teeth in the tin.

"Why did Lind even send us?" Susalee stands up, rocking the cruiser. We all grab our seats, but she's oblivious. "Why risk it?"

The answer is obvious. "Sit down, Susi," I say sharply. "The prefect told us. The coms link is down. They took their scrolls."

"Who took their scrolls?" Susalee demands.

Silence is all the answer we need. None of us asked if the Weave or scrags seized the scrolls. "No one in Holdfast knows what's happening in Pergama," Tem says softly.

"We need to get back to Holdfast as quickly as we can," Susalee says before returning to the pilot seat.

I wonder what our cruiser must have looked like to the prefect as we powered away: the shape and then a glimpse of a shape and then nothing. For the rest of the trip, I keep my hands from touching my leggings or the seat.

Leaving them at the mercy of hybas. And men.

12

Sons

As the cruiser settles into the mooring, I'm desperate to get to a sink and a stiff brush, to scrub the hands I touched to the slingshot cradle. To scrub away every cell and molecule of *male hair*.

Benit keeps disinfectant to treat battle dogs. I want to see 12: touch her, smell her, remind myself that something in this world isn't a lie. I don't bother going through the Gallery. The pens are just over the cinder cone. It's a rest day for the dog handlers, so the pens are empty. The dogs are all in their cages. By now, they think of me as part of 12, with my lingering burnt butter smell, and cower as I pass.

I keep my hands away from my body, as if they're fragile.

Virus. I should have paid more attention in Replicative Sciences. I should have paid more attention, period. Asta would be disappointed in me, again. I'm letting surprise and fear rule me. Of course, men can't be crossing the Rift. Or hybas. What is the Legion there for if not to protect the Weave from just this threat?

Those children didn't look protected. I can still feel the slick slingshot cradle. See the grin of the vendor as she praised it: *malehair*. The only truly logical answer is this: the Weave lied to us. All of us. Why should I be surprised? My assignment had nothing to do with my Sower formula, my drawing, all the tests I failed. The only way Pergamans can use malehair and collect hyba teeth is if scrags and hybas cross the Rift. Don't hide what you fear, I tell myself. Name it. Touch it. Smell it, like burnt butter. Trisk told me the Sowers she called traitors have sons. Are they the ones crossing?

Trisk named them once. Lam? Tim something?

The Pergamans trade with them.

Logical.

Generations ago, the Weave contained men to protect the Mother from violence. The whole point of the Great Quest is to eliminate men. Only then will the Mother and her children be truly safe.

Why would the Legion allow scrags to cross the Rift? Why wouldn't they just exterminate the hybas? My thoughts circle back to the slingshot cradle. The memory of how the glossy hair felt under my fingertips revolts me. The vendor touches the cradles all the time and obviously is still alive. I'm assuming the vendor is female.

Could the vendor have been male? How would I even know? I'm still carrying the butcher's bone, so place it on the hovuck. At the trough where Benit bathes the dogs, I take a scrub brush and rake my arms and hands with the flea-killing soap Benit swears by. My skin throbs, from the cold and bristles stiff as pine cones. With a knife, I pare the dirt from my fingernails, then scrub again. I walk myself through Pergama: the hanging meat, the slingshot vendor and her goaty eyes. The children staring. I suck in water through my nose and mouth, then spit it out. I hold my breath and duck my head under the faucet's freezing stream. I scrub my face and hair again under the coursing water.

My fear is turning to anger. Why am I kept in the dark? Why is everything a lie? Why am I not told the simplest things: males cross the Rift. Pergamans trade with scrags. Hybas crossed back over the Rift.

Susalee will always think I'm less than her. *Always.*

I'm angry at my professors. I'm angry at Susalee and Lind. I'm angry at Benit, who assured me no hybas prowled south of the

Rift. Most of all, I'm angry at Kesh, for bringing me here. If I could just see her again, I'd force her to answer my questions.

She'd have to answer me with 12 at my side.

Something bangs inside the shed. I call out, "Benit?"

I smell something: machine oil, rosemary salve. From inside the shed, a swear: "By the Mother's eyes."

The rasp is unmistakable: Kesh. My wish is granted, but I'm without my protector.

Four soft, paper-white bodies tumble through the shed door. Pups. The pups have long, rat-like tails and paws several sizes too big for their bodies. They sound like creaky windows.

They reek of burnt butter. Miniature 12s.

Kesh emerges through the shed door. Her one eye flicks over me: surprised. "I thought you wouldn't be back for hours."

My resolve to confront her vanishes. In her metal hand is a fifth pup, tail limp as a cooked noodle. "Bring me a rag," she orders gruffly.

Hanging over the trough is the net bag of rags I use to train 12. Kesh uses one to wipe a brown crust from the pup's eyes and the snot from its nose. She goes back inside the shed. When she reappears, she's carrying a tin of rosemary salve.

No pup.

The other pups play-fight beside a cage. The dog cowers in a corner. "Make yourself useful then," Kesh tells me. "I need fresh salve on my hip. Tell me about Pergama."

Kesh's tunic is slit at the sides, to accommodate the apparatus connecting her hip and spine to the machine legs. When she crouches, I see where a metal flange has dug a trench into her flesh. "Make sure to get the salve all the way inside," she says.

The salve is the same one Benit used on 132. As I press the gel into the wound, Kesh's one eye closes, from pain or relief I can't tell.

I'm careful with my words. "The people weren't welcoming."

"Why would they be? You're coming to take what little they have."

I'm shocked. "We were sent for monthly tribute."

Kesh speaks bitterly. "The Centrum would demand tribute from a pile of bones."

Then she stares at me. "What happened to your arms?"

My arms are still red from my scrubbing. My story pours out: male hair woven into a slingshot cradle, the virus, hyba teeth. The prefect told us never to return. The children: female or male?

"The virus isn't contagious," Kesh responds dryly.

"What about males?" I ask. "The hybas?" Kesh could say gravity's suspended for the day and it would make more sense. "Since when do males cross the Rift? For all I know they were there, in Pergama." I pause, watching her closely.

The answer is plain on her face.

"There were men there," I say slowly.

"Calm yourself." Kesh touches her wound gently, where the salve is thickest. "Fetch some gauze and tape."

I feel like I'm being run around an obstacle course, the truth secreted in a log or climbing net. This isn't a game. Under the racks of battle-dog armor is something new: a large box under a warming light. There, a battle dog is strapped down, teats exposed. The pup Kesh was carrying suckles weakly, its sharp claws scoring the dog's belly in moist, red stripes.

The battle dog's eyes roll with pain and fear. A muzzle muffles her whimpers.

I have no reason to feel pity for a battle dog. But this is cruel. I grab the gauze and tape and return to where Kesh crouches.

"That pup is hurting the dog," I say angrily. For once, I say what I think: "That's cruel."

"Benit will patch her up soon enough. It's not the first time she's nursed a litter. She nursed your 12." Kesh doesn't blink. "Fold the gauze into a cushion and tape it well."

The other pups tumble around her blades. Something black and slick leaks from their puckered anuses.

"I thought there were no more crosses," I say roughly. More lies. Benit told me 12 was the only one. "Are you making a pack of them? For who?"

Kesh doesn't react to my tone. "These are the last of them. A young Sower took the embryos without my permission. If she'd bothered to read my notes, she would have known the cross is corrupt. I brought them here for a little pleasure before they die."

She kneels and picks up a pup. "I should wring its neck," she says.

She sets the pup down, and the poor creature wobbles into the shed to suckle.

Kesh asks, "You want to know whether men cross the Rift? And hybas, too?"

"Yes."

With a soft groan, Kesh stands. When she looks down at me, there's something changed in her expression. There's a softness. "The answer to both questions is yes."

Before I can ask another question, she raises her flesh hand. "Let me explain."

Kesh starts with Pergama's mines, the richest in the Weave. As the miners dug deeper, the caverns filled with water. They had to bring in special miners able to swim and reach the ore. These miners got so far down the water boiled from the heat bubbling out of the volcanic vents. "The rest of the pergama is too deep to mine. There's not enough, in other words."

"Not enough for what?"

As she speaks, Kesh flexes her flesh hand. "They've used every ounce of pergama to build the new fleet. Once the fleet launches, the Legion will cross the Stairs and exterminate any scrags who remain."

So much for Becke's Population Management class. "You were going to tell me about the males and the hybas in Pergama," I say.

"North of the Weave, there are rich deposits of pergama still in the ground. The Sowers want them."

"To build the fleet," I say.

"To finish it," Kesh says. "You're a quick learner."

"What about the males? The hybas in the woods?" I was terrified of 12 when I first saw her. Multiply her and that's what the people of Pergama face.

"Without pergama, they have very little. Once the Weave eliminates the scrags, the town of Pergama will be moved north. To new mines."

I'm not giving up. If I can master my fear with 12, I can master it with the Legion Commander. I'm thinking of the prefect. She deserves better. They all deserve better. "I thought the whole purpose of the Legion was to defend the Weave. Not stand by while scrags and hybas cross the Rift. While the Pergamans suffer."

Kesh's expression is cool. "You are a sharp observer, Dinitra 584-KxA. This is part of your skill as a painter. You see things others miss."

Her praise is double-edged. How could any of us miss seeing Pergama's high walls, the faces of the wild children? I keep my voice even, but I'm roiling inside. "You'd have to be blind and deaf not to see it."

"There are worse things than men in this world," Kesh answers.

From inside the shed, the Keeper dog whimpers.

"Benit tells me you've bonded with the hyba cross," Kesh says. "You have a talent." Kesh says she went to the laboratory every day to watch 12 develop in the sac.

"A sac?"

"The sacs where the Sowers grow drafts. We fill them with nektar."

The only nectar I know comes from bees. Susalee crossed a bee with a sundew flower for her Biotics final. "What kind of bees?"

"Like no bee you've ever seen." There's a new gleam in Kesh's eye. "For weeks, I watched the cross develop—the tail, the jaws. Of course, the stripes came in later. When I cut her out, she was just like a hyba, white as snow."

I don't understand how Kesh can be a Sower and Legion commander. "If you were a Sower…"

"How did I come to be here? It's a long story, Dinitra 584-KxA. For another time." She pauses. "Soon, I hope. Tell me, Dinitra. What do you think about the cross now?"

No one, not even Benit, has asked me what I think about 12. Love sounds weak. "I think… I think she's the most astonishing creature I've ever seen."

An alarm blares. A transport has arrived in Northpen to collect dogs for the containment. "Lock the pups in the shed," Kesh orders. "I think what's outside will be of interest to you."

The beams in Northpen are harsh. Insects flurry near the bulbs, making the light into a vibrating soup. Benit and Trisk are watching a transport lower. At Trisk's feet is what looks like a heap of dirty rags. Since there's no cradle, the transport has deployed spindly struts to keep the belly off the hard ground.

Several handlers and their dogs wait to board. When Trisk sees Kesh, she shouts over the whine of the propellers. "Blazes, no mistake. Caught them near The Watcher."

The heap moves. I see an elbow, a dark eye. Dirty feet hobbled at the ankles. Their wrists are bound with rope.

I step back, into Kesh and the sharp rod of her metal arm. I search for the word Professor Wylla taught us in History: *boys*. Two of them. At first, I think the boys are collared like dogs. But the mark on their necks is blue and parceled into letters. A tattoo: REKREKREKREKREK.

They are no more than pups.

Trisk is wearing leather armor and gauntlets. She grabs one, then the other, and shoves them into a metal cage. They go spitting and hissing. Trisk and Benit cover the cage in burlap. A dog strains at the leash, eager to attack them.

A hoist grabs the cage and loads it on the transport. The handlers and their dogs follow. Soon, all I can see are the transport's blinking belly lights as it flies south.

Trisk pretends I'm not standing there. She beams with pride. "My squadron's keeping a close eye on Rek. She's moving east of the Crags. Wouldn't that be something, to catch old Rek with her boys!"

"You'll take her with you," Kesh says.

Trisk steps back. She looks from me to the commander. "You're not serious."

"Since when is a direct order not serious?"

Trisk folds her arms, defiant. "With all due respect, commander. This one ain't even been trained to shoot."

"She'll have the cross," Kesh says. "She doesn't need to shoot."

"What madness is this?" Trisk demands.

For once, I agree with Trisk.

In the terrible light of Northpen, Kesh's face is a mask. "Do you defy a direct order?"

Trisk's jaws work on a response. If it's *traitor*, she won't survive the hour. She relents. "As you wish, commander."

Kesh turns to Benit. "Fit 12 with the new armor. Give Dinitra three days of food. I want her across the High Rail within the hour."

With that, Kesh stalks back to Holdfast.

I'd rather walk to Pergama alone and naked than cross the Rift with Trisk, with or without 12. "What's Rek?" I cry. "Where are Crags? What does Blazes mean?"

"Quit your blubbering," Benit spits. "You heard the commander."

I can't help myself. Across the Rift with only the cross to defend myself? "You told me yourself never to turn my back on her. Never trust her. We're not ready!"

I'm really thinking I'll never be ready when Benit stops, turns, and slaps me hard. "You told me yourself the only obstacle course worthy of 12 are the Black Stairs themselves."

"I was just talking!"

"You'll live your words." Benit closes her eyes, her lips pressed together. When she opens her eyes, her look is hard. "You need to calm down and soon."

Benit uses her fingers to tick down the answers to my questions. "Rek is a rebel Captain. The only Arcadium girl ever to make Sower and a traitor through and through. There are dozens of Captains like her, each worse than the last. They each have hundreds of sons, every one bred to kill. Of them, Rek's Blazes are worst. Even those young ones you just saw. As dangerous as a dirty knife. The Crags are mountains east of here, just where the Stairs give way to the Wastes. Are you satisfied now?"

I've never seen Benit so angry.

"Blazes," I repeat. I could say "spoon" or "rivet" for all the meaning the word has to me.

"Did you pay no attention at all in History?" Benit cries. "To the news? Blast you Collegium girls!"

"What am I supposed to do?" I sob.

Benit grips me by the shoulders. "By the Mother's breath, she's caught me by surprise, so she has. She's the one who brought you here. She's the one who put you with 12. I have no quarrel with any of that. Listen to me Dinitra 584-KxA. My words may mean your life."

The information I've been yearning for comes at me like a hail storm. The Captains make sons to fight the Weave. They have what Benit calls "little names": Blazes, the Sea Hunt. The Harvest, the Birds of Prey, the Living Wood, the Mother Eyes.

"Like children," she scoffs, "but deadly. They have a single purpose: kill us all."

Benit's eyes glitter. "Ready or not, you cross the High Rail tonight. Thank the Mother you and 12 are as one. She is your best hope, Dinitra. Your only hope, to be honest. 12 will defend you, come what may. My advice? Let her."

13

The Rift

We pull supplies from the shed. The hyba-cross pups are splayed out in the warming box: all dead. The Keeper dog pants, her belly still weeping blood. Benit pays her no attention.

She pulls down a set of armor made especially for 12. On any other day, I'd take the time to marvel at its beauty: leather and embossed pergama, made to fit her shoulders and flanks.

The High Rail closes at dusk. Kesh wants us through now.

The straps are the same strange skin as 12's old collar. "Lither," Benit says, "indestructible. Not even a laser can split it. A kind of snake the Sowers made, then released."

The torso is assembled like fish scales. These scales are tinted brown and black, to match 12's tiger stripes. The chest shield is embossed pergama, in the shape of the Legion's three-crescent shield. "The armorer never finished the helmet, blast her," Benit says.

Benit tries to drag the armor onto the hovuck, but it's too heavy. Benit sobs once and wipes her eyes. "Don't just stand there like a hole in a bucket. Help me."

Suddenly, she turns her back to the camera nearest the shed. She cups her mouth so even her lips are hidden. "Never let 12 out of your sight. Never. If you hear a whistle, it's them. If you hear a twig snap: them. Run. Anywhere."

Together, we wrestle the armor onto the hovuck. She shoves supplies for me into a pack: dried meat, a flask of water, bread left from lunch.

"What will 12 eat?" The mash has so many ingredients.

"What she forages. Her hyba nature will prevail."

Benit taps the cage number into the hovuck's screen: 12. By the time we're at the Tower, 12 is already making her way down. It's unusual for me to come at this hour. She's agitated, chuffing. Though I've only been gone a day, she looks bigger, longer.

I make the gestures for sit, lie down, roll: our morning routine. 12 treats it like a game. I give her the bone I brought from Pergama. She licks it affectionately, then cracks the bone in two and swallows the halves whole, one after the other. 12 rubs against me, as if to remove any lingering Pergama smell from my clothing and replace it with her own.

I feel like I'm being loved by the Black Stairs themselves.

12 takes to the armor well. Once the pergama chest plate is properly buckled, the hyba cross explores with her tongue the image of the Weave's shield. The armor on her flanks–a second, impermeable skin–she nibbles with the tiny teeth between her fangs. She gives a terrific sneeze, as if to pronounce all is in perfect order.

The kennel keeper grabs one last thing from the shed: her sheepskin jacket. "The nights are cold. You'll be back tomorrow. Or the next day. Soon, anyway."

"I can't take this." I might not be able to return it.

Abruptly, Benit takes my face in her rough hands. "Trust the cross," she tells me, "and no other. Promise me."

"I promise."

"And bring my jacket back, Dinitra 584-KxA."

Benit walks me to the special tunnel they use to access the High Rail, reserved for the battle dogs. Trisk is there with 132. Like 12, 132 is armored. She wears a helmet, thistled in cruel-looking spikes. On Trisk's back is strapped a crossbow. A bandolier of glowing strela bolts crosses her chest. A comms unit covers one ear.

She ignores Benit. "You'll do as you're told," she says to me harshly. "You'll not say a word unless told to speak. When I say jump, you jump. When I say follow, you'll be on my heels. You'll do whatever I tell you to do without a second thought."

I nod. Of course, I nod. Behind her, a camera lens gleams. Others are watching. "Leave, Kennel Keeper. You're not needed anymore," Trisk says.

Trisk triggers a glowing switch on the floor. The High Rail opens with a whisper. 12's snout lifts and her ears swivel. I smell Beyond-the-Weave: pine and something mineral from the constant churn of the Rift River against rock far below.

"You first," Trisk says.

Benit's warning sounds in my head: never turn your back on Trisk. "I'll follow."

"Did I tell you not to speak unless told to? Did I not tell you no word is to pass your lips without my command when we're across the Rift?"

"We're not across the Rift." My hand searches out the space between 12's ears. I like to press the ridge of her brow. "I will follow."

Trisk's eyes go to the camera pointed at the Rail. Her jaws work. Abruptly, she jerks 132's leash. She knows someone is watching, too. "Get on with it, then."

As we walk up the metal ramp, 12's head swivels right and left, right and left. Where there are breaks in the mist, I glimpse through the glass the Rift's rock walls, black and slick with moisture. Above, the sky is a darkening strip blinking with the lights of the fleet tethered there. Under my feet, the floor is springy and muddied with boot and paw prints. If I look to the side, I can see the Rift river far below: white spume over a boulder tumble.

Mid-Rift, there's a split in the Rail, marked by a steel divider. Trisk bears right. Then we're on the other side of the Rift, in a rock tunnel that angles sharply up. My heart thumps from fear as much as the climb. My threats are worth nothing now, in a place Trisk knows well and I know not at all.

12 is so eager she's a bit ahead of me. I have to grab her ruff to slow her. Ahead, I see a carved arch, like the one at the Moorings. This one also has a saying etched in stone:

The Mother divides and unites. The Mother ends and begins. You serve the Mother until the end of your days.

We exit through the hatch and into an open bowl. The air is wonderfully sweet after the musty odor of the High Rail. Paths lead through pines on either side of a steep fall of boulders.

Trisk stops at a stump to speak into her comms.

I put 12 into a sit, then look back at the hatch. At the top is carved the three crescents. Someone's defaced it, making the crescents look like a pup's puckered anus.

To one side, a camera lens glints over a blinking blue light. 12 wraps her tail around me. Against my leg, she trembles with anticipation.

Trisk signs off, then stares at me. I wouldn't call her gaze friendly, but at least she's no longer enraged. "All settled," she says. She digs a length of rope from her pack. "Tie the cross to a tree."

"What?"

She repeats. "Tie the cross to a tree. Then run, little Chronicler."

Like an idiot, I repeat: "Run? Run where?"

"East, west. I don't care. Tie the cross and run."

My confusion goes straight to 12, as if we share the same veins and heart. She growls.

"You heard me. Run," Trisk repeats.

"We're supposed to stay together."

"Says who?"

"Kesh. You heard her. We're supposed to find Rek. Her Blazes."

"I don't give a hyba's fart for Rek. Kesh is the real traitor. I've just filed a full report with the Centrum. All her doings. Diverting to the Collegium when we only go to the Arcadium for new girls. Giving you the cross. Now this! She's a traitor, I've been telling them for months. She's cooking up something. I mean to stop her."

"She gave you an order."

"Traitors don't give orders. Run."

"You're a liar." I'm trembling in Benit's sheepskin jacket. "She'll have you thrown out."

"Thrown out?" Trisk cackles. "Don't you see where you are? She can't throw me any worse place than Beyond-the-Weave, yet here I stand, saying this to you: *run*."

I turn to the camera, to denounce her, to call for aid. But no light blinks.

Trisk had the camera turned off. No one is watching from Holdfast.

"Tie the cross or I'll shoot her." Trisk shoulders her crossbow. "Is that Benit's jacket? I'll take it, too."

"You wouldn't shoot her."

Trisk pulls a shimmering bolt from the bandolier, loads the crossbow, and aims at 12. "The jacket."

I throw it to her. 12's ears are pricked and she stares at Trisk.

"Tie her," Trisk says evenly.

"You won't shoot her. You want her too badly."

Trisk is thoughtful. "You're right."

She aims at my head. "Collegium girls. Not so smart." To 132, Trisk says, "Up."

The battle dog's tongue is vivid in the dappled light filtering through the pines: pink as Becke's favorite candies. "The cross is mine," Trisk says. "Always should have been. Now is. What a marvel!"

"I'd rather die," I tell her.

"Happy to accommodate. Tie her or I'll shoot. I guess Benit won't getting that jacket back."

I should take more joy in what I'm planning to do. Trisk hasn't given me a choice. Like Benit said, I only need one weapon. Still, I'm sad. It's an awful thing to ask of 12, on her first day, her first hour, in Beyond-the-Weave. Her bad luck, to love me.

I flick my hand. At the same time, I leap sideways into a heap of pine needles.

The flick means *Go*.

Trisk may not be cunning, but she doesn't scare easily. She squeezes the crossbow trigger. A strela bolt sizzles past my ear. There's a flash as the tree behind 12 shatters, then turns to dust.

12 is almost too fast to see. Her forepaws reach, her black and brown armor flashes. Her tail, her marvelous hyba tail, flows past like water. She smashes into Trisk. The crossbow flips into the air butt end first and clatters on a rock. The bow is so light, it doesn't stop, slipping down the slope and into the Rift.

I never hear it hit bottom.

The legionary rolls to her side. Trisk is used to this from practicing with battle dogs. Besides, this is the same attack she tried on me my first day. Compared to 12, 132 moves as if through honey. The battle dog catches only the tuft at the tip of 12's long tail.

The bite is enough to save Trisk's life. With a liquid chuckle, 12 turns and clamps her jaws around 132's neck, at the gap between the battle dog's helmet and armor. She slams 132 to the ground, so hard the thistling on the helmet buries in the hard ground, trapping the battle dog. There's a wet crack as 12 bears down, snapping 132's neck.

132's eyes roll in their sockets. Her legs flail, then go limp. I smell urine mixed with fresh blood. The battle dog is dead before Trisk wobbles to her feet.

I'll give Trisk this: she's stubborn. She fights back with her fists, with kicks, with shrieks. 12 doesn't respond since I've given no further command. I'm giddy with amazement, horror. 132's blood drips from 12's pergama shield.

"To me," I tell her.

12's tail lashes as she settles beside me. Trisk stumbles to 132's motionless body.

Trisk moans, "You killed her."

"You would have killed me."

"Traitor," she spits.

"I've done nothing wrong." My fingers bury between 12's ears. "Lead me back through the Rail. If you're right and Kesh is a traitor, I'll gladly tell the Sowers everything I know."

Trisk snarls, "You know nothing, Collegium girl."

"That's what I'm offering for your life."

Susalee and the others must be wondering where I am, worrying. I can't wait to get back into our quarters and tell them everything, from the first moment I met Kesh on the green until now. They'll help me figure this out. They know I've been loyal. I should have told them everything a long time ago.

A twig snaps. Neither one of us has moved. Trisk stares at the rock slide across from the Rail opening.

12's growl sets my heart racing. I look around the bowl: trees, rocks, a stump. Nothing. That delay is everything to Trisk. Before I can command 12 to block her, Trisk ducks into the High Rail. With a whoosh of stale air, she shuts the door.

12's hyba tail lashes, raising a storm of dust and pulverized tree. 132's dead body steams.

I'm alone in Beyond-the-Weave. I know it's pointless to pound on the door. I tell 12 to sit. I kneel, using her body to shield me from the rocks. I practice breathing: slow, slow. 12 pants, then swipes her blue-black tongue around her jaws. From over her shoulder, I scan the rocks: nothing.

Benit said, *If you hear a whistle, it's them. If you hear a twig snap: them. Run.*

Run where? *Anywhere.*

How can I find a new Rail? I remember: my tracker map. I give a thousand thanks to the Mother that I kept it in my boot. That Wylla gave it to me. That Flicke forced me to take it before I climbed the swinging ladder of the Legionship.

That Flicke loved Wylla enough to stay. I flatten the map against 12's tiger-striped shoulder.

Shapes swim into view. A large spot—me—beyond the Rift. A separate spot in Holdfast. I swipe the map's surface to magnify where I am. I see the Rail: straight back to Holdfast. The forested bowl where I'm crouching swims into view.

The spot I thought was me fractures.

Into three. Three separate spots.

Two of them are closing in.

12 pricks her ears. She chuffs a warning.

"Stop!" I shout. The map has the spots in the rocks. "She'll kill you. Leave us be."

Pine branches rustle. "Look what she did to the battle dog." Stupidly, I point, as if 132's steaming remains weren't obvious. "A bloody mess is what you'll be if you come any closer!"

I look higher, where the bowl rises almost vertical. 12 growls again. One rock has two eyes. "Who are you?" I scream.

12's snout thrusts into the air. "I'll set her on you," I vow. "She'll not stop until you are in pieces."

The other dot has moved to my right. I'm surrounded. A bird chirps again.

Or whistles. I see the scrag's crossbow first. A bolt flies so fast I barely have time to harden myself for the impact.

The bolt hits 12 right where her armor ends and her back haunch is exposed.

12 leaps vertically, gnashing pure air. Her great tail slams the ground, swirling up dust. Still, the bolt dangles from her haunch. Why didn't she explode? The bolt is silver, not glowing with light. I yank it from her, and clear liquid drips from a needle tip.

A second bolt smacks into her haunch in exactly the same spot. Twisting, 12 snatches out the bolt with her teeth. Then she sinks to her front knees, then falls heavily, her tongue lolling.

"What have you done?" I bellow. 12 looks dead.

A little scrag hops up and down, hooting. A second shadow detaches from the very tree Trisk pointed to when she told me to tie 12. The third spot on the tracker map.

This scrag is a tall and muscular, straps heavy with bolts crossing over its chest. Some bolts have clear liquid, and others glow with a strela's fatal charge.

This scrag has heavy dark hair and black eyes.

The little scrag hoots again. Something about the sound strikes me, a vibration, a tone. I think of Rek's boys.

The little scrag is male. *Mother help me.* A boy.

The boy takes aim a third time.

This time, the bolt smacks my shoulder. Something cold squirts painfully under my skin. Only much later do I imagine how it would have looked if the camera were still on: Dinitra falling, 12 already dead, 132 a steaming pile. Drawing this, I would have used quick, hard dashes. Something violent, sudden. Something hard. The only continuous line would have been 12 and her long, limp tail.

Too bad Trisk already escaped. She wanted a glimpse of my face when I saw my first male in Beyond-the-Weave.

Above, I hear a whir. Lights flash through my closed eyes. I don't know if I'm dying or dreaming. I am flying in darkness like that old nightmare. In my mouth, I taste metal.

What would the Chronicler have written at the top of this drawing, to record for the ages?

The simplest story of all. Killed by a male.

14

Petal

I open my eyes and close them again. Open or closed, I see black. It's so perfect and deep I know I could never match it with paint.

I put my hand in front of my face, feel the pain sharp in my shoulder where the bolt hit. My hand dangles, prickling from being asleep. Though my fingers are close enough to touch my nose, I see nothing. I feel a lump on my skin at the wound site, swollen and hot as fresh bread. Did I dream the arms hoisting me?

Or were those arms metal? I touch my cheek, crusted with dried spit. How long have I been unconscious? I search around me. No 12. No backpack. No boots. My tracker map is gone.

The worst pain—the searing, throbbing heart of the pain—is the back of my neck. Gently, I touch my fingerpads to the skin. There's a fresh cut sutured with thick thread.

My life fiber is gone. And Benit's sheepskin jacket. I feel suddenly naked. The Legion could have used the life fiber to track me. Without it, I'm invisible to them. The life fiber has my Sower formula. I feel like I've lost my past, what makes me Dinitra 584-KxA.

How far was I carried? What is this place? Where's the boy?

Did he touch me? I feel around me for the tracker map. *Gone.*

I fall asleep, wake, fall asleep again. The boy knew the other scrag was aiming. I was distracted and the boy shot me like he shot 12. My 12. My dead 12.

Something whimpers. I feel a surge of hope. Is 12 just a little further away? I feel the floor, solid planking. I whistle softly.

The whimpering vanishes.

I realize: the whimpering is me. I led her across the Rift and killed her. For love of me. I feel like I've been split open, my heart and lungs exposed. I've killed 12, entrusted to me. She protected me and died for it.

Died for nothing. My mouth opens and no sound comes out, a howl as dark as the room.

When I wake again, I want water more than food. I want boots more than water. There's no escape without them. Most of all, I want even a glimmer of light. Even with eyes enhanced with *Capra aegagrus*, I need some light.

Something tickles my ankle: a hairy centipede. I throw it hard. My reward is a soft plop.

There is a wall.

I'm woozy, but I manage to stand, humped like a question mark, like old Professor Wylla. *Trust what you see, not what you're told, dear girl.* How can I trust anything in this blasted darkness?

I hear footsteps. A door opens, the light blinding. It's the tall scrag.

I throw myself at her.

The scrag blocks me easily. Then she lifts me off the floor. I bite. All I get is hair. The scrag turns me so my back is to her, then hooks an elbow around my neck and squeezes.

Fleshy lips press to my ear. "*Ka Url,*" the scrag whispers. I struggle for breath. "*Ka Url.*" She squeezes harder as the room spins and I black out.

I wake exactly as before: laid out, bootless. I have no idea how much time has passed.

The door is still open. I see a light flickering orange and yellow. I smell a fire and something savory. My stomach clenches with hunger.

I struggle to my hands and knees. The floor seems to buck like a Legionship fighting a storm. Gradually, the walls shudder to a stop. Only in towns like Pergama do Weavers still make fires. I go through everything I remember like a list. The transport, the containment dogs. Rek's sons, Trisk and 132: *traitor*. And the little scrag who shot me.

A boy.

I am in Beyond-the-Weave.

In my bare feet, I stand and take a small step, then pause to balance. My head swims. I prop myself on the doorway and gulp down the sourness bubbling at the back of my tongue. Several steps later, I'm halfway down the hall.

I see the boy. He sits on a low stool beside a hearth with a lively fire. On another stool, strips of meat glisten. The boy lifts a strip of meat, threads it onto a metal skewer, then cooks the meat over the fire.

For a moment, I feel like I've stepped into a History class. No one cooks over an open hearth in the Weave. No one cooks meat like this. The Collegium cooks use a flame fueled by the Cyclon.

On the floor next to the boy is my backpack. My tracker map juts from the top.

Did he butcher 12 for the meat?

Still, he hasn't noticed me. He's muttering to himself, something about them and it and a word that sounds like *piggles*.

Sacks pile along one wall. There is a single door, to the left of the mantle. Beside it sits the other scrag. Her dark eyes are fixed to me.

"Why am I here?" My voice is weak.

The boy looks up, then back to his meat.

"Where are my boots? What did you do with 12?" I can't bring myself to say *her body*. "The beast with me. What did you do with her?"

The boy pulls back the skewer to check if the meat is done. "Things is changed for you, knobbie."

Slowly, the boy stretches out his leg. He's wearing my boots. My skin crawls. To get my boots, the boy must have touched me.

The boy's brown cheeks are sprinkled with rusty freckles. He has a stick neck and a thick cap of bright red hair. His hands look too big for his arms, like a pup's feet.

"They'll come for me," I blurt. "They'll rescue me."

Immediately, I regret it. The scrags must have seen Trisk shut the High Rail against me. Without a life fiber, I'm invisible. The next legionary to come through the High Rail will find 132's remains and assume I'm dead, too.

The boy hands the roasted meat to the tall scrag. She strips the skewer, shoves the meat in her mouth, then hands the skewer back. The boy takes a new length of raw meat to thread onto the skewer. "If your beast dies, them Captains will have my skin for a war drum. Anku is... not so gentle. I tried to fix your beast, so I did."

"Where is 12?" I insist.

The boy nods toward the sacks.

I see a brindled forepaw. Against the far wall, her tail lies like some dead thing, the white tuft splatted like spilled cream.

I rush to her side and use both hands to tear the sacking off. Around her back paws wraps a thick lither strap. Another winds her snout shut. At her right ear and down her neck is a long, deep gash that weeps pus.

Her armor is gone. Between slit lids, 12's golden eyes look dull as old coin.

"You didn't need to bind her!" I cry.

"Did so." The boy examines the sizzling meat. "While you was a-snoozing, that creature woke. Two bolts ain't enough, I said so to Anku myself." The boy nods at the tall scrag. "One such as you should be glad she's alive at all. Anku says the Captain would strangle us herself if the beast dies!"

I feel 12's black nose. It's dry and flaky. "I need to clean the wound. Dose her. Or else she will die."

The boy doesn't move.

"Didn't you hear me? I can save her," I shout at him. I try to remember what Benit used on 132: clean water, disinfectant, rags, forgetting. Gauze, thread, the curved needle.

All in the fysic kit Benit put in my backpack.

"My backpack. Bring it to me," I tell the boy.

Sullenly, the boy pulls gristle from between his teeth and flings it into the fire. "Ain't no son of yours to order."

"If she dies it will be your hide. Best bring me my backpack."

It takes a grunt from Anku to get him off the stool. "And cloth," I tell him. "Clean, warm water."

Inside the fysic's kit is a tin of salve, a curved needle, a vial of forgetting, a spool of thick black thread, gauze pads, and antibiotic powder. *Bless you, Benit*. Gently, I unwind the lither straps around 12's feet and snout. I pry open her jaws and with my finger smear antibiotic powder on her tongue.

How much? How often? She might not die from her wounds, but from my clumsy attempts to heal her.

I watched Benit sew up 132, I tell myself. I can do this.

With a thump, the boy sets a pot of steaming water beside me. He squats down to watch. With the needle tip, I pick out dirt behind 12's ear. I cup the warm water in my hand, then drip it through the wound to flush out any remaining dirt. Water courses down her snout. Then I douse her again with disinfectant.

Now the difficult part: sewing. I drip three drops of the forgetting on the back of 12's tongue before I make the first needle puncture.

She doesn't flinch. I have to pull hard to get the slightly broader eye of the needle up and through her flap of skin. Still, 12 doesn't move.

I make twenty stitches in all. "Give me a knife," I tell the boy.

"Gaw! You is no Captain here! You would stick me with it, so Anku herself would agree."

"To cut the thread." My glance at Anku is enough to move the boy toward the bench where he left the knife.

With all of my time with 12 in the pens at Holdfast I'm strong enough to flatten him. He's not much more than bones and a hank of red hair. Probably I could outrun him, even in bare feet.

But 12 can't run. I sprinkle the wound with the antibiotic powder, then maneuver 12's massive head to my lap. I run my palms down her snout, then massage her neck, hoping this comforts her. Even her burnt butter smell has ebbed. With my thumb pad, I gently press her brows all along the bone ridge, something I learned from Tem: it always feels good. I want her to know I'm there. I haven't abandoned her.

12 breathes fast and shallow. From the bucket, I take one sip of water for me, then drip some into 12's mouth.

The water puddles on the floor.

The boy returns to the fire. Idly, he pokes the coals with a skewer, sending up a flurry of embers. How did I know he was a boy? Something about his face, all angles. Close up, he smells of wet dirt and metal. His baggy tunic makes it impossible to guess his true size. Over his shoulders is draped a sheepskin.

Benit's sheepskin, given to me for good luck. I promised to return the sheepskin to Benit.

I have to get it back.

The boy roasts another strip of meat. This time, he brings the skewer to me. Ravenous, I pick the meat off, so hot it burns my fingers.

It's delicious—the most delicious thing I think I've eaten. I think I need to tell Becke, then I remember she's across the Rift. I wonder if she and the others think I'm dead. Are they weeping for me or did Trisk already tell them I'm a traitor?

That the commander is a traitor.

The boy stares at 12. "Gaw," he says softly. "She's like no hyba I ever seen."

"She's a cross," I tell him.

"She's crossed?"

"She's not pure hyba. She's part hyba. She's also dog."

"Ah," the boy says. "We find them drafts all the time."

"Find them?"

"Some are stranger than anything. Fish and bird together, maybe horse and snake. Whatever them knobbies wake up wanting. They wander until they is found. Or die."

I'll ask about "knobbies" later. This boy wants to talk. Maybe I can learn how to get back to Holdfast. "What's your name?"

I'm surprised at his quick answer. "Petal."

"That's a thing, not a name."

"It was a flower year."

12 groans softly. I lay my hand against her shoulder. "She'll need to eat," I tell Petal.

He brings me another strip of meat. I chew some and place the wad on 12's tongue. The meat falls out. I chew the wad again until it's almost liquid, then slowly drip the meat soup into her mouth.

"The beast's a dead one." Petal rests his head on his filthy arms. "What do you call her?"

"She is 12," I say.

"I'm twelve."

"You told me your name is Petal."

He shakes his head. "I notched the portal of my own dwelling place, twelve exact. Like my own breath I knows it, so I do. Twelve summers since my mother brought me into this world."

"Your mother?" Petal's talking about his age, twelve, and also a mother. Not the Mother of us all or a Sower. He means an actual person. Before I can ask about his mother, he shrugs. "Might as well call the beast one or two. Or twenty-two. It's a queer name, 12."

"Petal isn't even a whole flower. Why not call yourself stem or thorn?"

"Don't know any Stem." Petal's face brightens. "Thorn is a warrior, brother of Ash. The best fighter in all of Bounty. Timbe's son. Best ever, Ash says."

My heart is in my throat. Mother, warrior, and now this: a male warrior. "What is Bounty?"

"Where you are, knobbie! Council House, most beautiful in the land." He twirls his finger in the air to mean the room we're in. "Better than the old Centrum rock, so my mother says."

Petal eyes 12 again. "Sure you'll get her living?"

He reminds me of the younger girls in the Collegium: spiky at first, then friendly.

"They'll skin me sure if 12 is a carcass." He splits the word in two: car CASS. "We was to get the beast alive and with it the female. KxA female. You. Not TxS. Not NxN." In the firelight, Petal gazes at 12 with a mixture of loathing and fascination. "I have the KxA female and a car CASS."

His list of things the Captains will remove if 12 dies gets longer: a tongue, a finger, a foot. "Anku cracked its skull like a morning egg, she did. Would have stomped it, too, excepting I saves it. Not that you'll thank me. Not that they'll ever know."

Anku listens from the corner. "Why doesn't she say something?" I ask.

"Legion got Anku's tongue years ago." Petal digs a skewer end into the space between the floor planks. "Filthy fighters, those. Fed it to a battle dog while she was a-watching. All her words, swallowed. She hates them so. That creature ate every one of her words forevermore."

Petal wipes his face with his sleeve, rearranging the dirt. "We is to get the female with rolly hair. Skin the color of piney bark, they says. Rolly. You. KxA. We is to catch the beast while we're at it. Two bolts of forgetting, no more. Herself, she gave the order."

Herself? With the skewer, Petal scrapes letters on the floor: K, A. "I spied the letters on your nape. K, A. The very one. Rolly hair and the beast, too. Done and done. Except 12's a-dying."

I think of the moving dots on my tracker map. I saw Anku and Petal approaching. Why are these scrags connected to me? How can I be on a tracker map with a boy? I feel the cut on my neck, where my life fiber used to be. "You cut it out."

With the skewer tip, Petal points to the fire. A silvery blob bubbles on a log. "Anku did. Got to or..." Petal crabs his hand and wriggles the fingers, like a hungry creature. "Them croakers will be searching."

"Croakers?"

"Them ships! Cross the mountains, come searching for us. We call them croakers because of the sound. Croak, croak!"

Anku grunts. Petal's talking too much. Abruptly, the boy stands, adjust Benit's sheepskin, and returns to the fire.

I can still feel Anku's arms squeezing me. There's nothing to be done but wait for 12 to heal. I stroke her shoulder where the tiger stripes are broad and blackest, then slip my hand to her ribs, to feel her breathing. If she survives the hour, she may survive the day. Then the week, long enough to get back across the Rift.

There's a sudden patter on the ceiling: rain. My hand finds the soft spot between 12's ears, like a hatchling's feathers.

I stretch out against her and sleep.

15

Daughter Feast

I wake to a terrified shriek.

I reach out with my hand, but 12 is gone. I scramble to my feet, my head whirling.

12 is backing Anku and Petal against a wall, her spine hair stiff as nettles. Her tail sweeps Petal's stool against the wall with a crack, then the meat stool and skewers, then the bucket half filled with water.

Petal screams, "If you don't call off your beast, Anku will murder it!"

Tears slide dirt streaks down his cheeks. He looks like a stick toy, breakable, as he clings to Anku's leg.

Anku has raised a log, aiming to crack 12's skull. Through her plank of hair, she grimaces. I see an honest debate in her eyes: is one blow enough to take down 12? Or is it the exact thing to start a killing frenzy?

I'd put everything on frenzy. So, eventually, does Anku.

"Come," I say to 12. "Sit."

Benit would call her form perfect. 12 comes, her tail curling around me protectively, the white tuft ticking just below my chin.

"Eh," Anku says, lowering the log.

I don't want Benit's sheepskin anymore, covered as it is with

Petal's invisible goo. I do need my boots, even if they're dripping in it.

Petal blubbers. "Bind the beast! Bind it about the maw!"

"Shouting will only agitate her. Give me my boots."

Anku peels the boy from her leg. "Ooos," she says.

I'm starting to understand her. "Ooos": boots.

Petal flings first the left, then the right boot. I catch them easily. 12 stares at me, ready for my next command.

What would be the command for: *Take the rest of his legs?*

"Good girl." Then I smile at Petal, flinging his words back at him. "Things is changed for you now."

I pull on my boots, lacing them tight. "I am going to feed her. You stay right where you are, both of you. Then 12 and I are leaving. Don't follow. Don't shout. Or 12 will finish you both."

I feel taller, wider, heavier. Also giddy and afraid and still woozy. "You saw what she did to 132, I think."

12 makes quick work of the meat scattered across the room by her tail. Her shoulder is healing: the stitches holding, the swelling gone. For good measure, I put Petal's meat knife in my backpack.

I take out the tracker map and press my thumb to the corner. One large spot swims into view: the three of us together in Beyond-the-Weave, as expected. Holdfast is to the southwest. How many days away? I remember the sound of whirring as I passed out. Lights flashed. 12 is far too heavy for even someone as strong as Anku to carry that distance. Some sort of ship must have carried us.

On the map, this room is connected by a hallway to a circular space. Other hallways connect to the circle, making a sunburst shape.

The only way out is through the circle. I see the three dots: me, Anku, Petal. The fourth spot is no longer in Holdfast. The fourth dot is in the circular room.

Here.

Bless the Mother. The only way out is to pass whoever it is.

Petal grins. "Things is changed for you, Dinitra KxA." He flicks his fingers, an imitation of my hand commands to 12. "Go on then. Walk. See her who brought you."

I should have told 12 to rip off his legs.

My heart is in my throat as I open the door by the mantle. Again, a hallway. Again, the orange flicker of firelight. I wish my skin felt harder, like a lither strap. I hear the clink of utensils. I catch the smell of roast apple. Bread. Wet wool. There are voices, several.

I pause just inside the doorway to examine the room.

My first thought is *not so bad*.

Women, only women. They are unlike any I've ever seen. At least a dozen people crowd the room, more arriving through heavy doors flung open onto a rainy street. Their heads are shaved around a circlet at the crown. There, they gather their long hair and plait a dozen braids that fall past their elbows. The braids are woven with colored ribbon and beads.

As more women arrive, they shake the rain from their cloaks, hang them, and prop their crossbows against the wall. Many wear bandoliers, the sockets shimmering with live bolts and bolts filled with the same clear liquid Anku used to take down me and 12.

I don't need a boy or Anku to tell me these are rebel Captains.

Which one is the fourth spot on my map? Servers lay the table for a meal. Glasses of dark red licor crowd a side table. Against the far wall, a fire roars in a stone hearth. Like the room I woke in, this one is a circle. The end of the rays, the sun at the center.

Several chairs are pulled close to the fire. A red-haired Captain passes out licor, smiling and joking with the others. There must be thirty of them.

"273 or 274," one Captain says, lifting the glass. "A year of rains like this one if I'm not mistaken. The bellies of my Vessels were round as melons."

"What I wouldn't give for a ripe melon." This Captain is broad in the shoulder and with a bit of a belly.

Behind me, Anku speaks. "Oooo." Move.

A server sees me first. Her eyes go big as fists. Not because of me: 12, with her golden eyes and long snout, advances like a living shield. The server drops her jug, drenching the nearest Captain.

The Captain—white-haired, her face care-worn—is about to exclaim when she sees us.

To me, I motion to the hyba cross.

12 positions herself at my hip. As we advance, she swings her head back and forth.

From a large chair pulled close to the fire, someone speaks. I freeze. I've heard this voice before. "Stay calm," she says with her familiar rasp.

Kesh stands with a whir of her metal apparatus.

The Captains murmur in shock. "I never doubted."

"I see. I don't believe."

"The likeness. So telling."

"Magnificent."

"Blessed be the Bond."

"Blessed be the Bond."

"Blessed be the Bond."

I could kill any one of them with a flick of my wrist, release the mayhem I feel in my head. This cannot be happening. "I want to go home," I say, too loud.

Kesh says, "Welcome to Bounty."

"Traitor," I spit. "Trisk was right."

12's great head swivels to me. She snarls: *What command is this? What would you have me do?* Kesh is the same as the day I first saw her on the Collegium green: her metal apparatus, the black tunic over the sockets connecting the machine to her flesh hips, the pale, shattered face. Her smell is the same: machine oil and rosemary. Rosemary, I know from Benit, for pain.

The pergama sheaves have been ripped from her shoulders. "If being a traitor to the Weave is the worst you can say of me, so be it. I will betray the Weave every day of my life until it is defeated."

My mouth twists. "I should tell the cross to finish you. I would be praised, rewarded. They would honor me."

A shadow of amusement passes over her face. "Perhaps. Or perhaps my Captains would kill the both of you before you take your next breath."

At least three of the Captains are aiming crossbows loaded

with shimmering strela at 12. "Come," I say sharply. 12 moves with me as I step toward the door.

"You are free to go, but you must leave 12."

"She is mine." I'm about to say *you gave her to me*. I sound like some petulant first-year.

"I will make a truce with you, Dinitra 584-KxA." Kesh's tone has turned gentle, like she's speaking to a Holdfast pup. "If you choose to go after you hear my story, you may, with the cross. And my blessing. Go be the hero of the Weave if you still wish it."

Without 12, I'll never make it to Holdfast. Between me and any Rail are wild hybas, wild men. "Nothing you can say will change my mind."

"Let's put that statement to the test. Use logic and reasoning like a good Collegium girl."

I stab my finger at Anku, who has taken a glass of licor. "She almost killed me."

"Anku has no love for dogs or their drafts. But she would not have killed you. She had orders to bring you back. You and 12."

"Tell me why they are on my tracker map." I mean Petal and Anku. They were the spots I saw just before they shot us. With 12 beside me, I feel bold. "And who else? Someone else in this room? Who?"

"Come, sit with me," Kesh says evenly. "Have something to eat."

"I will not." With the rain pouring outside, I can't tell if it's morning or afternoon. "Tell me as I stand here and then 12 and I will be on our way."

"Very well." The joints of Kesh's metal apparatus whir as she lowers her torso. She looks me in the eye. "You are my daughter."

If she had said I was a fish or an oolieberry pie I would have been less shocked. Daughters belong to the past, when men ran wild and brought the world to the brink of destruction. It's a word as strange as *boy*. "Impossible."

Kesh has her one eye on me. In its depths, I see only conviction. "I should be more logical. I sowed you fifteen years ago. This celebration here," she says looking around the crowded room, "is called the Daughter Feast, when Sower and daughter are reunited. Our encounter here, in the Council House, has been many long years in the making. I am so pleased to welcome you to your new home."

It's as if all the answers I once yearned for are scribbled at once, in a horrible tangle. On the green, Flicke said legionaries have no patience for underfooting students. *Especially you*. I thought she was being mean. She meant it: *especially you*. Kesh didn't expect to come face to face with me at the Moorings. When she did, she didn't see a Collegium student. An inferior girl. She saw the child she'd sown.

She saw a *daughter*.

KxA. K for Kesh. The letter is tattooed on my skin. My mother has always been there, a secret in plain sight.

Kesh's raspy voice is patient. "I used the A extract. An older one, not generally preferred. I felt it had valuable qualities. Therefore, you and I have a Bond."

This is what Flicke meant when she growled at me, *For the Bond. For Herself*. She meant Kesh, my Sower. The Bond is between us. Mother and child. Mother and *daughter*.

"Anku is my sister," Kesh says. "Therefore, she appears on your map. The map is based on my genetic formula. That's how we make them in Bounty."

"Sister," I repeat. I don't know the word.

"Females with the same Sower and extract. Carried in the same Vessel. For his part, Petal is Anku's son. If you think back to Relational Diagrammatics…"

"No more lies. Just tell me."

Kesh's eye flashes. "I have never lied to you."

"The world is a lie," I cry. "Why have you brought us here?"

"Bring my daughter licor," Kesh says.

"I will not drink. I want to go home."

"Bounty is your home." Fury twists her face. "Have you no sense of how much has been sacrificed for you?"

Kesh's wavers on her black blades, and I think she may fall. Anku rushes to her side, steadying her.

"You did lie to me, on the Collegium green. You told me you would give me any assignment I wanted. A lie."

"I did not lie. I knew you wouldn't betray your friend. Asta, correct?"

The name in her mouth is like a gut punch. She knew the painting was for Asta all along. "I know everything about you, Dinitra 584-KxA. I am your Sower, after all."

"Maybe you don't lie," I say savagely. "You just don't tell the whole truth."

It's as if all of the emotion drains out of her. "I am weary. Come, let us sit by the fire. Let me tell the story, then do what you will."

Anku helps Kesh lower herself onto a chair. She remains at her side, watching me balefully.

The fact that I came from Kesh's body, the body sitting before me, fills me with revulsion, like peering inside my own stomach to watch food digest. I even touched her when I applied the salve to the inflamed flesh around her cables. To know your Sower, to speak to her, to touch her, is against everything the Mother stands for. We belong to the Weave, not another person. We serve the Weave, not some Sower.

Does Kesh expect me to belong to her because she assembled my genetic code? The empty socket, the scar halving her face. She is flesh and bone, breakable, like me. She is just a person. Why should I honor her and not the power of the Weave?

"About your tracker map." Kesh winces as she settles. "Anku and I had the same Sower and the same extract. The same Vessel carried us and we were nursed and raised by the same Keeper. Sisters," she says again, "that is our Bond. Anku's boy came another way. It's enough to say your formulas are linked through the two of us. In the old days, you would have called Petal cousin."

Cousin. The hair prickles on my neck. Not only did the boy touch me. We're connected by our tissues. Revolting.

Kesh seems not to notice my disgust—or care. "Putting it more simply, the four of us share elements of our formula. Our genetic code, in other words. The formula is embedded in the substrate of the map. When you touch the surface, the tracker map reads the formula connecting the four of us. Wylla gave it to you as a precaution. We—I mean Anku and Petal—wanted to be able to find you quickly once you crossed into Bounty."

Again, the word: Bounty. "What is this Bounty?"

Kesh opens her flesh hand. "This is Bounty. We are Bounty, daughter. Everything around you is Bounty. This is Bounty's Council Hall. And around you, welcoming you, are Bounty's Captains. The land, the mountains, east to the Wastes and north to the Deep. You will be Bounty also, you and 12, if you stay."

"Bounty is Beyond-the-Weave."

"Sister," Kesh says to Anku. "Show my daughter your map."

Anku keeps her tracker map in her sleeve. She flattens hers on the table in front of Kesh, then takes Kesh's map from the sleeve of Kesh's flesh arm. The maps knit just as they did in Holdfast, when the girls placed theirs together.

The four of us are one large dot in this room. Kesh tells me that Wylla and Flicke gave her regular reports. "For instance, I knew you had a talent for drawing. The wren. They'd smuggled the image to me and so many others. I know you have nightmares about falling. You sleep-walked, for a time."

I don't know where my courage comes from. Maybe from 12 herself, from the fur between her shoulders that I'm clutching. "Are you finished?"

Kesh is taken aback. "You must have questions."

"I'll be on my way." I stab my finger at Anku. "Your sister almost killed 12. Ask that..." I struggle with the word. "Boy."

12 knows her name and takes this as a command. I feel her tense with dreadful purpose. Benit told me that once she starts, she will never stop.

"Careful, Dinitra," Kesh says softly.

I imagine commanding 12 to attack her. The room would be a butchery. How would I make it back to the Weave then?

"Sit," I tell the hyba cross.

"The forgetting was sadly necessary," Kesh says, "to prevent worse injury. We underestimated how much was necessary. 12 woke up. She had to be subdued, for her safety as much as anyone's. If you want to blame someone, blame me."

I stand and press my palm to my chest. To 12, this means *walk with me.*

I make my way as far as the door. There, a young Captain blocks me. Like Kesh, her head is shaved to the skin. Behind her, the rain is a solid gray curtain.

My patience ends. "I control this cross to a point," I threaten. "Past that point, your life is yours to spend."

She holds her palms up, a gesture of peace. "My name is Mei. I am a daughter, also. I was brought here just like you. There, my mother stands."

She points to the white-haired Captain. "Lam, her name is. Captain of the Birds of Prey. I am Mei 574-LxX."

Mei bends her head to show me the tulip tattoo. She has the same little scar, from where her life fiber was removed. Benit mentioned the Birds of Prey. To her, it was a joke: *little names,* she called them.

"Ask me anything," Mei tells me.

I ask the only question that matters. "Why are you standing in my way?"

"Because you need to hear more. Before you risk the journey back to the Weave. You owe this to your mother."

"My Mother is the Mother of us all."

Mei has to blink to keep the rain spray out of her eyes. "You always had a mother. The Weave called her Sower and kept her from you. The Weave broke the Bond, the most sacred thing the Mother of us all gives us. The Bond, Dinitra, is what binds a living thing to its mother, the one who gives us life. To us, the Bond is everything."

"The Bond is for beasts," I spit. "I am no beast."

"For beasts and for us." Mei looks no more than a year or two older than me.

"Where were you schooled?"

"The Pronomicon. Near The Spices. For girls means to host and serve, make contracts and agreements and the like. We're meant to be talkers," she says, smiling.

I fire back, "I'm finished with talk."

"Then you must listen." I see no lies in Mei's face.

"Your Sower should be proud of you," I say, realizing I've lost this argument.

"There she stands," says Mei. "Ask her yourself."

The resemblance between Mei and Lam is striking: the same fine nose, the same high cheekbones, lightly freckled skin.

"I will sit beside you and answer any question you have," Mei is saying. "For as long as you want. You must eat before you make a decision as important as this one."

Fear and confusion ball up in my mouth and come out a sob. "They almost killed her."

"Yet she lives." Mei takes my arm. "Come, Dinitra. We have food for your cross as well. I will tell you anything you wish to know. I promise you, if you still wish to leave, I'll guide you myself to the nearest Rail."

"Before I sit," I say, "tell me this: where are the other scrags?"

The word displeases her. "To the Weave, we are all scrags. It's an ugly word."

"I mean the males. Where are the males?"

"Snug under their roofs. They are not allowed in the Council House. You will see them tomorrow, I think. If you stay."

My heart races. Males are near. Not just *malehair*. Actual males.

All 12 and I have eaten since leaving Holdfast were the meat strips Petal roasted. My stomach clenches with hunger. Mei is right: we need food, water, and a proper rest. My shoulder still aches from where the bolt struck me.

"Only I feed 12," I tell Mei.

"Of course."

I turn back to the table. A server sets down two bowls—one of mash and one of water, for 12. Mei pulls out a chair. "You sit here, beside me. 12 will eat at your side."

12 gobbles the mash, then drains the water. Once I sit, 12 pushes her way under the table, scratches the floor, turns three times, then settles her head on my feet. Her tail pushes up between my knees, the tuft resting against my chest.

The room is thick with the smell of burnt butter.

To eat, there's stew, potato bread, and a single roast apple, the sugar packed in the hollow core gone brown and bubbly. The red-haired Captain brings me another glass of licor.

"For the toast," Mei says. "This is Timbe, Captain of the Living Wood."

A maple-leaf clasp gleams against Timbe's dark throat. Her eyes shine as she approaches Kesh and lifts her glass. Her toast is simple. "To victory," Timbe says.

I leave my glass untouched as the others drain theirs and pass the bottles for more.

As we eat, I count thirty-seven Captains including Anku. Petal squats by the fire over his meal. Though he must have eaten half a goat in the other room, he's on his second bowl of stew before I take my first bite.

The walls are draped in tapestries woven with hares, leaping derak, tall pines entwined with woodland flowers, and foxums. Each tapestry has as its outer edge the curling tail of a hyba.

Mei tells me her mother brought her to Bounty. "Shan over there," she says, motioning at another young Captain, "is my sister."

Sister, I remind myself: same Sower, same extract. Unlike Anku and Kesh, Mei and her sister look alike: the same high cheekbones and slender build.

"Shall I tell you the story of how I came to Bounty?" Mei asks.

I nod since my mouth is full of baked apple.

Mei and Shan were brought to Bounty as second-years in the Pronomicon. One night, hands grabbed her from her bed. It was so dark, she couldn't see faces. She was loaded onto a stolen croaker and flown to Quillka.

"This is Quillka, our largest town," she adds.

Petal used the word croaker, too. "I understand that's a ship."

"We steal them from the Weave, then refit them to fly off the Signal Way. A croaker can go anywhere. As long as they're not heavily loaded, they can even cross the Black Stairs."

Professor Wylla warned me to trust what I see, not I'm told. What if I've been taught that everything I'm seeing is treason? That nothing I'm being told is natural or proper?

I challenge her: "The Captains want to destroy everything the Weave has built."

Kesh cuts in before Mei can answer. "Some things. Not all things."

"Why?" The Weave is plenty and peace. Order. Equality. Why ruin it?

What I don't say is that the Weave will win the coming fight, as Kesh must realize. The Weave has the Legion. The Weave has Benit's battle dogs. Most of all, the Weave has a new fleet. That's what Susalee and the others are training to fly.

"Don't the females fight?" I ask suddenly. If Bounty has any hope of defeating the Weave, everyone must fight.

"Of course!" Mei's eyes are bright, as if she's pleased with her best student. "Females command, as is right. They support Bounty as farmers, craftspeople, cooks, and the like. We put all of our resources to their best use."

Kesh stands, a little wobbly until Anku steadies her. Her face is flushed from the licor.

"Daughter, come with me," Kesh says abruptly. "I would have a word with you alone."

16

Mother-Bond

K esh's room is at the end of another long spoke of the sunburst. The room is empty but for a low couch, a thickly padded chair with a high seat, and a central brazier that has the room quite warm.

Kesh points to the couch. "Sit," she tells me.

I suppress an impulse to fire back that I'm no beast to be commanded. But her face is as forbidding as I've seen it.

I sit, 12 stretching at my feet.

One wall is entirely occupied by a great machine. The machine is mostly flat, stretching from the floor to a high ceiling. Kesh backs against it. Like a Keeper tending a small child, Anku lifts the hem of Kesh's tunic and slides it past where the metal connects to her flesh and over her head.

Kesh is naked. Her breasts are small, nipples the size of small coins. Like her face, her chest and belly are sectioned by scars. The places where machine meets flesh—where I once rubbed salve— are inflamed.

Steadied by Anku, Kesh lays the palm of her metal hand to a lever and pushes down.

The machine whirs. Two clamps attach to where the cables join to the metal apparatus at her hips. Two more settle on her shoulders. She winces as gears behind her turn. There are several clicks and soft exhalations as the tubes connecting her flesh to the apparatus detach. Her metal knees go limp as they suspend on the wall.

Her shoulders twist. With a groan, she releases her torso from the metal legs and the metal arm. The metal arm is flexed with the fingers hanging limply downward. The clamps at her shoulders lift her smoothly and deposit her on the chair. Behind her, nozzles and brushes begin to clean the apparatus.

12 lifts her great snout, gazes at the machine, and sneezes.

"Leave us," Kesh tells Anku.

Anku nods.

In the chair, Kesh's body looks as defenseless as the wren hatchlings I once drew for Professor Wylla. All that's left of Kesh is her torso and hips, one arm, and her scarred head. Dark half-moons of exhaustion sit under her eyes. Before Anku leaves, she wraps a vicuña shawl around Kesh's bare shoulders.

I don't know if it's the cordial or the dim chamber. Kesh's voice sounds softer. "As I told you, Anku is my sister. Birthed from the same Vessel, raised by the same Keeper. Always together, even at the Collegium."

Inhabiting the same Vessel's belly seems dangerously intimate, like trading blood or spit with a sick stranger. "I couldn't receive you across the Rail, Dinitra. It wouldn't have been wise. I knew Anku could handle 12. There is one thing you and she share, though she'd never tell you. She has a terror of battle dogs. And the hybas, well. They are their own special horror in the wild. Perhaps she was rougher than she needed to be with 12. Forgive her. Surely, you can understand her fear."

"Petal told me the Legion took Anku's tongue and fed it to a battle dog."

"So they did."

"Why didn't you stop them? You were Legion Commander, after all."

Kesh's flesh fingers clench. "That and much more I couldn't stop. My duty was to stay as long as I could, to help Bounty before I was discovered. I'm proud to say I succeeded, for the most part."

My response is cruel. "I doubt Anku would say the same since she can no longer speak."

Kesh takes her time to answer. "You may be right."

I'm taken aback. The Legion Commander—Kesh, my mother —is admitting that something she did was wrong.

When Kesh speaks again, it's with great control. "None of this has been easy. Would you like to hear how I first learned of Bounty? Perhaps that will help you as you judge things you know little about."

I can't say it isn't a little enjoyable, to see Kesh upset. What I wouldn't give now for paper to sketch her. *Traitor revealed*, I'd scrawl at the top. *My Sower. In pieces.*

My cruelty curdles in my mouth. I can't bring myself to think *mother*.

Kesh says her favorite subjects were Biotics and Vidantics, perfect for a future Sower. "I believed everything I was told: the Weave craved peace, prosperity. Beyond our boundaries lay only chaos. What I knew of scrags was this: few remained. Barely human. And wild males? We needed extract, only. Vary the gene pool of our containment males. Once we achieved the Great Quest and could brew new generations without them, they would be exterminated. Something I believed and looked forward to with all of my heart."

Like I still believe.

Kesh says out loud what I am thinking. "Like you."

She winces as she adjusts her flesh arm. "I got a first in Plant Analysis, a first in Bioregeneration. Ironic, no?" She glances back at the machine polishing her legs and arm. "Fastest, most agile, most promising. I was like your Susalee."

Kesh knows Susalee? How much does she know about my friends?

Kesh notices my surprise. "I followed the 584s closely. Because of you."

"Through Wylla," I say.

"And Flicke. They were my friends. I've offered to bring them to Bounty a thousand times. A thousand times they said they would rather stay to watch over you."

I blurt, "I thought Flicke hated me."

"She did." Kesh half-smiles. "Flicke loves Wylla. Always has, from the day they met as first years. A little like—which is it, Tem?"

"Tem and Edba."

"What curious names." Kesh clears her throat with a cough. "It was Wylla who loved you. Flicke loved Wylla. She refused to leave the Weave without her. Wylla refused to leave without you. They stayed."

"Wylla told me Flicke wanted to be a pilot." Was Wylla telling me about the past in her odd way? "She said it was their duty to watch over me. Their shared task."

Kesh nods. "More than she should have said."

"Then you came for me. That day on the green."

"A sacrifice I can never repay."

"What do you mean, sacrifice?"

"They are both imprisoned, daughter." Kesh watches me closely as the news settles.

"Imprisoned." I gasp. "Why?"

"As you say, I am a traitor to the Weave. So were they. Traitors the three of us. Trisk reported on the trip from the Collegium, 12 -- all of it. They were taken away immediately for questioning." Behind her, her metal legs gleam. Still, the nozzles travel from her blades upwards like mechanical bees. "I knew the Sowers would come for me eventually."

"What about Benit?"

Kesh shakes her head. "She was never a part of the rebellion. She does her duty. An Arcadium girl through and through."

Panicked, I think about Susalee and Mariza, of Becke, Edba, and Tem. "What about the other Collegium girls? They knew nothing."

"As I hope will be understood. Eventually."

"And Asta. What about Asta?"

Kesh shakes her head. "I don't know anything about Asta."

"If you only wanted me, why bring the others to Holdfast? Why not just me?"

"An entire Legionship coming to the Collegium, for the first time in anyone's memory, for a single girl? I had to take more."

The only reason Susalee, Mariza, Becke, Edba, and Tem are at Holdfast is because of me. Not, as I assumed, because I was included by mistake. Would they want to know me if they knew I was the reason they ended up at the Legion? "They're suffering for me," I blurt.

Her words are sharp. "They suffer because of the corrupt Weave."

Kesh draws her shawl close. The room is stifling. Still, Kesh shivers.

"Shall I do something about the fire?" I ask.

"No. The cold never goes completely away." She gazes at me fixedly. "Dinitra. Daughter. You must listen carefully. The Weave is no longer your home. Even if you returned tomorrow, you would not be welcome. Mei will take you back if you wish. But understand this. You would be arrested. 12 would be taken from you and killed."

The minute Trisk shut the Rail against me, I was a traitor. But what is my place in Bounty? What does *daughter* even mean? I don't understand how a Legion Commander, a Sower, can choose to betray the Weave. "You told me in Holdfast that you would tell me someday how you went from being a Sower to Legion Commander."

"I did."

"I need to know now."

Kesh takes a deep breath. "I warn you. This is a hard story to tell. Harder even to hear."

Kesh expected to become a Sower. During her last year at the Collegium, that's all she could think about. "Not just a Sower. I wanted to be *the* Sower, the Head Sower. The position, the power. I wanted to be in charge of everything, make the new generations that would secure the Weave. To me, scrags were simply a problem to be fixed. Eliminated. Kill them, burn them, drown them—I didn't care. Peace at whatever price as long as they paid. I vowed to become Head Sower so I could order the Legion to complete the Great Quest on my first day."

In the dim light, the flesh that covers her empty eye socket looks like a dark eye of its own. "One afternoon, Anku and I went to the boulder to talk. You know it."

The boulder: where Professor Flicke caught me drawing. It was Rest Day, Kesh says. "Anku and I were discussing a problem in fluid dynamics. I thought she'd made a mistake in her calculations. Of course, she hadn't. She was the most talented engineer of our generation. We were so absorbed in our argument that we didn't notice her at first."

A girl hid in a shadow. They'd never seen anything like her. "We smuggled her into the sleeping hall. Professor Wylla found her under Anku's bed."

"Professor Wylla?"

"She was our teacher, too. I am not so old, daughter. This was how dear Wylla began to learn the truth about the Weave."

Professor Wylla explained to Kesh and Anku that the girl was a draft. The Sowers must have lost her, she said. Only later did they understand the girl had been abandoned. "Another meaning of draft is a Sower formula that doesn't produce the expected results. It is one thing to create something in a classroom: say, a flower that withstands cold. Often, the Sower drafts are... complicated. To put it directly, Dinitra, they mix human formula with beasts and plants. Whatever interests them. Sometimes, the experiments go terribly wrong."

I think of my carnivorous potato. The word "draft" doesn't do it justice. What if I had mixed the potato with human code instead of skunk or orange?

Kesh watches me closely, to gauge my reaction. "Are you understanding what I am saying? I told you I could watch 12 grow. That I used the translucent sac, with the nektar."

"Yes."

"There was no need for a Vessel. I could do much more than I could with a human child. In fact, we were encouraged to. The sacs are reusable, the nektar, too. Nektar never loses its power."

Kesh is quiet for a moment. "You must understand. The Head Sower doesn't like failure. In fact, it fills her with rage. Sowers suffer. Instead of reporting the failures, the Sowers hid them. Abandoned them, actually."

"Abandoned?"

"Some died, like those hyba cross pups. Some were killed. Others were released on the Black Stairs."

It takes me a moment to process this. "Released? Why would anyone do that?"

"Because the Sowers wanted nothing to do with mistakes. They were afraid of being punished. Fear, I have found, is the most powerful human emotion. More powerful even than love."

Hybas were among the first drafts to be released on the Rift. "They were meant to be better than battle dogs. Stronger, more lethal," Kesh says. "But they were utterly untrainable."

That didn't bother the Head Sower. She ordered the hybas loosed north of the Rift, to finish off the scrags and save the Legion the trouble. Kesh ticks off the other drafts made and released across the Rift. "Lithers: awful creatures, with enough wild cat in them to make them solitary, yet the size of the largest constrictor you've ever imagined. 12's collar was made of lither, as you know. The armor, too. Speluks for the caves, with bodies slick as fish and eyes the size of my fist. Some drafts were released to provide the Legion with food: derak and dilidots. Foxums control their populations. I know the Sower who made derak: deer and springbok combined, for the smaller size, and sugar cane to sweeten the flesh. They believed the drafts wouldn't be able to cross back over the Rift."

She pauses as the machine behind her injects oil on the joints of the apparatus. There's a sudden smell of nuts. "The scrags learned how to protect themselves, as any Sower worth her position should have predicted."

Kesh looks at me pointedly. "Do you remember the dog that attacked you?"

I do: black and stinking. Even speaking of it makes my arm ache.

"It was no dog. It was an early hyba. Sick and near to death. The pack abandoned it or you wouldn't be here today."

"Flicke saved me."

"More than once."

"What about that girl you found? The one you brought to Wylla?"

Kesh describes her: face and arms covered in red blisters. Her back hardened into scales. Her fingers fused but for the thumbs. She was completely blind and without a single hair. She had clothed herself in some stolen blanket. The rough nap of the fabric only made her skin worse.

"Her Sower must have wanted photosensitivity, for what purpose we never knew. Why the shell? Her fingers? Somehow, she'd managed to keep herself alive just long enough to crawl to the boulder and beg for help."

Just then, the machine cleaning Kesh's apparatus beeps. The nozzles retract. The room is quiet. "We took her to Wylla. The next morning, she was gone."

Much later, Kesh and Anku learned that Professor Wylla knew some of the Captains. Girls who had studied under her, then fled north to Bounty. One came to guide the girl north.

"Anku is our best Guide," Kesh says proudly. "She has saved hundreds of drafts by bringing them north. Drafts and daughters both," Kesh says, looking at me pointedly.

"I don't understand. Why do the Sowers make such things? It seems so cruel."

"Because they can. Some say they must. We're built on drafts, Dinitra. Every single person in the Weave. Every single one of the Captains, too. Your eyes, for instance. *Capra aegagrus*. We learned that example in school. That gives us night vision, correct?"

Even now, I see her clearly in the dark room. "Before the Sowers put those eyes in you, they had to develop them, test them. Often, the early-stage installations go awry."

"Early-stage?"

"Every new human generation incorporates things the Sowers experimented on with drafts. We are all drafts, in a way. We are just drafts that succeed."

"You told me about bees like no other. About nektar. Are those bees drafts?"

Kesh pauses. "Some drafts have made their own places to live. In the east, principally."

All I know about the east is what we learned in Geography: the Eastern Wastes. Empty, barren. Like what we learned of Beyond-the-Weave. "Perhaps it's wrong to keep calling them drafts. They are free, their own kind. Queen Odide is such a one. From Hive Home, she sends us nektar. To the Weave, too. She sends nektar in exchange for peace."

Susalee made her Biotics final from a sundew crossed with a bee. The honey was delicious. From what I remember, queen bees are like Sower and Vessel combined.

This new information is almost too rich to take in. "Did you abandon drafts?"

"I'm ashamed to say I did. I'm no innocent." Kesh's one eye is fixed on me. "Anku and I—when we were your age, we thought the world was what we'd been taught. We thought we knew everything. In reality, we were chicks still inside the shell of the Weave."

Kesh reaches up to pull a lever. The machine starts up again in reverse, first reconnecting her metal arm, then clamping again to her shoulders to lift her torso. For an instant, I glimpse the wound I tended at Holdfast: still raw. Kesh groans as the apparatus reattaches to her hips. With a thump, her blades meet the floor, take her weight. She tests the knees, bouncing lightly, the yellow claws at the blade ends scraping the floor.

"It's better you see for yourself," she tells me.

I stand from the couch. 12 gives herself a terrific shake and follows us down the hall.

Kesh talks faster, as if she has to get this story out before something stops her. "I wanted to show everyone I was best. That I could make the best citizens. Valuable citizens, healthy, smart, able. Not like that poor girl. That was the lesson I learned. Not that this was wrong. But that her Sower made a mistake. I wouldn't. That was how wrong I was."

The large Council room is empty but for Timbe, waiting silently. The plates and glasses have been cleared away, fire banked. Kesh goes straight into the heavy rain, oblivious. I catch every other word. "I boasted I would eliminate every weakness... Terrible burns...I was wrong...taught me..."

She turns to me. Her ruined face courses with rain. For the first time, I see myself in her: she is paler, scarred, but I have her chin, her nose. "Your formula was nothing special," Kesh tells me. "A tweak here or there on the template. I placed the sprite in the Vessel and forgot about it. Until the day you were born."

The last thing I need is for anyone to remind me how unremarkable I am.

"You have enhanced sight, resistance to disease, all standard. But you weren't going to win me any prizes, certainly not Head Sower. I needed a living child, that was all, to prove I could sow."

When she first held me, she says, she remembered that draft at the Collegium. "I realized how much pain she'd been in. How terrified she'd been. She was brave, Dinitra, something no formula can distill."

She lowers herself, eye level with mine, just as she did on the green. "What I realized is that her life was as dear to the Mother as yours. As my single daughter. Failures don't exist. To make the drafts and discard them as if they are nothing is a cruelty I could no longer bear."

17

Sil

The place Kesh brings me to is low-ceilinged, divided into rows. For a moment, I think the rows are made of cages, like Holdfast's kennels. I look for mash buckets, battle dogs. As my eyes adjust, I see the rows are shelves. Not shelves: beds, stacked four high.

I see hundreds of eyes.

Timbe lifts the lamp she brought from the Council House and raises it high over her head. "Not for you," Kesh says to me. "For them. These are the drafts we've rescued from the Weave. Not all can see in the dark. Not all can see."

Nearest to me is a creature with stripes. The stripes are green as spring leaves. The draft has a human face with whiskers and neat, cat-like ears. Another is like a dog, with a slender snout. Instead of ears, the creature has a moth's brown, furred antennae. There is a draft with translucent skin over a network of veins and limp fins instead of arms. She opens and closes her lipless mouth. The blood coursing in her veins is as orange as her eyes.

Kesh speaks as she moves down the row. "That one with green stripes? A human crossed with a soya plant, among other things. She must be led everywhere, fed and clothed and cleaned since she has not the brain to care for herself.

"And that one," Kesh says, pointing to a creature with a mass for a head and no eyes. "I think the Sower intended to study tissue regeneration, so they made a tumor that never stops growing. She won't live much longer, we think."

I see something that looks like a sea creature entirely covered in tentacles. "The tentacles must be cleaned in the fountain daily. You cannot touch her or she will shrivel. We call her Darling, our only way of showing affection."

I realize the creatures are speaking, each in their own way: chitters, squeaks, pops. "Purpose-built every one, out of human formula mixed with animal and plants. Insects, too. Sea creatures. Even microbes, bacteria. Viruses. The Sowers make anything and everything."

Kesh turns at the end, to come back along the next row. I see what looks like a child with a stiff mane down its back and a tail with a brown tuft at the end. A girl completely covered in scales, with vertical pupils, like a snake.

"The Sowers know no boundaries. Some drafts were meant for the containments: cleaners, principally, so no Weaver would be risked among the males. Others for the factories, the mines. Others, as I said, the Weave discarded. Each less than perfect, according to their Sowers. They would have died had our guides not brought them north. There is a settlement in the north made up almost entirely of drafts."

"Do you mean Queen Odide?"

Kesh shakes her head. "Odide is East. The Deep, the draft settlement, lies past the peak we call The Sentinel. Only drafts go there, drafts and renegades."

"Renegades?" Another word I don't know.

"Humans who wish to live apart. More common than you might think. In Bounty, people are free to go where they will. Renegades is…affectionate. A word you might use for an unruly friend."

"I've never heard of such a thing. Neither renegades or colonies of drafts or the Deep."

"Of course not." Kesh moves down the row, greeting each draft with a touch of her flesh hand. She speaks soothingly "The Weave never speaks of the drafts they discard, though they are happy enough to trade with them when the drafts have something they want. Their nektar, for instance."

Kesh looks at me pointedly. "Many from Pergama have gone north, to the Deep. You saw their plight."

It seems so long ago that we landed the transport outside Pergama's walls. The people there were afraid and starving.

"They are trying to survive," Kesh says. For years, she tells me, the Weave has hidden the yearly harvest totals. "The harvests are falling for reasons their best Sowers don't understand. The villages suffer since they are the ones who have their rations cut. Their pleas fall on deaf ears. Or worse: they cannot even complain."

"They cut their comms," I say. The Pergama prefect told us the comms had been down for months.

"And more. The Weave is nothing if not efficient in its cruelty. The Weave makes ever new and more elaborate drafts while their own people starve. The exact thing they are doing, interfering more and more with the Mother's own arts, defeats them."

Kesh pauses by a bed. "Come, Sil. Meet my daughter."

A draft unfolds from a blanket. She wears a brown shift. In place of a nose, she has two black slits lipped in shiny gold. The draft's eyes are round circles: one orange, one light blue. The draft has no lids, lashes, or eyebrows. She is slightly shorter than me and quite slender. Her skin is green and slick with mucus. Even then, with a face so strange, the draft—Sil—has a fine look, made beautiful by the clear intelligence in her eyes.

Kesh extends her hand, the metal one, to Sil's shoulder. She gently moves the draft so she turns, to expose the nape at the neck. I see a scar like my own, over where I had my life fiber.

Kesh speaks with a gentle voice. "Sil was made to be a river miner. Remember I told you of Pergama, how deeply they had to dive for the metal? That they needed special miners? Sil was one. You don't find precious metals and stones lying on the ground, after all. And what human can dive so deeply?"

"Was Sil grown in nektar? From that draft Queen?"

I can't take my eyes from Sil, the strange skin, the gently moving gills.

Kesh nods. "Who digs until a vein is revealed? Until a diamond is knocked loose? Who braves the swells for the pearl, so that the jeweler and the metalsmith can ply their art? No citizen of the Weave, I tell you. Let me ask you this, daughter. Have you ever heard of a Collegium student selected for the pergama mines?"

"No," I say.

"To dig the cavern for new segments of Cyclon?"

"No."

"To quarry stone for the Centrum itself? Where does all of that beautiful white granite come from? Who blasts it from the mountainsides? Who loads it on the ships, filling their lungs with poison dust?"

Kesh tips up Sil's chin. The draft blinks rapidly, her blue and orange eyes going from Kesh to me and then to 12. Sil isn't frightened of the hyba cross—only curious.

"Pergama is the metal in your scroll, the metal in 12's armor, the metal used to launch the Weave's new fleet. The metal in crossbows. It's even in my legs and arm. Light as a feather and with a unique property. Pergama preserves energy, so what is absorbed is stored intact. A fully charged scroll sheathed in pergama will last a year or more."

Kesh turns the draft's hand palm up. Sil's fingers are long, the knuckles bulbous. Her palm is rippled, and I see tiny tentacles that seem to move in little waves. "Lam herself found Sil almost dead. Once there was little pergama to be mined, the Weave abandoned her like some broken tool. Lam's son Kestrel carried Sil all the way to Quillka. When Kestrel brought Sil to this building, I thought she was old rope. Moldy and good for nothing more than the Cyclon. We revived her with water brought in a barrel from a spring. Totally submerged for hours, isn't that right, friend Sil?"

I'm surprised to hear the draft speak. Her pink tongue is slender and forked at the tip. "I am grateful."

"Sil has become a leader among the drafts." Kesh examines me to gauge my reaction. I am fascinated and repelled in equal measure.

Kesh turns to Timbe. "What was the annual campaign when you escaped the Weave?"

"Thrift and science," she answers. "Then Mother's Good Gifts."

"Yes, Good Gifts. And the year before that?"

"Season of Plenty."

"And before that?"

"Abundance Above All," Timbe replies patiently.

"Greater economy, greater thrift, working as one," Kesh says. "Slogans change. The purpose is always the same. Beneath every one of those campaigns is a lie."

Her voice grows hard. "The Sowers have grown arrogant beyond measure. They create life and waste it. They abuse the Mother, thinking they are greater that her, that their powers of creation should take the place of hers. Meanwhile the people go hungry. Instead of hearing their cries, we cut their comms, isolate them, assuming they will just give up and die. If the Sowers can get no more metal from Pergama, they abandon it, as you saw, daughter. There's demand from the Centrum, always demand, and less and less for anyone but the Sowers and their followers. The only pergama left is here, in Bounty. They mean to take it all: metal, land. But what about the people? The drafts?"

The chittering in the hall grows louder. 12 whines, feeling their fear.

Kesh takes a breath. "Daughter. The Weave is a shell over a hollow core. All the Sowers have left are mere words. Empty words about the Mother, empty words about plenty and prosperity. While most of their people suffer. The Sowers seek wealth, power. Perfection. You must ask: at what cost?"

No one ever talked this way at the Collegium. No one even mentioned the word *draft*. No one talked of starvation, of isolated villages. My cheeks are hot with shame. How eager I was to rid myself of my carnivorous potato. Is that what the Sowers do, discard the drafts they don't want like I tossed that potato? All I wanted was to be rid of it: my mistake. I brought it to life, then killed it without a second thought.

A thing that was just as alive as this draft: Sil.

"Do you know who was the first to have enhanced night vision?" Kesh asks me.

I shake my head.

"Helse. On Founders Day, she was presented to everyone as a great achievement. You must have seen the recording in Wylla's class."

I remember. The recording showed a crowd gathered beneath the great prow of the Centrum. There stood the Head Sower with the council, like a constellation of moons with their eyebrows and eyelashes plucked. A woman stepped forward, her eyes swathed in bandages. The Head Sower herself removed them. The woman stepped forward and stumbled.

Proof, the announcer said, of a triumph: faultless night vision.

Kesh is still looking at Sil: the draft's orange and blue eyes, her skin with its leafy sheen. "That day and until she chose the Sleeping Chairs, Helse was completely blind. They lied. She chose to kill herself rather than live with the pain."

Kesh uses her metal hand to gently turn Sil's face to Timbe's light. Around the places where her fingers touch, Sil's skin gently flushes gray, matching the color of the metal. Pergama, I realize: from Kesh's hand. "By design, to mine Pergama's rivers. I'm guessing the formula of a frog introduced into a human embryo. And chameleon, to locate even the smallest speck of pergama."

Kesh takes my hand. "Here, let Sil touch you."

The draft's fingertips are tiny suction cups. They feel wet and sticky against my palm. As the cups warm to my skin, I think I hear the draft speak: *Don't be afraid.*

Sil's lips haven't moved.

I snatch my hand back. Sil's pink tongue flicks.

"Sil has a special skill." Kesh looks from Sil to me. "Through her touch, she can know the mind of anyone. I doubt Sil's Sower even realized she'd made a creature with this special gift."

Kesh taps a metal finger lightly on Sil's shoulder. "That's why I only use my metal hand with Sil. I've learned my lesson, haven't I?"

The draft's gills flare. There is something about this draft that matches Kesh: not in size, but in will.

"As you know, I made 12," Kesh says. "I mixed her formula for speed, size. Temperament. The ability to respond to command. And the ability to love her master. I chose those qualities carefully. In Bounty, this is how we also make our sons and daughters— strength, agility, ferocity in battle. Temperament. In that we are no different from the Weave."

This must be the Sower in her, to talk about constructing a human being like one might speak of making a machine: like her own legs and arm. Gears and sprockets and cables and the long bars of metal that are her thighs and shins.

Timbe scoffs. "Hisla's gone too far with her boys."

Kesh nods. "Dear Hisla brews her boys as much for looks as for strength. She wants those boys to match, with white hair and the whitest skin you can imagine. An oddity, but her choice. In all other things, Hisla's sons are good, strong warriors. I suppose the coloring is handy in the winter."

She and Timbe smile. "She calls her boys the Dreams," Kesh says. She shakes her head. "My dreams are always dark."

I venture a bold question. "How is that not the same thing?" I mean how is what Bounty does different from the Weave and its Sowers? "The Captains are Sowers, too. They brew sons to fight for them."

"Excellent question." Kesh moves toward the door. She seems almost spent. There's a twist to her face that I think must be pain. "What makes it acceptable, say, to make 12 and not Sil, you mean? To make a Dream, whatever color the hair, and not Thoth?"

She points at a squat little thing with livid yellow eyes and a skin of hard, black ridges, like an alligator. "Why should we not manufacture drafts to do our labor? To love us or bury us or sing to us when we're weary or sad? To improve our stamina, our strength? These are the Mother's gifts, after all. Or so the Head Sower herself says."

Her words are clipped. "I'll tell you. It's not the mixing. It's not the making. That is the Mother's gift to us, no one could deny it. As you see in the Weave, that technology is skill alone, no more special than mixing a soup or sewing a tunic. Here is what's wrong. The Weave denies the Bond. The Bond: the force that binds one to another, the draft to its creator. The Bond no matter what the result. It could be a girl covered in blisters, a draft like Darling, who can't bear another's touch. Timbe to her sons, me to you. Me to 12. It's not the making of a thing that's wrong. Without the Bond, the creature has lost its true link to the Mother. The maker must care for it, no matter what. The mother must give that creature its purpose in life. Must nurture that creature even though it's life may be short or painful. One life sheltered by another, cared for by another, owed to another: that is the Bond."

I think of the sick hyba cross pups. Kesh couldn't bring herself to wring their necks even though they suffered.

Her flesh hand lifts my chin so that I stare into her single eye. "This is the Bond and this is the meaning: I made you. I thought about you, I planned for you. I mixed you and chose a Vessel to carry you. Keeper, too. I had Wylla and Flicke protect you, Anku guide you to Bounty. Anku and Petal: her son. The son she made and who serves her. This Bond we honor in Bounty. It is not the laboratory, daughter. That's chemistry alone. It is not the use. It is the Bond, always the Bond. We may make a mistake, but we never abandon our own. Never."

"Males. I mean warriors," I say. This new way of thinking is hard. New ideas bring new thoughts. New possibilities. "Males are dangerous. Violent. That's why the Weave put the males in containments so long ago. That's why we have the Quest, to rid the Mother of them forever. That is our duty, to keep the Mother safe."

"The Quest." That's the name of the plan to eliminate men, once the Sowers can reproduce without males.

Timbe spits. "Our sons are as dear to us as daughters. They are not thrown away in some containment. Used only for extract. Then *exterminated*."

"Timbe." Kesh lays her flesh hand on the captain's shoulder. "The drafts are listening."

Timbe turns to me, her voice lowered. "We love them. We care for them. When they sacrifice their lives for us, we honor them."

Outside the building, Kesh stops by a stone fountain. The rain has stopped. There's a new heaviness in the air. A full moon hangs over the Black Stairs, low clouds scudding south.

Toward the Weave. Toward home.

I know I can't go back.

Kesh reaches down to cup water, drinks, then wipes her face. "I think we could all use a rest," she says.

Anku appears at Kesh's side. She moves almost as quietly as 12, a useful skill for Bounty's best guide. Petal trails behind, rubbing his sleepy eyes.

Kesh turns to me a last time. "After breath and sustenance, the Mother-Bond is the most fundamental part of life. Remember this. To be bound to the Sower who gave you life is to be linked forever to the Mother of us all. What is lost in the Weave is this, the link between two beings, how you come to the Mother in the first place."

Timbe's dark red hair gleams in the moonlight. "The Mother-Bond gives us life and history," she says to me. "Not some Sower fantasy of test tubes and formula and perfection. The Mother-Bond is flesh and blood and the tie of one being to another. The power of the Mother, to bring new life. Loyalty. Service. The Mother-Bond is our greatest weapon."

Anku uses her hands to speak. She points at me. *You.* Then *Bond*: her thumbs hooked together. She crosses her hands on her chest just under her collar bone. *I.* Her thumbs hook and she points to Petal, practically asleep on his feet.

I am Bonded to him, she is saying. Then she looks at Kesh. There's no mistaking the look of devotion in her eyes. *I am Bonded to Kesh.* Bonded as sisters.

Then her palms flip and press down, spreading apart. Without being taught the words, I grasp her meaning: *the Bond is all.*

18

Ash

Timbe leads me to my quarters opposite the Council House.

The younger Captains have rooms on the second floor. My room is simple: a bed with pillow and blanket, a flame lamp turned low, a table. On a small trunk is a jug of water and wash bowl. A window overlooks the street.

Timbe points to a square of cloth on the bed: a Captain's cloak and clasp. In the trunk are fresh tunics, underclothes, and leggings. For 12, there's a water bowl and her own cloak, for her bed.

"Kesh had the metalsmith strike the clasp last year," Timbe tells me. The clasp is a hyba head, with yellow stones for eyes. "She's been expecting you a long time."

There are two more gifts on the table: a leather-bound book with empty pages and a packet of drawing supplies: pressed charcoal sticks, brushes, a tiny paddle to mix paint. I marvel at them. I've never had brushes I didn't have to carve myself.

There are fresh vials, empty, fit like tiny bolts in the bandolier of a leather case. Timbe flips open the book's cover and points to the writing on the first page. *Draw what you see. Write what you will. Tell the truth.* Beneath is scrawled a name: *Kesh 544-DxL.*

Timbe turns to go. 12 has already scratched the floor, turned three times, and stretched out, using the cloak as a pillow.

"I've never slept alone." Even after the Rail, Anku and Petal were with me. I can still feel Sil's moist fingers on my cheek. Everything's a jumble. I don't know how to feel. Is knowing about the Mother-Bond supposed to change me? Am I supposed to look at Kesh and feel it, like a touch? A shared thought? A hunger? Is it embedded in the circuitry of my skin, like a tracker map?

I don't understand how a bond can be a weapon. To me, Kesh sounded crazy as she talked about defeating the Weave. She never mentioned the Legion, the new fleet. What possible weapon, what army could match the Weave's power?

Yet no one knows the power of the Legion better than Kesh. And the question I keep asking: where are the males? Where are the sons?

Timbe steps into the hall. "You are hardly alone with the cross at your side. Someone will come for you in the morning. There will be plenty of time for questions. Meanwhile, get some sleep."

Alone in the room, I pace. 12's eyes follow, as if at any moment I might jump out the window. I imagine telling the girls back in Holdfast everything I've seen—the Captains, a boy. Drafts stranger than any childhood tale. Kesh, a three-sheaf commander turned traitor. By her own admission, she's spent years plotting the Weave's destruction.

She spent years plotting to bring me to Bounty. To have me. I look at the clasp but can't bring myself to touch it.

Those girls in Holdfast, and Asta. Chicks inside their shells, as Kesh said she and Anku were before coming to Bounty. In every question, every thought, I circle back: where are the warriors?

I strip off my Legion tunic and leggings. With a cloth, I scrub myself as best I can using the wash bowl. The new clothes feel wonderful. By the time I pull on a fresh tunic, 12 is snoring softly.

The paper in the book is soft and thick. I press a corner, to see if shapes appear. This is no tracker map. It is paper: thick and soft to the touch. I take one of the charcoals and make a line. My fingers feel clumsy. I haven't drawn anything since leaving the Collegium.

I stare at the line. It could be a tail. I extend it: 12's tail. Quickly, her body appears on the page, her head turned toward me.

Hyba Cross, I write at the top. I use my own lettering style, not the Chronicler's. *This is 12. The only one who lived. She is mine.*

Perhaps that's what they mean by the Bond. I am 12's and she is mine. What would happen to her if I died? Does Kesh think of me like some dog she's trained?

I push the thought away. On the next page, I draw the draft Sil. At the top, I write: *Sil. River miner. Do not let Sil touch bare skin. She is a thought-walker.*

"Thought-walker," I murmur. I can do better.

I stretch out on the bed, then get up again. On the third page, I try to draw Kesh. Nothing feels right. I rip the page from the book. Crumpling it isn't good enough. I move the wash bowl to the table, remove the mantle from the flame lamp, and set the paper on fire. I watch the paper burn until it's a curl of ash.

I dab the ash where 12's paws should be on the page. *Perfect.*

Only then can I sleep.

In the morning, a gentle tap on the door wakes me. Sunlight shafts through the window. 12 is up, tail lashing. She's like last night's storm trapped in this tiny room.

In the hallway stands a young Captain, the one Mei said was her sister. *Sister*, I remind myself. The same Sower and extract, Vessel and Keeper.

"Good morning." Her brown hair is pulled into a top knot. She can't be much older than me. "I am Shan. Captain of the Gemstones."

"My name is Dinitra."

She cocks her head, smiling. "Everyone knows your name."

I feel exposed, like people know things about me even I haven't realized. Again, I think of how I came from Kesh's body, how we share things only Sowers with their microscopes can see.

"There's breakfast below," Shan says. "Kesh asks that you join her in the training pen when you're finished."

"Training pen." I thought I'd see warriors, not more battle dogs.

"Come," Shan says, "so we have time to talk."

In the common room, breakfast is laid on a side table. There's paddle loaf, berry jam, a bowl of pink and green apples, olives, hard-boiled eggs, a thick gelled cream cut in into squares, honey, and red and green pastes. On a side table is a bowl of mash for 12 and another of water.

A small fire crackles in the hearth. Outside, the day is clear and fresh.

I feed 12, then sit beside Shan. "Where are the others?" I ask.

Shan watches 12 with fascination and fear mixed. "It's late for us. Up and about with chores, planning. My mother asked me to wait for you."

"Your mother is Lam. Is that right?"

"You have a good memory."

"And Mei. Your sister."

She nods. "We came fourteen years ago last month. I was seven years old."

12 positions herself under the table. It's smaller than the one in the Council Hall, so her rump sticks out one side and her forepaws the other. 12's tail lies across the floor like a snake covered in brindled fur.

I'm ravenous. I sop up cream with strips of paddle loaf. I try the red paste and the green: delicious. To drink, there's hot, sweet coffee. At Shan's throat is a clasp, a circle of multicolored stones around a green gem. Her eyes are patient as she watches me finish off the honey with a crust of paddleloaf. "This is all a shock, I know. It was for me."

"You were scared when you came? You came the same way as your sister?"

"The same. We were always together. Remember, I was much younger. It's a blur to me now."

The wound over my life fiber still throbs. "Did they take your life fiber, too?"

Shan turns to show the scar above the collar of her tunic. The scar is the length of a finger. Shan 579-LxS. "They have to. Otherwise, the Weave could track us."

Since it's just the two of us, I ask, "Where are the males? I mean," I say, searching for the right words, "the sons. Warriors?"

"Sons is fine." Shan takes a last sip of coffee. "Come, I'll take you to them."

My heart races, and it's not from the coffee "Before we go, I have a question. I hope you don't mind."

"We had so many questions! Ask away."

"Do these males have virus? These sons? Like the ones in the Weave? Are they...safe?"

Shan laughs. "Of course they have virus! It would be irresponsible not to have that in the formula."

I'm relieved and take a breath. I'm remembering the slingshot cradles, my boot on Petal's skinny legs. "We can't catch the virus, can we? I'm sorry. Virology wasn't my best subject."

"Let me explain with my own boys. The Gemstones, remember?"

Shan gets a light in her eyes as she talks about them. "They're young, mind you. Fifteen beautiful sons. I made them to build things. You know, like if you need to cross something and have to have a bridge. Or a watchtower. They're smart like that and resourceful. By next year, three of them will be training with my mother's Birds."

"They have virus." I say this to convince myself there's nothing to worry about. The disgust I felt after I touched the slingshot cradles in Pergama is still fresh. "It's the same virus the Sowers put into males in the containment."

Shan nods. "At every morning meal, our sons get their Remedy." She thinks for a moment. "In the Weave, it's called supplement, right?"

Shan describes it: like brown flour. "So long as they have Remedy, our sons are as healthy as you or me."

"What's in this supplement? Remedy, I mean?"

"It's completely natural. Honestly, I don't know what Ular puts into it. Herbs and such. She gathers it and prepares it. It's all quite healthy."

"Ular?" There is so much to learn.

"Ular is a Captain. Her sons are the Harvest. They take care of the supplies, cooking and such. She's built like one of her barrels, like her boys."

Something about this doesn't connect. The Weave keeps men in containments for our safety. The virus is the ultimate cage, ensuring that any who escape will die within the week. Yet these warriors, these sons, do battle for their Captains. Their mission is to fight the Weave, uncaged. Why would they even need virus if they are bred to obey?

Shan notices the confusion on my face. "It's more of a tradition than anything. Our sons love us too much to ever leave. What would they do, anyway, on their own? They need us for so many things: clothing, food, instruction. Can you imagine 12 ever choosing to leave your side? That's what a son is like: loyal."

Shan hesitates. "There is one Captain," she says, "who doesn't use virus anymore."

Males without virus? It's like letting a wild beast, a hyba, loose in your bedroom with no cage. No: with no prod, like the one Benit had from the containment. "Which one?"

"Rek."

I tell her I've heard the name. Before I left the Weave, the Legion caught some of her boys near the Crags. The boys spit and scratched as Trisk forced them into the cage. She and Benit wrapped the cage in heavy cloth before loading it onto the containment transport.

Shan looks pained.

"I'm sorry," I say quickly. "I'm still learning about...about the differences."

"We mourn sons who are captured as if they are dead. I am sorry to hear this."

We are silent for a moment as Shan collects her thoughts. "Rek leaves them their tongues, too. The other Captains don't agree. Rek does as she pleases in the North."

"Tongues? What do you mean?" The Weave cut out Anku's tongue and fed it to a battle dog to torment her.

"It's logical," Shan says. "If a warrior is caught, we don't want them telling the Weave about our plans. About where we are. It's efficient, believe me. Some boys look forward to the docking. It means they are warriors. Think of it like your graduation in the Collegium. Did you not feast? Wear a purple hood?"

I correct her. "Collar."

"Well, there it is," Shan says, pleased. "We all have our ceremonies. This lets the boys know they are accepted. They all look forward to it."

Shan make the docking sound so normal. "This Rek," I ask. "You said north. Do you mean The Deep?" That's where Kesh said the renegades go.

"Not that far." Shan pushes her plate away. "Rek stays in Dolor, a town built entirely out of lava rock. A marvel. But her boys, the Blazes, can be rough."

I shake my head as Shan offers another slice of bread. "Come, they're expecting us at the training pen."

I swallow hard. "The warriors?"

Shan grins. "The very ones."

Unlike last night, when Quillka seemed abandoned, the streets are thronged with people. Every other one seems to be a Vessel with a round belly. With a little scream, all of them—male or female, I can't tell—scurry behind doors as 12 and I pass.

12 pays no attention, her head swinging side to side as she scans the street.

The gate opens onto a well-travelled road up a hill. At the top, I see the distinctive fencing of a training pen, like Auxpen at Holdfast.

Kesh stand just inside the gate next to Shan's mother, Lam. Timbe, the red-haired Captain, is several paces in, shading her eyes. Petal is at a climbing structure, kicking rocks.

Anku has climbed half-way up the structure, to adjust the netting.

12 whines eagerly when she sees the netting. At Holdfast, she goes up and over a hundred times a day without tiring. There are barrels like the ones at Holdfast, chained end to end. A trench filled with muddy water bisects the pen. The fence encircles a hilltop, the far side blocked from view.

I twist my right hand, telling 12 to press against me as we walk. I feel her eagerness, her delight.

She wants to run.

The ground trembles. 12 and I freeze. "Look," Shan points eagerly.

Fifty or more warriors appear from behind the hilltop. They're running at full speed, in close formation. One warrior leads: tall, with a mass of long, dark red hair. He leaps into the trench, the others behind him. The water explodes, then they're through, hardly slowing.

12's tail lashes. "Stay," I tell her. I wish I had that blasted leash. A pen. A wall. Anything.

Every cell in me vibrates with alarm.

The warriors wear light armor: leather chest plates and gauntlets on their arms and thighs. Anku drops off the climbing net just before the warriors fling themselves on it, scrabbling to the top.

12's snout goes high as she sucks in their smell. When the lead warrior drops to the far side, he throws his arms into the air and bellows.

12 stands and takes a step toward him. I didn't command her. I step in front of her, speaking with my mouth and my hand: *Stay! Sit.*

She sits, barely. "I should leave the pen," I tell Shan.

Shan's face is alight with the spectacle.

"Again!" Timbe shouts.

The warriors thunder to the far side of the hill.

Kesh beckons me to her side. Like Shan, she seems buoyed by what she's seen. "The Legion has never seen anything like it. These are by far our strongest crop of warriors."

Shan speaks with pride. "That one in the lead? Ash, Timbe's best."

Petal spoke of a warrior called Ash. The warriors are hairier than females, thicker. Their chests and backs look heavily muscled under their leather chest plates and gauntlets. The warriors finish a second circuit, then gather at a water trough. They look nothing like Petal, who skips among them. It's the difference between the pups in the warming box and 12. Their arms, chests, and legs are thickly muscled. Like the Captains, they sweep up their long hair up and let it fall in thick tails and braids from a top knot. Like their mothers, they wear the colors.

"See there, the Birds of Prey." Shan point at warriors wearing black and gray. "A Dream, there, with the white hair. There are some of Ular's Harvest. They tend to be shorter, stouter, like Ular. Ular likes them strong and doesn't care about how fast they are. They drive the supply ships, cook, and so on. Timbe's Living Wood have all colors of hair. Timbe just wants them brave, a little reckless to be honest. Tactical, they are, and stubborn: the best hand-to-hand fighters we have."

"What are they doing with their hands?" I ask. The warriors are moving their hands constantly.

"Speaking," Shan says. "It's called shape language. Much like you speak to 12. Or how Anku speaks since she lost her tongue."

"Call them to us," Kesh orders Timbe.

I brace myself. I feel no joy as the warriors approach. Though the morning is cold, I'm sweating under the tunic.

With the warriors assembled, Kesh points to me. "My daughter, at last!"

They raise their fists and pound their chests, howling.

Kesh calls out again. "Bounty, cradle of Captains. Cradle of warriors. For the Bond!"

Again, they howl. I can't make out a single word.

Kesh turns to Timbe. "Bring forward your best son."

I search for a resemblance between the warrior who steps forward and the slender Captain. He's easily three heads higher and twice as broad. His chest is furred beneath the armor stamped with maple leaves. Coarse black hair covers his cheeks and chin.

The hair in his top knot is hers: a deep red.

Timbe speaks with pride. "My best. Ash has fought seven battles against the Legion, as far West as the Great Sea, as far east as the Shield. Show her," Timbe says to him.

Ash holds out his forearm: seven blue tattooed stripes. Around his neck are blue letters: TIMBETIMBETIMBETIMBE.

"Put him through his paces, Timbe," Kesh says.

With a sweep of her hand, Timbe sends Ash away. Alone, he seems even faster. When he reaches the netting, he leaps from two body-lengths out, grasping the rope halfway up. In one powerful movement, he swings up and over the top.

The warriors cheer as he dives head first into a barrel. When he emerges, he laughs, using his fingers to brush his forearms.

I understand him: *Easy.*

12 kneads the ground. She looks at me and back again, at Ash. She wants to run. She wants to best him. Too many days we've spent cooped up when she thrives on running, climbing, leaping.

Like Timbe's son.

As Ash runs toward us, the warriors form two lines facing each other. They've picked up long staves, lifted like a tunnel. They brace, and he's on them like a thunderclap. Ash flips the first two warriors flat on their backs. "Harvest," Shan says, with orange and yellow ribbons. He has their staves and uses them, merciless. The warriors yelp and grimace and sprawl.

Ash mows down warrior after warrior until there's a single one standing. He's tall as Ash and gray-haired. Not as strong or as swift. He wears Timbe's colors: red and black.

Ash's brother, I tell myself, trying out the word.

The gray-haired warrior manages to jab his stave on Ash's ribs, then his shoulder. Ash grimaces. His face is fierce as he speeds at the older man, blasting him off his feet and onto the dirt.

The man crumples like a damp rag, his breath expelled.

Ash flings his arms up: victory! His neck veins are thick as fingers. He hurls the stave into the air and watches as the stave pierces the ground, shuddering.

Then Ash roars, his mouth agape. I am close enough to see his mouth and within, a black stump. When Ash the boy became Ash the man, it was at the cost of a tongue. His roar is no less terrible for want of a tongue. I clap my hands to my ears. I can't help the sound that pops from my mouth: *Ga.*

A mistake. 12 hears the sound as *Go.*

I stumble forward, screaming, my hands flying pointlessly through the air. "Stay, Stay, Stay!"

It's too late. 12 is on the hunt. Once she starts, Benit told me, she always finishes. I grasp at her tail, liquid as water. In a single leap, 12 covers half the distance to Ash.

He sees her: too late. Her jaws are open. She's all instinct now, the hyba freed, her blood singing.

I taught her none of this.

By the shoulder, 12 wrenches Ash to the dirt. To her, the lither strap of his chest plate is no more bother than a grass stem. She has it split, the plate careening off. Ash struggles beneath her. He's wasting energy. 12's snout buries in his shoulder. When she lifts, triumphant, she has in her mouth a glistening scoop of muscle. A white shoulder bone winks.

Another warrior—brown hair, face twisted in anguish—hammers her shoulder with his fists. With a flick of 12's front paw, the warrior goes flying.

12 strikes like a cobra at Ash's throat. Pointlessly, his fingers scrabble at her thick neck. I could have warned him: 12's neck is hard as a plank. Using the weight in her powerful shoulders, 12 thrashes him. The warrior, once so magnificent, flops like a worn-out cloak.

Ash's knees drop to the sides.

It takes me a moment to even feel Kesh's metal hand on my shoulder. "Call her, daughter. She'll listen now the killing's done."

She does. Obediently, 12 sits beside me. Ash's blood drenches her brindled chest, neck, and shoulders. Her blue-black tongue works fresh gristle off her snout.

12 reeks of death.

The other warriors stare. The gray-haired warrior Ash hurled against the fence kneels at his brother's side, both hands pressed to the gaping hole in Ash's throat. Ash's blood pumps through the warrior's fingers.

Then Timbe kneels at her son's side. She grips his wrist, oddly untouched by any blood or even dirt. His hair is matted with mud, blood, and 12's saliva. Timbe presses her lips to her son's ear. Fondly, she strokes his forehead.

Then she draws a knife from a sheath at her waist and swiftly slits his throat.

12 looks to me seeking praise. I stare back as if I've never seen her before. I want to wipe her from my mind as one wipes away dust.

Kesh crouches, her face in mine. "You must tell her she's done well. Tell her you're pleased."

"I can't."

"Unless you praise 12, that warrior's death is for nothing."

"No."

Kesh jabs her metal finger at Timbe. "Is her sacrifice for nothing? His sacrifice: nothing? Timbe has lost this valuable Bond. She has done this for the good of Bounty, her duty. Unless you praise 12, 12 will wonder. Have I done right? Have I pleased you?"

"It was a mistake. It wasn't supposed to happen." My voice is more groan than words. "He had no chance. I never meant to kill. You should have left me in the Weave!"

Kesh takes my shoulders with both hands, metal and flesh. "I brought you because you are my daughter. Because I made you. Because of the Bond. Ash was made to serve his mother. And you to serve me. You must praise her. You must. I order it."

I force myself to look at 12. Her golden eyes are eager, open. She loves me, as Benit said she would. My first thought is this: how terrible for her, to be with me. To love me.

Poor thing. Poor pup.

"Good girl," I say to 12.

19

Death Machines

Petal hauls a bucket of water from the trough. I rinse the blood from 12.

Petal is weeping.

I wish I could weep. I am stunned, as if Ash himself beat me with a stave.

Ash is dead. At 12's hand and his mother's.

At mine.

With my hands, I scrub 12's chest, her snout, her belly, her paws. Again and again, I rinse the blood in rivulets into the dirt. I wish the water would dissolve the memory, too. Dissolve me.

I can't look Kesh in the eye.

"They'll sing a praise verse for him tonight." Petal scrapes his sleeve over his face, smearing the dirt left, then right. "His brothers, they're young yet. The Living Wood's praise song ain't so long. Enough words to get the pyre going, I guess."

I watched 12 kill 132 and reveled in it. Trisk's shocked face made me happy. I thought 132 deserved that death. I thought 132 was nothing, less than nothing. The battle dog was meant to die. I loved 12 even more after she killed 132.

Now, I feel shame. Why am I happy when a battle dog dies and upset when 12 kills a male? Kesh told me Timbe made Ash for the same purpose as Kesh made 12. The death was for the Bond. Tenderly, his mother stroked his forehead, then drew her knife. That's the memory I can't bear. If only I had trained 12 better, spent more time with her. If only I had known what she was capable of.

If only she and I hadn't been made to serve the Sower we share. If only there were no Sowers to serve.

That's impossible. It's Bounty or the Weave. *Master your fear*, Benit told me in Holdfast. What about mastering my disgust as the warrior's blood coursed between 12's brindled paws. Is there such a thing as mastering grief? Mastering horror? How about mistakes—am I master of my mistakes?

A trail of snot leaks from Petal's nose. "Always proud, Ash was."

As he watches us, Petal plays with a stick figure. He shows it to me: wiry black goat hair gone stiff, seed eyes. "Ash made it for me. Said it were him. Said I was of the Living Wood, too, only smallish. Someday, I might run with them if I got strong."

Noisily, 12 laps water from the bucket. I want to walk and keep walking, up and over the Black Stairs. I'd go past Holdfast and as far south as the Collegium and then beyond, to the Salt Sea. Then I'd find a way to cross it, hoping one morning to wake and discover I'd left myself completely behind.

Or north to The Deep. With the renegades.

12 would find me. She'll always find me, pan-sized paws following every step. She's mine whether I want her or not.

I correct myself: I am hers.

Four warriors bear Ash away. Petal follows, the stick toy clutched in his fist.

Shan kneels beside me. 12's eyes are watchful as she speaks. "My mother wants you to work the warriors with 12. So that they know her, know how to parry her. It's for the best. Training."

"Your mother wants her to kill another one?" My anger boils in my throat. I turn my back on the dark spot where Ash died. Where his mother slit his throat, to end his suffering. "Does she want 12 to rip them up one by one? Until she has no more sons? I won't do it, Shan. I can't."

"We'll stake her."

My mouth gapes. "You saw her, Shan. Stake her? Tell me, what stake will hold her?"

Shan won't relent. She points to the climbing net. Next to it, several warriors are already digging a hole for the stake. "You can't be serious," I tell her.

She looks at me shrewdly. "I know this was a shock. It was a shock to all of us. You haven't even been here a day. Things are moving fast. Believe me when I tell you, we have no time to waste. Dinitra, the Weave is coming for us. Now more than ever, with Kesh revealed. They know their Legion commander—their three-sheaf commander—is a traitor. The Legion knows that all of their secrets, their plans, are known to us."

"What do I care?" I mean it. I care nothing for Bounty, nothing for the traitor who calls herself my mother. I care nothing for Anku, nothing for the snot-nosed Petal. I care nothing for any of the warriors, for the Captains. Not for Shan or Mei.

Most of all, I care nothing for myself.

"Listen to me, Dinitra. At Holdfast, the Weave assembles a fleet. You know this. Even now, as we speak. New ships, special ships. I've seen them myself, out with my mother's sons. The Birds of Prey are scouts, Dinitra, they are sent to watch. Over the Rift, I myself counted seventeen helios tethered. Seventeen."

"The Weave has thousands of ships. I am not stupid, Shan."

"You're not listening. These ships are helios. New ships. New technology. We've never faced them before. Every ounce of pergama left in the Weave is in those helios." She's relentless. "I shouldn't call them ships. They are death machines. They have a single purpose: to wipe Bounty from the Mother forever."

"What does this have to do with me?"

"You are one of us, now. Of course, it has to do with you."

"Did you not just watch 12 slaughter Timbe's son?"

"It's the least you can do," she says curtly.

"You've seen the least I can do."

"Your mother won't tell you this. I will. The only reason we've waited this long to attack the fleet is you."

"You don't know what you're talking about."

"My mother told me. Kesh refused to leave the Weave until a Guide had come for you. Until Anku had come. The other Captains begged and begged. We could have sabotaged the fleet months ago. Stopped the last pergama shipments, destroyed the construction slips. Rek crossed the Stairs herself last month and blew up three of the ships as they were about to launch."

"Then go to this Rek with your stories."

"Kesh would not have it. For you."

"That's a lie."

Shan looks as if she might pound me into the ground. "You are certainly not the smartest daughter I've seen." Shan takes a deep breath. "Believe me or not. She insisted on waiting until the cross was better trained. Until there was no chance of anything going wrong as Anku collected you. My mother pleaded with her. They all did. We feared there might be a hundred helios by then and no hope."

"Better trained? Do you not hear yourself?"

"No one believed Constance would win, either," Shan says. "She did and changed history."

From Quillka, the warriors have brought an iron post with a loop at the top. They tip it into the hole, then place rocks around the base to keep it upright. They shovel in the dirt.

Shan stands beside me. I say, "Tell me about these helios."

"For one, they're light as leaves. That means they're different from other ships, most too heavy to cross the Stairs. More than any other thing, the altitude of the Stairs has kept us safe. Worse by far is this: they carry no fuel."

I scoff. "Everything must have fuel. Even we must have fuel."

"I didn't say they didn't need it. I said they didn't carry it."

Shan talks about the Cyclon and energy cells and angles and how light bends. She sees she's lost me. "This is what you need to know. The Cyclon creates fuel, right? For everything. You remember that much."

At this moment she reminds me of Susalee at her most arrogant.

"I remember that much," I fire back.

Shan ignores the tone. "The Legion's fleet can collect that energy. They mounted a magnifier on the Centrum's prow right at the top, where the Sowers stand on Founder's Day. Anku can explain it better than me."

I snort. "Anku? She can't even talk."

Shan crosses her arms, irritated. "You should listen more. Anku was the most talented Cyclon engineer in the history of the Weave. And Bounty's best Guide. She built our Cyclon. Plus—and most importantly—she would have died for you on the Stairs, Dinitra. A little respect."

A prickle of shame flares on my neck. "I'm listening."

"The thing—let's call it the source—condenses light. The magnifier points that light in any direction. At strength, the light goes hundreds of miles. When the light reaches the Concave, the Concave refracts the light—splits it—downwards into dozens of streams. Each stream fuels a helio."

"You've lost me again. Concave?" I have a vague memory of hearing the word as I dozed in Geometry.

Shan struggles to keep her patience. "The Concave is a ship." Shan cups her palm. "The ship is shaped like a shallow bowl. In Geometry, that's *concave*. The Concave ship captures the beam sent from the magnifier. Then the Concave refracts that single beam into dozens of light streams. Each one of those streams feeds a helio. There can be hundreds of helios, thousands, powered by the same Concave. A single beam from the roof of the Centrum. The beam is fuel and lasts as long as the Cyclon lasts: forever, in other words. As long as the Centrum generates that light, as long as the Concave captures and refracts the light, the fleet can go anywhere for any amount of time at any strength."

Shan sound strangely celebratory about a fleet launched to kill her and everyone else in Bounty. It is a stunning idea—to send through the air a light beam that fuels an entire fleet. "I've never heard of such a thing."

"You never heard of Bounty until today. There's a lot you don't know, Dinitra."

There's a lot Shan doesn't know about me. For instance, that

I'm not accepting all this talk about bonds and docking and who owes what to who. But I hold my tongue.

"These ships can cross the Stairs," I say. "So what? They hover there making faces at us?"

"You are being very dense." Shan looks south to the Stairs, low blue humps on the horizon. "They're armed. Kesh calls the weapons pulsars. Pulsars use the same energy beam that comes from the Concave. The pulsars use the same technology as strela bolts, only a thousand times more powerful. When the Weave tested the pulsars on the Eastern Wastes, Kesh says not even a splinter was left to collect. Bodies evaporate. Towns turn to dust. The pulsars wipe everything away."

For a long moment, we're both quiet. Two of the warriors have heavy mallets and take turns pounding the stake into the ground.

"You win," I say to Shan. "I believe you. Again: what does any of this have to do with me?"

Shan folds her arms as she stares at me. "One day, if our plans don't work, the helios will cross the Stairs. That's the only thing that really protects us. Then the Weave will blast every one of our towns, every one of our farms and pastures. Our people, too. Unless we can stop the fleet first."

"And if we can't?"

"We'll evacuate. We regroup at Dolor."

I remember Kesh telling me that Dolor is Rek's city in the north, built within an old lava flow. "The Weave will send the Legion to confirm they've won. First, they'll send the helios home. Why risk such a powerful weapon on herds of derak and the stray hyba pack?"

Shan turns to me. "This is where you come in. Their legion and battle dogs will search the forests. Our sons need to be ready to fight back. We'll cut them off. Ambush them, trap them. We'll divide the Legion, drive them into the snows, off the cliffs. Into the Eastern Wastes. And finish them off."

I can't help blurting, "That sounds like a terrible plan!" A thousand things could go wrong. What if the Legion doesn't get cut off? What if I can't teach the warriors not to be afraid of the Legion and their battle dogs?

"Have you got a better plan?" Shan jabs her finger at 12. "You can't deny you have a part to play, Dinitra. Your mother waited for you, yes. She brought you here. She made 12 for you and you alone. Now, Bounty needs you. The Captains need you. Those warriors need you.

She pauses, closing her eyes. "Dinitra, you've never seen a full Legion battalion coming at you over a ridge." She stares at the warriors. "They have. The legionaries put the battle dogs in front. When they order them to attack, even I lose heart. Imagine those boys!"

Shan grips my arm. 12 chuffs in alarm but Shan ignores her. "With your help, they will have seen 12. They will have sparred with her in the pen. It may not be much, I grant you. But it's one thing you can do to keep them alive."

I feel like slapping her, slapping every one of the Captains. "You're not understanding. She'll pull that stake—any stake—from the ground. She'll kill more boys!"

Shan examines me coldly. "So be it. They have to learn for all of our sakes."

I feel like I'm in some nightmare as 12 and I approach the stake. The warriors pieced together a harness of rope and lither skin to fit over her neck and chest. I don't tell them it's flimsy as cobweb to 12. I don't say it won't last a minute let alone the day. They grunt and point at where to tie her.

I tie her. They'll see soon enough.

"Is there nothing to bind her muzzle?" I close my hand around her snout to show them, like the strap Anku used.

A warrior shrugs. I guess that means no.

On the opposite side of the pen, the warriors line up. When the first warrior charges 12, she leaps, just as she did with Ash. The rope goes taut. 12 does a flip, just like 132 did my first day in at Holdfast's kennel.

For a moment, 12 hangs vertically, her great snout up and her tail, like a fifth leg, pressed to the ground. She lands with a thud I feel in my bones.

The warrior stands within a tail-length. His leather breeches are soaked with piss.

12 doesn't make the mistake the second time. When the next warrior charges, she runs the length of the rope. Then she stops to lean until the rope is so taut it frays before our eyes.

Beside me, Shan names the warrior: "Vision, one of the more intelligent Dreams."

The warrior lets out a terrible scream that 12 ignores.

Which will snap first, the stake or the rope harness? When Vision retreats, 12 returns to the stake to sniff the loosened dirt at the base. Before the next warrior even takes a step, 12's has trotted to the end of the rope and is leaning in with a single-minded ferocity.

"The stake won't hold," I comment. I've lost any hope of changing anyone's mind.

On the third warrior, the rope separates from the stake with a little shriek. 12 does a happy chuckle. The warrior is one of Timbe's: a red sheen to his brown hair, red and black ribbon braided through, Timbe's name collaring his neck in blue ink. He was the one who tried to pull 12 off his brother.

12 leaps. *No.* She explodes.

Then something unexpected happens. The warrior tucks into a roll, sliding beneath her. 12 snaps only air. She thinks it's a game, though one with a bloody ending. She lands awkwardly, already twisting. The rope trails her like an extra, useless tail.

The warrior stands, watching. 12's tail lashes. Her ears flick when I shout "Stay!"

I see exactly when 12 chooses to ignore me.

She leaps at the warrior. Again, he tucks and rolls. 12 is ready. I have just enough time to grab the rope and haul back before she rakes him with her knife-sharp claws.

The rope burns my palms like fire.

12 has the warrior flat on his back. She swivels her head to make sure I'm safe. I use that split second to fling myself onto her shoulder. I swing down between her jaws and the warrior's chest. With bloodied palms, I grasp her cheeks. I press my face to her snout. "Good girl. Good girl," I repeat.

Beneath me, the warrior struggles for breath. With me and the cross pinning his chest, I'm surprised he can breathe at all.

"You. Can. Not. Move," I tell him. He holds his breath.

I stroke 12's shoulder. I angle to the left, just a little. I talk to her without a pause. I wrap my arms around her neck, shifting again, so that her body shifts too, toward where Shan and the others watch in horror. Gradually, I have her off his chest and turned toward the climbing net. I order her into a sit, my body blocking her from seeing Timbe's son.

I look straight into 12's golden eyes. "I know what you want." I smile as I point at the climbing net, then gesture: *Go!*

Once she's racing to the net, I turn on the warrior, "You have five seconds to vanish."

12 climbs the net twenty times before I let her stop.

Kesh is waiting for me at the gate. "You mustn't be sentimental with them," she says, frowning. Them: the warriors.

"One death was enough for today."

There's no kindness in Kesh's voice. "You risked teaching 12 to hesitate. To mistrust her instincts. That's not why I made her. I made her to be a weapon."

I'm surprised at my response. "Like the Bond is our greatest weapon?"

"Don't mock me, daughter."

"I'm doing nothing of the sort. One death was enough for the day. For her. For 12. You made me her master. That's my decision."

As I defy Kesh, I realize that Dinitra 584-KxA was one thing to the Weave. She was another to the Legion. In Bounty, I mean to be something else, something new. I mean to be myself no matter what anyone else wants.

Kesh's lips curl. "That dead warrior was a weapon. They are all weapons. They are bound to us, yes, as we are to them. But we are not the same as them. The Mother made them different for a reason. Don't ever confuse male and female, daughter."

I think of the warrior I saved. At that instant, he was neither male nor female. He was a living thing. His life could have been mine to spend and I chose not to. Not because he was male. I saved him because I could.

"I won't kill for sport," I tell Kesh. "I won't kill by mistake. And I won't have 12 do it, either."

Kesh's flesh hand is rigid as a claw. "I sowed you. I sowed 12. You belong to me through the power of the Bond. You'll both do as you're told."

20

Great Quest

The next day dawns bright and warm After the long rain, Quillka reeks of wood rot, urine, and soap. A group of children and drafts gathers across the street from the Council Hall. I recognize the draft with soya-green stripes and the sea creature they call Darling. Sil, the frog-girl, holds the hand of the draft with the mane and tufted tail.

They watch 12 closely. She's one of them, they must think, though Kesh put not a speck of human in her.

I head inside the hall for breakfast. I feed 12 first, then fill a plate. But I can only pick at the food. How can anyone enjoy food after seeing someone die? I don't know what to do once 12 finishes the mash. I'm not sleepy, and I don't want to talk with anyone, least of all Kesh. I pull a chair close to the fire and listen as the Captains talk.

They are discussing 12 as if neither of us is there.

"What about a stout muzzle strapped behind her ears?".

"The tanner has triple-strength straps. Lither hide melded with steel, or so she claims."

"More like used derak," another laughs.

They fall to boasting: this or that son would have bested her.

They still don't understand 12's power.

Mei comes up to me. "I know you're upset. I am, too. Ash was a fine warrior."

I can't say what I'm thinking. Males are what they are. They can't help their natures. I know it's still wrong to kill them as if they were nothing. One of the Captains—Hisla, I think, of the white-haired Dreams—lifts a rib to her mouth and tears off the juicy meat.

"Walk with me. You haven't got a proper look at Quillka yet. I have some scrip for you, to buy things. Better than sitting here and listening to this boasting."

We turn left from the Council Hall. Mei names the shops: cobbler, butcher, flower seller. Every roof is covered in shiny solar panels.

The sign with a human figure between two thick lines is for Stoya, the paper-maker. "Would you like to see her paper?" she asks. "I know you are a wonderful drawer."

Even that compliment doesn't lift my mood. "Alright."

The shop is steamy from a boiling vat of paper pulp Stoya is stirring in back. She wears a stained leather apron. A draft—the little alligator—uses a strainer to scoop pulp mash from the vat and spread it onto a flat mesh strainer.

"What's on the menu today," Mei asks.

"Old clothes, pine bark, sawdust, and cow piss," Stoya answers gruffly. "What do you want?"

"This is Kesh's daughter, Dinitra."

Stoya looks me up and down. "You paint."

The question is so direct I laugh. "I paint," I say.

"Them scraps there is for the taking," she says, pointing to a bundle on a shelf.

Mei tries to leave some scrip but Stoya refuses. "Whatever she doesn't need we'll burn tonight on that boy's pyre."

Down the street is the shop with a six-fingered hand. I know from the Book of Sowers that Constance had six fingers. "What's that?" I ask Mei.

"The Sower laboratory."

"Isn't that a Weave word?"

"Most of the Captains were Sowers before. Except the younger ones, like Shan and me. Come, let me show you."

Inside, a woman notes Mei's badge: a raptor with wings and claws outstretched, for her mother's bird of prey. We follow a red line painted on the floor.

In the next room, my eyes take a moment to adjust to the darkness. There are dozens of metal consoles against the wall, each with an angled screen. We had a few of these consoles in Biotics, to cut and assemble formula. I used one to assemble my carnivorous potato. Most of the consoles are white, with green ones set in the corners.

A few assemblers bend over the screens. There's a hum of injectors as they twist the knobs and adjust the dials to cut and join formula. The assemblers are goggled, gloved, and draped in shoulder-to-toe white gowns, with white booties over their shoes, to maintain a sterile lab.

Mei tells me that each assembler has instructions on how to construct a formula according to a Captain's wishes. Perhaps a Captain needs boys with more speed or more patience, Mei explains. A taller boy or a broader boy, one who can lift great weights or climb. Sometimes, there are special orders, like for Hisla's Dreams: boys with these qualities and white hair.

The assemblers fill their orders at the white consoles. Other specialists retrieve eggs from the Captains, insert the proper formulas, then insert the fertilized eggs into Vessels.

"Our women, the women who are not Captains I mean, may order their own Bonds. Perhaps a merchant needs a girl who can work a market stall without becoming bored or tired. The merchant must find a Keeper and provide for the girl, of course. It is their right to make the Bond."

The green consoles are to assemble drafts.

I've only seen pictures of a Sower laboratory in the Weave. The laboratory was bigger, but the consoles looked the same. In the middle of the room is a long lab table crowded with racks of flasks and long glass tubes. Shelved beneath are stacks of small, round dishes pre-coated in orange element, the gel that feeds growing cells. I remember the smell from Biotics: a little damp and musty, like cheese beginning to mold.

I'm worried 12's tail will sweep a flask to the floor. She seems to understand that she must keep her tail low.

"Where does the extract come from?" In the Weave, men kept in containments provide extract.

"That, too, is a great advance over the abuses of the Weave. Mei reminds me a little of Professor Wylla, at least what Wylla would have been when she was young. A sharp pang of sadness hits me. Wylla is imprisoned because of me.

Mei doesn't notice. "We keep careful record of every warrior's qualities. Those qualities are catalogued and cross referenced, so that the Captains or the people wanting fresh girls can select for whatever suits them best. The warriors are happy to provide, since this can mean new brothers. Some even compete, to see who will contribute most to Bounty's next generations."

Each spring, Mei says, the Captains put on offer any Vessels they are not using to Bounty women who wish for children. "Of course, the Vessels are eager to serve," Mei says. "As in the Weave, they are bred for this, to carry new generations. So long as they are healthy and rested, they carry as many babes as they like."

In this, Bounty is not so different from the Weave. Some things are just natural and right. Vessels are meant for this. Sons are meant to fight. I have to get used to this new way of thinking. After the death of Ash and news about the docking of the boys, I'm relieved that some things are in their proper place.

"Here's something that might please you." Mei pauses beside a green console that no one is using. Below the screen are the holes where assemblers insert their hands into permanent gloves, which hang like a cow's deflated udders. The materials are laid out: a round container, the laser injector, fresh hypodermic needles. "Girls who show special promise can be invited to become Captains," Mei says. "Maraz, for instance. Captain of the Mother Eyes. Her sons are scouts and advance fighters. Very different from Ash."

Mei gauges my reaction. "In the woods, you'd never see them

until they are practically next to you. Their skin is black, to match the shadows. Maraz was originally meant to be a herder. The Captains noticed she never lost a single lamb or kid to the hybas. Sharp eyes, like I say. They offered her a Captainship and sons."

Mei is quick to add that this not obligatory. "It takes a special kind. Willing to be a leader of men. Of course, only Captains are allowed to make and command sons."

"Where do you make all of this?" I mean the consoles. I've seen no factories, no freighters, no Signal Way.

"We steal the equipment from the Weave. Or rather the Sea Hunt does. Their specialty. Come, let me show you the nursery."

"And the power?" I've seen no central Cyclon.

"Aren't you the curious one!" she exclaims, pleased. "Solar, mostly. Anku designed portable Cyclons, much smaller than the ones in the Weave. Easier to manage and much more secure."

We pass through another curtain. Here, the Keepers who care for just-born infants bustle around dozens of cradles, positioned end to end and stacked four high. The nursery reminds me of the building where Bounty keeps the drafts. Here, the infant cradles hang from long poles that drafts turn back and forth, to rock them, Each cradle is marked by the badge of the infant's mother. Mei identifies them: the starfish for Quor's Sea Hunt, her mother's bird of prey, Timbe's maple leaf, the wheat sheaf for Ular's Harvest, the eyeless face of Hisla's Dreams, and so on.

Mei stops by a cradle marked by her sister's Gemstone emblem. The babe there is robust, with thick brown hair. "My sister's newest. Little Ruby."

The last room is for Recovery. There Captains rest after providing eggs. Low couches are pulled close to several braziers. Only one is occupied: Ular, of the Harvest. She has a powerful build and a cap of curly blonde hair. She's asleep, her mouth slack.

"The power of forgetting," Mei says softly. "Egg extraction can be painful."

Mei tells me that some Captains come as often as once a month, depending on their plans for sons.

Mei touches one of the couches. "You may be resting here one day with a hundred sons to your name and a hundred more to come. Don't look so surprised," she adds, "I know it's what Kesh wants."

Never once did it occur to me that I would have daughters let alone sons. I never aspired to be a Sower. And a Captain? I look down at 12, who feels my agitation. Her golden eyes ask: *What would you have me do?* Imagine if I were looking down on a boy. Or more than one.

Or if I were looking at a warrior made in my image. My hand goes to the soft fur behind 12's ear. Would I caress a son as I saw Shan caress her Gemstones? Timbe stroked Ash's forehead before she killed him.

Mei puts her hand on my arm. "Not all of us have sons. I don't." This is a choice, she says. "The Bond is not for everyone. That is as it should be."

I swallow my response. *Slitting a son's throat is not for everyone.*

Mei leads me into the room at the back of the Sower building. "Let me show you where they hang the drafts."

This room is crowded with hip-high glass vats filled with clear liquid. The smell is greasy and thick, like rotting meat. Mei grabs a metal pole with a hook on the end and dips it in a vat to fish out a baby not much older than Ruby, Shan's newest. The baby's face is sharp-nosed, like a lizard. The rest of the body is human but for a fragile sprout of tail.

Mei retrieves another: the skin transparent, the veins, muscle, and tendons traced like a tracker map. "They died soon after they were taken from the sacs," Mei says, "Bounty preserves them. We make few drafts compared to the Weave, so it is unusual to lose them. We save them for research, to try to understand our mistake."

Mei returns the pole to the hook. "Come, let me show you the drafts still in their sacs."

Along the back wall is a rack with what looks like giant cocoons hanging from metal hooks. At Holdfast, Kesh described these to me, when she told me how she brewed 12. The cocoon skin is yellow and veined. Beneath each one is a little pool of thick, yellow liquid.

"What you see there," Mei says, pointing at the pools of yellow liquid, "is nektar. That gives it the yellow color. See how the sacs are translucent?"

She puts her hand behind a sac and wiggles her fingers. Like a shadow, another hand with six webbed fingers lifts to mimic it. Mei laughs and pokes the sac. A thumb pokes back.

I'm fascinated and repelled. "What is it?"

Mei reads the tag at the top. "Quor's Sea Hunt. Some water creature, I suspect."

Once we are outside, I suck in fresh air.

"This is a lot to take in, I know," Mei says. "Come, let me get you a honey roll. Flora's the best baker this side of the Stairs."

She leads me to a small market. The aisles are crowded with Vessels: chatting, drinking tea, haggling over vegetables and cheeses. The contrast with Pergama is stark. The vegetables are plentiful and appealing. Vendors smile as they collect scrip. One butcher has to step around the many hinds she's hung to accept scrip.

There are children everywhere.

At a baker's stall, Mei orders two honey rolls and two coffees. Before serving us, the baker splits the rolls in halves and coats them with dark honey. The coffee is served in brown paper cups, Stoya's mark on the sides: human figure between two thick lines. The coffee is spiced with cinnamon and ginger.

I have to press my paper scraps under my arm to hold the bun and coffee. "Does this honey come from..." I'm trying to remember the name. "Odide, I think?"

Mei laughs. "This honey comes from Ular's hives. She would be offended if you suggested Bounty has to go all the way to some draft Queen for its honey."

We look for a quiet spot to eat. Mei returns to our conversation, speaking as much to herself as to me. "If the Weave prevails, the first thing they'll do is kill the males. You know this: the Great Quest they've been planning since Constance founded the Weave. It couldn't be easier. Stop supplying Remedy—supplement—and they'll die. What the Weave has worked for since the Sowers first birthed a living child."

For an instant, I wish Kesh had put rock into my formula, so I could hide what I'm feeling. My words come too quickly, with too much anguish. "You're saying Bounty is better because it uses males to fight? Because they die on some stupid battlefield? Or in a training pen, because some stupid girl couldn't control her cross? I don't see such a difference, Mei."

I'm weeping. It's all too much: 12 killing 132 and Ash. My fear as I woke up in the dark, thinking I'd lost 12. A war is coming that I can do nothing to prevent and can do nothing to escape.

Mei's arms are around me. I'm taller, so her head—hair warm from the midday sun—bumps my mouth. It's so awkward we both laugh. "Of course that's not what I'm saying."

"Please don't tell anyone I asked this question," I tell her.

"Of course."

I take a deep breath. "Everyone knows the male is naturally violent. Nothing I've seen so far has changed my mind."

I'm about to say something I don't believe anymore. But I have to hear Mei's answer. "If Bounty defeats the Weave—and forgive me, that seems impossible—why not complete the Great Quest? It doesn't matter what side of the Black Stairs you are on. Isn't the Mother better off without males?"

I watch her face carefully. The young Captain betrays no surprise. "Let us sit somewhere quiet."

Nearby is a small garden. A climbing structure rises at the center, with children playing around it. I've never been with children this small, at least since I can remember. Their cries are like wild birds: caws, squeaks, chittering. Among the children are drafts I haven't seen before: one covered completely in dense yellow fur, another with a rabbit's long ears. Under one of its eyes is a single white teardrop against the chocolate-brown fur.

To the side, Keepers and Vessels chat in the shade.

Mei and I settle on a bench. The children stare as 12 stretches at my feet, laying her head on her paws with a chuff. Since she doesn't move, they quickly lose interest.

Mei gazes at the children. "I know that's what you've been taught. I was taught the same. All of us born in the Weave were taught that males are must be eliminated. That they are violent and can never be truly tamed."

"I believe you can tame some males," I tell Mei. "You can sow them for things like obedience or strength. But they are still males. That doesn't change. They are still dangerous."

I scratch the hyba cross between her ears. Her eyes close in pleasure. "I trained her. Then she killed Ash. The wildness is inside her. I think it's beyond any trainer's skill. Any Sower's skill. Isn't it the same with men?"

Mei opens her mouth, then shuts it again. A finger presses to her lips. "I don't expect you to change your mind so quickly. It is true what you say about 12. Yes, there is a violence in men no Sower can truly erase. The challenge is to put that violence towards its true purpose. To harness it. Let me tell you how my mind was changed."

The warriors' quarters lie behind a wall, Mei says. Sometimes, warriors come to this playground to watch the children and get to know their little brothers before they become warriors themselves.

One day, Mei talked to a warrior, one of Timbe's sons. "You've seen him. The grey-haired warrior."

"Yes." He was the one who fought Ash with the stave, then tried to stop the bleeding after 12 attacked him.

"I'm a fysic, as you know. I heal Captains and warriors, the people of Bounty. I heal everyone. That day, this warrior—Thorn is his name—came here, to this garden." Mei nods. "I trained him. Thorn is a gifted healer."

The children and drafts organize a game of hide-and-seek. "He is still a male," I say to Mei.

"He does good in the world. He cares for his brothers. Males are human, like us. That is the essential difference between them and those drafts. They are as human as you and me."

"Are warriors allowed to play with the children? With the females??" I say, incredulous. I don't know the rules between females and warriors who are not their sons.

Mei's smile is gentle. "They are our sons, after all. We want them trained well. Now, I wouldn't recommend that you go to their dwellings at night. They do smell."

Mei laughs and I laugh with her. I feel like we could become very good friends. Maybe even lovers. "The Captains want their main contact to be with their mothers, for discipline. It's part of the Bond, to make them the very best they can be."

There's a problem with what Mei is saying. Kesh herself said as much. Mei and I are *mostly* human. We are also a little *Capra aegagrus*, from the enhancement to our night vision. Our life-span has been increased through experimentation with self-repairing lizards, to revive aging cells. Kesh showed me the draft she said was used to study tumors, as a way to improve the next generation of Weave citizens.

Who gets to say who is human and who no longer qualifies? How much of the human formula separates a human from a draft?

Mei seems to follow my thoughts. "You are thinking about the improvements Sowers have made. Let me be clear. Every human, female or male, still has a consciousness of the Mother that no Sower has ever erased. That is what sets us apart from plants or animals."

What if a draft is more animal than human? Is the Mother still inside? The little rabbit draft sidles close to 12, sniffing. The gold of 12's eyes flashes under her eyelashes. The white tuft at her tail tip jerks once, then is still: she is luring the little draft. The rabbit-draft jumps back.

But curiosity gets the best her. She creeps close enough to gently sniff 12's motionless tail tuft.

Suddenly, 12 chuffs. The draft leaps into the air, then scurries away, delighted.

12 lays her head down on her paws, the tail tuft twitching in satisfaction.

Mei is earnest. "These warriors, they feel love, too. They love their brothers. They love their mothers. They fight for Bounty, just as we do. The Great Quest is wrong, Dinitra. Can you see that? It's wrong to kill anything capable of love."

I'm not convinced. "What about all of the old stories? When men slaughtered women, when they bred them and kept them in slavery?" I sound like a Weave history book.

Mei takes my hand in hers. "No one here will say that our sons should be wild or sown without virus. That would be reckless and irresponsible. Men need to be cared for, yes. On that we agree completely. For their own protection! In many ways, males are like those children. You'll be helping them become warriors just as I helped Thorn become a fysic. Once the Legion crosses the Black Stairs—and they will cross, have no doubt—we need to make sure our sons are prepared to fight. To survive. Training them means you are saving their lives."

Mei's eyes are bright with certainty. "Our cause is just. You've seen the drafts. We've saved them, every single one. We're the good ones, Dinitra. Our sons fight, yes. Some of them die. Yes. The fight is to save lives, Dinitra. The fight is for good. Help us."

Ash's death and the sun and the dead drafts in the laboratory and the children screeching are suddenly too much for me. "I don't know what to believe anymore," I tell Mei. "I think I need to rest."

"I'll take you back to your room," Mei says. "One last thing. Ask a warrior what they believe. They'll tell you the same. They'd die to defend their mothers."

By the time we leave, most of the children are being taken back to their dwellings for a nap.

That evening, Mei collects me for Ash's pyre. Ash's brothers spent the afternoon building a platform over a great pile of wood just beyond the training pen. The villagers are there, too, along with too many children and drafts to count. I see Sil and the draft Darling, the one with slick, gray tentacles who can't bear touch. Thoth, the alligator draft, stands next to Stoya, the paper-maker, still in her stained apron.

Once everyone is gathered, Timbe and several dozen sons form a circle around the oil-soaked pyre. Alone, Timbe sings: *Born of Timbe, the warrior Ash, First in battle, first to the kill, Lucky was he to serve the Mother bravely, The Living Wood lifts him in thanks.*

Timbe places a flame lamp on one of the logs. The warrior I saved steps up, removing a long huaraca from around his neck. This is the type of slingshot the Pergama vendor tried to sell me, a long rope split by a woven cradle. The others part to give the warrior a clear path to the lamp. He fits a stone into the huaraca cradle, then lets the cradle fall to his ankle. Gracefully, he swings, until the rope whistles. He releases one end and launches the stone, which cracks into the flame lamp. The lamp tumbles it into the oil-soaked wood, and the pyre catches with a whoosh. Flames engulf Ash's body.

Timbe sings again, this time starting with a warrior named Pine. Then she names Juniper, Holly, Laurel, Pecan, and Pine before repeating the verse about Ash.

All of her dead sons. A hand rests on my shoulder: Kesh. When she wants to, she's like 12, moving without a sound. "Timbe wishes to express her thanks for saving her son today."

The flames from Ash's pyre turn her metal legs gold. "12 must learn to kill only when you want her to. She kills to please you. We will start again in the morning."

21

Shape language

A t breakfast, the armorer is waiting with a metal muzzle. The heat of mid-summer is intense, and she's sweating heavily. The tailor is there to adjust the muzzle's buckle and triple-lither straps she vows can't be ripped.

I struggle to slip the metal cage over 12's snout. She manages to wedge a paw beneath a strap, splitting it from the buckle, and bite a section of the muzzle into a bend.

"I should have used pergama." Then the armorer mutters, "As if I could spare it."

The tailor's mouth goes wide before she scurries off, to get fresh straps. An hour later, the armorer is back with lither straps welded into a hastily-forged pergama casing.

12's claws are like curved knives. She's got the tips pierced through and sawing at the triple-thick straps in as much time as it takes me to pull in a single, defeated breath. She chuffs in triumph as the muzzle clatters to the floor.

The armorer is either awed or terrified by this display of her abilities. Kesh demands a new muzzle, thicker straps, and a more robust buckle.

The armorer shakes her head. "She'll obey or she won't. That's all I can offer." She pockets the pergama buckle and leaves.

I sip second cup of sweet coffee. After crossing the High Rail,

12 killed 132, then backed Anku and Petal into a corner. Then she killed Ash and almost killed his brother. "I have to go back to basics," I tell Kesh. "She thinks the only way is to kill. I have to work her alone."

Lam explodes at my words. "More delays? We don't have time."

I remember what Shan told me about the dozens of helios Lam and her Birds of Prey spotted on the Rift. The Captains waited for me. Now I'm telling them they have to wait even longer to train their sons with 12.

"Isn't that better than to sacrifice them?" I say.

I'm remembering what Mei told me, that the Captains believe their sons are as human as females. They deserve protection. "If you're going to defeat the Legion, you need every one of them," I say to Lam. "Your sons need to know what it's like to fight one of these creatures. I understand that. But they have to survive her first. If they can face 12, they can face any battle dog the Legion can send over the Rift."

My words hit home. But Lam is still furious. "Let your daughter be the one to tell Rek there's yet another delay," she says, turning to Kesh. "Make sure the cross is with your daughter when she tells her. She'll need protection. Rek's temper is worse than ever."

Before I take 12 to the training pen, Shan and Mei invite me to come with them to the armory. Kesh has ordered a leather breastplate for me stamped with a hyba head. There's also a new pair of knee-high boots, laced with bancat gut laces.

"Those laces will last longer than you." Shan is admiring. "I still have the ones my mother gave me when I arrived."

The sisters look on as I pull on the boots and slip the breastplate over my head. At the tailor shop, we pick up a gift from the two of them: a blue cotton tunic with a soft lining.

"For special occasions," Shan tells me. "You can wear this at the docking of my Gemstones in the fall."

As we leave, a group of boys runs by. Shan calls out, "Here they are! Come, my darlings. Come meet our newest Captain."

The boys look warily at 12. I put her in a sit and allow them to stroke her brindled shoulder. "She smells like Flora's buttered rolls," one boy exclaims.

Shan introduces them by height. Jasper, the tallest, then Opal, Agate, Diamond, Quartz, and Emerald. If they were Collegium girls, I'd say they were between eight and fourteen.

The smallest—Emerald—strokes Shan's arm, then embraces her around the hips. Shan plants a kiss on his cheek. "My baby, at least until my Vessels give me a new crop, if the Mother smiles on me."

Since there will be a delay in training with 12, the Captains order most of the warriors to deploy to the Stairs, to gather information about the new fleet.

12 and I have the training pen to ourselves. From there, the distant rise of the Stairs is muted blues and grays. I promise myself that I'll start making paint again. I'll start with the Stairs, painting them from the north as I once did from the south. The same mountains in the end.

The thought comforts me as I send 12 over the climbing net a dozen times a day.

For several weeks, I run 12. My purpose is three-fold: to reassert to her that I am in charge, to tire her, and to put the deaths of 132 and Ash well behind us. Summer turns to fall. Though Lam and Timbe eye me suspiciously, I insist: I need more time.

Only a few Captains stay in Quillka: Shan and Mei, Kesh. Anku comes and goes. Quor stays close, too, awaiting the birth of eight sons and several new drafts.

I rarely see Kesh, even at meals. It's Petal who becomes my frequent companion. As I work 12, he lashes together stick toys with twine, nut shells, and bits of old cloth.

One morning, I decide to try 12 on a new command. After an hour of telling her to climb the net, I pull a thread from a seam inside my cloak. I have her sit, then I wind the thread loosely around her muzzle. It's nothing, barely there.

I show 12 a new hand sign: the fingers of one hand pressed together in a cone. *Jaws closed.*

She shakes off the thread.

I wind it around her snout again. Jaws closed. Again, she shakes off the thread. This time, she looks guiltily at the thread in the dirt.

"I told you to keep your jaws closed. I mean don't shake." I scratch her between the ears. She shakes herself once, as if she's shaking off the mistake.

"OK." I make the cone shape. "This means no killing the nice warriors. Not even a little bit. No bites, no licks. For playing only. Got it?"

Her ears prick up as if she understands my words. So long as my fingers press together, she refrains from picking up a rag or a ball or even the bit of meat I bring from my meals.

Some afternoons, I teach 12 tricks that have nothing to do with fighting: dancing with her front paws on my shoulders, barking the number of fingers I hold up. Soon, 12 can balance on her back legs and tail and even hop forward, hyba cross and human combined. Her jaws open in a kind of hyba grin. She's more silly than scary, like a mischievous pup with her long blue-black tongue flopping.

I teach her to bark to twenty. I teach her to play dead. I teach her to fetch pine cones, spoons, apples, the leather scraps I wind into balls. By the time the weather turns cold again, she's retrieving the smooth-shelled pecans we find on our walks. Once she's cracked them, I soak the hulls and make them into brown paint.

No one seems to care that we go further and further from Quillka. I find a swimming hole the younger boys use to swim. Often, I spot Sil and several drafts there. Sil catches silvery fish she gives to the others to eat.

I don't have the right green for Sil's pebbled skin, so I use a scrap of Stoya's paper and charcoal for a sketch. *Drafts for a draft.*

Once I have green paint–spinach mashed, drained, dried, and mixed with powdered corn silk–I paint Sil into Kesh's book.

This is what I write at the top:

Sil fishes for fingerlings to eat. Some she frees since they're too small. The rabbit drafts are called Teardrop and Shine, both brown. Teardrop

*gets her name from a small patch of white under an eye. No one knows
how Shine got her name. She is just Shine.*

The drafts dip their toes into the water and eat grass. In the
future, what will people think about my stories? They're not
grand like the Chronicler's. There are no heroes like Constance.
Can there be good stories about other things, when there's no
fighting or dying? How about when drafts swim? How about
when 12 moans in some dream chase, the white tuft at her tail tip
twitching?

In the light of day, the coming war seems like some terrible
dream. At night, war feels as close as 12's long body in my bed. To
put off my nightmares, I've been tiring myself out, drawing more
and more, experimenting with dyes and paints, as if I can scribble
the fear away. On my walks with 12, I collect marigolds for orange
and holly berries for red. When the weather turns colder and the
rose hips are ripe, I use them for a soft pinkish brown.

The rose hips have a sour, earthy taste I like. I often squeeze
the juice from the ones that have gone squishy and drip it on my
tongue. Their dry husks look like little feet. Several times, I see
Mei, Ular, and the farmers harvesting rose hips. Mei uses the
bright red berries for soothing teas to combat infection and fever.

Every week, Kesh asks me if I'm ready to bring the warriors
back into the training pen. Every week, I say I'm not ready. I don't
tell her that I may never be.

One morning, I'm surprised to see a warrior standing at the
training pen. I recognize him: Ash's younger brother, the one I
saved from 12. The one who tried to beat 12 off of Ash. Around
his neck is the huaraca he used to topple the flame lamp and light
Ash's pyre.

He is slighter than his brother. He looks more like his mother,
Timbe, than like Ash.

I put 12 in a sit. I've tried to push away the memory of Ash's
grisly death. In my dreams, Ash speaks to me: why I didn't train
12 better, why I didn't push myself between 12 and him, like I did
with his younger brother.

"I will tell your mother when I am ready. I am not ready." I
turn my back on him, assuming he'll go away.

"I can help you."

A club to my head would have surprised me less than his voice. I turn and stare. "You have a tongue!"

He waits for me to catch my breath. "A few of us do. I am Fir, Timbe's son." He wears the clasp his dead brother wore, the maple leaf. His eyes are his mother's: gray-green.

I feel betrayed. "I know whose son you are."

He gestures words as he speaks. "Thank you for saving my life." His palm is vertical in front of his mouth.

"I don't understand shape language."

Fir makes the gesture again. "This means, *Thank you.*"

"I'm no child to be schooled by a warrior."

Fir makes no move to leave. "I would like to ask a favor." His palm moves out from his forehead. "That is *please*. If I watch you train with her, it would help."

"Help what?"

His answer is blunt. "Help me master my fear."

Master my fear: what Benit told me when I first saw 12.

His presence irritates me, but there's no reason to say no. "Do what you like," I tell him.

All day and the next, Fir watches as I train 12. As the sun sets on the second day, he approaches me. He is holding a huaraca. The ends are bound in red and black thread: Timbe's colors. The cradle is brown, the same color as his hair.

"A gift," Fir says. "Thank you."

I feel a rush of anger. Who is this warrior to approach me so boldly? "I have no use for such a thing."

"You can throw things for 12 to chase. They will go much further. Let me show you."

Fir takes a leather ball and fits it into the huaraca cradle. With his left hand, he starts the swing. As the huaraca gains speed, the rope whistles. Suddenly, Fir releases one end. The ball shoots over the pen wall.

12 doesn't move to retrieve it. Since I didn't hurl the ball, she knows it's not for her.

Fir is left-handed, like me. "Try it," He holds the huaraca ends toward me.

I shake my head. Why is he being kind? I'm suspicious he wants something from me. I can't help thinking about virus. The huaraca must be crawling with it.

"It takes practice." Fir steps closer. "You are left-handed. So is my brother, Cedar. He can throw things furthest. Hold out your left hand and I will teach you as I taught him."

His face betrays no hesitation. 12 is unconcerned, methodically licking her paws.

I am itchy with discomfort. When I defended him from 12, I touched him. That was a reflex, to save his life. How can I say no now? As I reach for the huaraca, things slow down. The huaraca is braided rope that is surprisingly slick.

Fir presses the huaraca into my palm. He arranges my fingers to hold it. "After you swing it, you release just one of the ends."

Fir shows me which finger to lift.

I look around, to see if anyone's watching. Does it matter? Mei urged me to teach the warriors what I could. She never mentioned them teaching me.

Fir has a second huaraca around his neck. To show me how to swing and release, he fits a ball into his huaraca. I watch closely as he swings. Again, the ball sails over the pen wall.

When I try, the ball flops at my feet.

This time, 12 retrieves it. Obediently, she presses the ball into my hand. Even Fir sees that she looks disappointed.

Fir says, "It took me weeks to get it right. Try again."

I get the same miserable result. I press the two huaraca ends together and hand them back to Fir.

He won't take it. "A gift," he says.

"I can't accept it."

His gaze is steady. "You saved my life."

Fir speaks with a directness that unnerves me. I'm the one who finally looks down. Talking like this feels too close. At the same time, I wish I could just look at him. Everything about his body is different from mine.

Fir drapes the huaraca around his neck and returns to Quillka. I watch, expecting him to look back, to see if I am watching. He doesn't, and I'm disappointed. I would have like to talk to him a little more. I didn't even ask him for the gesture in shape language for *huaraca*.

That night is especially cold. 12 refuses to sleep on the floor, instead climbing into my bed. She buries her black nose under the pillow, then looks at me, expecting me to order her down. It's a little mischievous and probably something Benit would tell me not to do.

Benit's not here. I'm so far beyond what she taught me, what she expected of me or 12, that I don't think she'd have a single piece of advice.

The only one who knows what to do is me.

12's enormous paws dangle over the bedside. To sleep, I wedge between her spine and the wall. I rub her fine ears before falling asleep. I think of Fir in the warrior quarters. Will he come tomorrow when I train 12? I look at the huaraca on my table. It's beautiful with the tightly woven cradle and the colorful ends.

I bury my face in 12's wiry, sleek fur. I feel alone and not alone with 12 in my bed. I can never return to the Weave. Already, that life seems so far away. My life is in Bounty now, with my mother, with 12. Whatever happens, I can't be separated from 12. If a fight is coming, I must fight. If not for me, then for 12. I couldn't bear to see her hurt.

Or killed. If training the warriors helps save 12's life, then I must do it.

And save the lives of others: my mother, Petal. Fir. Fir needs me to be brave. So does 12.

They all need me to be brave.

22

The Fall

Over breakfast, I tell my mother I'm ready to train the warriors with 12. Lam orders her Birds of Prey to meet me in the pen. It's a blustery day, with early snow in the air.

By evening, my hand feels frozen in a single command: jaws closed.

12 responds perfectly.

The next day, I train the Living Wood. As their new commander, Fir is first in line to face 12. His brothers are anxious, their hands moving too quickly for me to pick up words.

Easily, 12 tumbles him. Fir lands hard on his back, breath knocked out. 12's tail lashes in delight. Deliberately, she plants her paws on either side of his chest, as if she wants to remind him of what she did before. Drool slings from her jaws to his leather breast plate. Her black nose flares with his scent. Once she's satisfied he's surrendered, she looks at me with golden eyes.

She wants to know: have I done well?

How could she not? I give her a long scratch between the ears. Then she takes down Fir's grey-haired brother, Thorn.

By late afternoon, every warrior has gone at 12 at least twenty times. She's perfect, taking them down and leaving only bruises. I pick up more shape language. *Run*: fingers dusting the palm.

Good: a cupped hand, palm up, at the lips. *Attack*: four fingers thrusting forward. Then another gesture: the second and fifth finger crooked in a fist.

I piece together the meaning: *12*.

That night, I use shape language to talk to 12 in my bed. I praise her: *Good* (cup) *12* (crook). *Good 12*. She gets an ear scratch each time.

The next morning, the Captains at Quillka gather to watch the warriors train. One of Ular's Harvest—his chest thickly furred, with stout, strong legs—pokes another warrior and points when he sees me using their shape language to speak to 12.

Good 12, he mimics.

I wait for the warrior to look at me. *Good* (cup), I motion. Then I point at the warriors. I'm asking the word for warrior. *Good* (cup), I repeat. I point at them. It's how I taught 12 to keep her jaws shut.

The warrior cups his hands at his mouth, then places his fists on his hips. *Good warrior*.

I point to myself. *Good*?

He lifts a forearm parallel to the ground. Shan shouts the translation. "That means Captain. You know they hear perfectly well. You don't have to learn the shapes."

"I want to." I turn back to the warrior. "I am no Captain," I say.

No: a fist. *Captain*. I point to my chest, then draw my little finger from my temple to my chin: *What is my name?*

The warriors confer. The Harvest warrior waves his hand at me to pay attention. He makes the sign for 12: the second and fifth finger crooked in a fist. Then over it, he slides a flat palm: *12's master*.

I nod, pleased with my shape name.

The rest of the winter and into the next, I train warriors. They come from the far reaches of Bounty to stay for a week or two. Some warriors are shorter and squatter, made to dig the tunnels and trenches they use to fight the Legion. Others, like the Birds, are long and lean, fast runners, with sharp, far-seeing eyes. One group comes on horseback: messengers. They call themselves

Bancats, after one of the wild drafts whose night howl can be heard for miles.

I'm more confident in 12. She understands her role: to teach the warriors how to parry her without hurting them. Since he was the first to survive her, Fir often comes to show the warriors that she won't kill them. He lets her tumble him again and again, then he reaches up to her ears to pull them playfully.

Sometimes, I feel a prickle on the back of my neck. When I look, I see Fir watching me. He's different from the others. He wanted to train with 12 to better fight the battle dogs. Now, he's observing me with some other purpose in mind.

I think Fir wants to learn me as he learned 12.

The thought makes me anxious and a little pleased. 12 and I are good with each other. For the first time in my life, I'm good at something. When I know Fir is watching, sometimes I do special things, like show off a new command or hug 12. It feels more important when someone notices.

And I like it that it's Fir.

One rainy fall day, Kesh asks me to do night training, to test 12. Unlike me, 12 has no enhanced night vision. It's hard to know for sure, but I think 12 switches to scent more than sight in the dark. She's runs just a little slower, careful not to run into one of the obstacles.

By the time I return to Quillka, I'm exhausted. I'm wet from rain, and my boots and leggings are covered in mud. A burst of early winter chill has me frozen to the bone. I return to my room long past dinner.

There's no Beckc to save me a plate. I search in the kitchen for a snack. The cooks are long gone, every cabinet locked up.

When I enter my room, there's a surprise: Petal asleep in my bed in a storm of broken charcoal, paint brushes, and Stoya's paper scraps. He's wrapped in Benit's sheepskin, like a dirty little lamb.

At night, I've been sketching warriors, one way to learn their names. It's also a challenge to get their bodies right, so different from a female's. Petal has been looking at them and, if the smudges are accurate, licking them.

Dumped on the floor are Petal's stick figures, some still wet with my paint. He's been dabbing them with the colors of the warriors called the Bancats: brown spotted on white, named after the forest drafts that inhabit the middle slopes of the Black Stairs. It looks like a battle has been waged in my room.

Several of my vials have tipped over, paint pooling. Kesh's book lies open, a hand print—Petal's hand—on one page. At my feet is a sketch of Fir that Petal traced, clumsy lines over my careful ones.

I see immediately that Petal made one improvement. On Fir's shoulder is the lightning bolt tattoo I missed earlier. Petal drew it in scarlet, a shade Stoya showed me how to make from the bugs she collects from the prickly pear cactus.

Pink and green dye streak Petal's forehead. Colored footprints show where he padded back and forth across the floor. I should roust him, put him to cleaning. If I still believed virus would infect me, I'd be frantic to get any trace of him off my sheets.

I know better now. The worst I'll get is a second layer of Petal's grime.

12 seems to agree and climbs into bed next to him. She scratches the sheet, a habit. Then she lays heavily down. She sets her head set squarely on my pillow.

Petal mumbles and sets his filthy foot on her rump, still deeply asleep.

I hang my cloak and pull off my boots. Then I grab a fresh paper scrap to sketch the two of them. Petal's lips part as he gently snores. Only when I start to droop over the table do I shake the boy awake. "Time for you to clean up," I tell him.

Petal rubs his eyes, leaving bright green circles. 12's eyes are golden slits as she sleeps through it all.

I watch Petal clean from my chair. As he stacks some sketches, he knocks others back to the floor.

"By the Mother's breath! What are you for besides making a mess?"

"You's *such* a knobbie."

I am out of patience. "You broke into my room, messed up my things. You tracked paint all over the floor." I point to the red, green, and yellow prints. "You've stained my sheets. You've wasted weeks' worth of paint. And I'm the knobbie? I don't even know what knobbie means."

"Knobbie." He pouts. "Mixed in a tube and dialed to order. With a turn of the knob, you come out tall or fat or red-haired. Before you was piped into some Vessel's belly, you got a turn or two. Knobbie," He crows, triumphant.

"Everyone's a knobbie."

I'm taken aback by the boy's shamed expression. "Not me."

"You are Anku's son."

Petal picks at a smear of dried pink paint on his wrist. "Weren't no knobbie. Knobbies took her tongue with one slice when they caught her. While I were in her belly, so they did. Hidden-like. They threw that tongue to a battle dog."

Kesh told me the Legion caught Anku and punished her by taking her tongue. Was she a Vessel?

"Left her for dead, so they did," Petal says. "I birthed from her alone. She let no one touch me. It was her and me at Dolor until I could walk. That's why I talk like Rek's kind."

"Is that the way of northerners?" I mean being Sower, Vessel, and Keeper in one.

Petal shrugs. "Here and there. My mother was with one of the Sea Hunt. See?"

Petal stretches his fingers out. At the base of his fingers are webs, slightly pink and almost translucent.

Mei told me Captains choose the warrior they want for extract to sow their new sons. For Petal, Anku chose the Sea Hunt. "What does the Sea Hunt have to do with you not being a knobbie?"

Petal cries out, "You ain't listening, is you, knobbie! Do I have to knock you over the head like Anku did with your beast?"

I think back to the times I've seen Petal eat. Not once have I seen Petal eat the supplement, what the Captains call Remedy. He eats what the Captains eat, what his mother eats: no Remedy. Anku raised him in the north. Perhaps Petal has no virus, like Rek's Blazes.

I try again. "The Blazes. Are they knobbies?"

"Why, of course they is, you dense stump." Petal's

determination to school me fights against his shame. "Them Northerners, they is opposed to virus alone, not the knobs. Rek's Blazes, they's loyal to their Captain without no virus to keep them. They're not like any of them here, no. Fiercer and oh! Them colors they put in their hair! You will like them colors."

Petal picks up one of the stick figures to show me. I recognize Ash. He's dipped another figure's hair in orange paint. "That's Burn," Petal says, "he of the Blazes. Burn, he is their leader, as Ash was."

Petal continues. "The Battle of the Bog convinced old Captain Rek. She has a thousand sons at Dolor, knowed you that? More soon, since the season of birthing is nigh."

Petal moves his figures to 12's exposed belly. He calls the wrinkle of sheet beneath her the Bog. "It were at Battle of the Bog that the Captain called Idriz fought the Legion. Years and years ago. This ain't Ash no more, nor Burn. He is the Anvil, this one," Petal says, wiggling the dark-haired figure, "and the Forge, mightiest of all the Iron Fist."

Petal has a figure with a blue cloth cape climb past 12's midsection, marked with a tawny line of fur. "Idriz. Captain of the Iron Fist. Ain't a one lived. Herself as well, Idriz. The croaker that killed her? Straight from the Weave. Long arms it had, pounding the tunnels where them Fists hid. Collapsing them. There Idriz lies buried to this day."

The tunnels: the tender skin at 12's hind leg, where it touches her belly. "The Anvil himself brought a croaker down with his mighty arm. Whoop, whoop."

Petal mimics the action of a warrior whirling a huaraca over his head. It was how Fir taught me, his fingers shaping mine.

I push the thought away. I can't let Fir touch me again.

Petal holds his fist over 12's ribs, then dangles his fingers. "A croaker, pshew!"

I'm losing patience. "This battle happened years ago. You weren't even born. How are you not a knobbie? You've haven't told me."

Petal's sullen. "Have so."

"Have not."

With a fist still over 12, Petal knocks over a stick warrior. "Pshew! Evil things, with legs that grab. Pshew! Pound the earth, so they do, to force us out of our hidey-holes. Pshew!" The battle makes its way up 12's ribs. "The Fountain, pshew! The Anvil, pshew, dead every one. Then, pshew, down goes the Forge, mightiest of the Fist, protecting his mother. A vibro blast, zound."

12's ear flicks.

"The air trembles with them vibros," Petal says. "Sucks the life from your ears and nose, the vibros do. All things with hearts and lungs fails if they is too near. Only plants can go about their daily business." Petal tips over another warrior ("dead by the croaker, pshew!"). He sets two standing on the Bog. "Far from Remedy, they was. Days away. So what warriors the knobbies didn't kill the Remedy sickness did. Hundreds at a time, a suffering. So Rek says: not my boys, not anymore. No virus for them dear ones. They is skant, as they says."

Petal sees my confusion. "Skant of virus. Free."

I finally understand what he's telling me. "You have no virus. I've never seen you eat Remedy. Like the Blazes, right?"

"Them Northerners," Petal says softly. "They're knobbies through and through."

Knobbie comes from knobs, like the ones on the consoles in the Sower lab. I am careful with my words. "You were made without knobs."

Tears sparkle in Petal's eyes. "Not so dumb now."

How else can a babe be brewed? "You were born... beast-like," I say softly. I might as well have said Petal was formed out of mud and leaves. *No wonder Petal is ashamed.* Petal is like one of his stick warriors. Nothing clean, nothing planned, like in a Sower lab. No consoles, no sterile tools. "Your mother and this warrior. This Sea Hunt. That's how you came to be. They...made you."

I can't even say the words. Anku and the Sea Hunt warrior mated like beasts.

A single tear slips down Petal's cheek. "He were good, she tells me. Cared for her. He were no beast and neither she. She says she loved him, so she did. He loved her. And I, she says, is made from love."

On Petal, there's no obvious sign, like a birth mark. As I stare, Petal moves his warriors around 12's belly.

I tell him the truth. "I didn't know that was possible. I thought... Well, I thought everyone except wild beasts were sown."

Now that Petal's in a truth-telling mood, I ask about my mother. "Tell me why Kesh went from being a Sower to the Legion. Was this about knobs?"

"Pshew!" The croaker—his fist—goes aloft over 12's shoulder. "They don't like it when I tell the sad stories."

A toy warrior—the Anvil? I've lost track—knocks another warrior to the floor. Petal buries two more figures in the fold of 12's hind leg.

"I'll trade you," I tell him.

"Ain't got a thing I want. Except..."

"What?"

"Them old boots."

He means the boots I brought from the Weave. The ones he stole from me. I have my new pair from my mother. "You may have them once you tell me the sad stories."

"And..." He stares at the paper scraps.

"And what?"

"I want you to teach me."

"To make paint?"

"No knobbie! To make that!" He points at the drawings of Fir he traced.

"You tell me the sad stories. For every story, I'll teach you something about drawing."

"You first," Petal says.

Then and there, I sketch his face: curious eyes, pointed chin, a swoop of filthy red hair across his forehead, then all the freckles. His ears have a slight point at the tops. I exaggerate them.

His hands fly to his ears, to see if they've suddenly grown peaks. "You make me look like Panta!"

Panta is a draft with a pinched, foxum face and cat-like ears. "Lines aren't hard," I tell him. "It's the seeing you have to learn. To really see, that's the trick. Your turn."

"Them Gemstones have their docking with the full moon."

"That's not a sad story. Besides, I knew the docking was coming. Tell me something else."

He thinks for a moment. "Kesh and Anku are sisters."

"I knew that."

"You was born of a Vessel, in year…"

"584. You have to tell me something I don't know. Something sad."

"My mother, she were the best Cycloneer the Weave ever knowed."

"Mei told me the same."

"Medals," Petal is saying, "what they call accolades. She had a-plenty."

"There is nothing sad about that. You need something better."

"In darkest night, Kesh climbed the walls. She fell."

"What?" This is new. "Do you mean the Keeper walls? Fell where?"

"Your turn," Petal says, triumphant.

I hand Petal a charcoal nub. "Hold it this way. Not too tight."

I can't rush this. I guide Petal's hand into a line that matches 12's shape on the bed. As he sees what he's drawn, he looks to the hyba cross, then the page, then the hyba cross again. "Gaw," he says, pleased.

"Your turn," I tell him.

"Like a vibro you cried, shaking the walls. The Keeper walls." He grips the charcoal nub, eager to keep drawing.

"Keep going." Before he can protest, I say, "You already told me about walls. Besides, I had you draw all of 12 and she is quite long."

Petal agrees to the trade. "It were as if the Bond burned you. Them other babes was a-sleeping. You cried and cried. The Keepers came a-running, thinking some rat had got in. It were her: your mother. Stealing you away in her arms."

My heart is in my mouth. Kesh tried to steal me from my Keeper when I was small. How could she have managed with those metal legs?

Petal's face is full of mischief. "Your turn."

With my hand guiding his, we draw 12's head, the slits of her eyes. Petal insists on capturing 12's black lips and the thicket of whiskers. "Piggles!" he cries as he smudges the nose. "I ain't a one for this hard chore."

"Finish the story," I tell him.

"That Kesh, she tried to scramble down fast as fast. The rope, it weren't right."

"She climbed with her metal legs? How is that possible?"

"Mei, she wrote of Kesh the saddest of all the songs: the Mother-Bond. Makes the Captains weep every time." Petal smiles cruelly. "I don't want to do more drawing. You've got nothing to trade now."

"Your warriors don't have faces." I point to the stick figures. "I can give them faces."

"Show me." He grabs the closest figure. Carved in the arm is a lightning bolt tattoo. Fir.

"Your turn," I say.

"Not fair!"

I shrug. "Then you'll have no faces."

"She fell from the top of the wall, the babe bound tight to her. The babe: you. Like a shell around a nut she curled. That babe got the breath knocked clean out. And lived. Not the Captain. Well, she cracked."

I open my mouth and close it. When she stole me, Kesh was whole. Because she stole me, she broke. Kesh has those metal legs and that metal arm because of me.

The Mother-Bond split her. Ever since, I've dreamed of falling. Kesh paid for the Mother-Bond with the coin of her limbs.

Wylla and Flicke paid with their love. For each other. For me.

"You was just a sprig, mired in your own offings!" Petal doesn't notice my stricken expression. He wipes his stained fingers on his tunic. "Kesh had the Bond strong-like. She wanted to bring you to Bounty. She were going to take you or die trying. The fall, well, that she didn't plan. They gave her them legs and sent her to the Rift, her punishment. Kill those on the far side. Well, she showed them! Quiet she kept, year after year. A-waiting and a-planning until you was old enough. And she made this here 12 too, to keep you safe."

Petal lays his stick figures out side by side, the hands touching. He says Kesh had to promise the Sowers never again to seek her daughter. "Some say them knobbie fysics in the Weave cut Kesh before the forgetting started to work. Awake, they drilled in them legs. Even her heart is part machine, my mother says. Don't know if she got forgetting for that. Kesh never talks about how much she hurt. How long she suffered before she could walk again. How much she pined for you, her dear daughter. You wouldn't know her, she kept saying. You wouldn't know she tried to take you to Bounty. That she never wanted to leave you. All that time, she had to plot her way. She had to get you, that was her everything—get you and bring you here, which she done with my mother's help. The best Guide in all of Bounty, my mother." Petal cocks his head. "Sad enough for you? Where's them warrior faces you promised me?"

23

Fir

It's almost dawn before Petal is satisfied with the faces on his stick warriors.

He leaves for breakfast, the stick figures in a sack at his waist. I stare at his colorful footprints. I can scrub the floor of them. But the strongest soap in Bounty won't erase what he's told me.

Kesh came for me and fell. They gave her machine legs and attached them while she could still feel the drills digging into her flesh. They didn't wait for the forgetting. They punished her with the Legion, thinking she'd never be able to find me again. That maybe she wouldn't want to, for fear or regret.

The Bond was stronger than her fear. Stronger than any of them could know. I remember the news Asta and I watched: Legion Commander reviews forces at Holdfast. Legion Commander rounds up scrags. Legion Commander announces new Campaign against the rebel Captains.

She won three sheaves, the highest honor the Weave has. Then she betrayed the Weave for me. She made her life's work the destruction of the Weave.

For the Bond.

Did Idriz die because of her? The warriors Petal named: the Anvil, the Forge? As she plotted and planned her betrayal, Kesh killed Captains and sons she knew. She rounded up sons and sent them to the containment. All that time, she also plotted against the Weave. Cherished the Bond she made with me. She waited until she could steal me again, this time for good.

"The Mother-Bond is our greatest weapon," she told me. How could I have known the enormity of what my mother did for the Bond? At the Collegium, I wondered what flaw my Sower put in my formula. I never belonged. In a way, I was right. My Compendium never mattered. My fails never mattered. Nothing I did mattered. It was never what I could do. It was always what I was.

Kesh was always coming for me. I always belonged to her and her alone.

My mother.

I pace the room, connecting all of the pieces. We weren't brought to the Legion because of Susalee's skill with a strela bow or Tem's healing ways. It wasn't the lie Kesh told Trisk, that they wanted Collegium girls to pilot the fancy new fleet.

At least, not at first. I wonder if my friends are all pilots now. If the fleet does cross the Rift, will they be the ones shooting at the Captains and their warriors? Will they shoot at my mother? At me?

From high up, they won't be able to tell the difference between me or Mei or Shan. Between me or the warriors of Quillka. My face drawn on, my limbs glued. Orange hair, black hair—it doesn't matter. To them, we are scrags to be killed or captured. I feel like one of Petal's stick figures, moved here and there. Only now, I see the hand moving me: Kesh's hand. For Kesh, I am her only Bond. She risked everything to get me back.

Trisk was right all along. She wondered aloud what Kesh was doing, why she diverted the Legionship to the Collegium. She vowed to reveal Kesh as a traitor. *I'll say this for the Arcadium,* Trisk said to me on the Legionship. *We may not be the smartest, but we're loyal.*

Why did no one notice that Kesh diverted an entire Legionship to the Collegium to get the daughter she'd been told never to see again?

Maybe the Weave just forgot. Between sowing me and taking me, Kesh earned three sheaves. The most successful Legion commander since Constance. Maybe her successes buried her past. Kesh bided her time until the only one who even suspected her was a low-level Arcadium girl, a battle-dog handler who stank of the kennel and whom no one would believe.

Not even Benit believed Trisk. No wonder Trisk hated me so much. She knew something was wrong, she said it, and no one listened.

I clap for 12 to wake. Her stretch as she steps to the floor is luxurious and long. "Get enough sleep?" I say to her. "You slept for the both of us."

12's wet nose bumps against my hand. I could be walking west to the sea or east to the Wastes and she'd follow, eager.

Two Captains lounge close to the fire in the common room. Breakfast is on a side table: paddle-loaf, cheese, hard-boiled eggs, honey. No sign of Shan or Mei, thankfully. They'd want to chat and I have no patience for words right now.

The server has left 12's mash for me to serve. There's a bucket of pebbles by the fire, and I rub a handful quickly between my palms before dropping them into her bowl. As 12 eats, I slip some cheese and bread into my pocket to eat later.

Outside, the streets are busy. There's a snap of snow in the air, though the sky is clear. Some children and younger drafts have a game with 12. They dart at her tail as it sweeps to see who can touch it. Just as one little draft approaches—three-legged and thickly-furred, with a bald pink snout—12 sweeps her tail high, causing the little draft to chatter with glee. Then 12 holds her tail steady, so the draft can at least feel the wiry white tuft at the end.

The only way Kesh could get away with something so bold is exactly what she said: there's something rotten at the core of the Weave. They can't see the harm they're doing. They don't see Bounty as a threat. Why would they? The Weave is mighty, with millions of people. The Weave has everything, not just a new fleet: the Signal Way, scrolls, the laboratories, the containment, the Centrum itself, so masterfully built. Above all, the Cyclon, providing the fuel that not only lights their lamps and powers their ovens and looms and metal presses: the Cyclon will lift a deadly fleet on an endless, weightless supply of fuel.

The people the Weave assumes are loyal are not. *Knobbie*, the slingshot vendor called me: made with knobs. If I'm a knobbie, then some people in Pergama were not knobbies. The thought brings out a cold sweat. Petal isn't the only beast-born child I've met. Any one of those children in Pergama could have been beast-born.

How could I tell the difference? Beast-borns aren't obvious like drafts. Are there beast-born girls? The only way to tell would be to look for a life fiber and a tattoo. Beast-borns wouldn't have them.

I told Petal a line may not look right at first but it ends up being just the thing. Where does that leave me?

Right where I am standing.

I don't want to fight. I don't want 12 to kill again. I don't want to kill the girls I grew up with—or anyone from the Weave. I especially don't want them to kill me or 12.

I'm never going to belong to Bounty as I belonged to the Weave. I have to start thinking my own way forward. I have to do what's best for me and 12. What's best for the people I love.

What's best for *everyone* I love.

I pass the training pen where some warriors are practicing with huaracas. There's a pecan grove not far beyond it, then a stream through a little copse of trees. I've seen Sil fishing there.

A little hill overlooks the stream. There's a spot where 12 and I can sit, hidden.

And think.

In the grove, I pause for 12 to take a long pee. I do, too, behind a bush. The corn fields to the north are brown. A low blue haze clings to the stalks, like the Mother's own cloak.

At the spot, I settle against a rock. 12 scrapes at a shallow ditch she's made during our visits over the past weeks, turns three times, and lies down, nose tucked beneath the white tuft of her tail.

The words wind around my brain like strands of matted hair.

Kesh wanted me so badly she stole me from my Keeper's cradle. Then she fell, curled around me like a shell.

And cracked, Petal said.

In my nightmares, I fall. I never hit the ground. Kesh took the blow for me. My mother curled around me and protected me.

For the Bond.

Why don't I feel anything for her? Why can't I? Does the Bond go only one way, from Sower to child? The Captains don't call it daughter-bond. Son-bond. The Captains put virus in their sons to keep them loyal. The sons know that if they leave their mothers, they'll die.

They put no virus in daughters. Does that mean we cannot be other than loyal? Can I betray my mother?

If I had known Kesh as a mother, as Petal knew Anku, as the warriors know their Captains, would I feel differently? Would I feel the Bond, like a different skin?

Kesh called the Bond a weapon, the most powerful of all. How? Why? I think she means that the Bond is loyalty. I feel nothing. No: I still feel disgust. I don't want to know where I came from. I wish I was mixed like a draft, by order: inserted into a sac and suspended in yellow nektar. Simple, direct. Without complications. I don't want to owe anyone my life. Knowing Kesh sowed me from her own flesh and expected me to be bonded to her makes me feel unclean, compromised.

Like her personal battle dog.

Yet Kesh fell for me. How could I not be grateful her sacrifice? How could I not appreciate what Bounty stands for, the right of mothers to know their children, the right of males to exist?

No matter what I feel about Kesh, I know the Captains are right. The Great Quest to exterminate men is wrong. Males are born just as females are: fruit of the Sower's art and the assembler's skill, carried in the Vessel, nurtured by the Keeper, then trained and formed by teachers. So long as those males are bonded to their Captains, they should be allowed to live. I've seen Captains hug their sons. They love them and speak of them with great pride.

Yet. Timbe slit Ash's throat as if he were no more to her than an animal. The two places, Weave and Bounty, are like pictures reflected through different glass, one blue and one orange, like Sil's strange eyes. Between them, how can I choose? Must I follow my mother, follow the Bond? Or is there another path that is neither Weave nor Bounty?

Just then, there's a rustle at the stream bank. Two warriors—Ular's Harvest by their girth and hair color—appear. One carries a small sack of taffies from a Quillka shop. Swiftly, they take off their clothes. I see their maleness, a soft tube in the thicket of hair where their legs join.

Is that all maleness is, a soft tube?

The warriors slip into the water, splashing loudly.

With fistfuls of leaves they scrub themselves. Once they're on the bank again, they dress quickly, then huddle together against the cold. They take a taffy each from the sack.

I make out a little of their shape language. Something is *good*: a cup of the hand. They're talking about the taffy. A circle of thumb and forefinger. One laughs, opening his mouth for the other to see how the taffy sticks to his teeth. *Look at me*, he is saying.

Then give me another. That's easy to understand: his fingers flick in a loose fist. The brothers are careful to divide the taffies equally. When the sack is empty, they put on their clothes and leave.

12 pants at my side. I see the sense of it, males put to good purpose. Not wasted or loosed, to start up the old wars. They're cherished by their Captains. I only recently met my mother, even had the idea of a mother that was not the Mother of us all. Despite the violence I saw when Timbe killed Ash, perhaps this is a better way. To be tied to others by the Bond: Mother-Bond, Sister-Bond. Even the Bond I have with 12.

A faraway bell peals to announce the start of a new training session in the pen. Then 12 chuffs in warning. Someone is approaching. I scramble to my feet, my hand at 12's shoulder.

It's Fir. "You scared us," I confess.

Sorry. A palm circle over the heart. "I wanted to speak to you."

His huaraca hangs around his neck. He has an old cloak he wraps close to his body. He stares at his boots as if they're suddenly the most interesting things he's ever seen.

"Then speak," I say.

He bristles. "I'm not yours to command."

Somehow, this exchange has gone terribly wrong. "You said you wanted to speak to me. That's all I meant."

Gripping the ends of his huaraca, he looks more boy than warrior. "Blast it all." Fir's mouth twists in frustration. "I practiced all week what I would say. It never went like this."

"Practiced...speaking?"

To his boots, Fir declares, "A question. I practiced asking a question." His green eyes are sincere. "I didn't think I would frighten you. I am sorry. Please forgive me."

I can tell Fir has cleaned his armor and boots. His tunic is freshly washed. "You are forgiven. Ask what you will."

His voice lowers. "Can this be between us alone? It is a question I don't wish to share."

This exchange is suddenly much more dangerous than the one I had with Petal: sad stories for drawing lessons. No one has ever told me I cannot speak with a warrior or answer a question in confidence. Now that I know there are beast-borns—that Petal is a beast-born—I can't look at Fir the same way.

"Were you followed?" I ask.

A slow smile spreads across his lips. "No one sees me if I don't mean them to."

I can't help smiling back. "You are confident."

"I could say the same for you."

I didn't expect this ease between us. "I have questions, too," I tell him. "We can trade."

"Trade?"

"Yes," I say. "One question, one answer. A trade."

This definitely feels like we are breaking some rule.

"A trade," Fir repeats. "Just between the two of us."

"And 12. But she is not much of a talker."

Another smile from Fir. Something changed in his expression, and it takes me a moment to understand. He's less afraid.

Fir clears some twigs and leaves away from where I was sitting, as if to make the rock more appealing to me. "Please sit," he says. "This may take a little time."

"You first."

Fir sits with his back against the rock. Then he looks at the space he cleared for me. "Is it not good?" He makes the shape for good: a cupped hand, palm up, at his lips.

Good, I motion back. I sit, 12 stretching out between us.

"Ask me your question," I say.

"You have been in Quillka since last summer. Almost a year now." Fir measures out each word.

"That is not a question."

"Give me a moment. I am not used to this."

I look at his hands, which I remember well from when he taught me how to use the huaraca. They are larger than mine, rougher. From the opening in his cloak, I see that the sleek brown hair on his forearms matches the hair on his chest.

He cups his hands over his knees. "How have you found Bounty so far?" he asks.

I have to laugh. "You walked all the way from Quillka to ask me about Bounty?"

"I did not promise a large question." His cheeks flush. "Sometimes one can trade for small things. What is your answer? Isn't that our agreement?"

"I have found it strange." I tell him I knew nothing about Captains before arriving at the Legion. I didn't know about the Bond or that I had a mother. "I don't know what I'm supposed to feel about the Bond. Do you feel the Bond?"

"Is that your question?" His gaze reminds me a bit of Petal: mischievous.

"Yes. That's my question."

Fir considers his answer. "Yes, I feel the Bond. The Bond has been there since I was small. I always wanted to be a warrior. To be with my brothers and serve my mother."

"Do you love your mother?" I don't know why this matters, but it does. I never knew my mother before coming to Bounty. Now that I've watched her, I see something in her eyes when she looks at me, something that frightens me. I don't think I will ever love her the way she loves me.

"It is not your turn." Again, he looks as me with mischievous eyes.

I motion *Sorry*.

Fir looks out across the swimming hole to the fields beyond, spiky with dried corn stalks. I've never spoken to anyone so openly, not even Asta. With her, I always had to prepare myself for her to find some fault. I think Fir would see my faults and not care.

"You have seen many warriors since you came last fall." Fir's green eyes have golden flecks. "You have been told what we do."

"Yes."

"What would you call us?"

"Call you? Beside warriors?" I think this is another light-hearted question, but Fir is serious.

"Yes."

"What you are. Sons. Warriors. Is there some other word?"

Fir is watchful. "We speak between the two of us, yes? You will tell no one?"

"Is that an extra question?"

"An assurance. You will not speak of this to the other Captains. Promise me." His voice is a thrum I feel against my skin.

I look over his shoulder, to make sure no one else is coming. No one sits at the swimming hole. I don't want to have to lie to Mei or Shan. Or my mother.

"I will not tell anyone. Tell me what you mean. What other word is there is for warrior?"

Fir crosses his wrists.

"I do not know that word," I confess. A sharp wind tosses the tree branches. 12 is calm and that calm transfers to me.

"We use it among brothers," Fir says. "And with some warriors who feel the same."

I have a feeling our trade is at an end. We've started a longer conversation. "Teach me the word."

He catches my eyes to gesture again "That word is slave."

I'm surprised. "Slave?" Like *boy*, *slave* is an old word. I shake my head. "There are no slaves. No person can keep another in..." I am about to say *slavery*. Is that what Fir means, that sons are kept in slavery? They fight out of loyalty to their mothers, as 12 is loyal to me. "The Mother would not allow slavery."

"I don't know about the Mother," Fir tells me, "or about the past. This is the word we use."

If I close my eyes, I think I can hear him breathe. A few stars wink against the darkening fringe of sky. "You are sons. You have the Mother-Bond. You said yourself that you've always felt the Bond."

His eyes are like an open gate: no defenses. "I have felt the Bond, yes. To us, the Bond is slavery."

"No one may keep slaves," I insist. We are talking past each other.

"What would you call it, Dinitra?"

I've never heard him say my name. The silence is filled by our breaths and 12, who twitches and softly moans in a dream.

"You are sons as I am a daughter," I finally say. "Your mothers make you, they raise you. Your mothers love you. You are Bonded to them, as I am to my mother. But I am no slave."

By now, I've lost the thread of questions I had for Fir. We could be outside of Bounty, outside of time. Against this rock, rules have vanished. Like me, Fir has tucked his boot toes under 12, our own private heating fire.

"I would choose the Bonds I honor, not be forced," he says. "This Bond, to fight and die for Timbe…I would break it."

That's like declaring up is down and black is white. "But how can you break the Bond? Isn't that the whole purpose of your mothers making you?" The next words are out of my mouth before I can stop them. "Not even I could break the Bond."

Fir's voice is patient. "You were not raised with the Bond, Dinitra. You asked me yourself. How does the Bond feel? I thought that maybe, out of all of the Captains, you might understand what I mean when I say slave. To have the Bond forced on you."

To hear him say my name is intimate as a touch. "What do you mean by forced?" I hesitate before I say his name. "Fir."

"That you would be made to die for it. Against your will. To die and know that your brothers die too or are still slaves."

I don't know what it must feel like to be Fir, to have the Bond and know it means you must give up your life. I don't know what it feels like to be a son, a male. My only parallel is 12: brewed to fight and die for me.

When I thought Anku and Petal had killed her, that she had died to protect me, I felt gutted, like someone had opened me and removed my insides. It didn't matter that she was male or female, that she was a draft. What mattered was that I loved her and didn't want her to die.

I don't want Fir to die.

"Your mother loves you," I tell him. "I see how she looks at you. How the other Captains look at their sons. I saw Timbe sing the praise song for Ash. She would grieve for you."

Fir squeezes one hand with the other. His anguish charges the air around us. With each second, a new star winks into view. I don't want this night to end.

"My mother praised my brother because he sacrificed for her. Then she put me in his place. When I die, she will praise me for the same sacrifice. Another brother will come behind me: Tanoak, our strongest. Behind him come a hundred others who are still sprigs or in their Vessel's bellies. Each one she expects to sacrifice. Each one she knows may die for her. Because we are slaves, Dinitra, not because we choose it."

I thought I knew the Weave, but I was wrong. Then I thought I knew Bounty. What Fir is describing is showing me I am wrong again. What can I do? There is no safe place for him north or south of the Stairs. There is no place where I could still be his friend. Except right here, at this rock. From Quillka, a bell rings to announce that the gates will soon be closed.

"You came to ask something," I say. "Ask me."

He clasps his hands. "It is impossible. I know that it is impossible. I will trouble you no more."

He starts to stand. I grab his wrist. Fir is trembling. "I didn't know you were so cold. You should have said something."

"This is not from the cold." His expression is a swirl of fear, longing, excitement, and uncertainty.

"Ask me," I repeat. I think he must want me to speak to Timbe. To talk to the Captains and explain that some of their sons think they are slaves.

Fir takes my hand from his wrist and envelops it between his palms. They are rough and warm. "We need enough Remedy for a week, Dinitra. We'll go east, where there is a Master of men. Myself and my eldest brothers. A single sack."

"Steal it?"

"We want to escape. Before this war starts. Or we will all die. I beg you."

"That's treason."

Fir recoils. "It's our lives."

I have a thousand questions. What if they run out of Remedy? What if there is no Master? What if we're attacked by the Legion? What if the Captains force them back? What if a pack of hybas hunts them down in the Wastes?

None of this do I say.

I touch his hand. "Give me time to think."

I watch him as he makes the long walk back to Quillka.

24

Gemstones

Under Timbe's command, Fir and the Living Wood leave the next morning for the Black Stairs. Anku goes with them. Petal is desolate when I see him at the training pen, his sack of toy soldiers spilled at his feet.

Fir's word—*slave*—echoes in my thoughts for days, a sound that won't go away. I don't want steal Remedy or think about this Master in the east. I was stupid to assume that asking questions posed no danger. Questions lead to more questions and then to answers I don't want to hear. When I first met my mother on the Collegium green, she asked me who I was making my painting for. I refused to answer because I knew that would get Asta in trouble.

Since, the questions have only become more dangerous.

Once Fir and his brothers escape, I'll never see him again. But can I call him friend if I keep him caged?

I can't go to anyone for advice, certainly not Mei or Shan. Not even Petal. Without sons, the Captains have no hope of defeating the Weave. They won't even be able to defend themselves.

Every day, I take the huaraca Fir gave me and warm up 12 by shooting balls for her to retrieve. Every time, she leaps with joy, oblivious. I should be more like her: no questions.

As the days pass, my questions get more serious. If I stole a sack of Ular's Remedy, the Living Wood would escape and perhaps other warriors, too. Bounty would be undefended. The Concave, the helios, and the vibros would sweep Bounty away.

Just because Fir and his brothers want to be free. That's selfish. All that their mothers have done for them, and they would repay them with betrayal.

Is the freedom of a few warriors worth so many deaths?

I imagine starting a conversation with Kesh. "A warrior told me he is a slave. He'd rather die than fight this war. They would like a sack of Remedy and also the source. Shall I ask Ular myself?"

Men were contained generations ago because of their violence. So now I, Dinitra, all on my own, will release men upon the world, undoing all the good the Weave and even Bounty have done. What gives me the right? Isn't it better that he and his brothers remain bound to their mothers, slaves if need be, for the good of all?

At the Collegium, I believed everything I was told about why things were the way they were, why the Weave put men in containments and judged me by my Sower's plan. When Kesh told me of the Weave's crimes, I believed her, too. Now this: Bounty is built on slavery.

I should keep my mouth shut. That's the safest course. I didn't set out to save anyone, least of all a man.

But I did save Fir, when 12 attacked him. I never meant to. Saving him was what happened. If 12 had leaped at any other warrior, I would have done the same thing, forced myself between him and the hyba cross.

Fir meant to be first. For weeks, Fir has watched me. Out of all of the Captains, he thought I would understand. Because I never felt the Bond. I go back over my weeks in Bounty. Every time I approached the training pen, every time I watched the Captains with their sons, he was watching me.

Did Fir see something in me that even I missed? I once told Petal he had to learn how to see to be able to draw well. *To really see, that's the trick.*

Yet I missed everything about Fir.

I've never had a friend who made me feel warm and cold at the same time. When he said my name, his voice felt like a caress.

A week after my conversation with Fir, I use fresh paper scraps to make lists. I don't want to write any of this in Kesh's book. I title the first scrap WEAVE. I used to think the Weave was everything, that Bounty—Beyond-the-Weave—was a wasteland. *Wasteland*, I write. I make a tick on the paper. *Wrong*.

I used to think I'd never know my Sower.

Sower. Tick.

I knew nothing about drafts. *Tick.* I used to believe that my achievements mattered, that my Compendium would determine my fate.

Nothing mattered. Kesh was always coming for me no matter what I did. *Tick.*

I make a second list, to compare the two. This one I title BOUNTY. I don't feel this Bond. *Tick.* Fir loves his mother, yet he is determined not to be a slave. *Tick.* Is everything my mother told me, everything Shan and Mei told me, a lie? Or are they truths hiding something ugly: slavery. *Tick, tick, tick.*

Some warriors have tongues. Sowers make flawed drafts they kill or discard. Sil, the leader of the drafts, can read thoughts with a touch of her suction fingertip on my skin—is Sil a slave, too? The Captains mean to defeat the Weave they were born to, that made them. If I kept listing things under WEAVE and BOUNTY, I'd need enough of Stoya's scraps to go up and over the Black Stairs. A Signal Way of old clothes, pine bark, sawdust, and cow piss.

On the third list, the list for Fir's world, I write absolutely nothing. I can't even imagine what the Eastern Wastes look like. Or The Deep up north, where the drafts and the renegades go.

Through my window, the streets are empty, the doors and windows of the dwellings shuttered against a light snow. I have to figure this out myself. The only way I've ever known anything is to draw. I go through my sketches. Will I notice now that Fir was watching me all the time? There's Sil at the pool with fish, Petal and his stick figures, the warriors at the trough. Teardrop and Shine, the rabbit drafts, curl around each other by the fire in the

Council Hall. A Captain—Maraz, of the Mother Eyes, with striking gold-flecked eyes—watches her sons train.

I find a portrait of Fir I made soon after I started training the warriors. I was so pleased with the way I captured him that I copied the portrait into Kesh's book.

Now, I see I missed something in his eyes. A knowledge. He knew I was drawing him.

When he taught me how to use the huaraca, his callused hand cupped mine. Cup: *good*. I can still feel the warmth.

I redo the sketch on a fresh scrap. I stop and close my eyes—Fir whirling the huaraca. Fir tumbled by 12 in the training pen. The questions that made me smile. I want to believe him, I want to help him. What would that mean for Bounty? For Shan, Mei, and Petal?

For me?

A new question sends a shiver through me—am I free?

Questions are terrible.

Stretched out in my bed, 12 twitches as she dreams. Are they dog or hyba dreams? Baboon, tiger, or hyena? From the common room below, I hear the clink of dishes, low voices. Sometimes, the younger Captains talk and tell stories late into the night, as I sketch. I feel an urge to go to them, to listen to them.

I'm not fooling myself. What I want is to feel Fir's touch. To go beyond what I know into his embrace.

The shame of it burns my skin. Anku mating with the Sea Hunt warrior. What if someone saw Fir cup my hand? What if someone understood the way he looks at me, as if he will never look away?

What if someone saw how I look at him?

Kesh would die before she'd share the Remedy with the warriors. Every one of the Captains would.

Would I? My answer scares me. *I don't know.*

With a ball of sourwood gum, I erase every sketch of Fir I put in Kesh's book. The scraps—except one—I burn over the flame lamp.

The scrap I keep is the first sketch I drew of Fir. The sketch that shows how he watched me.

It's the only sketch that's true.

I decide to roll the sketch inside my tracker map. I keep the tracker map with me always, in my boot.

I press my thumb to the corner. I'm pleased when it glows just as before, shapes swimming up. There are three spots in Quillka: me, Kesh, and Petal. This time, Anku's spot is in the Weave, just outside the Centrum.

She is Bounty's best guide, I tell myself. But there are no schools in the Centrum. No girls to guide to Bounty.

I take my thumb off the map, press it again. The same.

What could Anku possibly be doing in the Weave?

Awful questions.

This has to be part of the Captains' plan. But after so many lies, I'm suspicious. Could Anku betray Bounty?

Treason, I write on the third scrap of paper. Then I scratch it out. Impossible.

The next morning, the streets are loud with people arriving for the Gemstone docking. I'm deeply asleep, 12 stretched out beside me like a living furnace, when Mei taps at my door. Hurriedly, I scoop up the scraps that litter the floor and place them under Kesh's book.

Mei grins. "There's breakfast laid. All of the Captains are here. No lunch today, so get something while you can. We're feasting this afternoon."

I call 12 to me. Mei shakes her head. "Aren't you forgetting something?"

I panic. Has she found out that I spoke to Fir last night? That he asked me for Remedy so he and his brothers could escape?

"The blue tunic. The one Shan and I gave you. Everyone's wearing their finery." She pulls aside her cloak to show me her tunic, dyed a deep rose.

"Of course."

By the time we get to the Council Hall, there's hardly any room. Dozens of Captains have come to Quillka to honor Shan and her sons. They've brought their Vessels and Keepers, too, and their children and drafts are everywhere.

The servers have decorated the Council Hall ceiling with

paper Stoya made for the occasion, dyed Shan's colors: a rose pink and emerald green. Outside, Stoya is selling whirligigs on sticks, dyed rose and green.

The rabbit drafts, Teardrop and Shine, have retreated to a corner. They watch with wide, brown eyes.

Lam is back from a week-long patrol with her Birds. Her hair is still wet from the baths. She wears the same rose-colored tunic as Mei. But Lam's face is troubled as a thundercloud in the midst of the merriment. As I set down 12's mash and water, she delivers ominous news. "Osprey spotted more helios tethered above the Rift. That makes more than one hundred."

A Captain I don't recognize scoffs. Like Kesh, she's part machine. A metal arm is wired into her shoulder. Her face is thickly tattooed with curling lines. She is broad and almost as tall as Anku. "How many times have I said we should not wait? More times than all of the knobbies I've caught!"

She stretches her flesh hand flat on the table. From wrist to elbow are parallel scars, each no longer than a fingernail. "I'll tell you," she says, looking at her fresh scars. "Seventeen last month alone."

Lam shakes her head. "We voted at Council, Rek. You lost."

This is Rek, the northern Captain. Under her lower lip are studs that give her a permanent metal frown. "You'll curse the day, Lam, when you voted against me. Mark me: this plan you have, this secret plan you Quillka Captains whisper about, will get us all killed."

When 12 returns to my side, her blue-black tongue circles her jaws to get the last crumbs of mash. Rek sees her, then her eyes move to me. "There she is. The famous daughter, so long awaited. The one we've delayed for, the one that cost me boys. Her and that... thing."

I feel like a prize cow. Rek grins as if someone's told a marvelous joke. The Council Hall grows quiet. "What, no metal legs? No springs, no coils? A tender spawn for such a formidable Captain. I expected at least a rivet or two from Kesh's get."

Maraz, Captain of the Mother Eyes, interrupts her. "She

brought the cross as promised. Once you see 12 work, you'll change your tune."

"Why, my youngest boy would have that creature's heart in a pot for my dinner by sundown," Rek fires back.

Rek comes around the table to get a better look at 12. "That's all? That's it? Why by the promises Kesh made, I thought the thing would be big as a mountain, ferocious as a whole pack of hybas."

She shakes her head. "There it lies—a dog."

12's eyes follow the northern Captain.

"What say you, daughter of Kesh?" Rek says to me. "Shall we put your cross to the test against one of my boys? In the street, why not? Help pass the time before the butchery planned for the afternoon."

Shan's been listening with growing anger beside the fire. At Rek's challenge, she pushes her way forward. "There'll be no fighting. Today we celebrate my sons. You offend me, Rek, with your idle threats. This is no Butchery. It is a docking, same as every other son."

"Every other son." Rek responds, "but my own. My threats aren't idle. You should have learned that by now, Shan. My Scream is ten years old. I think he's ready for a fight. Too much peace and food make him fidget. Of all of my boys, he's most like me."

"Save your boasting for battle, Rek."

"In battles, I don't boast. I win." Rek turns her back on Shan. "You're too like your mother, Shan. No fun."

Shan's having none of Rek's lip. "We're here to honor my boys. Respect the day. At Quillka, we've grown weary of your antics."

"Says the Captain whose sons still shit themselves." Rek drains her coffee and sets the cup sharply on the table. "Here's a thought. Let's have my Scream fight any one of your little ones. I'll sweeten the challenge—my Scream against all five of your boys. Blindfolded. I'll put 300 scrip on him. And an empty Vessel for your next batch. I've already got twenty-seven carrying this month. One has twins."

"Enough." Shan is pale with anger. "Today is about becoming

men. It's about my sons. Your boasts, Rek, only insult our Mother."

Rek shrugs. "Our Mother knows full well who'd win. The only insult to the mother are these things." She points at Teardrop and Shine. "Impure. A waste of resources. Corrupted. They'll turn on you one day. You worry about the Weave. I tell you that allowing these laboratory concoctions to live is more dangerous to us that anything in the Weave."

Lam ends the argument. "Shan and Rek. You are both Captains and both pledged to the Council rules."

Lam looks at her daughter. "Shan, you are right to say that ceremony days are to honor the Mother. You must welcome all of our guests, including Rek. And Rek," she says, turning on the northern Captain. "I will take you up on your challenge. Tomorrow. Bird to Blaze, our choice: in the pen. I will sweeten the challenge. Five of my Vessels I will give to you if your Blaze wins. They are experienced and ready for new sons. Does that appeal?"

Rek's metal smile is broad. "With you, Lam? My pleasure. Tell me, Bird Captain. What do you gain from this if I lose?"

"This is what I'll take when my son bests yours." With her height and gray hair, Lam looks like a heron eyeing a squat toad. "I will take one, only one of your Vessels. The one you boasted of, the Vessel carrying your twins. Those twins will be mine."

Rek's face boils with fury. "Never have I heard of one Captain taking the other's sons. Quillka ways, like refusing to fight and refusing to move against the Weave. Like brewing more of these monsters you call drafts." Rek battles to control her words. "I will take that bet and I will take your Vessels to Dolor." Contemptuously, Rek pushes her way to the door. She turns on Lam for a last insult. "Make sure every one of those Vessels is a solid bearer. I expel fallows."

Once Rek is gone, Mei lays a hand on my shoulder. "Every time she comes, there's a terrible argument. Rek is too much alone with her sons. She takes on their violent ways."

"You need Rek for her sons," I say. From listening to the Captains at meals, I know the Blazes are by far the most numerous of the warriors and the most ferocious.

Mei nods. "To keep up that pace, they raid the Weave for Vessels. An ugly thing." Mei notices my shock. "Not many. At least that we know of."

"You mean girls like us?" I say. "Taken by force?"

"No," Mei says quickly, "not like us. Farm girls mostly. They're bred to be Vessels in the Weave. I don't think their lives are much different at Dolor than they would be if they stayed in the Weave. Rek treats them well, so long as they bear."

"And expels Vessels who don't bear. She said it herself. Did you not hear her? Where do they go when they are expelled? Do you even know?"

Mei bites her lip. Rek's use of Vessels concerns her, too. "In the end, every Captain has the right to have their children in the way she deems best. There are rules, Dinitra. If Rek had her way, your 12 would be killed and spit roasted. She thinks drafts are impure. A drain on the Mother. We would never allow her to hurt 12 or any of the drafts. A vessel or two—it's a small price to pay for her loyalty."

"A small price for you. Not for some poor girl taken by the Blazes."

"Rek always does this to us, makes us fight." Mei takes a breath. "Believe me, Dinitra. If I could keep her from taking Weave girls or expelling the Vessels who can't bear, I would. Some Vessels go to The Deep. There are settlements there."

I want to ask her then and there: would the Captains ever let their sons go to The Deep? My brain screams no. The warriors are different, she'd tell me. Their natural state is the Bond. She'd ask: where did you get this idea?

This time, no Captain would call me *brave* for refusing to answer.

"Come." Mei takes my arm as a kind of apology. "Let us go and find a good place to watch the ceremony.

Outside, the streets of Quillka are teeming with farm folk. For them, the Gemstone ceremony is a harvest festival. Vegetables, cheeses and meats, cloth, pumps, huaracas, toys, new boots and armor, all are laid on tables and blankets spread on the street.

The same slingshots I saw in Pergama are being sold here,

dyed bright red. Bones, too, and new cloaks and boots, new crossbows and fresh derak and lither hide.

In the early afternoon, the ceremony takes place in the warrior compound. The compound is inside Quillka's walls, separated from the rest of the town by a low mud barrier. The warriors themselves built the barrier, to mark their own place, Mei tells me.

The warriors' dwellings are rough, raw boards and roofs of straw, circling an open fire pit. The pit is cold, ashes swept away. The armorer is already there, stoking a portable brazier on a stand. The fire sinks into hot coals as the armorer pokes it with the tip of her iron rod.

Spread in a circle around her are pine branches. Inside the circle is a small table with a clay jug, a metal cup hooked to the rim. The armorer wears a thick leather apron and gloves.

The people of Quillka gather on the low barrier, some using it to sit or lean back. It seems that everyone has a treat: spun sugar cones, grilled chicken hearts on sticks, hot pasty pies, ears of fall corn slathered in melted cheese and spicy sauce. One old woman has a cart filled with cheese wheels wrapped in gauze. A thick wedge of the milky-white cheese sells for half a scrip apiece.

The warriors assemble on the other side of the armorer, facing us. They are in formation, a tight half circle several rows deep. Their chests are bare and dusted in white chalk. The chalk coats their eyelids, too, making their eyes flash when they blink.

I can pick out Rek's Blazes. They have the same lip studs as their mother. They've shaved everything on their heads except for the crowns, where their hair is unbound and falls like horse tails to their shoulders. Their scalps are thickly tattooed with the same circles their mother has on her cheeks.

Fir is in back, beside gray-haired Thorn. The ceremony doesn't start until Kesh arrives. Her blades make a muffled thud as she approaches the armorer. Beside her comes Shan, followed by her five young Gemstones.

Shan holds the hand of the eldest. He holds the hand of his brother and so on. The youngest can't be more than eight.

The boys' hair adornments match their mother's: green and rose ribbon woven into elbow-length braids. The last two in line are weeping. Shan places a kiss on their heads before passing the two youngest boys to Mei.

Mei tries to soothe them. "Your time will come." She tucks one under each arm, then takes them to buy spun sugar cones.

Over the Black Stairs, a bank of clouds creeps north. Overhead, the sky is still clear. The air is surprisingly pleasant so late in the year.

My hand rests on 12's brow, which twitches as she scans the crowd.

Lam, elegant in a dove-gray cloak, joins Shan to face the armorer. Kesh stands with her, watchful. The warriors start the ceremony with a welcome dance. As one, they raise their arms. They stamp their feet, then stamp again, their eyes a white flame. The warriors shout a wordless song. With the dust rising, they turn and flick out their tongues. They pound their chests, sending up puffs of white chalk.

The hair on 12's neck bristles. Her tail sweeps against my legs. "Stay," I tell her softly.

Petal sidles up beside me, mouth dusted in pasty-pie crumbs.

"Is that water?" I ask about the jug next to the armorer.

"Naw." For once, Petal doesn't call me knobbie. "Forgetting."

"Pardon?"

"Distilled from whatnot. For the pain," Petal says.

Shan kisses the tallest boy on the forehead, then lays his hand on the armorer's leather glove. I wonder if Shan's weeping, since her cheeks sparkle. I look more closely. Lam has it, too: a powder of crushed mica that catches catch the orange glow of the coals.

The armorer pours a splash of forgetting into the cup. Shan gives the cup to the boy, making sure he drinks deeply. He slumps into her arms.

Still supporting him, Shan grips the boy's hair and pulls sharply back. His chin rises and his mouth opens. The armorer pulls a knife she's had heating in the coals. With one hand, she pulls the boy's tongue out. With the other, she severs his tongue.

Blood spurts from the boy's mouth. The armorer shoves the knife back under the coals as she tosses the tongue into the pine branches. She lifts the iron rod. With its red-hot tip, she sears the boy's wound closed.

12 sneezes, the stench of burning flesh sharp in the air.

Shan carries her eldest son to one of Lam's Birds. One by one, each of the Birds holds him. The last Bird carries the boy into one of the dwellings, then returns alone.

My tongue feels heavy in my mouth. The armorer completes the same procedure two more times: forgetting, the knife, the searing rod. The third Gemstone weeps openly as his mother leads him forward. Instead of taking the armorer's hand, he grabs Shan by the waist and buries his head against her.

Her embrace is tender. She whispers in his ear. The boy allows the armorer to pull him to the brazier.

"In the Weave, they'd call this cruel," I say to Petal. I don't care who hears.

"Cruel it is." Petal scuffs his boot in the dirt—my old boot. "The docking makes them warriors. Some say, who cares about that lump in your mouth? Have you no crook?" He wiggles his thumb at his crotch, to mimic the male appendage. I saw it when Ular's two Harvest sons bathed at the swimming hole. Boys with tongues aren't considered fully male, Petal is saying.

When the armorer's finished, she dumps the coals into the boughs then fans them.

Everything—the boughs, the blood, the severed tongues—burns with a sharp, nauseating smell.

25

Mother's Kiss

I wish I had a jug of forgetting to drink. I'd bathe in it, wash my hair in it, scrub the calluses of my feet with it. I'd dive into it like Sil does water, then open my eyes to wash them clean of what I saw at the docking.

There's not a drop of forgetting at the feast laid in the Council Hall. Ular, the Captain of the Harvest, is pouring mugs of beer from a barrel that's been tipped on its side. Froth drips down her thick forearms.

"I call this Gemstone Ale, for my lovely Shan," Ular announces loudly. She's clearly been sampling a fair amount of beer. "A bit of ground apple skin, for the color. And the tenderest hops this side of the Crags."

The servers have filled long tables with beet slaw and lamb shanks glistening with mint and butter, wheat puddings crusted with candied pine nuts, golden pasty-pies fragrant with onion and still steaming. Along one wall, there's a whole row of cheeses, the sour-faced cheese-maker standing by to slice with her long knife.

Rek's Vessels and Keepers mix with their Quillka friends. In a corner, a trio of musicians plays pipes and a drum as children and drafts dance.

Kesh is there, congratulating Shan. At her throat, Shan has her Gemstone clasp.

I push my way into a corner with 12. This is surprisingly hard since everyone has become used to 12. Hands reach out to stroke her sides. Some offer their crusts, even though they know she will accept nothing. One little draft finally gets a good grab of her tail. 12 suffers the draft to slide behind her for several steps, the draft shrieking with delight, before she shakes the draft off.

We find a narrow bench. 12 stretches out in front of me, her head on her paws, watching the crowded room.

The docking made up my mind. I will help Fir. Nothing about the docking is necessary. Those boys would become just as much men with their tongues intact.

But it's not just the docking. It's Rek, too, and her boasts about expelling Vessels. About capturing Weave girls south of the Rift.

About exterminating drafts.

Trust what you see, not what you're told, Professor Wylla said.

I can't change the war. But I can protect my friends. Protect Fir. I'm planning on slipping into the kitchens to search for a sack of Remedy when I see Sil approaching through the crowd. Behind her comes Darling, the sea creature draft that can't be touched. Behind her waddle the two rabbit drafts, Teardrop and Shine. They are still chewing on the corn they bought at the docking. They've gone past the kernels and into the cob itself.

"They wanted to see the fun," Sil tells me. "It's not often Darling can be near so many people. No one must touch her. Perhaps she can sit with you and 12? 12 can keep her safe."

"Of course."

I direct 12 to lay in front of the drafts, a mountain range to protect them. Sil sits next to me on the bench. For several minutes, we watch as Captains hug friends who've been away on patrol and boast about how many legionaries and hybas they've encountered on patrol.

Through the crowd, Ular spots me. I remember seeing her dozing in the Sower laboratory. She offers me a dripping mug of beer. "Shan's compliments!"

Froth sprays me and 12 both as The Harvest's Captain

stumbles. "Drink with us, fine daughter of Kesh! Someday, it will be your turn to celebrate the docking of your sons!"

12 shakes her head, tentatively lickings the froth from her paws. "To the Gemstones!" Ular shouts, raising her mug.

"To the Gemstones!" Fresh beer splashes to the already sticky floor.

Ular leans close, her cheeks mottled from drink. "Don't be so glum, Kesh's daughter. It's a hard thing to see the first time. Remember this. Without their mothers, our sons would be unprotected as pups. It's our duty to do what's best for them."

I don't bother pointing out that without their mothers, there would be no sons. Another cheer goes up across the room.

"Eat your fill tonight," Ular says, swinging her mug up, "for who know what comes tomorrow!" She stumbles off, arcs of beer splashing to the floor.

Sil's gold-lipped gills flare with amusement. "She is always the happiest at parties."

I have to bend close to hear. Sil stretches out her suction-cupped fingers to share thoughts without speaking.

I pull back. My thoughts are full of Fir and stealing a sack of Remedy. Not for sharing. "The docking is horrible," I say.

Sil nods.

"How many dockings have you seen?"

"Many." Now that I'm used to her strange aspect, Sil is pleasing to look at: even features, the slick pebbled skin. Her striking eyes, one blue and one orange.

"I don't understand how they can celebrate such a thing. The Gemstones may be males, but they're not beasts."

"Beasts." Sil's voice is liquid, soothing. "You would not care if they did such things to beasts? To drafts like me?"

"I'm sorry, I didn't mean that. It's a saying."

"A saying," Sil repeats.

My cheeks flush red. "It's wrong whether it's a male or a beast. I would care, of course I would."

My voice quavers. "One of them cried. He was afraid. He knew what was happening."

"Agate," Sil says. "He swims with me. He is a good boy."

"Do they always cry?"

"Sometimes. They are with each other constantly until they are docked. There are many reasons why a boy may cry."

"Like what else?"

"These are emotions one can only know from the inside. They are excited. They have been waiting for this their whole lives. They have been told they will be warriors after this day. They are frightened. They have seen their older brothers wounded. They are eager, to fight. Many things."

I barely hear Sil over the talk and laughter. I wish I could touch the draft without revealing what I plan to do for Fir.

Sil seems to understand my hesitation. "There is no need to be afraid of me wandering your thoughts," Sil says. "I will not hear what you do not want me to hear."

"You hear everything. That's what Kesh said."

"I do not hear everything," Sil answers.

"What if there is something a boy doesn't want you to know? Would that boy still let you touch them?"

"Sometimes. I can also touch to speak only. I don't have to wander." Sil's smile is gentle. "That's what I call it. Wandering thoughts. Have you ever wandered that way, without a place to go?"

"12 and I go for walks."

"Just so. I don't always wander. Sometimes, I sit where I sit and talk."

"With Kesh, my mother. Did you wander? She said she only touches you with her metal hand."

"The first time. Yes. I wandered. That was before I was able to control my ability."

"What did you see?" I blurt. "Did you see her fall?"

"I do not share what I see with others without their permission. I do not wander if you wish me to stay in one place."

The more I know, the better I will be able to help Fir. Protect 12. And maybe someday find my own way to The Deep.

"May I?" I make the shape for please: my palm moving out from my forehead. I'm nervous, but willing to trust Sil. Instead of having Sil touch me, I place my hand on the back of Sil's hand.

"It doesn't work that way," she says gently. The draft places a single suction cup on my inner wrist. *There*, I hear in her liquid voice. *I will take it off whenever you wish.*

The sound of the celebration fades. Sil speaks in a delicate tremor. "The last thing they remember is their mother's kiss. That's the warriors' word for the ceremony you saw: the mother's kiss."

I speak to Sil's mind. "It's horrible. I'm told Rek's sons all keep their tongues and have no virus."

Sil's voice in my mind is both young and like a grown human. "They believe what they've been taught. We all do, until we teach ourselves."

"Rek was taught. Yet she refuses to follow the others. She refuses to harm her sons. She puts no virus in them. That is something."

"There are things Rek does that you might not find so admirable."

"Like what?"

Sil looks at Darling. "Rek hates drafts. She thinks these Captains waste valuable resources on us. She thinks humans should be pure, animals and plants, too. No mixing. No experiments. If she had her way, we'd all be exterminated. She proposes this at every Council. Burdens, she calls us. Worse: thieves, criminals. That someday we will kill them in their sleep. She even made a shape for burden, so the warriors would speak of it."

Without removing the suction cup that allows us to communicate, Sil lifts her other hand. Burden: three fingers curled, like something hanging on a back.

"Are drafts slaves? Couldn't the drafts leave if they wanted to?"

"They are not slaves. Some leave. Others stay."

My heart beats faster. "And the warriors, are they slaves?"

Sil's tone doesn't change. "Some believe so. None can leave regardless of what they think."

"Because of Remedy."

"Yes."

"The males without virus. Are they slaves?"

I feel Sil's hesitation. "What you speak of is not wise."

"Petal has no virus." I state this as a fact. "Neither do the Blazes."

"True."

I feel like I'm on the edge of a precipice. The edges of Sil's golden gills tremble. "Some who have no virus leave," Sil says. "Blazes and the beast-born. The beast-born are called wildmen. Like the Blazes, they do not need Remedy. Rek has many warriors in Bounty. The Master has three times that number."

Fir spoke of a Master. "He is...east of here?"

Sil's eyes flick to see if anyone is watching. "There is Seven Lake. A city. There, a Master dwells. Many of these warriors would go to him if they could free themselves of virus. If they had Remedy or knew its source."

"Do you know the source?"

Sil pauses. "That is a dangerous question. Even a Bond may not protect you."

"What could Kesh do?"

"I don't know. And I don't want to test her."

For a long moment, we are silent. Sil's finger is light on my skin. "Did you notice the direction the Living Wood placed the feet of Ash before he burned?" Sil asks.

I shake my head.

"East. The warriors believe that when they die, their ghost travels there, to join the Master in the world of men."

"And what of drafts? Do you point the feet of drafts east before they burn?"

"The Master has no love of drafts. He is like Rek. He would have us all burn. All of us," Sil says, looking at 12.

Her gills flare. Through touch, I feel Sil's emotion. She is frightened for me. "Fir spoke to you. I know what he asked. He has spoken to me of this, too. He risks everything. His mother would be ruthless if she knew."

"As she was with Ash."

"Like it or not, that was a kindness. An end to his suffering. Timbe would make an example of Fir."

I feel Sil wandering my thoughts, to my feelings for Fir. I can tell those feelings frighten her far more than any chance I would give Fir Remedy. "You promised you wouldn't wander in my mind."

"I see this on your face, Dinitra. I have no need to wander. Others may see it, too. Every time you look at Fir, it is there: an affection, I think you call it. This cannot be hidden."

I recoil. With her free hand, Sil grasps mine. Her voice is unchanged: slow, sinuous. "I am Fir's friend. Believe me when I tell you that the punishment for him would be far worse than anything you saw today."

12 raises her head. The tip of her tail twitches and she stands, shielding us.

It's Rek, waggling a half-gnawed rib. Scornfully, she tosses the rib to 12. At any other time, I would look forward to examining her face tattoos: swirls and circles punctuated by the studs in her lower lip. She plants her feet aggressively just an arm's length from 12.

12's tail tuft ticks.

"Here is our reason for delaying our actions against the fleet. A daughter and a dog. Tell me, girl. Why have we risked so much for a single life?"

Mei appears beside her, already agitated, as if she and Rek have been arguing. "You yourself reclaimed your daughters, Rek. Would you deny Kesh this Bond? Dinitra is the only Bond she has."

Rek's face twists. "Yes."

Rek turns on Mei. "Are you so stupid? Remind me. How many sons have you? How many daughters?"

"Keep talking." I've never seen Mei so fierce. "Maybe that hot air will blow the helios back across the Stairs."

A thrum of amusement runs through the crowd.

Rek sends a wad of spit to the floor, just missing my boot. "I'll put my boys against your tinctures and potions any day, Mei. You'll see tomorrow how my Burn bests any one of your mother's sons."

"I'll be sure to remember that when one of your sons is ailing and needs a fysic."

"My Torment is the best fysic in all of Bounty!" Rek picks meat from between her teeth. "Mei, I am truly moved by seeing Kesh's daughter befriend that frog-thing. Is that the future for Quillka, this mixing of daughter and frog? What babes will they make? Gills, certainly. Perhaps their spawn will hop!"

The Northern Captain slaps her thigh as she guffaws. Rek's eyes go to Darling, who is trying to make herself small in the corner. "And by the Mother's eyes, what thing is that?" Rek reaches for one of Darling's tentacles.

I block her.

Rek tries to shove my arm away.

Then the floor trembles.

12 is up and growling. She would take down a Captain as easily as a warrior.

Good, I think. I find 12's golden eyes. "Sit," I say, repeating the command with my hand. "The draft is not to be touched," I tell Rek. Without turning, I say to Sil. "Take Darling, Teardrop, and Shine outside."

As Sil leads the drafts away, people are careful not to touch Darling's tentacles.

"Your tongue's had enough exercise this day," Mei says to Rek. "Ular's beer barrel needs draining. Drink, be happy for my sister. Then go back to Dolor."

Rek is not so easily banished. Her real argument is with Kesh and I am Kesh's daughter. "We waited," she says, biting every word, "and we waited. We waited more. For a dog. For a girl. Kesh betrays us, she betrays us with that tongueless lump she calls a sister."

I haven't seen Anku for weeks. That's why Petal has been moping around, sneaking into my room.

There's commotion at the door. Several Blazes push toward their mother.

Lam rushes toward them, Timbe, Hisla, and Maraz behind her. "Order them out, Rek! No warriors are allowed in the Council Hall. You know this."

They stop a Blaze from entering. He has flame-orange hair in a messy tail down his back. No braid, no ribbon or beads. Around his neck is hung a string of yellow hyba teeth.

"At Dolor, my sons go where they will," Rek says.

Lam towers over her. "This is not Dolor"

"No need for shouting." Rek's smile is malicious. "I only wish to show you the Vessel you will not win tomorrow. She bears my twins."

Behind the Blaze, I see the swell of a Vessel's belly. Rek jabs her finger at Lam. "You need us, sister, more than we need you. Any one of my Blazes can split this draft-dog in a stroke."

The warriors step aside. The Vessel raises her head. "I'll get a whole squadron out of this one," Rek says, pulling her forward.

I want to scream. The Vessel is Susalee.

It can't be Susalee. She's at Holdfast.

It's absolutely Susalee, with her red-gold hair. Her belly is enormous, but her legs and arms are stick thin.

"Twenty more Blazes will I have by months end." Rek pulls Susalee close. "You, sister Mei. You and all of the others. All you have are useless drafts. Drafts you should have put out of their misery long ago."

26

Susalee

Rek talks about Susalee like an enhanced cow or nanny goat.

I don't think Susalee sees me. Her eyes are cupped in dark circles. What would I even say? I crossed the Rift in July, over a year ago. By the looks of her belly, Susalee must have been taken last fall, while I trained alone with 12.

While I was in Bounty, she was too. With Rek.

I wish I had Sil's gift to communicate with a touch. "I know Rek's Vessel," I whisper in Mei's ear, "she was with me at the Collegium."

I babble. "Susalee wasn't brewed to be a Vessel. She wanted to be a Sower. She was always the best. She was a legionary, Mei. How is that possible?"

"Walk with me."

We leave Rek boasting about her twins, her son at her side, as the Bounty Captains fume. Mei leads me to the Sower laboratory. "No one's here today," she says. "We can talk."

The cold is penetrating, and I wish I had my regular wool tunic. Mei walks through the empty waiting room and past the hooded consoles and stacks of little dishes half-filled with orange medium. In the Captains' resting room, the braziers are cold. She sits on a couch, a pillow and blanket folded neatly at the end.

"I feel like you're going to tell me something awful," I say.

Mei pats the space next to her. "Rek has a way of making everything complicated."

I sit and Mei drapes a blanket over our laps. 12 lays herself at our feet but stays vigilant. In the street outside, people are still celebrating the docking. "Rek is a brilliant fighter. She and her boys. Within reason, she gets what she wants."

"Within reason," I repeat.

Mei takes my hand. "Dinitra, it hasn't been easy. I know you see Bounty as peaceful, with food and buildings. Heat. It wasn't always that way. For many years, they suffered. When Rek came, she questioned a lot of the old ways. It's partly because of her that Bounty is able to even challenge the Weave and its evil."

"Girls in the Weave aren't forced to be Vessels, Mei. Something they're not even brewed for!"

Mei's eyes are guarded. "Are you so sure of that?"

I'm not, but that doesn't make it right whatever side of the Rift you're on. "We're talking about our own kind, Mei. Girls like us."

"Yes. And we need more sons."

"To fight."

Mei nods. "Sacrifices have to be made. It's unfortunate you knew her."

"Knew? That's someone I grew up with! I know her. Her name is Susalee."

"I'm sorry. Yes. *Know.*" Mei cups her hand around my cheek. "I wish this war was over so we could all live in peace. I think you and I...well, I think you feel it, too."

Gently, Mei presses her lips to mine. She tastes of oolieberries.

I let her draw me close, our fingers entwined. I've long wondered what it would feel like to have a particular affection. When we part, Mei's brown eyes search mine. I want to kiss her again.

Yet I hesitate. Why has she brought me here, to this laboratory? Why only after I recognized Susalee? Trust what you see, Dinitra, not what you're told, Professor Wylla told me.

What I see is Mei trying to keep me from talking to Susalee.

I pull away. "I'd like to think I would be upset if anyone was forced to be a Vessel." Even as I say that, I know I'm lying. If I hadn't known Susalee, I wouldn't have thought twice about seeing her dragged forward by the Blaze.

"We need Vessels, Dinitra. We need sons," Mei says. "Rek's Blazes are our most numerous warriors. It's about numbers, not what's easy."

"Easy? What if that were Shan?"

"It's not Shan," Mei snaps. "We had our mother to protect us."

"Doesn't Susalee have a mother somewhere, too?" My mother sacrificed her body for me. For years, she planned to bring me out of the Weave.

Susalee has no one.

Mei runs her hand over her close-cropped hair. She goes on about the Bond and the coming war and how the Weave throws away drafts. All things I know. How does any of that justify what Rek did to Susalee?

It's natural to look the other way when people you need do something awful. It's also easy to turn your back when the people they hurt need you.

Mei splays her hands out. In shape language that's *forgive*. "These are hard choices. Where would you draw the line, Dinitra?"

I draw lines to see, to understand, not choose someone's fate. I motion for 12 to stand. "That's not what you said before. You said you'd stop it if you could."

It's not about the drafts or the Bond or even all of us. It's not about men, either. It's about who gets to decide. I hear the words in Sil's liquid voice as she wandered my thoughts: *humans should be pure, animals and plants, too. If Rek had her way, we'd all be exterminated. Burdens, she calls us. Thieves, criminals.* Does Rek get to decide Susalee's fate? Does she get to say who is a burden? How long until Mei lays out her hands apologetically to say that 12 is a burden?

That Bounty no longer needs the warriors.

Slaves.

Once, all I wanted was to belong. I wanted to do what I was told, fit in. I didn't understand what that meant.

In Susalee's desperate eyes, I saw the price. In Sil's, in Fir's. Belonging has a price I'm not willing to pay.

I'm lucky Mei has none of Sil's ability to wander my mind. "If it makes you feel better," Mei says, "none of the other Captains take Weave girls. They use Vessels meant to carry sons."

"For now."

I mean my words sarcastically, but Mei nods. "We have to do what we can to win."

I want to scream at her. Where does it stop? I'd sound like some mewling pup. The Weave is coming to kill us, Captain, son, and draft. What are the Captains supposed to do?

Mei's sister Shan told me once not to judge things I knew little about. How can I not judge a world that gives one person the right to force another. To make another a slave. To kill another?

Mei looks at me imploringly. "I'm not saying Bounty is perfect. I chose not to have sons, as you know. That's my decision. Rek made a different decision. We all do this for the greater good. You have to believe me, Dinitra. It's terrible for your friend. In the end, it will be the right thing for the rest of us. Why, I've seen Vessel after Vessel weep when they've been chosen to bear sons."

"Chosen?" I interrupt. "Susalee was forced."

"Enough." It's the first Mei has been impatient with me. "When those sons are born, when the Vessels see them, they're proud. Proud. Making new life like that? Your friend—Susalee—may not have chosen this. But once those sons are born, she'll change her mind, I'm sure of it. She'll see the bigger picture."

Mei shakes her head. "If only we could have brought you earlier. You would better understand the Bond."

"If only my mother hadn't fallen, you mean, when she tried to take me as a baby."

Mei looks at me coldly. "Rek's right, you know. Kesh refused to move against the Weave until she had you back. We've lost Captains, Dinitra, and sons because of that decision. You are quick to judge others. Remember, your life has cost us dearly. You owe us this much: loyalty."

27

Renegades

Rek and her sons are slowly making their way down Quillka's main street to their ships, tethered beyond the training pen. As they go, they are buying spun sugar cones and roast corn and the last of the rose and green paper whirligigs.

They are leaving for Dolor.

I duck back into my room to scribble a note to Susalee. I have to let her know that I am here. I saw her. I wish I had time to look at my lists again, puzzle out what I should do.

I know what I have to do.

I will rescue her. She may not know her mother. Her mother may not know the Bond or want to protect her.

Susalee knows me. I am going to be brave for her.

It's all tied together: Susalee, Fir. Sil and the drafts. In exchange for Remedy, Fir will show me how to get to Dolor. I'll find some way to rescue Susalee. From there, we can head for The Deep.

We'll be renegades together. It's a crazy plan, awful, impossible.

I have 12. I have a tracker map. How is this any crazier than being assigned the Legion? Climbing a twisting, icy ladder into a

Legionship? Training a draft who smells of burnt butter and would give her life for me if I asked?

I push aside any thought of my mother, who sacrificed for me. Of the Bond. I am betraying her just as she betrayed the Weave.

No Bond should force me to stand by while people I love are hurt.

Dearest Susalee: I am in Bounty. Scrags took me when I crossed the Rail. I will come for you in Dolor. Don't despair. Dinitra.

As I push through the crowd toward Rek's ships, I think I will try to convince Fir to come with me to The Deep. When I kissed Mei, I felt desire whirl up inside my chest, a force I've never felt before. It wasn't for Mei. I wish Fir had been the one pulling me close.

I never knew I was a daughter. If I am a beast as well, so be it.

Rek's dozens of Vessels and Keepers accompany her. Among them are little Blazes, who jump and race around their warrior brothers. They have the same tattoos as the boys I saw captured at Holdfast, their necks collared in her name: REKREKREKREKREKREKREK.

12 lifts her snout high to catch their scents, her tail lashing.

Rek's ships are a battered collection of croakers and old transports, refitted to use the fuel of Bounty's solar arrays. I've tucked Susalee's note in my satchel of drawing things. I'm always carrying it. No one will think to know I have a secret message tucked in Kesh's book.

I just have to get close enough to Susalee to give her the note without anyone seeing.

Easy, right? I feel the first glimmer of fear that this plan is not so well thought out.

Petal appears at my side, doing his peculiar skip-walk. His mouth is smeared with red sugar from the cone. It's the first time I've seen him happy since Anku left.

The largest croaker's hull is patched with lither scraps and slashed with orange and red paint. On the side is a name: Destiny.

"That's Rek's alone!" Petal crows, pointing. "Famous that one is. From Destiny, Rek directs every battle."

I spot Susalee: trailing behind the other Vessels, painfully slow. Rek struts in front, as if she's leading a joyous parade. Burn, the orange-haired son who brought Susalee into the Council Hall, walks beside her.

Petal tells me Burn will fight one of Lam's Birds in the training pen before Rek leaves. I know Rek won't take her eyes off him. That's my chance to give the note to Susalee.

Kesh and Lam are grim-faced as they follow the Blazes to the training pen.

"Osprey it is." Petal hoots with delight. "There with his shield? He'll best that bloody Burn!"

Beside Lam walks a warrior. His hair is pulled up and freshly braided with gray and black ribbon. He has a confident swagger. Despite the cold, Osprey has no cloak. His chest is bare over his leggings and boots.

"Gaw." Petal's thoughtful. "Wish I could see old Dolor again. Formidable it is, made of lava rock. Rek's labyrinth is at the very center."

"Formidable. That's an interesting word for a place."

Petal shrugs. "Ain't beautiful or fine. Formidable fits."

As Osprey and Burn reach the training pen to fight, there's a commotion behind them. I think it must be other warriors sparring. A whisper races through the crowd. A Vessel is down.

12 clears a way through the crowd.

The commotion is Susalee. She crouches, moaning deeply. A Blaze pulls at her arm to get her standing. A wet spot spreads down her cloak.

Susalee falls to her side. A figure pushes his way forward: Thorn, Fir's gray-haired brother.

Fir bends over Thorn's shoulder as Thorn gestures, *Bring me my supplies.*

Susalee's face clenches in pain. I use 12 and her bared fangs to clear a space around her and Thorn. Even Rek, red-faced, can't get close.

Susalee's face glistens with sweat. "Whoever you are," she says to Thorn, "kill me. Kill me before this thing does."

Her belly heaves. Susalee screams. Thorn motions for me to support her head. I whisper in her ear, "Hold on, dear Susalee."

She doesn't know me. "Why don't you kill me?" she weeps.

"Put her on the ship!" Rek screams. "It will be hours yet. My son Torment will birth the twins."

Thorn reaches under her cloak. He shakes his head. I don't understand the sign he makes. When he lifts his hands, the meaning is clear. They are slick with blood.

Susalee is having these babies now.

Someone brings a blanket, to shade her. A flask of water appears. I wet my hand, then press it to Susalee's forehead.

She grunts, oblivious. Fir kneels beside his brother with the fysics kit: alcohol, disinfectant, forgetting. Thorn has Fir douse his hands in clear alcohol, sharp in the warm air.

Thorn removes a vial of forgetting and presses the opening to Susalee's lips.

Fir looks at me and for the first time I know I am weeping. "The Vessel won't remember a thing," he says.

I want to punch him. "Her name is Susalee. *Susalee.* She was forced. You of all people should understand that."

I immediately regret my words. But everyone is staring at Susalee, not me.

"Susalee." Fir says. His eyes find mine. "Susalee won't remember a thing."

Fir's brothers push back the crowd, even Rek. She's boxed in and fuming between Lam and Ular. Several little Blazes stare at their mother with wide eyes.

Susalee is oblivious. When her belly heaves, Thorn gently parts her knees. There's a fluttery feeling under my ribs, like I've eaten a moth or bee. I never thought I'd see a babe being born.

Suddenly, Susalee screams again. The pain has knifed through the forgetting. Thorn reaches beneath her cloak. Susalee twists, almost wrenching away from me.

Thorn's hands are a blur as he motions to Fir. "He says the first son is backwards. Thorn has to turn him. Hold her tightly, Dinitra."

He's close enough for me to touch. From somewhere, Petal

slips in to grip Susalee's hand. Thorn hums, as if the tune, whatever it is, will help Susalee and the babies live.

With both hands splayed, Thorn presses firmly below Susalee's belly, then up. He's shifting the babies while they are still inside her. On the surface of Susalee's skin, I see bumps moving: knees, elbows. I can't help remembering the sac in the laboratory, when Mei waved and the little Sea Hunt draft waved back.

Thorn reaches between Susalee's legs. She groans again. After several minutes of pushing, Thorn lifts up a squirming infant. The infant is dripping blood and mucus, a stout flesh cord still attaching him to his Vessel.

To Susalee.

Someone hands Thorn a cloth. He wraps the child just as it starts to wail. Petal takes it, his face alive with wonder.

The next son comes quickly. Again, Thorn wraps it. By then, Rek has broken free and takes the babe from him.

"Eleventh twins!" Rek's face is triumphant.

Kesh is there, and Rek lifts the baby's still-bloody body into the air. "These sons I name for you, Kesh. This one I call Ruin. What we will make of the Weave. The other I call Rage. Is that not a lovely name for such a strong warrior? He forced his way out before his brother. This Vessel will deliver me a squadron before I'm through with her."

Rek looks around for Petal, still holding Rage. Her voice is deceptively kind. "You are Anku's beast-born son. I remember you when you were this small." She looks admiringly at her boy. "Come with me to Dolor. Learn what it means to be a Blaze. Board Destiny with me and these fresh boys."

Kesh steps forward. "He stays with Anku."

Rek's eyes are malicious. She would hurt Petal if given half a chance. "Where, bless the Mother, is Anku? I did not see her at the docking."

The last time I looked at my tracker map, Anku was in the Weave. Rek strokes the studs under her lip. "I wonder, friend Kesh, if you and your sister are entirely loyal to Bounty. Once a traitor..."

Lam moves toward her. "I will gut you."

Rek doesn't flinch. "My Burn will best your Osprey, Lam. Let us go and watch. If we have time, he will give you a proper lesson in gutting. Are your Vessels ready to board my Destiny?"

Rek turns her back on Lam: an insult. To one of her sons, she shouts, "Get this Vessel boarded! Then to the pen to watch your brother gut a Bird!"

By now, with the babies born, only Thorn is still with Susalee. He's wrapped Susalee in her bloody cloak.

I pull out my note.

Susalee has no pocket or bag or hat or anything to hide a note. Still, she does not know me, another blurred face through the haze of forgetting.

Then a Blaze shoves me aside. He lifts Susalee onto his shoulder and carries her away, her red-gold hair like a pelt down his broad back.

I feel like I'm the one who's been gutted. She won't remember I was there. She won't know I'm coming to rescue her.

Dolor, I tell myself. When I reach Dolor, she'll know me.

From Quillka, I hear a shout. A Dream pounds toward us, his white hair flying. Behind him run the townspeople. Their screams hit me a second later. 12 chuckles, unusual for her. It means she sees the fight coming. Her snout is tipped up and she stares at the sky. Far above hangs a black crescent. The crescent is vertical, like a sliver of dark moon facing south and speared on a dense, pulsing cable of light.

The Concave. The great ship refracts the light downwards, to dozens of helios speeding across the Stairs. They look like embers from an enormous fire.

Kesh opens her arms wide. Her great blades churn against the ground as she runs toward Quillka. "Scatter!" she bellows.

A pulsar blast whirls from the closest helio and smashes the Council Hall. The roof collapses. A huge mushroom of smoke billows up. The blast wave comes a second later, hurling Kesh into the air. Her back arches and she slams backwards into a tree.

For an instant, the blast wave peels 12's lips into a snarl. I roll helplessly, eating dust.

When I'm able to stand again, Kesh is gone.

Rek is boarding Destiny, Susalee dragged behind her by two Blazes. I've lost track of the babies and Petal. Another pulsar hits Quillka: the warriors' quarters. A woman pounds past me carrying a rack of spun sugar cones that fly off like pink and green birds. A Keeper drags two children, boys or girls, I can't tell. Fir is looking for something and I think it's me.

I count forty bright embers.

Rek was right. The fleet was ready.

Another pulsar hits Quillka's gate. I feel the rumble of falling timbers through my boots. The next pulsar hits a solar array, and it pops, then bursts into flame. One of Rek's cruisers explodes. The smoke throws a quick shadow. Metal shards whirl into the air.

A flock of hens brushes my ankles. The armorer stumbles by, waving an iron pincer. I fall to my knees, my ears stabbed by a thousand knives. Vibros. Petal told me about them: *zound, zound*. A warrior—a Mother Eye—opens his mouth and vanishes in a puff of brilliant ash.

Blood streams from 12's ears. I can't hear a thing. I see her muscles strain as she howls. She'd rip the fleet from the air if she could, take them in her jaws and dismember them rudder to prow. She'd shake loose the pilots and rip those threads of fuel apart.

Pilots who could be Mariza and Edba. Becke. Helma. I want to wave my hands, beg them to stop.

They would not stop for a scrag like me. *Mother save Fir and his brothers. My mother. Susalee.*

A vibro zounds again. I know because blood from my ears gushes down my neck. One of the drafts—not Darling, a different sea creature, with long yellow tentacles and a protruding nose—bursts like a sack filled with purple jam.

A Vessel lumbers past. Behind her, a Keeper collapses where she stands, the baby she was carrying rolling from her like a toy.

A shape swoops in: Thorn, Fir's brother. He checks the Keeper. She's dead. Thorn scoops up the baby and keeps running.

Petal tucks Rage like a ball under his arm. His sack of toy

warriors is slung over his shoulder. With his free hand, Petal pulls me away. *We have to run*, he motions.

He thrusts his hands at my stunned face, his fingers flicking across his palm. *Run or be dust.*

I run.

28

Cheese seller

I run as far as I can. Petal is always ahead, carrying little Rage. Every other step, I see 12's great snout raised, her whiskers trembling, then the spasm: a sneeze in perfect silence.

I walk only when the people of Quillka are too exhausted to run anymore. 12 keeps pace next to me, her great tail sweeping back and forth. All of that training with the warriors. Yet Quillka burns behind, great billows of smoke trailing toward the Black Stairs. For hours, the Concave hovers, pouring light into the helios that smash Quillka to bits.

As the sun sets, the ash turns the sky a brilliant orange and purple. The snow starts as swirling flakes and then I see this is not snow but freezing ash.

None of us can hear a thing. With my hands, I ask Petal, *Will the Legion follow?*

Petal gestures glumly. *They don't need the Legion no more. From the sky, they'll kill us all. Or we'll starve.*

A pulsar blast flattened Kesh. What happens to a dot on a tracker map when that person dies? I'm about to pull the map from my boot when I see Petal whispering in little Rage's ear, to soothe him. If he finds out his mother is in the Weave—that Anku may have betrayed us—he'll shrivel up with grief.

Where are the warriors? I ask Petal.

His fingers skim his palm. *Scattered.*

Will they fight?

I hope they run.

Where are we going?

Petal circles his ears with a finger. *Did you lose your brain and your ears? The only place we can: Dolor.*

The milk cow in front of us carries two full sacks of flour strapped across her bony back. Each plodding step sends a white puff into the air. From slings on the Keepers' backs, infants stare with frightened eyes.

The cheese-seller harnessed herself between the prongs of her cart, still loaded with the cheese wheels she was selling at the Gemstones' ceremony. She has a few pots, knives, and blankets as well as a nanny goat tied to a side rail. She is Keeper to two of Maraz's youngest Mother Eyes, who walk beside her.

When the goat opens its mouth to bleat, I hear nothing. The two rabbit drafts—Teardrop and Shine—sit on a cheese wheel and weep. Huddled under a blanket is the draft Darling, her grey tentacles pale and sickly.

For them, the Weave's victory is a death sentence.

Rek's victory would be death, also: to me, to 12, to Petal. To every one of the drafts.

Tiring, Petal hands little Rage to Teardrop, who presses the baby against her furry belly.

My plan to steal Remedy for Fir, rescue Susalee, and go like renegades into The Deep seems like a child's foolishness. Like Petal playing with his stick figures. In Spectronomy, we learned that light is infinite unless something blocks it. Or snuffs it out at the source. What can possibly stop that murderous light from feeding the Concave and the helios all the way to Dolor?

Or past it, anywhere the Weave decides to go?

Nothing. In shape language, the fingers circle a hole.

A gritty, freezing wind seems to want to push us back to Quillka's ruins. Dust coasts my eyelashes and the inside of my mouth. I'm relieved to see Lam's son Kestrel carrying Sil on his back. For a second, I glimpse Fir running with his brothers to the side of our straggling column, then melting in the pines to the east.

As night falls, we pause only to redistribute things to carry: a braid of onions, a shovel, more cloaks for the little ones, a pepper plant. I end up with seven potatoes and a bag of salt. Seven normal potatoes. My Biotics final seems like part of someone else's life.

High above us hangs The Eternal Keeper. The Chronicler wrote in the Book of Sowers that men came to abduct a woman and her child. Maybe this was a mother or maybe a Keeper. Rather than surrender, the woman took the Mother's hand and climbed with the child into the sky.

Once the night deepens, I lose the constellation in the dense spread of stars.

My ears, I motion to Petal. *12's ears. Do you think we'll be deaf forever?*

He can't see me since his eyes aren't enhanced. I tap his shoulder, then point to my ears.

The warriors heal, he motions. *Heal*: fists under the chin and moving out.

I point to 12.

Petal flicks his fingers at his temple. He means, *I hope so* or *Who knows*.

12 shakes her head vigorously, as if she can shake off the pain. Blood has dried in the pink hollow of her ears. Someone passes around a flask of water. I take one of the cheese-maker's pots and pour my share for 12.

12 seems to understand she must lick up every drop.

Rek was right. My mother waited too long for me and 12. Kesh said the Bond was our greatest weapon.

She was wrong. A dark thought occurs to me. Was my mother a traitor too?

I saw the fleet. No Bond can defeat it. The Bond is a feather against a forest fire. More than fire: the sun itself in a pulsing, endless cable of light.

We walk through the night. Once, I hear a hyba chuckle from the trees. 12 chuckles back, eager to join them.

Or fight. *To me*, I tell her with my arm.

She looks longingly at the trees, then obeys. None of the warriors had time to grab crossbows and strela bolts before the fleet attacked. Some warriors—Fir with his brothers and several Dreams—unspool their huaracas and vanish into the forest. I hear no more hyba sounds for the rest of the night. They have only stones. But it keeps the pack at bay, at least for tonight.

By dawn, we're climbing a narrow valley that angles up. I hear the name of it whispered back: Hyba's Throat. Farmers join us, convinced the Legion is on our heels.

Some see 12 and quickly move to the rear. Others are curious, hanging to the sides to examine her. Every time a cart joins us, new food makes its way back: apples, bread, dried peas.

And the whispered hope that Rek will protect us.

I know she'll be no friend to me or 12. Or to Petal, or to Sil and all of the drafts.

Maybe we will become renegades together.

As the sun sets on the second night, we have to rest. One by one, the refugees drop their bundles. Some sit where they stopped walking, in the middle of the road.

It's a good place, with a nearby copse of trees and a slender creek that burbles beneath a bridge.

Sil is the leader of the drafts. She walks among them, checking to see who survived, who needs medical attention or food. Others she sends in a group to collect firewood and buckets of water.

Sil herself dives into the creek and brings up small silvery fish and handfuls of tiny clams and crawfish.

The cheese-seller sets to boiling a cow bone. Once there is a broth, she removes it to stir in corn meal. "I have only bone for the beast," she tells me.

I'm starting to hear as if from far away. "12 will find her own food," I say.

"Not while that hyba pack shadows us. They'll take her down or them boys will crack her in the skull. Better she stays here for now."

I wait for the bone to cool. 12 swallows it whole.

Despite her mournful look, the cheese-seller gives me hope.

We'll deal with whatever the road brings us. As long as we're together, we'll make it. The warm corn mash helps. After two days of walking and only eating what comes down the road, the mash is delicious.

The cheese-seller's name is Abiqua. She short and humped, with cheeks that look like crumpled paper. Her knife is quick as she cuts cheese wedges, releasing a pungent, goaty smell. She distributes apples, carrots, strips of dried derak, a handful of sugar cubes, and half a bread loaf.

Abiqua milks the nanny goat into a cup. Then she lifts a sack from her cart and dips a spoon inside to bring up a brown powder. The sack is marked with a symbol: Ω.

It takes me a moment to place the symbol. Ω is on every Weave coin. The Sower wears the symbol on a chain around her neck.

This has to be Remedy.

Abiqua stirs a spoonful of the brown powder into the milk and shares it between the two Mother Eyes.

Little Rage gets none. For him, Abiqua milks the nanny goat a second time, filling a glass bottle. A rubber teat fits over the top. Teardrop won't let anyone else feed him. The rabbit draft keeps a close eye on the baby as he suckles and is careful to burp him when he's finished.

"May I taste it?" I ask Abiqua.

Abiqua looks at me sourly. "It ain't poison. Why do the likes of you need Remedy?"

"Just curious."

"A taste is all," Abiqua says morosely. "That might be all the Remedy left in blasted Bounty."

The powder is dusty, a little sour.

I recognize the taste immediately: rose hips.

Abiqua draws the string on the top of the sack tight, then protects the sack with old cheese gauze still coated in stinky wax. "Young Rek doesn't need it. Unless Ular has a stash, them boys will have to hunt the heights to harvest more."

All of the secrets that were kept from me and this one is handed to me like a piece of old cheese wax. The Remedy is rose hips. I use it for a pinkish brown paint. As I've plucked berries, I've squeezed the juicy ones on my tongue.

Rose hips. Fir's freedom. The freedom for any warrior who wants to go east. I wish I has something of Fir's, a cloth or shred of cloak, so that 12 could find him. I want to tell him that I'm ready to trade. If he helps me find Susalee, I'll hand him his freedom.

I step away from the cart to look, and I trip over a sleeping warrior.

Fir. He looks sheepish as he stands, brushing the dust from his cloak. He takes pride in being invisible, and I tripped over him. As he rubs sleep from his eyes, he looks young, only a little older than Petal.

"Why didn't you walk with us?" I ask.

He taps his ears: still deaf. Dried blood cakes down his neck.

You can walk with me, I motion.

Behind is better.

No one will punish you.

Better to keep you safe, he answers. *My brothers are in front. A hyba pack has been following.*

I will make you a trade for Remedy. Help me get Susalee from Dolor. I will give you some and tell you how to find more.

How much?

I have to leave some for Maraz's sons. For the other warriors. Suddenly, I'm unsure. By giving Fir the Remedy, will I condemn those boys to a horrible death? What about Lam's Birds, The Harvest?

Half a sack, I tell him.

That's not enough, he motions.

And how to find more.

Fir waggles his fist. *But.*

But what?

I can't leave you. I can't leave all of them —he motions at the refugees —*to die.*

You can tell all of the warriors about Remedy.

And the Weave? The helios?

There's nothing any of us can do to stop them.

I wish we were alone. I'm newly aware of how Fir moves his hands, how he stands. I wish I could touch his hands. Feel how he breathes. I wish I could put my hand on his cheek as Mei put her hand on mine. I wish we could carve out of the air a place to stand where no one would think twice about seeing a Captain and a warrior together.

Where no one would call us beasts.

Particular affection feels like a dose of forgetting. I'm suddenly unsure of where to put my arms, how to move my head.

Fir watches every move, every blink, every breath. What does he see? Dinitra cloaked in dust, dark circles under my eyes, smelling of bone broth and corn mash.

It's hopeless, we're hopeless. He will go east with his brothers. I will go north to The Deep. Apart from a few flame lamps, the camp lies in darkness. Even with my enhanced eyes, I can't see a path forward for us. There's a mad chuckling in the nearest copse of trees. 12 lifts her head to howl, longing and warning both. I can see the dark shapes of hybas moving through the tree branches.

Fir pulls the huaraca from around his neck and runs toward the trees.

At Abiqua's cart, Petal sleeps next to Shine, with Teardrop and Rage between her and the two Mother Eyes.

Abiqua is awake, staring at the forest.

I hear splashing as someone crosses the creek. "What is it?" I ask her.

"That hyba pack is chasing more than us. There's wildmen, too. Got more reason to fear the Legion than you or I. They is moving fast to The Sentinel, to cut east. Drawing the hyba packs with them."

I step up on the cart. A group of about fifteen men with wild hair and bodies have crossed. On the far bank, they've met up Fir and his brothers. I can pick up some of the words they shape: hyba, night, safety, wait.

"If they're smart, they'll wait for morning," Abiqua says. "Rare is the pack that hunts in a morning."

The wildmen move to the edge of the forest to make a camp with a roaring fire.

Roughly, Abiqua wakes Petal. She grabs the Remedy sack and dumps half into a pot. Then she seals the pot in cheese wax and thrusts it at Petal. "Best you be off, boy. Them Mother Eyes will get no mercy from the knobbies. Half the Remedy have you, so they can reach that Master. Half a spoon a day, mind you."

Petal shakes his head. "The knobbies will never catch me. Never have, never will."

Abiqua pinches him until he yelps. "Your mother ain't coming back, I reckon. Best be off with you while you can. Dolor won't open its doors to you or any one of these poor mites. Rek hates them, so she does."

She means Teardrop and Shine. Abiqua looks at 12 and shakes her head. "Things is changed for all of us. It's a kindness you would do, taking them Mother Eyes to the wildmen and yourself with them. At least they'd have some hope."

Woken by Abiqua's voice, Teardrop whimpers. She's sicker, her nose bright pink with fever. Abiqua spoons a bit of the cold corn mash into her mouth. "This one's no more use than a cow crossed with snake. No milk, no meat, no good leather."

"Maraz would gut me if she knew I'd sent her little Winds away," Petal says.

The cheese-seller spits. "I myself saw Maraz blown to bits."

Petal claps his hands over his mouth and bursts into tears. Then he takes Maraz's two sons each by the hand. When he returns, his cheeks are streaked with tears, and he's left the boys with the wildmen.

When Petal returns, Abiqua grumbles that he is a no good, lazy, selfish boy. As she doles out cheese, Petal gets the thickest slice and a swipe of her palm across his head.

That day, I pull the cart. Petal walks beside me, Teardrop in a sling on his back. If only the wildmen would take the drafts, too. But they are safe nowhere unless the Captains win this war. I check to see if Fir is behind us and he is, his brothers walking around him.

"Why didn't you go with them?" I ask Petal.

"Addled Abiqua is, from too many years." Petal chews a hard strip of cheese rind. "Nothing safe about that journey for me."

"East is where wildmen go. You told me yourself," I remind him. "You have no virus. You can go to the Master."

"My mother would section me if I left," Petal says.

"You'd be gone, dummy. Anku's not even here." I don't tell him I know Anku is in the Weave. "Besides, she doesn't want you dead. Abiqua said it—everything's changed."

"What do you even know about the East, knobbie?" Petal cries. "There be hybas in the trees, lithers in the caves. Them wildmen, when they get free. Hoo! They ain't so nice!"

I think for a moment. "There's a draft Queen, I hear. Drafts go to The Deep."

He gives me a squint, as if to prove how foolish I am. "From what I'm hearing, that Deep ain't so nice neither. And the Queen? Great fangs, she has. She eats men whole. You know nothing, knobbie!"

With that, Petal skips ahead, his too-large boots—my old boots from the Legion—slapping around his skinny shins. I don't see him again until three days later, when we finally reach Dolor.

By my count, the warriors have only two days until they sicken from lack of Remedy. What's left in Abiqua's sack is barely enough to stave off sickness for the Living Wood for a week, let alone all of the other warriors.

Rek's decision not to sow her Blazes with virus is looking smarter and smarter.

We have to climb a long hill with low brush to both sides. Petal told me Dolor is formidable, built in an old lava flow. The lava is gray, pocked stone, in huge lumps that fold in on each other in massive defensive walls. Some of the pocks are windows that overlook a flat plain. Brush and stunted trees have grown up the sides.

On the walls, guards walk high parapets. The gate is closed.

From window, a Blaze peers down. "Dolor is for Blazes alone."

12 could scale the wall easily. To what purpose? Muttering darkly, Stoya, the paper-maker, lays down her sack, spreads a blanket, and throws herself onto the ground.

The moon lifts high above the plain. The lava stone seems to generate its own thick, foul-smelling mist.

I help Abiqua drape blankets over the cart and make sure little Rage and the drafts are warm.

Just as the Eternal Keeper appears over our heads, I hear a shout. A figure approaches over the plain. The figure is unusually tall, with a predatory walk: Kesh. Behind her come dozens of Captains and their warriors.

Ular is at Kesh's side, with several of her Harvest. All the merriment I once saw in Ular is drained out of her face. One son carries a dead brother. Another is borne by two Dreams, a stump of leg wrapped in bloody gauze.

Kesh doesn't pause to greet us. Her eye flicks over our ragged camp. I know she takes me in, 12 beside me. The metal in her legs is smoke-stained. One of the bars is bent, giving her a limp.

She hammers Dolor's gate with her metal fist.

A Blaze peers from the parapet, just as he did before. "Only Blazes."

Kesh points to 12. "Open or that draft will climb up and through that window and rip out your very guts. Believe me, she knows exactly where to tear."

The Blaze vanishes. The gate cracks open enough for Kesh to go inside. The gate closes behind her.

Suddenly, I'm taken up in a fierce embrace: Mei. The way we parted at in the laboratory is forgotten. "I was so worried," she cries.

She pulls me after her. "I need your help with the wounded."

"Me? I'm no fysic."

"I saw you with the Vessel. You've stitched 12. They need you," she says, motioning toward the wounded warriors being laid on the ground.

Mei shoves a fysic's kit at me. "Dose the forgetting. Clean and stitch what you can. I can tend the more serious wounds. That Harvest first." She points to the Harvest with half a leg. "His name is Carrot. The brother carrying him is Sweet Pie."

The warrior's leg bone winks white under the flesh. I give Carrot five drops of forgetting.

"Blast that Rek," Mei mutters. She's carefully stitching Carrot's gruesome wound. "We need supplies, blood, fluids. She's taking full advantage. We have to do what we can until Kesh can pry loose what we need."

Our next warrior is one of Fir's brothers burned by a pulsar blast. Mei uses another five drops of forgetting before removing burned skin from his back. She sprinkles the raw flesh with antibiotic powder before layering him in gauze.

Two Night Skies are permanently deaf from the vibros. Seven Vessels have lost babies. Another gives birth soon after we arrive, her son emerging with a thicket of white hair: a Dream.

The celebration of the Dream's birth is brief. The warriors have a new word: a fist held high, then opening and closing rapidly: *helio.*

29

Labyrinth

In the morning, Kesh emerges from Dolor. The scar dividing her face is so pale it looks like a strip of ice. Exhaustion makes her stumble on her blades. I don't have Anku's strength, but I go to her side to steady her.

Behind her come the people of Dolor bearing supplies: tents, blankets, beds, clothing, heaters. Fifteen hovucks deliver vats of soup and baskets of bread. Ten more have medical supplies: tubes and bags of fluid, needles, and cryo-cannisters of blood.

The warriors set up a hospital tent in a lava crevasse, to block the biting wind that daily scrapes up the valley from south to north.

Once Kesh sees that the wounded are being treated and the refugees fed, she calls the Captains to her. They will council in Rek's labyrinth.

"It's a mistake." Lam pounds her fist into her palm. "Rek and her Blazes alone know where the halls lead. I hear there is no pattern to follow. The halls cross and re-cross. They use them for sport. Some who enter never leave, intoxicated by the blasted mist that rises from the rock."

"We have 12," Kesh says confidently. "She'll know the way out."

I'm not so sure. 12 can find things, actual things. I've never asked her to lead me out of a labyrinth.

Lam insists. "Rek could be laying a trap. She has no need of us, friend Kesh."

"She does have need and she knows it." Kesh winces as her blades slip on the lava stone. "She is one Captain. We are many. Look around you. Little grows at Dolor. Most of the Vessels and food comes from Quillka."

"Came from Quillka." Lam is not persuaded. "She promised us Remedy. Where is it? We have one day, Kesh, a single day, before we begin to lose our sons."

Kesh's face is impossible to read. "Rek is angry. She lost several ships and many sons. We have no choice, Lam. We have to keep her with us. We have to find some agreement while we wait."

"Wait for what?" Lam demands.

Kesh stares at her for a long moment. "While we wait," she says ominously.

I know we must be waiting for Anku. But what can she do so far away in the Weave? Whatever she's doing, Kesh is betting our lives on it.

Kesh takes me aside. "Get Petal. I want him close. All of this Rek blames on Anku. She will kill the boy if she can."

Kesh has my shoulder with her metal hand. She squeezes. "You've seen Anku on your tracker map."

I nod.

Kesh breath is a rasp. "Say nothing. If she succeeds, even at this dark hour, we will be victorious."

Petal is with Abiqua. I tell him I'm there to grant his wish, to go into old Dolor and even Rek's Labyrinth. He cocks his head and gives me an odd look. "Rek asks for me?"

"My mother does. She says if you don't come, I have permission to tear you limb from limb and feed you to 12."

"Aw, piggles." Petal hop-skips his way through the gate and into Dolor right behind 12. I tell him to stay within tail range, no further than 12's white tuft.

Dolor is nothing like Quillka or even Pergama. The dwellings are placed where the lava bulges and folds on itself, creating hollows that are boarded in with wooden walls and doors. Roofs of thatch and scrap metal are propped on top.

I'm not sure formidable is the right word. Ramshackle is more like it. Only the smell is the same: smoke, rotting potatoes, urine, sour milk.

I keep my eye out for Susalee or any Vessel.

As we climb, the people shut their windows and bar their doors. I don't know if Kesh or 12 scare them more.

Lam limps behind me, with Timbe, Hisla, and Ular. Lam's hip was badly injured when she was hit by a tree branch blasted by a pulsar. An hour earlier, I watched as Mei plucked splinters from her thigh. Lam told her that she saw Shan, Mei's sister, disappear in a pulsar blast. So far, they've found none of the Gemstones.

Lam's hand lay on her daughter's shoulder as they wept.

I came to distrust Mei, and I hate that Shan took her sons' tongues. But I grieve for her and her boys. All of this is too much to bear.

At the top of the hill, a great fold of lava has been carved into a gate. The gate has none of the grace of Holdfast. The arch is carved with terrible faces: monsters, snakes with human feet, enormous vultures. Two Blazes guard it, leather breastplates marked with the shape of a flame.

I know one of them: Burn, with the furred snake on his chest. His hair is loose, a cascade of orange to his elbows. "No weapons," he tells us.

The Captains have nothing to set down. "That thing." Burn points at 12. "It stays here."

"With you?" Kesh lets her words hang in the air. "You would command her? Can any of your brothers command her?"

Fear darkens Burn's face. It's a brilliant threat. The only one able ensure her obedience is me.

"You must tie her. Bind her in some way." He glares at the other warrior. "Get rope."

I have to suppress my smile. We've done this before, but not with the Blazes. It seems an easy enough thing to allow, since a rope is no more to 12 than a string of cobweb. I loop the rope around her neck, then offer it to him. "Would you like to hold her?"

Burn's face twists with disgust. "Your words mean nothing in Dolor."

Burn leads us down a series of tunnels: to the left, right again, right and down a flight of hardened lava steps. Rek stands in a large room with windows overlooking Dolor's plain. She's examining a large map spread on a polished rock table.

Kesh has to hunch to keep her head from touching the low ceiling. Several Blazes stand in the shadows. The room is lit by torches.

Rek's eyes fix on 12. "I said no weapons."

She points to Burn. "Bring a chain. Better yet, a fresh bolt."

"She is tied," Kesh says evenly.

Rek's look is murderous. "This is my city. Get that draft out of this room."

"I respond for Bounty." Kesh's blades scrape the floor. "Stop wasting time with your little fears."

Rek's jaw tightens. "If it moves, kill it," she orders Burn.

"Kill it, sister Rek, and I will kill you." Kesh's voice is soft, as if she's complimented Rek on the table or remarked on the weather. She leans over the maps, as if Rek's threats are no more than flies buzzing. "Let's get to planning."

She's treating Rek like a petulant child. Rek's cheeks flush with anger. If I weren't so worried about finding Susalee and getting Fir the Remedy, I'd enjoy the sparring.

"Captains, join up your maps," Kesh says. "Let us look at the state of things."

The Captains take out their tracker maps and lay them flat on Rek's table. For a moment, the individual maps go gray as the symbols shift and rearrange. As the maps knit, the seams vanish.

The Black Stairs are prominent. Quillka is a charcoal smudge.

"The losses are severe." Lam runs her hand over the hundreds of gray pinpricks: the dead. "Half of my Birds. There the Harvest, the Mother Eyes. Maraz. Shan."

Lam glances at Kesh, impassive. "Our worst losses yet."

My map is in my boot, wrapped around my sketch of Fir.

Kesh rests her flesh hand on the table. "It looks like Quor and her Sea Hunt…"

Rek cuts her off. "Where is your map?"

"Lost."

Rek shakes her head slowly. "I don't believe it. You are hiding Anku. Show your map."

"Gone," Kesh says. "You saw how they attacked. My map was in my quarters. Destroyed."

Rek glances quickly at me. She knows I have no sons. Why should I have a tracker map?

"We should have attacked the fleet months ago," Rek fumes. "Yet we waited for this useless daughter and her creature."

I have no love for Rek. But she's right. Kesh waited until the fleet destroyed half their army and Quillka with it.

"Unavoidable." On the map, I see the Centrum, a sharp point, the green around it like a splash of paint.

Rek speaks forcefully. "Now more than ever we must reach out to the Master. Make our alliance. With his forces, he can attack the Weave from the east."

I stop breathing. This is the Master Sil spoke of, the one Fir wants to find. The wildmen we saw on the road are going to him, with the little Mother Eyes.

Rek is proposing an alliance with men.

Kesh shakes her head. "Never."

Rek's grin is terrible. "Were you not at Quillka, Kesh? What would you call what you saw there? Feasting? A fine sip of licor from the helios?"

The Captains are loyal to Kesh. But even I can see Rek's point. With the Concave feeding the helios a constant stream of fuel, with the fleet able to go as far and as long as they wish, there's no hope for Bounty. If they want to survive, they have to do something different.

Kesh's voice has an edge of anger. "We have other friends."

Rek explodes. "Years you spent as a spy in the heart of the Weave. Years we spent waiting—for that sprite, for that creature." She stabs her metal hand at me. "Whose city lies in ruins? Still you don't see. Kesh, you told us to wait. Wait we did. What we get in return is fire and death."

I can't fault anything the Northern Captain says. I steal a look at Kesh, her shattered face a mask.

Rek's next words are ominous. "You ask too much of me. Too much of us. One day, you may not have so many Captains to command."

Rek turns to the Captain of the Dreams. "Hisla, what say you? How many Dreams do you mourn? Ular—do you desire another helio barrage for your fat sons?"

The lava walls of Rek's labyrinth surround us. Like the other Captains, I know even these walls are nothing against the Concave and the helios and their pulsars.

Hisla runs her finger over the map, a faint glow following. "There are others in the east who may come to our aid."

"That is rich," Rek scoffs. "You mean that draft Queen, Odide. Not a wildman who comes near Hive Home escapes her."

I'm practically vibrating. Kesh told me about this Queen in the east. The Sowers use her nektar to make drafts. Is that a place Fir and I can go? Neither the Master nor The Deep: a compromise. Someplace where we can be together. But not if she imprisons the men. Eats them, Petal says. I have no reason to trust the boy, but how could I urge Fir to take his brothers someplace even worse than Bounty?

"It's true, she has an army," Ular says thoughtfully. "They fly. As far as I could see, neither the Concave or the helios have a defense against air attack."

Rek throws up her arms. "That bee-thing? Treacherous and fickle. Corrupted in some Sower sac. The Master will deal with her in good time. And you propose to send her little bees against those helios? Ha!"

Lam looks at Rek pointedly. "She's provided the Weave with nektar for longer than you've been alive. I have seen her army, Rek. Those are no little bees."

Rek folds her arms, metal over flesh. "Granted, I am no Collegium girl. In the Arcadium, we learned about loyalty. If this mongrel Queen has had such long association with the Weave, then I think I can predict that her allegiance is with the Head Sower, not us." Rek's face is thunderous. "The Master will help us, I know he will. He loathes the Weave, that I know for a fact. His Hundred-Hundred can be across the Wastes in a week. Why, they could take the Centrum itself, catch those miserable Sowers in their soft beds. He is pure human: no concoction. We can trust him."

The room explodes in insults: "Northern filth." "Vessel piss." "Draft-lover." "Son-lover." Petal slips his shaking hand into mine. More than the insults, I'm afraid Rek is making headway among the other Captains. She wants them to see the drafts as a burden. A danger. She wants to win their loyalty from Kesh.

Is it working? I am my only guide, and I have to say yes. If I did not have 12, I might follow her.

Kesh hammers the rock table with her metal fist. "Quiet!"

Rek's voice is cold "Here is my question for you, Captain Kesh. I will do anything you ask if you answer a single question. I will even give you Remedy. Yes, though my boys don't need it, I keep a store just in case. Tell me. I see your sister's beast-born spawn standing there. Where is its mother? Where is your sister?"

A Blaze has crept up behind and roughly seizes Petal. The boy squeals, but it's too late to command 12. I couldn't be sure she'd go after the Blaze and not Petal or one of the Captains in the way.

The Blaze drags the boy to Rek's side, then lifts him by the shoulders of his tunic. Petal writhes, his little crook exposed. A boot–my old boot–thunks to the floor.

Rek's face twists in triumph. "Look no further for evidence of who betrays us. Your sister. Confess, rat-boy! Where is your traitor of a mother?"

The Blaze grins, "Squeak, squeak!"

Rek turns on my mother. "Tell me, Kesh, or I'll split him head to toe."

I don't know what Anku is doing in the Weave. Petal is my friend, crook or no. "Let him go," I say.

"Another mistake!" Rek pretends to laugh. The tattoos make her face into a terrible picture. "For that you sacrificed your legs?"

"Let him go," I repeat.

Rek stares at Petal as if he's rotted meat. "Sliver, take him away," she orders the Blaze.

My fingers curl in the air. 12's response is immediate: a growl. "Let him go, I said."

"You wouldn't dare."

Even I, who love her, know that 12 is terrifying. "I will say this one more time, Captain Rek. Let the boy go."

There is fear in Rek's gaze, and fury. There's also the will to vengeance. Rek will come for me.

That works in my favor. Fear is a powerful emotion. I disagree with my mother on this, I think. The only one more powerful is love.

I tell 12 to stand. "Why would I waste a blade on such a puny thing?" Rek says, smirking. "Let him go, Sliver."

Petal scurries to my side.

To the northern Captain, Kesh speaks calmly. "My sister is no traitor. She will strike our greatest blow yet against the Weave."

"Greatest blow," Rek snorts. "Says you who waited. Says you who lost your own Council Hall to the fleet then comes begging to mine. We should have put Anku out of her misery the moment she appeared with that sprig in her arms."

"Watch your words," Kesh warns.

"Oh, are words weapons?" Rek mocks. "Will words give us our greatest blow yet against the Weave? All you have, all you ever have Kesh, is words. While I do the real fighting. Me and my dear boys. I think I know who my real friends are. I guess I'll put that Remedy to the flame."

Rek saves her last words for me. "When it's over, I will come for you. I will have that thing's heart for my dinner."

I meet Rek's eyes. "Both of them?" I rub 12's ears. "I'd like to see you try."

30

Queen

P etal can't help a jig as we leave through Dolor's gate. "Bested that filthy Captain, so you did! Dinitra and the cross, hoo!"

No Captain sees the humor in it. Rek vowed to burn whatever Remedy she has. By tomorrow, the warriors will feel the first signs of Remedy sickness. I can't expect Fir and his brothers to wait any longer for me to find Susalee. They must take their share of what Abiqua has and head east.

Somehow, I have to find Susalee. I'll take her and 12 into The Deep. Maybe Petal, too, and the drafts. Abiqua was right. Petal should have left with Maraz's two little Winds. Maybe, we all should have left. I won't wait for my mother's foolishness to kill us all.

Luckily, there's no one at Abiqua's cart. I take Kesh's book from my satchel and rip off a page. Quickly, I sketch a rose bush and the berries it bears. Fir can use this to identify the rose hips they need. I dump everything out of my satchel and scoop in half the Remedy from Abiqua's sack.

I find Fir at the pyre where he and his brothers are placing the dead warriors.

I'm shocked to see a furry body among them: Teardrop. She died while we were in Rek's labyrinth. Sil crouches beside her, worried that the vultures circling high above the plain might take this tiniest of the bodies.

Teardrop's feet point east.

I motion to Fir, *We need to speak.* I find a spot hidden by a fold of lava. 12's ears are pricked, a troubling sign. Still, there are no Blazes near and nothing visible on the horizon.

Protected from the wind, the spot is surprisingly warm. Little rock plants have survived the first blast of cold and still bloom in the cracks of the lava stone.

There's no time to think about what I am feeling. I don't even feel ashamed. I just want Fir to flee.

"Remedy," I say, thrusting my satchel at him. "Rek is putting the torch to what she has."

Fir face pales. "The others…"

I show him my drawing. It's rough, more a suggestion of a plant rather than a careful drawing. But it's enough. "This is the plant you must find. Teach them. Look for it near the ridges. It can be dried and ground. That is all you need for Remedy. For all of the warriors."

Fir shakes his head. "Some will not leave."

"Then let them stay. Leave them the Remedy. But you and your brothers need to go. Today. Now. The fleet is coming."

"I can't leave you," Fir blurts. "The fleet will destroy Dolor." Fir grabs me by the shoulders. "You must come with us. You and 12. There is no point in staying to die." Fir uses shape language. *Come with me and be free.*

"East is for men." I don't know if I'm laughing or crying. "They would not take a Collegium girl."

I know I'm right by the stricken look in his face. There is nothing for me with this Master. He hates drafts as much as Rek. I can't go a place that puts 12 at risk.

Fir is fighting his Bond to his brothers and what he feels for me. "You must leave, Dinitra. You cannot stay."

"I can neither leave nor stay," I say, so desperate it comes out as a laugh. "You know I can't leave Susalee. She is as much a slave as you."

The list just gets longer. Abiqua, Shine, Petal. The alligator draft, the paper maker, Stoya. Is there anywhere we could be free together?

"I won't leave without you." Fir's face is weary and streaked with tears. "You must come."

I'm shaking my head. "When I have a hard decision to make, I write a list. Here is my list for you. The Weave will kill you if they capture you. Or worse: contain you and your brothers for the rest of your lives. They'll kill the drafts. You have to go, for your brothers, at least."

I see the truth of what I'm saying sink in. "Is there no other way?" Fir asks.

I didn't want to mention the Queen. I am putting his fate, the fate of his brothers, on the angry words of Captains shouting in Rek's Labyrinth.

"There is this Queen. You have heard of her."

"The Queen with the nektar?"

"Yes. The Weave and Bounty trade with her. Queen Odide, they call her. You must know of her."

"Past the Eastern Wastes is what I've heard." Fir thinks for a moment. "My brother Tanoak speaks to the wildmen. Few men who see that Queen ever walk free."

My hope is fading. "The Deep?"

Fir shakes his head. "I know nothing of The Deep. Some call it the edge of the world."

"Well, there it is." I will never see Fir again. "Give me something with your smell. In case...well, in case there's a place for us somewhere that's not the end of the world."

Who knew that when I trained 12 to find things by smell it might mean breaking the Mother-Bond?

I'm making a new Bond, to a male: to Fir.

He tears off a piece of his tunic hem and hands it to me.

"This will do," I tell him.

I cradle Fir's two hands between mine. They smell of rosemary. I remember how Tem and Edba would look at each other, how they touched each other and kissed. How Mei kissed me. Is this how love feels, when you are drawn by a force impossible to resist? I place both hands on Fir's cheeks—rough with stubble, streaked with tears—and draw him to me.

He tastes of flowers and dust.

Within the hour, the Living Wood is gone.

It doesn't take long for Timbe to realize her sons have fled. Soon, the word gets to Rek. Kesh's face is thunder as she calls the Captains to confer with Rek at Dolor's gate.

Rek does nothing to conceal her triumph. She has Burn, her lead Blaze, take a head count of Blazes. The only ones missing were killed at Quillka.

Rek announces she's had a change of heart. An old hovuck bears several large sacks of Remedy. As a gesture of peace, she says slyly.

"I'm guessing some of you might want to call a new vote for Commander. Who should you choose, the one who lost Quillka and a whole squadron of sons or the one who can still summon every one of her sons by name from the safety of her own dear city?"

Lam steps toward her. "You betray Bounty with that Master in the east. With men."

Rek shakes her head, her lip studs gleaming. "You know, friend Lam, my Dolor is twice Quillka's size. We would never hurt your sons on purpose. It was just the emotion of the moment got the best of me."

Rek gives Lam a mocking bow. "I will offer this as my apology. I'll send my sons Burn and Hunger, the best I have, to follow that Living Wood and bring them home to their grieving mother. I would ask only this in exchange: a vote. Let us vote again for who is to be Commander."

"Impossible." Lam looks to the others. Ular is still bloody from carrying one of her sons. Timbe's faced is an agonizing mix of shame and fury.

"A vote we shall have." Kesh stares down at Rek like some insect. "And we will have that vote tomorrow. After our sons have their Remedy."

If the vote goes to Rek, she'll order 12 killed. And the drafts. Likely Petal too.

I have to find Susalee and run for The Deep.

I can see no way into Dolor from this gate. To scout around it, I take 12 up one of the lava flows and through one of the low scrub forests that manage to dig their roots into the porous stone.

The bushes rattle as we approach. Furry little dilidots send up a squeaky alarm. 12 hasn't eaten more than Abiqua's bone and some cheese for days. I let her hunt through the trees. I've never seen her so graceful as she uses her long tail to swing from branch to branch, snapping up the dilidots as they scurry.

I'm startled by a rustle behind me.

Petal.

"Gaw," he says, dejected. "My mother ain't no traitor."

Then a ragged laugh bursts from the brush. Two Blazes emerge, bows aimed at us.

Rek herself follows. She has a crossbow too, and a full bandolier of strela bolts. She's loaded a bolt into the chamber.

12 drops directly in front of me, a squealing dilidot still in her jaws. She snaps its spine and swallows.

"We've been looking for you. Splinter, Blight. Go behind," Rek orders.

The Blazes circle us. Despite the cold, Blight's chest is bare. The wings of a tattooed bird flare on his chest, its long, skinny neck snaking up beneath his chin and opening its beak around his blackened lips.

Blight flips his crossbow to his back and starts to swing his huaraca. "Don't fire the bolt, mother," he says. "It would be a sad waste of fresh meat. Didn't you say you wanted to taste its heart? The beast-boy we'll leave for the vultures."

"You won't shoot," I tell Rek.

Rek grins as if I've made some quick joke. "I've had enough of waiting. You're the start of the doing. With you and that beast out of the way, there won't be a need for any vote."

Splinter wears a hyba ear necklace. I remind myself: he never trained with 12. He may have killed his share of hybas. But he's never faced something as lethal as my cross. A mixture of glee and anticipation animate his face.

A deep chuckle comes from 12, her teeth bared. Even my blood runs cold at the sound of it.

Blight's huaraca is just starting to whistle when the ground shakes. A column of smoke twists from the gate of Dolor. In the sky, helios are dropping fire.

The fleet has come.

My first thought isn't relief. It's that I failed Susalee. I've failed 12. It's not weak to love something. It's the bravest thing I've ever done, to love 12, and now I'm going to pay.

A helio drops directly over us. The curved pergama belly shimmers with light. Rek screams, aiming her crossbow. The air seems to ripple. Blight is agog, his huaraca limp at his side. The flash is so bright my eyes sting. Blight explodes in a flurry of ash. For an instant, his huaraca hangs in the air, then falls to the ground and bursts into flame.

Run or be dust. What if there's nowhere left to run?

Susalee, I think. All of her Sower's art, all of her accomplishments, about to be blasted by the very Weave that made her.

The helio lifts and slides toward Dolor.

I count more than twenty helios spread out. All are attached to the Concave by a pulsing cord of light.

I run toward Dolor, 12 bounding ahead.

Petal holds my hand, sobbing, "They is come!"

Pulsars pound the gate, as if they want to trap people inside and bury them. I pass Abiqua wisely running for the trees, little Shine clutched to her. The Captains are bellowing to gather sons.

12 tears the air. She howls, her neck muscles rigid. She wants to rip flesh, taste blood.

I see Timbe: her face black with ash, her eyes two green holes. Alone. Her russet tail of hair is mostly gone, burned away. The back of her tunic is still smoking. "Where are my sons?" she screams.

A helio maneuvers over us, so close I see its delicate silver whiskers lash. Under its radiant light, everything throws a shadow: leaves, the pebbles at my boot heel. For an instant, I see the capillaries in Timbe's outstretched hand. "Run!" she bellows.

The helio's nose tips down. The whiskers stiffen and vibrate. The pilot's helmet glows as she works the levers. I know her: Helma, the Collegium girl who invoked the Rule. She sees me—I know she sees me and maybe even knows me—and she fires.

The snow puddles sizzle into water, then steam. The air is too hot to breathe. I'm flying, falling. As if suspended, I see Kestrel, one of Lam's sons, in mid-swing with his huaraca. The pulsar blasts him. A single red ribbon curls in the updraft.

The helio turns to the right. Over Dolor, I see black cruisers rise—one, two, then five stacked in the air. Rek is fleeing. The last one, closest to the ground, bursts into flames.

The helio that shot the cruiser rocks in celebration.

Lam's warriors swing their huaracas, the rocks pinging off the helio skins. They might as well be hurling peas. Insults. The helios pound the city and the lava rocks burst apart.

I wrap my arms around 12's thick neck and huddle over Petal.

Helma's helio tips its nose down again. Her smile is gleeful as a beam sears a black trench through a tent. Even 12 trembles, the stench of burnt flesh nauseating.

12's glittering, golden eyes go from the helio to my face and back again. What would I have her do, she asks? She kneads the steaming mud with her paws.

Nothing physical holds her. Only duty to me. Love for me. Our Bond. This is the end of everything. I hope I die. I hope Petal and 12 die before the Weave takes them.

What I think next shames me. If I live, I'll draw this. The helios and their whiskers, the croakers exploding. Most of all, this: Timbe, screaming alone as a helio positions itself over us. If I have no paper, I'll draw on stones. I'll draw on my own skin. I'll be a living Book of Sowers.

I'd rather be paper toasted over Stoya's fire than what I am right now: a miserable, trembling thing.

I was never brave.

Heated water courses through the mud. Even the air smells cooked. Blood trickles down my neck, from what I don't know. 12 licks my face. Her tail lashes. Petal's fists are balled in his eyes.

But there are no vibros. What's changed is this: no sound. No pulsars. We're swathed in steam from the blasts heating the ground water into steam. Nearby I see the shadow of a body. We crawl to it: one of Lam's Birds, still wearing feathers in his hair. His lower half is a pile of ash. The huaraca—the ridiculous, useless huaraca—is a charred snake at his side.

I see parts of warriors, too, like Petal's stick figures waiting to be assembled.

I look up, to see the helio that will end us. There are no more golden embers. The helios are dull silver. There are no more trails of light.

Timbe's face turns upwards. My eyes follow hers, to the Concave. The clouds have vanished, cooked by the sizzling beams. The Concave is a black gash. There is no light fuel any more.

It's as if someone has turned the entire fleet off with a switch.

No fuel. No fleet.

I know what's happened with a certainty that sends me to my knees. Anku. The most talented Cyclon engineer of her generation. A Collegium girl. The best Guide in Bounty, able to slip in and out of the Weave without a trace.

Anku has destroyed the Weave's Cyclon. With the fleet in the air, she took it, too.

A single woman defeated an entire fleet.

And every light in the Weave. Every heater. Every freighter, every comms link. Every factory, every oven, every sensor, every door.

Everything.

Helma's helio tilts. The rear rises, the nose points down. The whiskers hang limp as old string. The rudder clunks back and forth, back and forth as Helma, panicking, realizes she's going to crash.

For a split second, Helma's eyes meet mine. Then she throws up her arms and the ship smashes to bits.

One after another, the helios spin down and shatter. The last to crash is the Concave, which hits with a terrific boom.

Bounty has won.

31

Anku

A nku's croaker appears from the south early the next morning. No thread of golden light trails it. The battered ship coughs out a dense blue smoke.

Shards of helio skin make the plain of Dolor sparkle. People wander the wreckage marveling: pergama is so light, transparent. The croaker settles near where Helma fell.

I think back to when I stood at the hatch of the Legionship, my painting sucked inside. This time, it's Kesh who waits for someone to emerge. When Anku steps out, Kesh reaches for her and lifts her in a tight embrace.

Something passes me in a blur. Petal. Anku squeezes him so hard he squeaks. She gives him a terrific shake before setting him down.

"Aa-uh," she says.

"Gaw." He buries his face in her belly.

Anku climbs onto the wreckage of the Concave to tell the story of what happened. The people of Dolor don't know shape language, so Kesh stands near the twisted rudder to translate.

"I was trained as a Cycloneer. I knew everything about the system. I knew that the Cyclon was the Weave's prime vulnerability. Unfortunately, the Head Sower feared the very same sabotage."

Sabotage: her laced fingers sliding apart. "I thought I could disable the Cyclon months ago. We kept it between us, my sister and me. For safety. Months ago, the Head Sower ordered the Cyclon codes changed. I had to redo many calculations. But it was done."

Kesh helps her down, then turns to the crowd. "It was always our intention to draw the Weave far into Bounty. To make them think this would be the final blow. That way, they would commit the entire fleet. With a single blow we have destroyed all of it. Every last ship is shattered."

A great cheer goes up.

But Anku raises her hands to her face. Her body heaves.

Kesh translates. "Anku wishes me to say that she deeply regrets what you lost at Quillka. What you lost at Dolor. She takes the blame. She wishes she could have stopped the Cyclon sooner."

Kesh pulls Anku forward. "I reject that entirely. Anku saved us all. Yes, this comes at a price. But it is price that lies on the Weave, not on her. She has rid the world of a great evil. We owe her our thanks."

"For the Bond!" Lam shouts. The call is taken up until the plain of Dolor shakes with it.

"The Legion is powerless," Kesh says when the cheers die down. "The central command console is destroyed. None of their ships or weapons work without the Cyclon and none of the sub-Cyclons work without these central controls. They cannot communicate. The people hide in their homes, afraid. There is no light, no heat. Only stored food since the greenhouses have gone dark."

"That is all good news," Lam says.

"Quor and her Sea Hunt seized the Centrum as soon as it went dark."

Kesh looks at her sister. Anku motions, *I am sorry. There is more I must tell you.*

"Something unforeseen." Anku's hand movements are sharp. "I saw ships flying south."

Anku's words hang heavy in the air. So much loss and more to come.

"Ships," Kesh repeats. "We launched no ships. Quor and her Sea Hunt hold the Centrum. I saw this on the tracker maps."

Her metal fist clenches. "I would speak the Captains alone."

The Captains gather beneath a section of the Concave's shattered skin balanced on pillars of lava stone. For a table, they have a small wedge of pergama, edges sharp as cut glass. "Tell us the rest, sister," Kesh says.

Rek will bring the Hundred-Hundred. An army of men. She means to take the Weave and with it Bounty. And your sons.

"Impossible," Lam hisses. "My sons love me."

Anku makes sure they see the words she shapes. *She promises freedom from the Remedy if they serve her.*

Lam interrupts. "That is well beyond her poor skill at a console."

The Master claims he has done it. Perhaps he lies, but some warriors...

Timbe pushes forward. "She hinted as much in the labyrinth. My sons believed this lie. That's why they abandoned me."

I don't correct her. Fir never mentioned to me a Remedy cure. I put the Remedy in his hands, not Rek's. And I didn't give him Remedy and my drawing to defeat Bounty. I gave it to him because I wanted him and the other warriors to be free.

Lam speaks next. "We have another war to fight."

Kesh is brutally quick with her decision. "Three Captains and as many warriors who can fit in Anku's croaker must go to the Centrum now. Lam, Mei, Anku. Myself and my daughter, with the cross. The rest must follow on foot. We need to keep the Blazes and whatever vermin Rek has gathered in the east from seizing it."

I blurt. "What about Dolor? The drafts? Who will defend them?"

Kesh's answer is brutal. "If Rek takes the Centrum, she'll turn the Weave against us. We must sacrifice."

Sacrifice? A hole opens inside me. "You pledged to protect the drafts. The Bond."

"How can I protect any Bond if Rek and this Master rule?" Kesh turns from me. "The decision is made. We leave at first light."

Timbe stops her. "What of my sons? Who will bring them back to me? Rek sent her boys. But they'll take them."

Timbe kneels in front of Kesh. "I beg you. Send the Birds. There are still Mother Eyes. Send them to get my dear boys."

Kesh looks down on her with great compassion. "My brave Timbe. We cannot spare warriors. Your sons betrayed you. By now, they are dying of Remedy sickness. Even if they returned, you couldn't trust them. Think to the future, Timbe. I promise you will be the first to sow new squadrons of sons."

Timbe weeps openly. Kesh isn't moved. "You can have the orphans. The Mother Eyes. They will serve you better than those traitors did."

I know what I have to do. I search the wreckage of Dolor for a single Vessel with red-gold hair.

I don't have a swatch of clothing to share with 12, but I think the hyba cross senses my urgency. We find Susalee slumped beside a lava rock just inside Dolor's gate, little Ruin in her lap.

This time, she knows me.

"Dinitra," she says dully. "You are dead."

I take her in my arms. "Do I feel dead?"

"They told us scrags killed you." She bursts into tears.

I remember what she said just after I'd failed the Biotics final. "At least it's over." I'm not angry with her anymore. "Let's get you some food," I tell her.

She leans on me heavily as I take her to Abiqua. Over and over again, I tell her, "I will take care of you. Don't be afraid."

Abiqua takes one look at Susalee and Ruin and starts bustling among her pots and pans. Swiftly, she has a pot of corn mash bubbling. She milks the nanny goat and tucks Ruin in Shine's lap to feed. Rage has already fed, and sleeps beside a cheese wheel.

Abiqua spoons mash into a bowl. With a clink, a spoon follows.

"Every last morsel," she says as she hands the bowl to Susalee.

When Susalee's finished, she looks a little better. "Where is Rek?"

"Gone." I tell her about the croakers that left Dolor before the fleet fell.

She looks at Ruin. "Poor him."

"He's lucky," I tell her. "He has Abiqua now. And his brother."

In one of Abiqua's old Remedy sacks, I pack food, a blanket, and a flask of water. I should leave behind Kesh's book, but I can't part with it. It's a piece of me, like a hand.

Maybe I'll use the pages for a fire. Or bandages. We'll suck off the paint and get sustenance from the bit of eggplant in the purple or what's left of carrot in the orange.

I don't want to think too hard about what I'm doing. If I do, I'll be useless as a carnivorous potato.

Abiqua sees me smile and waggles her spoon. "You're not taking these mites," she tells me. She means Ruin and Rage.

"They are better off with you. On one condition. Rek must never have them. Promise me."

"She'll not get within a stone throw," Abiqua vows.

I let Susalee sleep. She'll need her energy. I go to speak with Sil to see what she knows about the Queen. I know she will keep this in confidence.

Sil is soaking in a water barrel. The dust and smoke of the attack clogged her gills. Her back is seared from the edge of a pulsar blast.

Darling, the sea creature, has her own barrel. The water seems to boil with the movement of her tentacles.

I tell Sil what I heard at the Captains' Council. Kesh will leave them behind. Rek and her Blazes plan to take the Centrum. Rek is allied with this Master, who also hates the drafts.

There's no more protection at Dolor. They need to protect themselves.

Her gills gently flare. "And you?" Sil asks.

"I am taking my friend to the Queen."

"The Vessel."

"Yes." Sil holds out her hand and I let her place her suction cups, surprisingly tender. She sees Timbe begging, my reaction: a

About the Author

Robin Kirk's short fiction has been published in *Tomorrow*, an anthology of speculative fiction from Kayelle Press; in *Beyond the Nightlight*, an anthology published by A Murder of Storytellers; and in *The Moon Magazine*. She won an honorable mention in the Chicago Reader's 2014 Pure Fiction contest. She is also an award-winning non-fiction writer. Her essay on Belfast is included in the *Best American Travel Writing* of 2012; she won the *Glamour* magazine non-fiction contest; and she was featured in *Oxford American's* "Best of the South" issue. Her writing has appeared in the *New York Times*, *Mother Jones*, *The Washington Post*, *The American Scholar*, and *Sojourners*, among other publications. She writes a regular column for the Durham *Herald-Sun*.

Kirk has also published nonfiction books, including *More Terrible Than Death: Massacres, Drugs and America's War in Colombia* (PublicAffairs) and *The Monkey's Paw: New Chronicles from Peru* (University of Massachusetts Press). She coedits the *The Peru Reader: History, Culture, Politics* (Duke University) and is an editor of Duke University Press's World Readers series.

Kirk is a Faculty Co-Chair of the Duke Human Rights Center and is a founding member of the Pauli Murray Project. She is a lecturer in Duke's Department of Cultural Anthropology. She is a graduate of the University of Chicago and holds an MFA in Children's and Young Adult literature from Vermont College of Fine Arts. Visit her website at robinkirk.com.

The Bond is her first novel.

running with a single sack of Remedy, Burn and Hunger on their heels.

I have to believe there is a world in which he'll live. Where I'll see him again. On this side of the edge or another.

We walk the path we are given, not the one we think we should have. Maybe there's a way to make my own path. Maybe it will lead me to him.

"Tell me where we are going?" Susalee asks.

"East" won't make any sense to her. "A draft Queen," I tell her. "A Crimson Valley."

I always thought a girl like Susalee would get what she wanted. Susalee has me and 12.

I hope that's enough.

Ω

savage glee that I helped Fir escape. She sees Fir as I saw him last: a kiss and his taste, flowers and dust.

The Deep is closer, Sil tells me. *Warmer, at least. Or so Kestrel told me once. That is where I will take the drafts, once I heal. You would be with us.*

Why risk the Deep? It's off the edge of the world, I say, quoting Fir.

If it's this world we're leaving, I see no problem in stepping off the edge.

I can't hide my response. *I will be closer to Fir in the east. Maybe...maybe I'll find him. Besides, a draft Queen sounds like someone 12 should meet.*

When Sil laughs, her gills flutter.

Sil tells me to go north until we see The Sentinel, a single peak with a flat top. "That is the entrance to The Deep. From there turn straight east. Go no further than the Crimson Valley. You will know it by the crimson flowers that bloom no matter the season. That is the Queen's valley. And stay off any path. The Master watches them closely."

Sil points up, to the sky. "He has many spies, as does the Queen."

"Will the Queen welcome us?"

"I do not know her."

"But do you think she will?"

Sil blinks: one orange eye, one blue. "I hope she will."

I return to Abiqua's cart to get Susalee and my sack. Susalee is obedient, following my orders without complaint. Our goodbyes are quick. My only regret is that I don't see Petal. He will miss me and 12. I know he is happy with his mother returned.

The Captains are intent over their maps, Kesh with them. Strangely, I don't feel any sadness at leaving my mother. At betraying her. I never asked for the Bond. Once I had it, the Bond brought me mainly fear and sorrow.

I'd rather make my own Bonds.

We climb quickly up the lava fall out of Dolor, leaving the wreckage behind. 12's tail lashes as she takes in every smell. A hank of some warrior's ribbon has caught on a bush, blown there during the battle. Somewhere ahead of us, Fir and his brothers are